SHOOT TO KILL

"You will not leave this place alive!" the captain bawled, firing again. This time, the bolt stuck harmlessly in a wooden doorframe, which Ezio had ducked behind. But there was very little wrong with the captain's shooting. So far, Ezio had been lucky. He had to get away, and fast. Two more bolts sang past him.

"There's no way out!" the captain called after him. "You might as well turn and face me, you pitiful old dog." He fired again.

Ezio drew a breath and leapt to catch hold of the lintel of another doorway, swinging himself up so that he was able to get onto the flat clay roof of a dwelling. He ran across it to the other side as another bolt whistled past his ear.

"Stand your ground and die," hollered the captain. "Your time has come, and you must accept it, even if it is far away from your wretched kennel in Rome! So come and meet your killer!"

Ezio could see where soldiers were running around to the back of the village, to cut off his line of retreat. But they had left the captain isolated, except for his two sergeants, and his quiver of bolts was empty.

The villagers had scattered and disappeared long since.

Ezio ducked behind the low wall surrounding the roof, unstrapped his bags from his back, and slipped the pistol harness onto his right wrist.

"Why will you not quit?!" the captain was calling, drawing his sword.

Ezio stood. "I never learned how," he called back in a clear voice, raising his gun.

ASSASSIN'S
CREED

REVELATIONS

OLIVER BOWDEN

ACE BOOKS, NEW YORK

THE BERKLEY PUBLISHING GROUP
Published by the Penguin Group
Penguin Group (USA) Inc.
375 Hudson Street, New York, New York 10014, USA
Penguin Group (Canada), 90 Eglinton Avenue East, Suite 700, Toronto, Ontario M4P 2Y3, Canada
(a division of Pearson Penguin Canada Inc.)
Penguin Books Ltd., 80 Strand, London WC2R 0RL, England
Penguin Group Ireland, 25 St. Stephen's Green, Dublin 2, Ireland (a division of Penguin Books Ltd.)
Penguin Group (Australia), 250 Camberwell Road, Camberwell, Victoria 3124, Australia
(a division of Pearson Australia Group Pty. Ltd.)
Penguin Books India Pvt. Ltd., 11 Community Centre, Panchsheel Park, New Delhi—110 017, India
Penguin Group (NZ), 67 Apollo Drive, Rosedale, Auckland 0632, New Zealand
(a division of Pearson New Zealand Ltd.)
Penguin Books (South Africa) (Pty.) Ltd., 24 Sturdee Avenue, Rosebank, Johannesburg 2196,
South Africa

Penguin Books Ltd., Registered Offices: 80 Strand, London WC2R 0RL, England

This is a work of fiction. Names, characters, places, and incidents either are the product of the author's
imagination or are used fictitiously, and any resemblance to actual persons, living or dead, business
establishments, events, or locales is entirely coincidental. The publisher does not have any control
over and does not assume any responsibility for author or third-party websites or their content.

ASSASSIN'S CREED® REVELATIONS

An Ace Book / published by arrangement with Penguin Books Ltd.

PRINTING HISTORY
Ace premium edition / December 2011

ISBN: 978-1-937007-42-3

ACE
Ace Books are published by The Berkley Publishing Group,
a division of Penguin Group (USA) Inc.,
375 Hudson Street, New York, New York 10014.
ACE and the "A" design are trademarks of Penguin Group (USA) Inc.

PRINTED IN THE UNITED STATES OF AMERICA

10 9 8 7 6 5 4 3 2

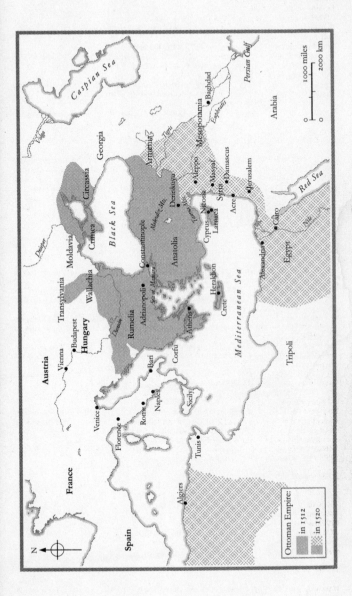

Caspian Sea

Volga

Georgia

Circassia

Armenia

Tigris

Mesopotamia

Baghdad

Euphrates

Persian Gulf

Arabia

1000 miles

2000 km

Crimea

Black Sea

Aleppo

Diyarbakır

Maraşh

Damascus

Jerusalem

Red Sea

Moldavia

Transylvania

Mähe ole Mts

Cyprus

Nicosia

Syria

Latakia

Acre

Wallachia

Constantinople

Anatolia

Cairo

Sea of Marmara

Alexandria

Nile

Egypt

Budapest

Adrianople

Heraklion

Vienna

Rumelia

Danube

Hungary

Crete

Mediterranean Sea

Austria

Bari

Corfu

Athens

Venice

Rome

Naples

Sicily

Tripoli

Florence

France

Tunis

Algiers

Spain

N

Ottoman Empire:
in 1512
in 1520

PART I

At one point midway on our path in life,
I came around and found myself now searching
through a dark wood, the right way blurred and lost.
How hard it is to say what that wood was,
a wilderness, savage, brute, harsh and wild.
Only to think of it renews my fear!

—DANTE, INFERNO

ONE

An eagle soared, high in the hard, clear sky.

The traveler, dusty, battered from the road, drew his eyes from it, pulled himself up and over a low, rough wall, and stood motionless for a moment, scanning the scene with keen eyes. The rugged snowcapped mountains fenced in the castle, protecting it and enclosing it as it reared on the crest of its own height, the domed tower of its keep mirroring the lesser dome of the prison tower nearby. Iron rocks like claws clung to the bases of its sheer grey walls. Not the first time he'd seen it—a day earlier he'd caught his first glimpse, at dusk, from a promontory he'd climbed a mile west. Built as if by sorcery in this impossible terrain, at one with the rocks and crags it joined forces with.

...d arrived at his goal—at last. After twelve weary months on the journey. And such a long journey—the ways deep and the weather sharp.

Crouching, just in case, and keeping still as he instinctively checked his weapons, the traveler kept watching. Any sign of movement. Any.

Not a soul on the battlements. Scuds of snow twisting in a cutting wind. But no sign of a man. The place seemed deserted. As he'd expected from what he'd read of it. But life had taught him that it was always best to make sure. He stayed still.

Not a sound but the wind. Then—something. A scraping? To his left ahead of him, a handful of pebbles skittered down a bare incline. He tensed, rose slightly, head up between ducked shoulders. Then the arrow whacked into his right shoulder, through the body armor there.

He staggered a little, grimacing in pain as his hand went to the arrow, raising his head, looking hard at the skein of a rise in the rocks—a small precipice, maybe twenty feet high—which rose before the front of the castle and served as a natural outer bailey. On its ridge there now appeared a man in a dull red tunic with grey outer garments and armor. He bore the insignia of a captain. His bare head was close-shaven, and a scar seared his face, across from right down to left. He opened his mouth in an expression that was part snarl, part smile of triumph, showing stunted and uneven teeth, brown like the tombstones in an unkempt graveyard.

The traveler pulled at the arrow's shaft. Though the

barbed head snagged on the armor, it had only pene-trated the metal, and the point had scarcely penetrated his flesh. He snapped it off the shaft and threw it aside. As he did so he saw a hundred and more armed men, similarly dressed, halberds and swords ready, line up along the crest on either side of the shaven-headed captain. Helmets with nose guards hid their faces, but the black eagle crests on their tunics told the traveler who they were, and he knew what he could expect from them if they took him.

Was he getting old, to have fallen into a trap so sim-ple? But he'd taken every precaution.

And it hadn't succeeded yet.

He stepped back, ready for them as they poured down to the rugged platform of ground he stood on, fanning out to surround him, keeping the length of their hal-berds between themselves and their prey. He could sense that despite their numbers, they feared him. His reputa-tion was known, and they were right to be wary.

He gauged the halberd heads. Double-type: axe and pike.

He flexed his arms and from his wrists his two lean, grey, deadly hidden-blades sprang. Bracing himself, he de-flected the first blow, sensing that it had been hesitant— did they want to try to take him alive? Then they started digging at him from all sides with their weapons, trying to bring him to his knees.

He whirled, and with two clean movements sliced through the hafts of the nearest halberds, seizing the head of one as it flew through the air, before it could fall to earth; and taking the stump of its haft in his fist, he buried the axeblade in the chest of its former owner.

They closed in on him then, and he was just in time to stoop low as a rush of air signaled the passage of a swung pike as it sickled over him, missing his bent back by an inch. He swung round savagely and with his left-hand hidden-blade hacked deep into the legs of the attacker who'd stood behind him. With a howl, the man went down.

The traveler seized the fallen halberd, which a moment earlier had almost ended him, and swiveled it round in the air, slicing the hands off another of his assailants. The hands arched through the air, the fingers curled as if beseeching mercy, a plume of blood like a red rainbow curve trailing behind them.

That stopped them for a moment, but these men had seen worse sights than that, and the traveler had only a second's respite before they were closing again. He swung the halberd again and left its blade deep in the neck of a man who, an instant before, had been moving in for the kill. The traveler let go of its pole and retracted his hidden-blades in one action in order to free his hands to seize a sergeant wielding a broadsword, whom he threw bodily into a knot of his troops, seizing his sword from him. He hefted its weight, feeling his biceps tense as he took a double grip and raised it just in time to cleave the helmet of another halberdier, this time coming from his rear left quarter, hoping to blindside him.

The sword was good. Better for this job than the light

scimitar at his side, acquired on his journey. And the hidden-blades for close work. They had never let him down.

More men were streaming down from the castle. How many would it take to overpower this lone man? They crowded him, but he whirled and jumped to confuse them, seeking freedom from their press by hurling himself over the back of one man, finding his feet, bracing himself, deflecting a sword's blow with the hard metal bracer on his left wrist, and turning to drive his own sword into that attacker's side.

But then—a momentarily lull. Why? The traveler paused, getting his breath. There was a time when he would not have needed to get his breath. He looked up. Still fenced in by the troops in grey chain mail.

But among them, the traveler suddenly saw another man.

Another man. Walking between them. Unobserved, calm. A young man in white. Clad as the traveler was, otherwise, and wearing the same cowl over his head, the hood peaked, as his was, to a sharp point at the front, like an eagle's beak. The traveler's lips parted in wonder. All seemed silent. All seemed at rest, except for the young man in white, walking. Steadily, calmly, undismayed.

The young man seemed to walk among the fighting like a man would walk through a field of corn—as if it did not touch or affect him at all. Was that the same buckle fastening his gear, the same as the one the traveler wore? With the same insignia? The insignia that had been branded on the traveler's consciousness and his life for over thirty years—just as surely as, long ago, his ring finger had been branded?

The traveler blinked, and when he opened his eyes, the vision—if that was what it had been—had disappeared, and the noise, the smells, the danger, were back, all around him, closing on him, rank upon rank of an enemy he knew at last that he could not overcome or escape from.

But somehow he did not feel so alone.

No time to think. They were closing in hard, as scared as they were angry. Blows rained, too many to fend off. The traveler fought hard, took down five more, ten. But he was fighting a hydra with a thousand heads. A big swordsman came up and brought a twenty-pound blade down on him. He raised his left arm to fend it off with the bracer, turning and dropping his own heavy sword as he did so to bring his right-hand hidden-blade into play. But his attacker was lucky. The momentum of his blow was deflected by the bracer, but it was still too powerful to glance off completely. It slid toward the traveler's left wrist and made contact with the left-hand hidden-blade, snapping it off. At the same moment, the traveler, caught off balance, stumbled on a loose rock at his feet and turned his ankle. He could not stop himself from falling facedown onto the stony ground. And there he lay.

Above him, the circle of men closed in, keeping the length of their halberds between themselves and their quarry, still tense, still scared, not yet daring to be triumphant. But the points of their pikes made contact with his back. One move, and he'd be dead.

And he was not ready for that, yet.

The crunch of boots on rock. A man approaching. The traveler turned his head slightly to see the shaven-headed captain standing over him. The scar was livid across his face. He bent close enough for the traveler to smell his breath.

The captain drew the traveler's hood back just enough to see his face. He smiled as his expectation was confirmed.

"Ah, the Mentor has arrived. Ezio Auditore da Firenze. We've been expecting you—as you have no doubt realized. Must be quite a shock to you, to see your Brotherhood's old stronghold in our hands. But it was bound to happen. For all your efforts, we were bound to prevail."

He stood erect, turned to the troops encircling Ezio, two hundred strong, and snapped out an order. "Take him to the turret cell. Manacle him first, and strongly."

They pulled Ezio to his feet and hastily, nervously, bound him fast.

"Just a short walk and a lot of stairs," the captain said. "And then you'd better pray. We'll hang you in the morning."

High above them, the eagle continued its search for prey. No one had an eye for it. For its beauty. Its freedom.

Two

The eagle still wheeled in the sky. A pale blue sky, bleached by the sun, though the sun was a little lower. The bird of prey, a dark silhouette, turning and turning, but with purpose. Its shadow fell on the bare rocks far below, torn jagged by them as it passed over.

Ezio watched through the narrow window—no more than a gash in the thick stone—and his eyes were as restless as the movements of the bird. His thoughts were restless, too. Had he traveled so far and for so long, only for it all to come to this?

He clenched his fists, and his muscles felt the absence of the hidden-blades, which had for so long stood him in such good stead.

But he had an idea of where they'd stowed his weapons,

after they'd ambushed him and overpowered him and brought him here. A grim smile formed on his lips. Those troops, the old enemy—how surprised they'd been that such an old lion could still have so much fight in him.

And he knew this castle. From charts and diagrams. He had studied them so well that they were printed on his mind.

But here he was, in a cell in one of the topmost towers of the great fortress of Masyaf, the citadel that had once been the stronghold of the Assassins, long since abandoned, and now fallen to the Templars. Here he was— alone, unarmed, hungry, and thirsty, his clothes grimy and torn, awaiting every moment the footfall of his executioners. But not about to go quietly. He knew why the Templars were there; he had to stop them.

And they hadn't killed him yet.

He kept his eyes on the eagle. He could see every feather, every pinion, the fanned rudder of the tail, speckled black-brown and white, like his own beard. The pure white wingtips.

He thought back. He traced the route that had brought him there—to this.

Other towers, other battlements. Like the ones at Viana, from which he had flung Cesare Borgia to his doom. That had been in the year of Our Lord 1507. How long ago was that? Four years. It might as well have been four centuries, it seemed so distant. And in the meantime, other villains, other would-be masters of the world, had come and gone, in search of the Mystery, in search of the Power, and for him, a prisoner at last, the battle to counter them had gone on.

The battle. His whole life.

The eagle wheeled and turned, its movements concentrated. Ezio watched it, knowing that it had located prey and was focusing on it. What life could there be down there? But the village that supported the castle, crouched low and unhappy in its shadow, would have livestock, and even a scrap of cultivated land somewhere nearby. A goat, maybe, down there among the tumble of grey rocks that littered the low, surrounding hills; either a young one, too inexperienced, or an old one, too tired, or one that had been injured. The eagle flew against the sun, its silhouette momentarily blotted out by the incandescent light; and then, tightening its circle, it hung, poised, at last, hanging there in the vast blue arena, before it swooped down, crashing through the air like a thunderbolt, and out of sight.

Ezio turned away from the window and looked around the cell. A bed, hard dark wood, just planks on it, no bedding, a stool, and a table. No crucifix on the wall, and nothing else except the plain pewter bowl and spoon which contained the still-untasted gruel they'd given him. That, and a wooden beaker of water, also untasted. For all his thirst and hunger, Ezio feared drugs that might weaken him, render him powerless when the moment came. And it was all too possible that the Templars would have drugged the food and drink they gave him.

He turned around in the narrow cell, but the rough

stone walls gave him neither comfort nor hope. There was nothing here he could use to escape. He sighed. There were other Assassins, others in the Brotherhood who knew of his mission, who had wanted to accompany him, even, despite his insistence that he travel alone. Perhaps, when no news came, they would take up the challenge. But then, perhaps, it would be too late.

The question was, how much did the Templars already know? How much of the secret did they already have in their possession?

His quest, which had now come to such an abrupt halt at the moment of its fruition, had begun soon after his return to Rome, where he had bid farewell to his companions, Leonardo da Vinci and Niccolò Machiavelli, on his forty-eighth birthday, Midsummer Day. Niccolò was to return to Florence, Leonardo to Milan. Leonardo had spoken of taking up a pressing offer of much-needed patronage from Francis, heir apparent to the throne of France, and a residence in Amboise, on the River Loire. At least, that was what his letters had revealed to Ezio.

Ezio smiled at the memory of his friend. Leonardo, whose mind was ever teeming with new ideas though it always took him a while to get around to them. He thought ruefully of the hidden-blade, which had been shattered in the fight when they'd ambushed him. Leonardo—how he missed him!—the one man he could have really trusted to mend it. But at least Leonardo had sent him the plans he'd made for a new device, which he called a parachute. Ezio had had it constructed back in Rome, and it was packed with his kit, and he doubted if the Templars would make much sense of it. He would put it to good use as soon as he got a chance.

If he got a chance.

He steeled himself against dark thoughts.

But there was nothing to do, no means of escape, until they came to get him, to hang him. He would have to plan what to do then. He imagined that, as so often in the past, he would have to extemporize. In the meantime, he'd try to rest his body. Still fit, he'd made sure of that in training before this journey, and the journey itself had hardened him. But he was glad—even in these circumstances—of the chance to rest after that fight.

It had all started with a letter.

Under the benevolent eye of Pope Julius II, who had aided him in his vanquishing of the Borgia family, Ezio had rebuilt and restructured the Assassins' Brotherhood in Rome and established his power base there.

For a while at least, the Templars were in abeyance, and Ezio left the running of operations in the capable hands of his sister Claudia; but the Assassins remained vigilant. They knew that the Templars would regroup, secretly, elsewhere, insatiable in their quest for the instruments by which they could at last control the world in accordance with their somber tenets.

They were bested for the moment, but the beast was not dead.

Ezio drew comfort and satisfaction from the fact—
and he shared this dark knowledge with Machiavelli and
Leonardo alone—that the Apple of Eden, which had fallen
into his care, and which had caused so much anguish
and death in the battle for its possession, was buried and
hidden deep in the vaults below the Church of San
Nicola in Carcere, in a secret sealed room whose location
they had marked only with the sacred symbols of the
Brotherhood—which only a future Assassin would be
able to discern, let alone decipher. The greatest Piece of
Eden was safely concealed from the ambitious grasp of
the Templars—as Ezio hoped, forever.

After the damage wrought to the Brotherhood by the
Borgias, there had been much to retrieve, much to put in
order, and to this task Ezio had devoted himself, uncom-
plainingly, although he was far more inclined to open air
and action than to poring over papers in dusty archives.
That was a job more suited to his late father's secretary,
Giulio, or to the bookish Machiavelli; but Machiavelli
was busy commanding the Florentine militia these days,
and Giulio was long dead.

Still, Ezio reflected, if he hadn't saddled himself with
the responsibility for what was to him a dreary task, he
might never have found the letter. And if another had,
that person might not have guessed its significance.

The letter, which he'd found in a leather satchel, brittle
with age, was from Ezio's father, Giovanni, to his brother
Mario, the man who'd taught Ezio the art of war and
initiated him into the Brotherhood three long decades
earlier. Mario. Ezio flinched at the memory. Mario, who

had died at the cruel and cowardly hands of Cesare Borgia in the wake of the battle of Monteriggioni.

Mario had long since been avenged, but the letter Ezio found opened a new chapter, and its contents proffered him the chance of a new mission. It was 1509 when he'd found it, and he'd just turned fifty; he knew that the chance of new missions seldom came to men of his age. Besides, the letter offered him the hope and the challenge of closing the gates of opportunity on the Templars forever.

Palazzo Auditore
Firenze
iv febbraio MCDLVIII

Dear Brother—

The forces against us are gathering strength, and there is a man in Rome who has taken command of our enemies who is perhaps the greatest power you and I will ever have to reckon with. For this reason, I impart to you, under the seal of utmost secrecy, the following information. If fate should overtake me, ensure—with your life, if necessary—that this information never falls into our enemies' hands.

There is, as you know, a castle called Masyaf in Syria, which was once the seat of our Brotherhood. There, over two centuries ago, our then Mentor, Altaïr Ibn-La'Ahad, greatest of our Order, established a library deep beneath the fortress.

I say no more now. Discretion dictates that what else I have to tell you of this must be in conversation and never written down.

This is a quest I would have longed to accomplish myself, but there is no time now. Our enemies press upon us, and we have no time except to fight back.

Your Brother
Giovanni Auditore

With this letter was another sheet of paper—a tantalizing fragment, clearly in his father's handwriting but equally clearly not by him—a translation of a much older document, also there with it, on parchment that accorded very closely with that on which the original Codex pages, uncovered by Ezio and his companions nearly thirty years earlier, had been written:

I have spent days with the artifact now. Or has it been weeks? Months? The others come from time to time, offering food or distraction; and though I know in my heart I should separate myself from these dark studies, I find it more and more difficult to assume my normal duties. Malik has been supportive, but even now that old edge returns to his voice. Still, my work must continue. This Apple of Eden must be understood. Its function is simple. Elementary, even: dominion. Control. But the process . . . the methods and means it employs . . . THESE are fascinating. It is temptation incarnate. Those subjected to its glow are promised all that they desire. It asks only one thing in return: complete and total obedience. And who can truly refuse? I remember my own moment of weakness when confronted by Al Mualim, my Mentor, and my confidence was shaken by his words. He, who had been like a father, was now revealed to be my greatest enemy. Just the briefest flicker of doubt was all he needed to creep into my mind. But I vanquished his phantoms—restored my self-confidence—and sent him from this world. I freed myself from his control. But now I wonder, is this true? For here I sit—desperate to understand that which I intended to destroy. I sense it is more than just a weapon, a tool for manipulating men's minds. Or is it? Perhaps it's simply following its design: showing me what I desire most. Knowledge . . . Always hovering at the edge. Just out of reach. Beckoning. Promising. Tempting . . .

The old manuscript tailed off there, the rest lost, and, indeed, the parchment was so brittle with age that its edges crumbled as he touched it.

Ezio understood little of it, but some of it was so familiar that his skin tingled, even his scalp, at the memory.

It did again, as Ezio recalled it, sitting in his cell in the prison tower at Masyaf, watching the sun set on what might be his last day on earth.

He visualized the old manuscript in his mind. It was

this, more than anything, that had determined him to travel east, to Masyaf.

Darkness fell quickly. The sky was cobalt blue. Stars already speckled it.

For no reason, Ezio's thoughts turned to the young man in white. The man he'd seemed to see in the lull in the fighting. Who had appeared and disappeared so mysteriously, like a vision, but who had, somehow, been *real*, and who had, somehow, *communicated* with him.

THREE

Preparations for his journey had taken Ezio the rest of that year and spilled into the next. He rode north to Florence and conferred with Machiavelli, though he did not tell him all that he knew. In Ostia, he visited Bartolomeo d'Alviano, who had filled out with too much good food and wine but was as ferocious as ever though he was a family man now. He and Pantasilea had produced three sons and, a month ago, a daughter. What had he said?

"Time you got a move on, Ezio! None of us is getting any younger."

Ezio had smiled. Barto was luckier than he knew.

Ezio regretted that there was no time to extend his journey farther north to Milan, but he had kept his weaponry in good order—the blades, the pistol, the bracer—and there was no time, either, to tempt Leonardo into finding yet more ways of improving them. Indeed, Leonardo himself had said, after he'd last overhauled them, a year earlier, that they were now beyond improvement.

That remained to be seen when they were next put to the test.

Machiavelli had given him other news in Florence, a city he still set foot in only with sadness, so heaped was it with memories of his lost family and his devastated inheritance. His lost love, too—the first and, he thought, perhaps the only true one of his life—Cristina Vespucci. Twelve years—could it really be so long since she had died at the hands of Savonarola's fanatics? And now another death. Machiavelli had told him about it, hesitantly. The faithless Caterina Sforza, who had blighted Ezio's life as much as Cristina had blessed it, had just died, a wasted old woman of forty-six, forgotten and poor, her vitality and confidence long since extinguished.

As he went through life, Ezio began to think that the best company he'd ever truly have would be his own.

But he had no time to grieve or brood. The months flew by, and soon it was Christmas, and so much still to do.

At last, early in the New Year, on the Feast of St. Hilary, he was ready, and a day was set for his departure from Rome, via Naples, to the southern port of Bari, with an escort organized by Bartolomeo, who'd ride with him.

At Bari, he would take ship.

FOUR

"God go with you, brother," Claudia told him on his last morning in Rome. They had risen before dawn. Ezio would leave at first light.

"You must take care of things here in my absence."

"Do you doubt me?"

"Not anymore. Have you still not forgiven me for that?"

Claudia smiled. "There is a great beast in Africa called the elephant. They say it never forgets. It is the same with women. But don't worry, Ezio. I will take care of things until you return."

"Or until we have need of a new Mentor."

Claudia didn't reply to that. Her face became troubled. She said: "This mission. Why do you go alone? Why have you said so little of its import?"

"'He travels fastest who travels alone,'" Ezio quoted by way of reply. "As for details, I have left our father's papers in your keeping. Open them if I do not return. And I have told you all you need to know of Masyaf."

"Giovanni was my father, too."

"But he entrusted this responsibility to me."

"You have assumed it, brother."

"I am Mentor," he said, simply. "It is my responsibility."

She looked at him. "Well, travel safely. Write."

"I will. In any case, you won't have to worry about me between here and Bari. Barto will be with me all the way."

She still looked worried. Ezio was touched that the tough woman his sister had grown up to be still had a tender spot in her heart for him. His overland journey would lead him through Italy's southern territories, and they were controlled by the Crown of Aragon. But King Ferdinand hadn't forgotten his debt to Ezio.

"If I'm after action," he told her, reading her thought, "I won't get any until I set sail. And my course leads pretty far to the north for me to have to worry about Barbary corsairs. We'll hug the Greek coast after Corfu."

"I'm more worried about your completing what you're setting out to do. Not because I'm worried about you personally—"

"Oh really? Thank you for that."

She grinned. "You know what I mean. From all you've said, and Santa Veronica may hold witness that you've told me little enough, a good outcome is important for us."

"That's why I'm going now. Before the Templars can regain strength."

"Seize the initiative?"

"That's about it."

She took his face in her hands. He looked at her one last time. At forty-nine, she was still a strikingly beautiful woman, her dark hair still dark and her fiery nature unquenched. Sometimes he regretted that she had not found another man after the death of her husband, but she was devoted to her children and her work, and made no secret of the fact that she loved living in Rome, which, under Pope Julius, had once again become a sophisticated international city and an artistic and religious mecca.

They embraced, and Ezio mounted his horse, at the head of the short cavalcade that was accompanying him—fifteen armed riders under Barto, who was already mounted, his heavy horse pawing the dust, impatient to be gone, and a wagon to carry their supplies. For himself, all Ezio needed was in two black leather saddlebags. "I'll forage as I go along," he'd told Claudia.

"You're good at that," she'd replied with a wry grin.

Raising his hand as he settled into the saddle, Ezio wheeled his horse, and, as Barto brought his own steed alongside, they made their way down the east side of the river, away from the Assassins' Headquarters on Tiber Island, toward the city gates and the long road south.

* * *

It took them fifteen days to reach Bari, and once there, Ezio bade leave of his old friend hastily, in order not to miss the first available flood tide. He took a ship belonging to the Turkish merchant fleet managed by Piri Reis and his family. Once installed in the after cabin of the large lateen-sailed dhow, the *Anaan*—a freighter on which he was the only passenger—Ezio took the opportunity to check—once again—the essential gear he had taken with him. Two hidden-blades, one for each wrist, his bracer for the left forearm, to deflect the blows of swords, and the spring-loaded pistol that Leonardo had made for him, along with all his other special armaments, from ancient designs found in the pages of the Codex of the Assassins.

Ezio was traveling light. In truth, he expected to find Masyaf, if he succeeded in reaching it, deserted. At the same time, he admitted to himself that he was uneasy at the scarcity of Assassin intelligence about Templar movements in the present days of apparent, or, at least, relative, peace.

As far as this second leg of the journey, which would take him to Corfu, was concerned, he knew he had little to fear. Piri Reis was a great captain among the Ottomans, and had once been a pirate himself, so his men would know how to handle them if fear of Piri's name alone didn't keep them at bay. Ezio wondered if he'd ever meet the great man himself one day. If he did, he hoped Piri, not known for his easygoing nature, would have forgotten the time when the Brotherhood had been constrained to "liberate" some of Piri's precious maps from him.

The Ottomans themselves now held sway over Greece and much of eastern Europe—indeed, their territories almost touched those of Venice in the west. Not everyone was happy with the situation, and with the presence of so many Turks in Europe; but Venice, after a standoff, had continued to trade with its Muslim neighbors, and la Serenissima had kept control of Corfu, Crete, and Cyprus.

Ezio couldn't see the situation lasting—the Ottomans had already made unfriendly advances on Cyprus—but for the moment, peace held, and Sultan Bayezid was too preoccupied with internal family squabbles to make any trouble in the west.

The broad-beamed ship, with her great sail of white canvas, cut through the water more like a broadsword than a knife, but they made good time despite adverse headwinds, and the short voyage across the mouth of the Adriatic took little more than five days.

After a welcome from the governor of Corfu, a fat Italian called Franco who liked to be called Spyridon, after the local patron saint, and who long since had clearly abandoned politics for lotus-eating, Ezio had a talk with the ship's captain as they stood on a balcony fronting the governor's villa, and looking out over palm trees to the harbor, which nestled under a sky of blue velvet. In exchange for another pouch of Venetian *soldi*, they agreed between them that Ezio should continue on to Athens.

"That's our destination," the captain told him. "We'll be hugging the coast, I've done the trip twenty times, there will be no problem, no danger. And from there it will be easy to take a vessel bound for Crete and even on to Cyprus. In fact, I'll introduce you to my brother-in-law Ma'Mun when we reach Athens. He's a shipping agent. He'll take care of you."

"I'm obliged," Ezio said. He hoped the man's confidence was well placed. The *Anaan* was taking on an important cargo of spices for transfer to Athens, and Ezio remembered enough from his early days when his father was one of the major bankers of Florence to know that this cargo would make the *Anaan* a tempting target for any pirate, no matter how great a fear the name of Piri Reis might strike in them. If you fight on a ship, you need to be able to move fast and lightly. In the town, the following morning, he went to an armorer and bought a well-tempered scimitar, beating the man down to one hundred *soldi*.

"Insurance," Ezio told himself.

The following day at dawn, the tide was high enough for them to begin their voyage, and they took advantage of it, together with a brisk northerly wind, which filled their sail immediately. They coasted south, keeping the shore about a mile to their port side. The sun sparkled on the steel blue waves, and the warm wind caressed their hair. Only Ezio could not quite bring himself to relax.

They'd reached a point just south of the island of Zante when it happened. They had pulled out farther to sea to take full advantage of the wind, and the water had turned darker and choppier. The sun was dipping toward the western horizon, and you couldn't look in that direction and see anything without squinting. The mariners were casting a log over the starboard side to take the speed, and Ezio watched them.

Afterward, he couldn't have said what it was that had caught his attention. A seabird, perhaps, dipping along the side of the ship, attracted his eye. But it was no bird. It was sail. Two sails. Two seagoing galleys, coming in out of the sun, taking them by surprise and almost upon them.

The corsairs had lain alongside almost before the captain had had time to summon his crew to arms and action stations. The pirates threw grappling irons on ropes over the *Anaan*'s sides and were soon scrambling aboard, as Ezio raced aft to arm himself. Luckily, he had the scimitar already at his side and was able to put it to its first tests, slicing his way through five Berber seamen as he struggled to reach his goal.

He was breathing heavily as he hastily strapped on his bracer and his gun. He had enough faith in the scimitar by then to dispense with his hidden-blades, which he stowed quickly in a hiding place in the cabin, and he judged the bracer and the gun the better weapons for this combat.

He sprang out into the fray—around him the familiar clashing of weapons and already the smell of blood. A fire had started forward, and the wind, which had chosen that moment to turn, now threatened to drag it aft the length of the ship. Commanding two Ottoman sailors to grab buckets, he ordered them back forward to where the ship's water reservoir was. At that moment, a pirate flung himself from the rigging onto Ezio's shoulders. One of the sailors yelled out a warning. Ezio spun round, flexed the muscles of his right wrist, and his gun sprang from the mechanism strapped to his forearm, into his hand. Swiftly, with no time to aim, he fired, stepping back immediately to allow the still-falling body to crash past him onto the deck.

"Fill, quickly, and put out the flames before they spread," he yelled. "The ship will be lost if the fire takes hold."

He hacked away at three or four Berbers who had raced toward him, sensing already that he was the one man aboard to neutralize, if their attack was to be successful. He then found himself confronted with the corsair captain, a burly brute with an English cutlass in each hand—booty, no doubt, from some earlier unfortunate victims.

"Yield, Venetian dog!" the man snarled.

"Your first mistake," replied Ezio. "Never insult a Florentine by mistaking him for a Venetian."

The captain's reply was to bring a savage left-armed blow ringing down toward Ezio's head, but Ezio was ready for it and raised his own left arm, letting the cutlass blade slide harmlessly the length of the bracer and off into the air. The captain hadn't expected this and was thrown off balance. Ezio tripped him and flung him headlong into the reservoir in the hold below.

"Help, *effendi*! I cannot swim!" the captain burbled as he surfaced.

"Then you had better learn," Ezio told him, turning away to cut at two more pirates, who were almost upon him. Out of the corner of his eye, he could see that his own two sailors had succeeded in lowering their buckets on ropes into the reservoir and that now, joined by a handful more of their shipmates, similarly equipped, they were beginning to get the fire under control.

But the most ferocious fighting had moved to the rear of the ship, and there the Ottomans were getting the worst of it. Ezio realized that the Berbers had no desire for the *Anaan* to burn, for that way they'd lose their prize; so they were letting Ezio's sailors get on with the job of dousing the fire while they concentrated on taking the ship.

His mind moved fast. They were badly outnumbered, and he knew that the *Anaan*'s crew, tough men as they were, were not trained fighters. He turned to a stack of unlit torches stowed under a hatchway in the bow. Leaping over and seizing one, he thrust it into the dying flames of the fire, and once it had taken, he threw it with all his force across into the farther of the two Berber ships lying alongside. Then he seized another and repeated the action. By the time the Berbers aboard the *Anaan* realized what was going on, each of their ships was well ablaze.

It was a calculated risk, but it paid off. Instead of fighting for control of their prey, and realizing that their captain was nowhere to be seen, they panicked and beat a way back to the gunwale, as the Ottomans, taking heart, renewed their own efforts and launched a counterattack, lashing out with sticks, swords, hatchets, bit ends, and whatever else came to hand.

In another fifteen minutes, they had driven the Berbers back to their own ships and cast off from them, cutting the grappling irons free with axes and using poles to push the burning galleys away. The Ottoman captain barked a number of rapid orders, and soon the *Anaan* was clear. Once order had been reestablished, the crew set about swabbing the decks of blood and stacking the bodies of the dead. Ezio knew that it would have been against their religion to cast any body overboard. He just hoped the rest of the journey wouldn't take long.

The Berber captain, a soggy mess, was hauled from the reservoir. He stood on the deck, abject and dripping.

"You'd better disinfect that water," Ezio said to the *Anaan*'s captain, as the pirate chief was led away in irons.

"We have enough drinking water for our needs in barrels—they will take us as far as Athens," the captain replied. Then he drew a small leather purse from the pouch at his side. "This is for you," he said.

"What is it?"

"I'm refunding your fare," said the captain. "It's the least I can do. And when we reach Athens, I'll see to it that your feat is spoken of. As for your onward journey, rest assured that everything will be arranged for you."

"We shouldn't have relaxed," said Ezio.

The captain looked at him. "You are right. Perhaps one should never relax."

"You are right," Ezio replied, sadly.

FIVE

Athens had prospered under the Turks, though as he walked the streets and visited the monuments and temples of the Greek Golden Age, being rediscovered and revered in his own country, and saw with his own eyes the statues and buildings that were inspiring his friends Michelangelo and Bramante in Rome, Ezio understood something of the proud resentment that gleamed unmistakably in the eyes of several of the men and women of the local population. But he was fêted by Ma'Mun, the Ottoman captain's brother-in-law, and his family, who showered him with gifts and urged him to stay.

His stay was longer than he had wanted it to be in any case since unseasonable storms had boiled up in the Aegean north of Serifos, battering the cluster of islands to the south of Athens and effectively closing the port of Piraeus for a month or more. Never had such tempests been seen at that time of year. Street prophets inevitably muttered about the end of the world, a topic much discussed at the time of the half millennium in 1500. In the meantime, Ezio, having no time for such things and only chafing against the delay, brooded over the maps and notes he had brought with him and vainly tried to glean intelligence on the Templars' movements in the area and in the region south and east of Greece.

At one celebration in his honor, he made the acquaintance of a Dalmatian princess and had a dalliance with her, but it was no more than that, a dalliance, and his heart remained as isolated as it had been for so long. He had ceased, he told himself, to look for love. A home of his own, a real home, and a family—these held no place in the life of an Assassin Mentor. Ezio had read something, dimly understood, of the life of his remote forebear in the Brotherhood, Altaïr Ibn-La'Ahad. He had paid dearly for having a family. And even though Ezio's own father had managed it, he, too, had paid a bitter price in the end.

But at last—not too soon for the impatient Ezio—the winds and the seas abated and were replaced with the fine weather of spring. Ma'Mun had made all the arrangements for his onward passage to Crete, and the same ship would take him farther—as far as Cyprus. This vessel was a warship, a four-masted *kogge*, the *Qutaybah*, with one of its lower decks armed with a line of ten cannon on each side, and more guns in emplacements in the hull fore and aft. In addition to lateen sails, she was square-rigged, European-style, on the mainmast and mizzen-mast; and there was an oar deck below the cannon, thirty oars to a side.

Chained to one of them was the Berber captain Ezio had tangled with on the *Anaan*.

"You will be free from the need to defend yourself on this ship, *effendi*," Ma'Mun told Ezio.

"I admire it. It has something of the European design about it."

"Our Sultan Bayezid admires much that is gracious and useful in your culture," replied Ma'Mun. "We can learn much from each other if we try."

Ezio nodded.

"The *Qutaybah* carries our Athens envoy to a conference at Nicosia, and will dock at Larnaka in twenty days. The captain stops at Heraklion only to take on water and supplies." He paused. "And I have something for you . . ."

They were seated, drinking *sharbat*, in Ma'Mun's office in the port. The Turk now turned to a huge iron-bound chest that stood against the far wall, taking from it a map. "This is precious, as all maps are, but it is a special gift from me to you. It is a map of Cyprus drawn up by Piri Reis himself. You will have time there—" He held up his hands as Ezio began to object, as politely as he could. The farther east you traveled, the less urgency there seemed to be about time. "I know! I am aware of your impatience to reach Syria, but the *kogge* will only take you so far, and we must arrange your onward transport from Larnaka. Fear not. You saved the *Anaan*. We will be suitably grateful for that act. No one will get you to your destination faster than we."

Ezio unrolled the map and examined it. It was a fine, detailed work. He thought that if he was indeed obliged to spend time on that island, he knew from clues he had already picked up in his father's archives that Cyprus was not without interest to the Assassins, in the history of their eternal struggle with the Templars, and that it could well be that there he would find clues that might help him.

He would make good use of his time at Cyprus, but he hoped he would not have to tarry there long, effectively controlled as it was by the Templars, whatever appearances might be to the contrary.

But it was to be a longer journey than anyone might have anticipated. Hardly had they set sail from Crete after their brief landing at Heraklion—a matter of no more than three days—than the winds began to rage again. Southerly this time, fierce and warm still from their long journey out of North Africa. The *Qutayah* battled them bravely, but by degrees she was beaten back north up the Aegean, fighting her retreat through the tangle of islands of the Dodecanese. It was a week before the storms abated, not before claiming the lives of five mariners and an uncounted number of galley prisoners, who drowned at their oars. At last, the ship put into Chios for a refit.

Ezio dried his gear and cleaned his equipment of any rust. The metal of his special weapons had never shown the least sign of tarnish in all the years he had had them. One of the many mysterious properties they had, which Leonardo had attempted to explain to him in vain.

Three precious months had been lost before the *Qutaybah* at last limped into the harbor of Larnaka. The envoy, who'd lost twenty pounds on the voyage, through seasickness and vomiting, and who'd long since missed his conference, made immediate arrangements to travel back to Athens by the most direct route, traveling overland as far as he could.

Ezio wasted no time in looking up the Larnaka agent, Bekir, whose name Ma'Mun had given him. Bekir was welcoming and even deferential. Ezio Auditore da Firenze. The famous rescuer of ships! He was already the talk of Larnaka. Auditore *effendi*'s name was on every lip. Ah—the question of passage to Tortosa. The nearest mainland port to Masyaf. In Syria. Yes, yes of course. Arrangements will be placed in hand immediately—this very day! If the *effendi* will be patient, while the necessary wheels are set in motion . . . The best possible accommodations will be at his disposal . . .

The lodgings arranged for Ezio were indeed splendid—a large, light apartment in a mansion built on a low hill above the town, overlooking it and the crystal sea beyond. But after too much time had passed, his patience grew thin.

"It is the Venetians," explained the agent. "They tolerate an Ottoman presence here, but only in a civil sense. The military authorities are, regrettably, wary of us. I feel that"—the man lowered his voice—"were it not for the reputation of our sultan, Bayezid, whose authority stretches far and whose power is mighty, we might not be tolerated at all." He brightened: "Perhaps *you* could help in your own cause, *effendi*."

"In what way?"

"I thought, perhaps, that as a Venetian yourself . . ."

Ezio bit his lip.

But he was not a man to let time hang idly. While he waited, he studied Piri Reis's map, and something drew him, something half-remembered that he had read, to hire a horse and ride down the coast to Limassol.

Once there, he found himself wandering through the motte and bailey of the deserted castle of Guy de Lusignan, built during the Crusades but currently neglected, like some once-useful tool whose owner has forgotten to throw it away. As he walked through its empty, drafty corridors and looked at the wildflowers growing in its courtyards, and the buddleia that clung to its crumbling ramparts, memories—at least, they seemed to be memories—prompted him to explore more deeply, to delve into the bowels of the keep and explore the vaults beneath it.

There, shrouded in crepuscular gloom, he found the desolate and empty remains of what had undoubtedly once been a vast archive. His lonely footfalls echoed in the dark labyrinth of rotting, empty shelving.

The only occupants were scuttling rats, whose eyes glinted suspiciously at him from dark corners as they scurried away, giving him slanting, evil looks. And they could tell him nothing. He made as thorough a search as he could, but not a clue of what had been there remained.

Disheartened, he returned to the sunshine. The presence of a library there reminded him of the library he sought. Something was prompting him though he could not put his finger on what it was. Stubbornly, he remained at the castle two days. Townspeople looked oddly at the dark, grizzled stranger who roamed their ruin.

Then Ezio remembered. Three centuries earlier, Cyprus had been the property of the Templars.

Six

The Venetian authorities—or someone behind them—were clearly blocking his onward passage. This became clear to him as soon as he had confronted them. Florentines and Venetians might have been rivals, might have looked down on one another, but they shared the same country and the same language.

That cut no ice at all with the governor there. Domenico Garofoli was like a pencil—long, thin, and grey. His black robes, exquisitely cut in the most costly damask, nevertheless hung from him like rags from a scarecrow. The heavy gold rings, set with rubies and pearls, clattered loosely on his bony fingers. His lips were so narrow that you could hardly say they were there at all, and when his mouth was closed, you could not see where it was in his face.

He was, of course, unfailingly polite—Ezio's action had done much to warm Ottoman-Venetian relations in the region—but he was clearly unwilling to do anything. The situation on the mainland eastward—beyond the coastal towns that clung to the shore of the Mediterranean like the fingertips of a man hanging from a precipice—was fraught with danger. The Ottoman presence in Syria was mighty, and further Ottoman ambitions westward much feared. Any mission not sanctioned by official diplomacy could trigger an international incident of the most dire proportions. That, at least, was Garofoli's excuse.

There was no way Ezio was going to find allies among his countrymen on Crete.

Ezio listened, and listened, sitting politely, with his hands on his knees, as the governor droned on in a desiccated voice. And decided to take matters into his own hands.

That very evening, he made his first reconnaissance of the docks. There were ships aplenty moored there, dhows from Araby and North Africa bumping against Venetian roccafortes, galleys, and caravels. A Dutch fluyt looked promising, and there were men working aboard, loading thick bales of silk under an armed guard. But once Ezio had recognized the cargo, he knew that the fluyt would be homeward bound, not outward, and he needed a ship sailing east.

He wandered farther, keeping to the shadows, a dark

form still as lithe and fluid as a cat. But his search yielded him nothing.

Several days and nights passed in reconnoitering. He always took all his essential equipment with him, in case he struck it lucky and could get away there and then. But each foray ended with the same result. Ezio's notoriety had marked him, and he had to go to some lengths to keep his identity secret; but even when he succeeded, he found that no ship's master was headed in precisely the direction he wanted, or that they were—for some reason—unwilling to take him, no matter how big the bribe offered. He considered returning to Bekir but resisted this in the end. Bekir already knew too much about his intentions.

The fifth night found him again at the docks. Fewer ships by then, and apart from the Night Watchmen and their crews, who passed seldom, their lanterns swinging on long poles and their swords or truncheons always at the ready, no one else was about. Ezio made his way to the most distant quaysides, where smaller vessels were tied up. The distance to the mainland was not that great. Perhaps if he could . . . acquire . . . some boat of his own, he might be able to sail the seventy-five leagues or so alone.

Cautiously, he set foot on a wooden jetty, its black boards shiny with seawater, along which five small single-sail dhows were ranked, fishing boats from the smell of them, but sturdy, and two of them had all their gear stowed aboard, as far as Ezio could see.

Then the hairs on the back of his neck prickled.

Too late. Before Ezio had time to turn, he was knocked flat on his face by the force of the weight of the man who'd thrown himself on him. Big man, that much Ezio could sense. Very big. He was pinning Ezio down by the size of his body alone; it was like struggling under a massive, muscular eiderdown. Ezio wrenched his right hand free so that he could unleash his hidden-blade, but his wrist was instantly grasped in a grip of iron. He noticed out of the corner of his eye that the hand that held his wrist was cuffed with a manacle from which two broken chain links dangled.

Gathering his strength, Ezio twisted violently and suddenly to his left, digging his left elbow hard into a part of the eiderdown that he hoped was tender. He was fortunate. The man pinioning him grunted in pain and relaxed his hold a fraction. It was enough. Following through, Ezio heaved with his left shoulder and managed to roll the body off his own. Like lightning, he was up on one knee, his left hand on the man's throat, his right poised to strike.

Ezio's moment of triumph was short. The man knocked his right hand away, the iron manacle on the man's left hand, similarly adorned with a couple of chain links, striking Ezio's wrist painfully despite the protection of the hidden-blade's harness, and Ezio found his left wrist now caught in another viselike grip, which slowly but inexorably forced his hold on the man's throat to weaken.

They rolled over, each trying to get the better of the other, putting in blows where they could, but although his assailant was bulky, he was quick, and Ezio's blade never found a mark. At last they separated and stood, grunting, out of breath, hunched, facing each other. The man was unarmed, but the iron manacles could do a lot of damage used as weapons.

Then, from a short distance away, there was a flash of light from a lantern and a cry.

"The Watch!" said the man. "Down!"

Instinctively, Ezio followed the big man's lead as they dived into the nearest dhow, flattening themselves in its bottom. Ezio's mind was racing. In the flash of light from the lantern, he had seen the man's face and recognized him. How could it be?

But there was no time to worry about that. They could hear the footfalls of the Watch scurrying toward the jetty.

"They saw us, may Allah blind them," said the man. "Better see to them. You ready?"

Astonished, Ezio nodded mutely in the dark.

"I'll finish *you* off once we've seen to *them*," the man added.

"I wouldn't bet on it."

There was no time for any more talk as the five men of the Watch were already upon them. Fortunately, they hesitated before throwing themselves down into the dark well of the boat, where Ezio and his unlikely ally now stood, and contented themselves with standing on the jetty, waving their weapons and yelling threats.

The big man regarded them. "Easy meat," he said. "But we'd better take them now, before they attract too much attention."

In reply, Ezio braced himself, crouched, and leapt up to the jetty, catching its edge and hauling himself onto it in one—these days—not-quite-fluid movement. In the

moment it took him to catch his breath, three of the
Watch were upon him, bludgeoning him to the ground
with heavy truncheons, while a fourth man approached,
swirling a short but wicked-looking sword. He raised it
for the coup de grace, but in that instant he was lifted
bodily by the scruff of the neck from behind and hurled,
howling, backward and upward, to land with a sickening
crash a long way farther down the jetty, where he lay
moaning, several of his bones broken.

At the moment that Ezio's three other attackers were
distracted by this, Ezio sprang to his feet and snapped
out his hidden-blade, slicing down two of them in two
quick, efficient strokes. Meanwhile, the big man was
struggling with the lampholder, another giant, who had
thrown his pole aside and drawn a massive Damascus,
which he waved threateningly over the head of his opponent, who held him in a wrestler's body grip. Ezio could
see that at any moment the thick blade would come
down square into the broad back of the big man. He
cursed himself for not having strapped on his gun, but it
was too late for that. He grabbed a fallen truncheon and,
shoving the remaining watchman aside with his elbow,
hurled it at the head of the lanternman.

His aim had—thank God!—been true. The truncheon
struck the lanternman square between the eyes and he
staggered back, falling to his knees. Then Ezio felt a
sharp pain in his side. The surviving member of the
Watch had drawn a dagger and stabbed him. He sank,
and before his world went black, he saw the big man
running toward him.

SEVEN

When Ezio came to, he was lying on his back. somewhere, and the world was rocking beneath him. Not violently, but steadily. It was almost comforting. He stayed where he was for a moment, eyes still closed, feeling a breeze on his face, not quite wanting to come back to whatever reality was waiting to confront him, smelling the sea air.

The sea air?

He opened his eyes. The sun was up, and he could see an unbroken expanse of blue sky. Then a dark shape came between the sky and him. A head and shoulders. A concerned face, looking down at him.

"You're back. Good," said the big man.

Ezio started to sit up, and as he did so the pain from

his wound hit him. He groaned and put a hand to his side. He felt bandages.

"Flesh wound. Not too deep. Nothing to make a fuss about."

Ezio raised himself. His next thought was for his kit. He looked around swiftly. There it was, neatly stashed in his leather bag, and it looked untouched. "Where are we?" he asked.

"Where do you think? At sea."

Painfully, Ezio stood and looked about him. They were in one of the fishing dhows, cutting steadily through the water, the sail above his head fat with wind. He turned, and could see Larnaka, a speck on the coastline of Cyprus, on the distant horizon behind them.

"What happened?"

"You saved my life. I saved yours."

"Why?"

"It's the Law. Pity though. After what you did to me, you had it coming."

The man had had his back to him, working the tiller, but now he turned to Ezio. For the first time Ezio had a good look at his face and recognized him instantly.

"You wrecked my ships, curse you. I'd been stalking the *Anaan* for days. That prize would have taken me back to Egypt a rich man. Instead, thanks to you, they made a galley slave of me. Me!" The big man was indignant.

"Egypt? You're not a Berber then?"

"Berber be damned. I'm a Mamluk though I may not look like one dressed in these rags. Soon as we get there,

I'm treating myself to a woman, a decent plate of *kofta*, and a good suit of clothes."

Ezio looked around him again, stumbling then regaining his balance as an unexpected wave chopped aslant the bow.

"Not much of a seaman, are you?"

"Gondolas are more my line."

"Gondolas? Pah!"

"If you wanted to kill me—"

"Can you blame me? It was the only reason I hung around in that cesspool of a Venetian port after I'd escaped. I couldn't believe my luck when I saw you. I'd almost given up—I was looking for a way out myself, down there."

Ezio grinned. "I don't blame you."

"You chucked me in a tank and left me to drown!"

"You could swim well enough. Any fool could see that."

It was the big man's turn to grin. "Ah! I might have known I couldn't appeal to your compassion by pretending that I couldn't."

"You repaid your debt to me, you saved my life. But why did you bring me with you?"

The big man spread his hands. "You were wounded. If I'd left you, they'd have come for you, you wouldn't have lasted the night. And what a waste of my effort that would have been. Besides, you can make yourself useful on this tub, landlubber though you are."

"I can look after myself."

The big man's eyes grew serious. "I know you can,

effendi. Maybe I just wanted your company—Ezio Auditore."

'You know my name."

"You're famous. Vanquisher of pirates. Not that that would have saved you after killing a team of watchmen and trying to escape."

Ezio thought about that. Then he said, "What do they call you?"

The big man drew himself up. His dignity belied the galley slave's rags he still wore. "I am Al-Scarab, scourge of the White Sea."

"Oh," said Ezio wryly. "Pardon me."

"Temporarily on my back foot," Al-Scarab added ruefully. "But not for long. When we get there, I'll have a new ship and crew within a week."

"When we get where?"

"Didn't I tell you? The nearest port worth anything, that's also in Mamluk hands—Acre."

EIGHT

The time had come.

It was hard to leave, but his mission was imperative, and it called Ezio urgently onward. His time in Acre had been one of rest and recuperation, forcing himself to be patient as his wound healed, for he knew his quest would come to nothing of he were not fully fit for it. And meeting Al-Scarab, disastrous as it would have been if things had gone differently, had shown him that if any guardian angel existed, he had one.

The big pirate, whom he had bested in the battle aboard the *Anaan*, had proved himself to be more than just a lifesaver. Al-Scarab had extended family in Acre, and they welcomed Ezio as the rescuer of their cousin and as his brother-in-arms. Al-Scarab said nothing of his defeat in the *Anaan* incident and enjoined Ezio on pain of unmentionable retribution to follow suit. But the escape from Larnaka was boosted into a fight of epic proportions.

"There were fifty of them . . ." Al-Scarab would start his story, and the number of perfidious Venetian assailants they'd been obliged to fight off had reached ten times that number by his tenth telling of the tale. Open-mouthed and wide-eyed, his cousins listened spellbound, and never breathed a word about any of the inconsistencies that crept in. At least he didn't throw in a sea monster, Ezio thought, drily.

One thing that was not invention were the warnings that came from Al-Scarab's family of the dangers Ezio would have to be prepared for in his onward journey. They tried hard to persuade him to take an armed escort with him, but this Ezio steadfastly declined to do. He would ride his own road. He would not subject others to the perils he knew he must face.

Soon after his arrival at Acre, Ezio took the opportunity to write a long-overdue letter to his sister. He chose his words with care, conscious that this might be the last time he would ever communicate with her.

Acre
xx novembre MDX

My dearest sister Claudia—

I have been in Acre a week now, safe and in high spirits, but prepared for the worst. The men and women who have fed and sheltered me here also give me warning that the road to Masyaf is overrun by mercenaries and bandits not native to this land. What this could mean, I fear to guess.

When I first set out from Roma ten months ago, I did so with a single purpose: to discover what our father could not. In the letter you know of, written the year before my birth, he makes a single mention of a library hidden beneath the floors of Altaïr's former castle. A sanctum full of invaluable wisdom.

But what will I find when I arrive? Who will greet me? A host of eager Templars, as I fear most strongly? Or nothing but the whistling of a cold and lonely wind? Masyaf has not been home to the Assassins for almost three hundred years now. Does it remember us? Are we still welcome?

Ah, I am weary of this fight, Claudia . . . Weary not because I am tired but because our struggle seems to move in one direction only . . . toward chaos. Today I have more questions than answers. That is why I have come so far: to find clarity. To find the wisdom left behind by the Great Mentor, so that I may better understand the purpose of our fight and my place in it.

Should anything happen to me, dear Claudia . . . should my skills fail me, or my ambition lead me astray, do not seek revenge or retribution in my memory but fight to continue the search for truth, so that all may benefit. My story is one of many thousands, and the world will suffer if it ends too soon.

Your brother,
Ezio Auditore da Firenze

Al-Scarab, in the course of fitting out for his own new ventures, had also seen to it that Ezio had the attention of the best doctors, the best tailors, the best chefs, and the best women Acre could provide. His blades were honed and sharpened, his kit was fully cleaned, repaired, replaced where necessary, and thoroughly overhauled.

As the day approached for Ezio to leave, Al-Scarab presented him with two fine horses—"A present from my uncle—he breeds them—but I don't have much use for them in my trade"—tough little Arabs, with soft leather tack and one fine, high-ended, tooled saddle. Ezio continued to refuse any escort but accepted supplies for his journey, which from now on would carry him overland, through what had once, long ago, been the Crusader Kingdom of Jerusalem.

And now the time of parting had come. The last leg in a long journey, and whether it would it be completed or not, Ezio had no way of telling. But for him there was *only* the journey. It had to be made. Old men ought to be explorers. At its end, he would see.

"Go with your God, Ezio."

"*Barakallah feek*, my friend," Ezio replied, taking the big pirate's hand.

"We'll meet again."

"Yes."

Both men wondered in their hearts if they were telling the truth, but the words comforted them. It didn't matter. They looked each other in the eye and knew that in their different ways they were part of the same fellowship.

Ezio mounted the larger of the two horses, the bay, and turned her head around.

Without a backward glance, he headed out of the city, north.

NINE

Masyaf was two hundred miles—as the crow flies—away from Acre. The seemingly gentle desert land that lay between the two points was very far from gentle in fact. The great Ottoman outward thrust from its original core had been going on relentlessly for two hundred years, and had culminated in the taking of Constantinople by the twenty-year-old Sultan Mehmed II in 1453. But still the Turkish tentacles extended, reaching westward as far as Bulgaria and beyond, and south and east into Syria and what had once been the Holy Land. The eastern coastal strip of the White Sea, with its vital ports and its access by water westward, was a jewel in the crown, and the Ottoman grip on it was as yet fragile. Ezio was under no illusions about what battles he would have to face as he made his lonely way north. He followed the coast for most of the way, keeping the sparkling sea in view to his left, riding the high cliffs and the tattered scrublands that topped them, traveling in the hours of dawn and dusk, hiding for four hours when the sun was at its highest and resting again for four hours at night under the stars.

Traveling alone had its advantages. He could blend in far more easily than would have been possible if he'd had an escort, and his keen eyes discerned danger points ahead well enough in advance either to skirt them or wait until they had passed. This was bandit country, where half-disciplined gangs of unemployed mercenaries roamed, killing travelers and each other for what they could get, surviving, as it seemed to Ezio, merely for the sake of it, in a countryside still reeling in the aftermath of centuries of war. Men turned feral and no longer thinking, no longer hoping or fearing; men who had lost any sense of conscience. Ruthless and reckless, and as callous as they were remorseless.

Fights there were, when they could not be avoided, and every one of them pointless, leaving a few more dead for the vultures and the crows, which were the only crea-tures truly to thrive in this wasteland forgotten of God. Once, Ezio saved a frightened village from marauders, and once, a woman from torture, rape, and death. But for how long? And what would become of them after he had passed by? He was not God, he could not be every-where; and here, where once Christ had trodden, God showed no evidence of looking after His own.

The farther north he rode, the heavier Ezio's heart became. Only the fire of the quest kept him on the path. But he tied brushwood to his horses' tails to eradicate his tracks as he passed, and at night, he spread branches of thorn to rest on, so that he would never quite sleep. Eternal vigilance was not only the price of freedom but of survival. Though the passing years might have robbed him of some of his strength, that was compensated for by experience, and the fruit of the training which had been drummed into him by Paola and Mario so long ago in Florence and Monteriggioni had never rotted. Though Ezio sometimes felt that he couldn't go on, that he wouldn't go on, he went on.

Two hundred miles as the crow flies. But this was a harsh winter, and there were many detours and delays along the road.

Finally, Ezio saw the mountains rearing ahead of him.

He drew in a deep breath of cold air.

Masyaf was near.

Three weeks later, on foot, both horses dead in the frozen passes behind him, and on his conscience, for they had been more stalwart and loyal companions than many men, Ezio stood in sight of his goal.

An eagle soared, high in the hard, clear sky.

Ezio, battered from the road, drew his eyes from it, pulled himself up and over a low, rough wall, and stood motionless for a moment, scanning the scene with keen eyes.

Masyaf. After many weary months on the journey. And such a long journey—the ways deep and the weather sharp.

Crouching, just in case, and keeping still as he instinctively checked his weapons, Ezio kept watching. Any sign of movement. Any.

Not a soul on the battlements. Scuds of snow twisting in a cutting wind. But no sign of a man. The place seemed deserted. As he'd expected from what he'd read of it. But life had taught him that it was always best to make sure. He stayed still.

Not a sound but the wind. Then—something. A scraping? To his left ahead of him a handful of pebbles skittered down a bare incline. He tensed, rose slightly, head up between ducked shoulders. Then the arrow, coming from nowhere, whacked into his right shoulder, through the body armor there.

TEN

The dawn was cold and grey. In its stillness, Ezio roused himself from his memories and snapped all his concentration to the present as the heard the footfall of guards' boots on the flagstones of the castle, approaching his cell. This was the moment.

He'd pretend to be weak, and that wasn't too hard a thing to do. He was thirstier than he'd been in a long time, and hungrier, but the beaker and the food still stood untouched on the table. He lay on the floor face-down, his hood pulled low over his face.

He heard the door of his cell crash open, and the men came in. They reached under his shoulders and half lifted him, dragging him out and along the bare grey stone corridor outside. Looking down at the floor as he was dragged over it, Ezio saw marked on it, laid out in a darker stone, the great symbol of the Assassins, their insignia since time immemorial.

The corridor gave way at length to a wider space, a kind of hall, open on one side. Ezio felt keen fresh air on his face, and it revived him. He raised his head slightly and saw that beyond him there were tall openings demarcated by narrow columns, and beyond them a wide-open view of the pitiless mountains. They were still high in the tower.

They pulled him to his feet, and he shook himself free of them. They stood back slightly, halberds at the ready, lowered but pointing at him. Facing him, his back to the void, stood the captain of the day before. He held a noose in his hand.

"You are a tenacious man, Ezio," the captain said. "To come all this way for a glimpse inside Altaïr's castle. It shows heart."

He gestured to his men to stand farther back, leaving Ezio standing alone. Then he went on: "But you're an old hound now. Better to put you out of your misery than see you whimper to a sad end."

Ezio turned slightly to address the man directly. That tiny movement, he noted to his satisfaction, was enough to make the halberdiers flinch and steady their weapons on him.

"Any last words before I kill you?" Ezio said.

The captain was made of sterner stuff than his men. He stood firm. He laughed. "I wonder how long it will take for the buzzards to pick your bones clean, as your body dangles from these parapets?"

"There's an eagle up there somewhere. He'll keep the buzzards away."

"A lot of good that'll do you. Come forward. Or are you afraid to die? You wouldn't want to have to be dragged to your death, would you?"

Ezio moved forward slowly, every sense taut.

"That's good," said the captain, and Ezio immediately sensed his slight relaxation. Did the man really think he was giving in? Was he that vain? That stupid? If so, all the better. But perhaps, after all, this ugly man, who smelled of sweat and cooked meat, was right. The moment of death had to come sometime.

Beyond the wide window between the columns, a narrow wooden platform projected over the void, perhaps ten feet long and four wide, constructed of six rough planks. It looked ancient and unsafe. The captain bowed in an ironic gesture of invitation. Ezio stepped forward again, waiting for his moment, but at the same time wondering if it would come.

The planks creaked ominously under his weight, and the air was cold around him. He looked at the sky and the mountains. Then he saw the eagle coasting, fifty or one hundred feet below him, its white pinions spread, and somehow that gave him hope.

Then something else happened.

Ezio had noticed another similar platform, projecting from the tower at the same level some fifteen feet to his right. And now, on it, alone, walking fearlessly forward, was the young cowled man in white he had glimpsed in the battle. As Ezio watched, his breath suspended, the man seemed to be turning toward him, to be making the beginning of a gesture . . .

And then, again, the vision faded, and there was nothing but the wind and the occasional scatter of gusting snow. Even the eagle had disappeared from sight.

The captain approached, noose in hand. Ezio fleetingly noticed that there was plenty of slack in the rope that trailed behind it.

"No eagle here that I can see," said the captain. "I wager it'll take the buzzards no more than three days."

"I'll let you know," Ezio replied, evenly.

A knot of guards had come up behind the captain, but it was the captain himself, now standing close behind Ezio, who pulled down his hood, slipped the noose over his head, and pulled it tight around his neck.

"Now!" said the captain.

Now!

At the very moment that he felt captain's hands on his shoulders, ready to shove him into oblivion, Ezio raised his right arm, crooked it, and drove his elbow violently backward. As the captain fell back with a cry, stumbling into his companions, Ezio stooped and took up the slack of the rope where it still lay on the planking, and, dodging between the three men, spun round and looped the slack round the stumbling captain's neck. Then he himself leapt from the platform into the void.

The captain had tried to recoil, but too late. He was slammed to the planks under the impact of Ezio's weight as he fell, and the planks shuddered as his head struck them. The rope snapped taut, all but breaking the captain's neck as it did so. Turning blue, his hands went to his neck as he kicked and struggled against death.

Uttering all the oaths they knew, the guards drew their swords and moved forward fast, hacking at the rope to free their officer. When the rope was cut, the accursed Ezio Auditore would plummet to his death on the rocks five hundred feet below, and as long as he was dead, what did the manner of it matter?

At the rope's end, twirling in space, Ezio already had both hands between the noose and his neck, straining to keep it from cutting into his windpipe. But as he did so he was already scanning the scene below him. He was dangling close to the walls. There had to be something he could catch to break his fall. But if there wasn't, this was a better way to meet death than going to it meekly.

Above, on the dangerously swaying platform, the guards at last succeeded in severing the rope, which by now was drawing blood from the captain's neck. And Ezio found himself falling, falling . . .

But at the moment he felt the rope go loose, he swung his body closer to the walls of the castle. Masyaf was built for Assassins by Assassins. It would not forsake him.

And he had seen a piece of broken scaffolding projecting from the wall fifty feet below. He guided his body toward it as he plummeted downward. He caught it, wincing in pain as his arm was wrenched almost free of its socket. But the scaffolding held, and he held and, grinding his teeth with effort, hauled himself up until he could get a grip with both hands.

But it wasn't over yet. The guards above, leaning out,

had seen what had happened, and began to lay hold of anything they could to throw down and dislodge him. Rocks and stones and jagged pieces of broken wood hailed on him.

Ezio looked around desperately. Over to his left, an escarpment ran up to the wall, reaching it perhaps twenty feet away from where he was. If he could swing from the scaffolding and gain enough momentum to throw himself across that distance, there was a faint chance that he could roll down the escarpment, at the foot of which he could see the edge of a cliff top, from which a crumbling stone bridge stretched over a chasm, to where a narrow path clung to the side of the mountain opposite.

Ducking under the rain of debris from above, Ezio started to swing backward and forward, his hands slipping on the ice-smooth wood of the scaffolding; but they held, and he soon built up impetus.

The moment came when he felt he just couldn't hold on anymore, he'd have to risk it, and he summoned all his energy into one last powerful backswing, hurling himself into space as his body moved forward again, and spread-eagled himself in the air as he flew toward the escarpment.

He landed heavily, badly, and it winded him. Before he had time to recover his balance, he was tumbling down the slope, bouncing off the rough ground but gradually able to guide his battered body in the general direction of the bridge. He knew this was vital, for if he did not end at exactly the right spot, he would be hurled over the cliff's edge into God knew what void beneath. And he was going too fast. He had no control over his speed.

But he kept his nerve somehow, and, at last, he was thrown to the ground—ten feet onto the trembling bridge itself.

A sudden thought struck him: How old was this bridge? It was narrow, single-span, and far, far below, Ezio could hear the crashing of angry water over rocks, invisible in the depths of the black chasm beneath.

The shock of his weight thrown upon it had shaken the bridge. How long was it since anyone had crossed it? Its stonework was already crumbling, weakened with age, its mortar rotted; and, as he got to his feet, to his horror he saw a crack snap open right across its width not five feet behind him. The crack soon widened, and the masonry on either side of it began to fall, tumbling crazily down into the dark abyss.

As Ezio watched, time itself seemed to slow down. There was no longer any retreat. He realized immediately what was going to happen. Turning, he started to sprint, summoning every muscle in his straining body to this one last effort. Across the bridge to the other side he ran, the structure fracturing and plummeting behind him. Twenty yards to go—ten—he could feel the stonework plunging away just as his heels left it. And at last, his chest practically splitting with the effort of breathing, he lay upright against the grey rock of the mountainside, his cheek pressed to it, his feet secure on the narrow path, unable to think, or do, anything, listening to the sounds of the stones of the bridge as they fell into the torrent below, listening to the sounds ebb, and ebb, until there was nothing, no sound at all but the wind.

ELEVEN

Gradually, Ezio's breathing calmed and leveled, and the aches in his muscles, forgotten in the crisis, began to return. But there was much to do before he could allow his body the rest it needed. What he had to do was feed it. He hadn't eaten or drunk anything for nearly twenty-four hours.

He bandaged his grazed hands as well as he could, using a scarf drawn from within his tunic and tearing it in two, and cupped a palm to capture a trickle of water that was running off the rock against which his cheek was pressed. Partly assuaged, he pushed away from the surface he'd been leaning on and checked himself over. No broken bones, a slight sprain in the left side, where he'd been wounded, but nothing else, nothing serious.

He surveyed the scene. No one seemed to have set out in pursuit, but they would have watched his fall down the escarpment and his run across the collapsing bridge— perhaps they hadn't noticed that he'd made it—perhaps they'd just assumed that he hadn't. But he couldn't discount the possibility that there'd be search parties out, if only to recover a body. The Templars would want to be quite sure that the Mentor of their archenemies was indeed dead.

He looked at the mountainside next to him. Better to climb than to use the path. He didn't know where it led, and it was too narrow to afford him room to maneuver if he had to fight. And the mountain looked climbable. At the very least, he might be able to reach some pockets of snow and really slake his thirst. He shook himself, grunting, and set about his task.

He was glad that he was dressed in dark colors, for he had no need to make any effort to blend with the rock face he was crawling up. Handholds and footholds were easy to find at first though there were times when he had to stretch hard, times when his muscles shrieked in protest, and, once, a shard of rock flaked off in his hand, nearly causing him to crash back down the hundred feet or so he'd already covered. The worst thing—and the best—was the thin but constant stream of water that fell on him from above. The worst, because the wet rocks were slippery; the best, because a waterfall meant a creek—at the very least a creek—up above.

But half an hour's climb brought him to the top of what turned out to be not a mountain but a cliff, since the ground he finally hauled himself up onto was level and covered with patches of rough, tussocky grass. A kind of all-but-barren Alpine meadow, bordered on two sides by more walls of black and grey rock, but opening westward quite some way, as far as Ezio could see. A mountain pass, except for the fact that, behind him, it led nowhere. Perhaps once, long ago, it had. An ancient earthquake might well have caused the cliffs he'd just climbed, and the gully into which the bridge had fallen.

Ezio sped to one side of the little valley to reconnoiter. Where there were passes, where there was water, there could also be people. He waited, near motionless, for another half an hour before venturing forward, shaking his muscles to keep them warm as they had begun to stiffen with the long period of immobility. He was wet, he was getting cold. He could not afford to be out there for too long. It was one thing to escape the Templars, but his effort would be wasted if he now fell victim to Nature.

He moved closer to the stream, locating it by the chuckling of its water. Stooping by its bank, he drank as much as he dared without glutting himself. He followed on. A few woody shrubs began to appear by its banks, and soon he came upon a stunted coppice by the side of a pool. There, he paused. It would be a miracle if there was anything living so high, so far from the village that squatted below the castle of Masyaf, any animal he could catch and eat; but if there was a pool, there was also the faintest chance that there might be fish.

He knelt and peered into the depths of the dark water. Still as a fishing heron, he disciplined himself to be patient.

And then, at last, a ripple, a faint one, which disappeared as soon as it had unsettled the water's surface, but enough to show him that there was something alive in there. He continued his watch. Little flies hovered low over the pool. Some flew over and harassed him, attracted by his body heat. Not daring to swat them away, he endured their tickling attentions and their tiny, vicious bites.

Then he saw it—a large, plump body, the color of a corpse, moving sluggishly six inches below the surface. Better than he'd dared hope—it looked like a carp, maybe, or something very like it. As he watched, another, much darker, joined it, and then a third, its scales coppery gold.

Ezio waited for them to do what he expected them to do—put their snouts to the surface and gulp air. That would be his moment. All his attention focused, he tensed his body and steeled his hands.

The dark fish made its move, bubbles erupted as a fat mouth appeared.

Ezio sprang.

And fell back, elated, the big fish wriggling frantically in his grasp but unable to slide out. He laid it on the ground beside him and dispatched it with a stone.

There was no way he could cook this. He'd have to eat it raw. But then he looked again at the stone he'd used to kill it and remembered the shard that had flaked off in his hand during his climb. Flint! With luck, he could start a fire—to dry his clothes as much as to cook with. Raw fish didn't bother him—he'd read, besides, that somewhere in an unimaginable country far away to the east there was a people who actually regarded it as a delicacy. But wet clothing was quite another thing. As for the fire itself, he'd take the risk. From what he'd seen, he was probably the first human in this valley in a thousand years, and its towering sides hid it from view for miles.

He gathered together some brushwood from the coppice, and, after a few moments' experiment, he had managed to start a tiny red glow in a handful of grass. Carefully, he placed it under a prepared tent of twigs, burning himself as his fire immediately flared. It burned well, giving off little smoke, and that was thin and light, immediately whisked into nothingness by the breeze

For the first time since his first sighting of Masyaf, Ezio smiled.

Despite the cold, to save time, he took off his clothes to dry them by the fire on rudimentary brushwood frames as the fish cooked and bubbled on a simple spit. Less than an hour later, the fire kicked out and its traces scattered, he felt a certain warmth in his belly and was able, soon afterward, to don garments which, if not laundry-fresh, were warm, and sufficiently dried for him to wear comfortably. They would have to finish drying as he wore them. As for his exhaustion, that would have to keep. He'd resisted the desire to sleep by the fire and the pool, a fight as tough as any he'd had on the road, but he was rewarded by a second wind.

He felt equal to the task of returning to the castle. He needed his gear, then he needed to unlock the secrets of the place if his quest was to mean anything.

As he retraced his steps, he noticed, shortly before he

reached the cliff he'd climbed, that on the southern side of the valley another pathway led upward along the side of that rock face. Who had hewn these pathways? Men from the dawn of time? Ezio had no leisure to ponder this but was grateful that this one was there. It rose steeply eastward, back in the direction of Masyaf. Ezio started to climb.

After an ascent of some five hundred feet, the path ended on a narrow promontory, where a few foundation stones testified to the presence long ago of a lookout tower, where guards would have been able to scan the country around and give the castle advance warning of any approaching army or caravan. Looking eastward and down, the great complex of Masyaf, with its rearing walls and cupola'd towers, spread out beneath him. Ezio focused hard, and his eyes, as keen as an eagle's, began to pick out the details that would help him return.

Far below, he discerned a rope bridge across the same chasm formerly spanned by the stone one he had run across. Near it was a guard post. There was no other access to the castle, as far as he could see, from the side he was on, but at the far side of the bridge, the way to the castle was relatively clear.

The way down to the bridge, on his side, was another matter. An all-but-sheer cascade of black rock—enough to daunt the surest-footed ibex. And it was in full view of the guard post on the castle side of the bridge.

Ezio looked at the sun. It was just past its zenith. He calculated it would take four to five hours to reach the castle. He needed to be inside before darkness fell.

He clambered down from the promontory and began his descent, taking it slowly, taking care not to dislodge the jumble of loose rocks, in case they tumbled down the mountainside and alerted the Templars guarding the bridge. It was delicate work, but the sun would be setting behind him and, therefore, shining in the eyes of any watchers below, and Ezio was grateful for its protection. He'd be down before it set behind the rock face he was on.

At last he reached the security and concealment of a large outcrop on level ground not fifty yards from the west side of the bridge. It had grown colder, and the wind was getting up. The bridge—of black-tarred rope, with narrow wooden slats as its walkway—swung and rattled. As Ezio watched, two guards emerged from the post and walked a little way to and fro on their side but did not venture onto the bridge itself. They were armed with crossbows and swords.

The light was dull and flat, it was difficult to judge distances. But the lessening light was to Ezio's advantage, and he blended in easily with his surroundings. Like a shadow, crouching, he made his way closer to the bridge, but there would be no cover once he was on it, and he was unarmed.

He paused once more about ten feet away, watching the guards. They looked cold and bored, Ezio noted to his satisfaction—they would not be alert. Nothing else had changed except that someone had lit a lamp within the post, so he knew there were more than two of them.

But he needed some kind of weapon. On the climb down and on his final approach, he had been too preoccupied with not giving his position away to look for something, but he hadn't forgotten that the mountain stone was flint, and there were plenty of loose shards at his feet. They glinted black in the dying light. He selected one with his eyes, a bladelike flake about twelve inches long and two wide. He picked it up and in doing so was too hasty, causing other stones to clatter. He froze.

But there was no reaction. The bridge was thirty yards across. He could be halfway, easily, before the guards noticed him. But he'd have to make a move immediately. He braced himself, stood up, and hurled himself forward.

But it wasn't easy going once he was on the bridge. It swayed and creaked alarmingly in the now-savage wind, and he had to grab its guide ropes to retain his balance. All that cost time. And by then, the guards had seen him. They shouted challenges, which gained him a second or two, but seeing him come on, they unslung their bows, fitted bolts, and fired. As they did so, three more guards, bows already primed, came rushing out of the post.

The bad light affected their aim, but it was close enough, and Ezio had to duck and dodge. At one point in the middle of the bridge an old plank snapped under him, and his foot caught, but he managed to pull it free before his leg sank through the gap—then he would have been done for. As it was, he was lucky to be able to avoid more than a grazing shot as a bolt caressed his neck, ripping through the back of his hood. He could feel its heat on his skin.

They'd stopped firing, and were doing something else. Ezio strained to see.

Winches!

They had plenty of slack rope on the winches, and they were preparing to let it go, let it spin out as soon as they unlocked the winches. They could haul the bridge up again after they'd tumbled him into the gulf below.

Merda, Ezio thought, half-running, half-stumbling, forward. Twice in one day! With five yards to go, he threw himself into the air as the bridge fell away beneath him, sailing forward and landing on one guard, knocking another flat, plunging the flint blade into the first man's neck and trying to bring it out again fast, but it broke off where it must have snagged on bone—then finding his feet, spinning around as he hauled the second guard, not yet recovered, roughly toward him, and swiftly drawing the man's own sword, he pulled it back and ran him through with it.

The other three had abandoned their bows and drawn their own swords, penning him in with his back to the precipice. Ezio thought fast. He'd seen no other men around, no one had gone to raise the alarm; he'd have to finish these three, then get into the castle before anything was discovered. But the men were big, and they hadn't been on guard; they were fresh and rested.

Ezio hefted the sword in his hand. He looked from one face to the other. But what was it he saw in their eyes? Fear? Was it *fear*?

"You Assassin dog!" one of them spat though his

voice all but trembled. "You must be in league with the Devil!"

"If the Devil is anywhere, he's with you," snarled Ezio, throwing himself forward, knowing that he could take advantage of their fear, of their fear that he was in some way filled with a supernatural force. *Se solo!*

They closed then, shouting oaths so loudly that Ezio had to make haste to cut them down, to silence them. Their blows were wild and panicky, and the job was quickly done.

He dragged the bodies into the guard post, but there was no time to haul the bridge back up; besides, that was an impossible job for a man alone. Briefly, he considered changing clothes with one of the guards, but that might have wasted precious time, and the gathering darkness was on his side.

Ezio started up the path leading to the castle, grateful for the shadows that had begun to gather at its sides.

He reached the foot of its walls on its blind side, unmolested. The sun had all but set, only a red glow showing behind the distant cliffs and mountains to the west. It was cold, and the wind insistent. The castle, old as it was, had weathered stones and they afforded enough handholds and footholds for a climber who knew what he was doing. Ezio, keeping in mind a picture of the plan of the fortress, which he had studied in Rome, drew on the last reserves of his energy and began the ascent. One hundred feet, he calculated, and he'd be within the outer sanctum. After that, he knew where the connecting gates that led to the inner fortifications, the towers, and the keep were.

The climb was harder than he'd thought. His arms and legs ached, and he wished he had some kind of implement that would help extend his reach, one that could grip the holds inflexibly, extending the power of his hands. But he willed himself upward, and, as the last embers of sunset died behind the black ramparts of mountain, giving way to the first pale stars, Ezio dropped onto a walkway that ran a few feet below the crenellations of the Outer Wall. Fifty yards on either side of him were watchtowers, but the guards in them were looking out and down—there was a commotion, dimly heard, from the direction of the guardhouse by the bridge.

He raised his eyes to the keep tower. They would have stowed his kit—his precious saddlebags with his weapons—in the secure cellar storeroom below it.

He dropped from the walkway to the ground, always keeping to the shadows. He bore left, toward where he knew the gate giving access to the keep lay.

TWELVE

Soft-footed as a puma, and ever seeking the darkest routes, Ezio reached his goal without further confrontations. Just as well, for the last thing he wanted was another noisy fight. If they found him again, they wouldn't let him linger or give him the ghost of a chance of escape—they'd kill him on the spot, skewer him like a rat. And there were few guards about—all he'd seen were those on the battlements. They must all be out, looking for him in the pale uncertain light afforded by the myriad stars—and the skirmish at the guard post would have made them redouble their efforts, for that had given them proof beyond doubt that he was not dead.

There were two older Templar guards sitting at a rough wooden table near the entrance to the cellar storeroom, but on the table was a large pewter jug of what looked like red wine and two wooden beakers, and the guards both had their heads and arms on the table. They were snoring. Ezio approached with extreme caution, having seen the ring of keys hanging at the side of one of the men.

He had not forgotten the pickpocketing skills which the Assassin *madame* Paola had taught him as a young man in Florence. Very carefully, trying to keep the keys from jangling—for the slightest sound, which might awaken the men, could spell his doom—he lifted the ring and, with his other hand, awkwardly untied the leather thong that attached it to the man's belt. At one point the loosening knot snagged and stuck, and in Ezio's efforts to free it, he tugged too hard, and the man stirred. Ezio became a statue, watching vigilantly, both his hands engaged and unable to make a move for either guard's weapon. But the man merely snuffled and went on sleeping, creasing his brow uncomfortably, perhaps at some dream.

At last, the key ring was in Ezio's hands, and he crept stealthily down the torchlit aisle beyond the guards, looking at the heavy ironclad wooden doors, which ran along either side.

He had to work fast, but it was a long job, checking which key on the big steel ring fitted into what lock, and at the same time checking that the keys didn't make any noise as he manipulated them. But at the fifth door, he struck lucky. It opened into a veritable armory, weapons of various sorts stacked neatly on wooden shelves that ran the length of the walls.

He'd taken a torch from its sconce near the door, and by its light he had soon found his bags. A quick inventory indicated that nothing seemed to have been taken, or even, as far as he could see, touched. He breathed a sigh of relief because these were the last things he wanted the Templars to get their hands on. The Templars had some good minds working for them, and it would have been disastrous if they'd been able to copy the hidden-blades.

He gave them a brief inspection. He'd traveled with only what he considered to be his essential gear, and he found, after double-checking, that everything he'd brought with him was definitely in place. He buckled on the scimitar, drawing it to make sure its blade was still keen, then slid it into its scabbard, slamming it firmly home. He strapped the bracer to his left arm and the unbroken hidden-blade to his left wrist. The broken blade and its harness he stowed in the bags—he wasn't going to leave that for the Templars, even in its current state, and there was always the chance that he'd be able to get it repaired. But he'd cross that bridge when he came to it. He stored the spring-loaded pistol with its ammunition in the bags and, taking as much time as he dared, took out his parachute and checked that it hadn't been damaged. The parachute was new—an invention of Leonardo's that he hadn't used in action yet. But the practice runs he'd made with it had more than proved its potential.

He folded the tentlike structure up neatly and returned it to the rest of his kit, slinging the bags over his shoulder and strapping them securely, and made his way back the way he'd come, past the still-sleeping guards. Once outside, he started to climb.

He located a secluded vantage point on a high turret of the keep. He'd selected the place because it overlooked Masyaf's rear garden, under which, if his research on the castle plans had been correct, the Templars would be concentrating their efforts to locate the library of the great Assassin Mentor, Altaïr, who'd ruled the Brotherhood from here three centuries ago. The legendary library of the Assassins, and the source of all their knowledge and power, if his father's letter was to be believed.

Ezio had no doubt at all that nothing less than a search for it would explain the Templars' presence in the castle.

On the edge of the turret's outer wall, looking down at the garden, was the large stone statue of an eagle, wings folded, but so lifelike that it appeared to be about to take flight and swoop down on some unsuspecting prey. With his hands, he tested the statue. For all its weight, it rocked very slightly when he applied pressure to it.

Perfect.

Ezio took up his position by the eagle and prepared to settle down for the rest of the night, knowing nothing would happen before dawn and realizing that if he did not take that opportunity to rest, he would not be able to act with efficiency when the moment came. The Templars might have taken him for some kind of demidevil, but he knew only too well that he was just a man, like any other.

But before he rested, a sudden doubt assailed him, and he scanned the garden below. There was no sign of any excavations. Could it be that he was mistaken?

Drawing on the lessons he had learned and the powers he had developed in training, he focused his eyes so that they assumed the power of an eagle's and examined the ground beneath him minutely. By concentrating hard, he was at last able to discern a dull glow emanating from a section of mosaic flooring in a once-ornamental, now-overgrown bower immediately beneath. Satisfied, he smiled and relaxed. The mosaic depicted an image of the goddess Minerva.

The sun had scarcely brushed the battlements to the east when Ezio, refreshed by his short sleep and alert, crouched by the stone eagle, knowing that the moment had come. He also knew that he had to act fast—every moment he spent there increased the risk of detection. The Templars would not have given up on him yet, and they would be fired up with hatred—his escape, when they had him in the very grip of death, would have left them howling for vengeance.

Ezio gauged distances and angles, and when he was satisfied, he placed his boot against the stone eagle and gave the statue a good, hard push. It rocked on its plinth and fell out and away over the parapet, tumbling end over end toward the mosaic floor far below. Ezio barely watched it for a second, to verify its course, before he threw himself into the air after it, executing a Leap of

Faith. It was some time since he had performed one, and now the old exhilaration returned.

Down they fell, the eagle first, Ezio plummeting in the same trajectory fifteen feet above it. Toward what looked like very solid ground.

Ezio didn't have time to pray that he hadn't made a mistake. If he had, the time for praying—for everything—would soon be over.

The eagle landed first, in the center of the mosaic.

For a split second, it seemed as if the eagle had smashed to pieces, but it was the mosaic that had shattered, revealing beneath it a large aperture reaching down into the earth, through which the eagle, and Ezio, fell. He was caught immediately on a chute that traveled deeper into the ground at an angle of some forty-five degrees, and he slid down it feetfirst, steering himself with his arms, hearing the stone eagle thundering its way ahead of him, until, with a mighty splash, it tumbled into a large subterranean pool. Ezio followed.

When he surfaced, he could see that the pool was in the middle of a great antechamber of some kind. An antechamber, because its architectural focus was a door. A door of dark green stone, polished smooth by time.

Ezio was not alone. A party of Templars on the granite embankment of the lake near the door had turned at the sight and sound of the crashing intrusion and were waiting for him, yelling, swords at the ready. With them was a man in workmen's clothes, a dusty canvas apron wrapped round his waist and a leather tool bag on his belt. A stonemason, by the look of him. A hammer and a large stone chisel hung in his hands as he watched, mouth agape.

Ezio hauled himself up onto the embankment as Templar guards hurried forward to rain blows down on him, but he fended them off long enough to get to his feet. Then he braced himself and faced them.

He sensed their fear again and took advantage of their momentary hesitation to attack first. He drew his scimitar firmly with his right hand and unleashed the hidden-blade beneath his left. In two swift strokes to right and left, he brought the nearest men down. The others circled, just out of reach, taking turns to make sudden stabs at him, like striking vipers, hoping to disorient him.

But their efforts weren't sufficiently concerted. Ezio managed to drive his shoulder against one, pitching him into the pool. He sank almost immediately, its black waters cutting off his anguished cry for help. Swinging round and keeping low, Ezio hurled a fourth man over his back onto the granite. His helmet flew off and his skull cracked with a noise like a gunshot on the diamond-hard stone.

The surviving fifth man, a Templar corporal, barked a desperate order to the workman, but the workman did nothing, too petrified to move. Then, seeing Ezio turn on him, the corporal backed away, his mouth slavering, until the wall behind him arrested his retreat. Ezio approached, intending merely to knock the Templar unconscious, but then the corporal, who'd been waiting for his moment, struck a treacherous dagger blow toward

Ezio's groin. Ezio sidestepped and seized the man by the shoulder, near the throat.

"I would have spared you, friend. But you give me no choice." With one swift stroke of his razor-sharp scimitar, Ezio severed the man's head from his body. *"Requiescat in Pace,"* he said, softly.

Then he turned to the stonemason.

THIRTEEN

The man was about Ezio's age, but running to fat and not in the greatest shape. At the moment, he was trembling like an outsize aspen.

"Don't kill me, sir!" the man pleaded, cowering. "I'm a workingman, that's all. Just some poor nobody with a family to look after."

"Got a name?"

"Adad, sir."

"What kind of work is it you do? For these people?" Ezio stooped to wipe his blades on the tunic of the dead corporal and sheathed them. Adad relaxed a fraction. He was still holding his hammer and chisel, and Ezio had kept a careful eye on them, but the stonemason seemed to have forgotten they were in his hands.

"Digging, mostly. Wretched hard work it is, too, sir. It's taken me a year just to find this chamber alone." Adad scanned Ezio's face, but if he'd been looking for sympathy, he hadn't found it. After a moment's silence, he went on. "For the past three months, I've been trying to break through this door."

Ezio turned away from the man and examined the door himself. "You haven't made much progress," he commented.

"I haven't made a dent! This stone is harder than steel."

Ezio ran a hand across the glass-smooth stone. The seriousness of his expression deepened. "I doubt if you ever will. This door guards objects more valuable than all the gold in the world."

Now that the menace of death was past, the man's eyes gleamed involuntarily "Ah! Do you mean—gemstones?"

Ezio regarded him mockingly. Then he turned his gaze to the door and examined it closely. "There are key-holes here. Five of them. Where are the keys?"

"They tell me little. But I know the Templars found one beneath the Ottoman sultan's palace. As for the others, I suppose their little book will tell them."

Ezio looked at him sharply. "Sultan Bayezid's palace? And what is this book?"

The mason shrugged. "A journal of some kind, I think. That ugly captain, the one with the scarred face, he carries it with him wherever he goes."

Ezio's eyes narrowed. He thought fast. Then he appeared to relax, and, taking a small linen pouch from his tunic, he tossed it to Adad. It jingled as the man caught it.

"Go home," said Ezio. "Find other work—with honest men."

Adad looked pleased, then doubtful. "You don't know how much I'd like to. I'd love to leave this place. But these men—they will murder me if I try."

Ezio turned slightly, peering back up the chute behind him. A thin ray of light came down it.

He turned back to the mason. "Pack your tools," he said. "You will have nothing to fear now."

FOURTEEN

Sticking to the less-frequented stairways and corridors of the castle, Ezio regained the high battlements unseen, his breath pluming in the cold air. He made his way round them to a point that overlooked the village of Masyaf, crouching in the castle's shadow. He knew there would be no way of leaving the castle by either of its heavily guarded gates, but he had to track down the scarred, shaven-headed captain. He guessed that the man would be outside, supervising the search for the escaped Assassin. Templars would be scouring the countryside, which explained the relative absence of men within the confines of the fortress. In any case, Ezio knew that the next step in his mission lay beyond Masyaf's walls. But first he had to leave the place.

Once he had a clear view of the village, he could see that Templar guards were making their rounds of it, interrogating its inhabitants. Making sure that the sun was at his back, obscuring any clear view of him from below, he unstrapped his bags and took out the parachute, unfolding it and erecting it with as much speed as care would allow, for his life would depend on it. The distance was too far and the descent too dangerous for even the most daring Leap of Faith.

The parachute took the form of a triangular tent, or pyramid, of strong silk, held in place by struts of thin steel. Ezio attached the rope from each of its four corners to a quick-release harness, which he buckled round his chest, then, pausing to gauge the wind and to ensure that no one below was looking up, hurled himself into the air.

It would have been an exhilarating feeling if Ezio had had the leisure to enjoy it, but he concentrated on guiding the device, using the convection currents and thermals as best he could, imitating an eagle, and brought himself to a safe landing a dozen yards from the nearest building. Swiftly stowing the parachute, he made his way into the village.

Sure enough, the Templars were busy harassing the villagers, pushing them around and beating them without mercy if they showed the slightest sign of not answering clearly and instantly. Ezio blended in with the people of the village, listening and watching.

One old man was pleading for mercy as a Templar bravo stood over his cowering form. "Help me, please!" he begged anyone who would listen, but no one was.

"Speak, dog!" the Templar shouted. "Where is he?"

Elsewhere, a younger man was being beaten by two thugs even as he implored them to stay their hand. Another cried, "I am innocent!" as he was clubbed to the ground.

"Where is he hiding?" snarled his assailants.

It wasn't only the men who were being cruelly handled. Two other Templar cowards held down a woman as a third kicked her mercilessly, stifling her cries as she writhed on the ground, piteously beseeching them to stop: "I know nothing! Please forgive me!"

"Bring us the Assassin, and no further harm will come to you," sneered her tormentor, bringing his face close to hers. "Otherwise . . ."

Ezio watched, aching to assist but forcing himself to concentrate on his search for the captain. He arrived at the front gate of the village just in time to see the object of his search mounting a horse-drawn wagon. The captain was in such a hurry to be gone that he flung the driver out of his seat, onto the ground.

"Get out of my way!" he bellowed. *"Fíye apó brostá mou!"*

Seizing the reins, the captain glared around him at his troops. "None of you leave until the Assassin is dead," he snarled. "Do you understand? Find him!"

He'd been speaking Greek, Ezio registered. Formerly, Ezio had mostly heard Italian and Arabic. Could the captain, at least, be a Byzantine, among this Templar crew? A descendant of those driven into exile when Constantinople fell to the sword of Sultan Mehmed, sixty-five years ago? Ezio knew that the exiles had established themselves in the Peloponnese soon afterward, but, even after they'd been overrun there by the triumphant Ottomans, pockets still survived in Asia Minor and the Near East.

He stepped forward, into the open.

The soldiers looked at him nervously.

"Sir!" said one of the bolder sergeants. "He seems to have found us."

For reply, the captain seized the whip from its socket by the driver's seat and lashed his horses forward, yelling, "Go! Go!" Ezio, seeing this, exploded into a run. Templar troops tried to impede him, but, drawing his scimitar, he cut his way impatiently through them. Making a dive for the fast-disappearing wagon, he just missed gaining a hold on it but managed to seize a trailing rope instead. The wagon checked for an instant, then surged forward, dragging Ezio with it.

Painfully, Ezio started to haul himself hand over hand up the rope toward the wagon, while behind him he heard the noise of thundering hooves. A couple of soldiers had mounted horses themselves and were hot on his heels, swords raised, striving to get close enough to cut him down. As they rode, they screamed warnings to the captain, who lashed his own horses into an even more furious gallop. Meanwhile, another, lighter wagon had set off in pursuit and was swiftly drawing level.

Crashing across the rough terrain, Ezio continued to haul himself up the rope. He was within two feet of the wagon's tailgate when the two riders behind him closed in. He ducked his head, waiting for a blow, but the horsemen had been too hasty, and concentrated more on their quarry than their riding. Their mounts collided sickeningly inches behind Ezio's heels, and fell, in a pandemonium of screaming horses, cursing riders, and dust.

Straining hard, Ezio forced his aching arms to make one final effort, and, breathing heavily, he wrenched, rather than pulled, himself the last foot onto the wagon, where he clung for a moment, motionless, his head swimming, catching his breath.

Meanwhile, the second wagon had drawn abreast of the first, and the captain was frantically signaling the men aboard to bring it in closer. But as soon as they had done so, the captain leapt from his wagon to theirs, pushing its driver from his seat. With a dull cry, the man fell to the ground from the speeding vehicle, hitting a rock and ricocheting off it with an appalling thud, before lying inert, his head twisted round at an unnatural angle.

Gaining control of the plunging horses, the captain raced forward and away, as Ezio, in his turn, scrambled to the front of the wagon he was on and seized the reins, his arm muscles yelling in protest as he hauled on them to steady his own team. His two horses, foam-flecked and wild-eyed, blood gathering at the bits in their mouths, nevertheless kept up their gallop, and Ezio remained in the chase. Seeing this, the captain steered toward an old open gate across the road, supported by crumbling brick columns. He managed to sideswipe one of these without hindering his onward rush, and the column smashed down in a welter of masonry, directly in front of Ezio. Ezio heaved at the reins, drawing his team to the right in the nick of time, and his wagon bumped and crashed off the road into the scrubland at its edge as he struggled to bring his horses back around to the left, to regain the beaten track. Dust and small stones flew everywhere, cutting Ezio's cheeks and making him squeeze his eyes into slits to protect them and keep focused on his quarry.

"Go to hell, damn you!" screeched the captain over his shoulder. And now Ezio could see that the soldiers hanging on precariously in the back of the first wagon were preparing bombs to hurl at him.

Zigzagging as best he could to avoid the explosions, which went off on both sides of him and behind him, Ezio fought hard to keep control of his terrified and, by now, all-but-stampeding team. But the bombs had failed to find their mark, and he kept on track.

The captain tried a different tactic and a dangerous one.

He suddenly slowed, falling back, so that Ezio, before he could make a countermove, drew level. Immediately, the captain caused his team to swerve so that his wagon crashed broadside into Ezio's.

Ezio could see the whites of the captain's half-crazed eyes, the scar livid across his strained face, as they glared at each other through the swirling air.

"Die, you bastard!" yelled the captain.

Then he glanced ahead. Ezio followed his gaze and saw, up ahead, a guard tower and, beyond it, another village. This village was larger than the one at Masyaf and partially fortified. An outlying Templar stronghold.

The captain managed to coax one more burst of speed

from his horses, and as he drew away with a cry of triumph, his men threw two more bombs. This time one of them exploded beneath the left-hand rear wheel of Ezio's wagon. The blast threw the vehicle halfway into the air, and Ezio was thrown clear as his horses made sounds like banshees and plunged away off into the scrubland, dragging the remains of the ruined wagon behind them. The land fell away sharply to the right of the road, and Ezio was pitched twenty feet down into a gully, where a large outcrop of thorny shrubs broke his fall and hid him.

He lay prone, looking at the unforgiving grey ground inches from his face, unable to move, unable to think, but feeling that every bone in his body had been broken. He closed his eyes and waited for the end.

Fifteen

Ezio heard voices, far away, as he lay in a kind of dream. He thought he saw the young man in white again, the man whom he'd seen at the time of the ambush and again when he was on the makeshift scaffold, but he couldn't be sure. Who had neither helped nor hindered him, but who seemed to be on his side. Others came and went: his long-dead brothers, Federico and Petruccio; Claudia; his father and mother; and—unbidden and unwanted—the beautiful, cruel face of Caterina Sforza.

The visions faded, but the voices remained, stronger now, as his other senses returned to him. He tasted soil in his mouth and smelled the earth against which his cheek lay. The aches and pains in his body returned, too. He thought he'd never be able to move again.

The voices were indistinct, coming from above. He imagined the Templars were leaning over the edge of the little cliff he'd fallen down but realized that they couldn't see him. The thick shrubs must be concealing his body.

He waited awhile, until the voices finally receded, and silence fell. Then, tentatively, he flexed his hands and feet, then his arms and legs, as, gratefully, he spat out the dirt.

Nothing seemed to be broken. Slowly, painfully, he wormed his way out of the bushes and got to his feet. Then, cautiously, and keeping to what cover there was, he clambered back to the road.

He was just in time to see the Templar captain passing through the gate in the walls of the fortified village, a couple of hundred yards away. Keeping to the side of the road where bushes grew and he could conceal himself, he brushed himself off and started to walk toward the village, but it seemed as if every muscle in him protested.

"This used to be so easy," he murmured to himself, ruefully. But he willed himself onward and, skirting the wall, found a likely place to climb it.

Having stuck his head over the parapet to check that he was unobserved, he pulled himself over and dropped into the village. He found himself in the stockyard, empty except for a pair of heifers which shunted off to one side, eyeing him warily. He took time to wait, in case there were dogs, but after a minute, he passed through the wicket of the stockyard and, following the sound of raised voices, made his way through the apparently deserted village toward them. Nearing the village square, he caught sight of the captain and stepped out of sight behind a shed. The captain, standing on the top of a low tower at one corner of the square, was berating two unhappy sergeants. Beyond them, the assembled villagers stood mutely by. The captain's words were punctuated by the *chop-chop* of a waterwheel on the other side, worked by the rivulet that ran through the village.

"I seem to be the only one around here who knows how to handle a horse," the captain was saying. "Until we're *sure* he's *dead* this time, I command you not to drop your guard for a moment. Do you understand?"

"Yessir," the men answered sullenly.

"How many times have you failed to kill that man, hmn?" the captain continued angrily. "Listen up and listen close: If I do not see his head rolling in the dust at my feet within the hour, yours will take its place!"

The captain fell silent and, turning, watched the road from his vantage point. Ezio could see that he was nervous. He fiddled with the cocking lever of his crossbow.

Ezio had made his way into the crowd of villagers during the captain's tirade, blending in with them as best he could, which, given his battered and downtrodden appearance, wasn't difficult. But the crowd was breaking up, returning to work. The mood among the people was nervous, and when a man in front of him suddenly stumbled, jostling another, the second turned on him irritably, snapping: "Hey, get out of my way—get a move on!"

His attention caught by the disturbance, the captain scanned the crowd, and in an instant his eye caught Ezio's.

"You!" he shouted. In another moment he had cocked his bow, fitted a bolt, and fired.

Ezio dodged it adroitly, and it flew past him, to embed itself in the arm of the man who'd snapped.

"Aiëë!" he yelped, clutching his shattered biceps.

Ezio darted for cover as the captain reloaded.

"You will not leave this place alive!" the captain bawled, firing again. This time, the bolt stuck harmlessly in a wooden doorframe, which Ezio had ducked behind. But there was very little wrong with the captain's shooting. So far, Ezio had been lucky. He had to get away, and fast. Two more bolts sang past him.

"There's no way out!" the captain called after him. "You might as well turn and face me, you pitiful old dog." He fired again.

Ezio drew a breath and leapt to catch hold of the lintel of another doorway, swinging himself up so that he was able to get onto the flat clay roof of a dwelling. He ran across it to the other side as another bolt whistled past his ear.

"Stand your ground and die," hollered the captain. "Your time has come, and you must accept it, even if it is far away from your wretched kennel in Rome! So come and meet your killer!"

Ezio could see where soldiers were running around to the back of the village, to cut off his line of retreat. But they had left the captain isolated, except for his two sergeants, and his quiver of bolts was empty.

The villagers had scattered and disappeared long since.

Ezio ducked behind the low wall surrounding the roof, unstrapped his bags from his back, and slipped the pistol harness onto his right wrist.

"Why will you not quit?!" the captain was calling, drawing his sword.

Ezio stood. "I never learned how," he called back in a clear voice, raising his gun.

The captain looked at the raised weapon in momentary panic and fear, then, shrieking "Out of my way!" at his attendants, he shoved them aside and leapt from the tower to the ground. Ezio fired and caught him in midjump, the bullet catching him in the left knee joint. With a howl of pain, the captain hit the ground, dashing his head against a sharp stone, and rolled over there. The sergeants fled.

Ezio crossed the deserted square. No soldiers came back. Either their fear of Ezio had persuaded them that he was indeed a supernatural being, or their love of their captain could not have been very great. There was silence except for the steady clatter of the waterwheel, and the captain's agonized whimpering.

The captain caught Ezio's eye as he approached. "Ah, dammit," he said. "Well, what are you waiting for? Go on—kill me!"

"You have something I need," Ezio told him calmly, reloading his gun so that both chambers were ready. The captain eyed the weapon.

"I see the old hound still has his bite," he said through gritted teeth. Blood flowed from his knee and from the more serious wound on his left temple.

"The book you carry. Where is it?"

The captain looked crafty. "Niccolò Polo's old journal, you mean? You know about that? You surprise me, Assassin."

"I am full of surprises," Ezio replied. "Give it to me."

Seeing there was no help for it, the captain, grunting, drew an old leather-bound book, some twelve inches by six, from his jerkin. His hand was shaking, and he dropped it onto the ground.

The captain looked at it with a laugh that died, gurgling, in his throat. "Take it," he said. "We have gleaned all its secrets and found the first of the five keys already. When we have the rest, the Grand Temple, and all the power within, will be ours."

Ezio looked at him pityingly. "You are deceived, soldier. There is no ancient temple at Masyaf. Only a library, full of wisdom."

The captain looked at him. "Your forebear Altaïr had the Apple of Eden in his control for sixty years, Ezio. He gained much more than what you call wisdom. He learned . . . *everything*!"

Ezio thought about that fleetingly. He knew the Apple was safely buried in a church crypt in Rome—he and Machiavelli had seen to that. But his attention was drawn back immediately by a sharp gasp of pain from the captain. Blood had been streaming from his untended wounds all the time they had been speaking. Now the man had the death pallor on him. A curiously peaceful expression came over his face, and he lay back as a huge long, last, sighing breath escaped him.

Ezio watched him for a moment. "You were a real *bas-tardo*," he said. "But—for all that—*Requiescat in Pace*."

He leaned forward and gently closed the man's eyes with his gloved hand.

The waterwheel hammered on. Otherwise, there was silence.

Ezio picked up the book and turned it over in his hands. On its cover, he saw an embossed symbol, its gilding long since faded. The emblem of the Assassin Brotherhood. Smiling slightly, he opened it to the title page:

LA CROCIATA SEGRETA
Niccolò Polo

MASYAF, giugno, MCCLVII
COSTANTINOPOLI, gennaio, MCCLVII

As he read, Ezio drew in a breath.

Constantinople, he thought. *Of course . . .*

SIXTEEN

The breeze freshened, and Ezio looked up from Niccolò Polo's book, open on his lap as he sat under an awning on the afterdeck of the large, broad-bellied baghlah, as it cut through the clear blue water of the White Sea, both lateens and jib set to take full advantage of a favorable wind.

The journey from Latakia on the Syrian coast had first taken him back to Cyprus. The next port of call had been Rhodes—where his attention had been caught by the arrival on board of a new passenger, a beautiful woman of perhaps thirty wearing a green dress that perfectly accorded with her copper-gold hair. Then on through the Dodecanese north toward the Dardanelles, and, at last, the Sea of Marmara.

Finally, the voyage was drawing toward its close. Sailors called to each other as passengers lined up along the gunwale to watch as, a mile distant, glittering in the sharp sunlight, the great city of Constantinople rose on the port bow. As he watched, Ezio tried to identify parts of the city from the map of it he had bought in the Syrian port before embarkation. Near him stood an expensively dressed young man, an Ottoman, probably still in his teens but also clearly acquainted with the city. Ezio had struck up a nodding acquaintance with him. The young man was busy with a mariner's astrolabe, taking measurements and making notes in an ivory-bound copybook, which hung on a silk cord from his belt.

"What's that?" Ezio asked, pointing. He wanted to have as much knowledge of the place as possible before landing. News of his escape from the Templars at Masyaf would not be far behind, and he'd need to work fast.

"That's the Bayezid Quarter. The big mosque you can see was built by the sultan about five years ago. And just beyond it you can see the roofs of the Grand Bazaar."

"Got it," said Ezio, squinting in the sun to focus and wishing that Leonardo had got around to making that instrument he was always talking about—a kind of extendable tube with lenses—which would make distant things seem closer.

"Watch your sleeve purse when you go to the Bazaar," advised the young man. "You get a pretty mixed bag of people there."

"Like in any souk."

"*Evet.*" The young man smiled. "Just over there,

where the towers are, is the Imperial District. That grey dome you can see is the old church of Haghia Sofia. It's a mosque now, of course. And beyond it, you see that long, low, yellow building—more of a complex of buildings, really—with two low domes close together and a spire? That's Topkapi Sarayi. One of the first buildings we erected after the conquest, and we're still working on it."

"Is Sultan Bayezid in residence?"

The young man's face darkened slightly. "He should be—but no—he is not. Not at the moment."

"I must visit it."

"You'd better make sure you have an invitation first!"

The breeze slackened, and the sails rippled. The sailors furled the jib. The master brought the ship's head around slightly, bringing another aspect of the city into view.

"You see that mosque there?" the young man continued, as if anxious to take the conversation away from Topkapi Palace. "That's the Fatih Camii—the first thing Sultan Mehmed had built, to celebrate his victory over the Byzantines. Not that there was much of them left by the time he got here. Their empire was already long dead. But he wanted his mosque to surpass Haghia Sofia. As you can see, he didn't quite make it."

"Not for want of trying," said Ezio diplomatically, as his eyes scanned the magnificent building.

"Mehmed was piqued," the young man continued. "The story goes that he had the architect's arm cut off as a punishment. But, of course, that's just a legend. Sinan was far too good an architect for Mehmed to want to damage him."

"You said the sultan was not in residence," Ezio prompted, gently.

"Bayezid? No." The young man's troubled look returned. "A great man, the sultan, though the fire of his youth has been replaced by quietness and piety. But, alas, he is at odds with one of his sons—Selim—and that has meant a war between them, which has been simmering for years now."

The baghlah was sailing along under the southern walls of the city and soon rounded the corner north into the Bosphorus. Shortly afterward, a great inlet opened out on the port side, and the ship steered into it, over the great chain that hung across its mouth. It had been lowered, but could be raised to close the harbor in times of emergency or war.

"The chain has been in disuse since the conquest," the young man observed. "After all, it did not stop Mehmed."

"But a useful safety measure," Ezio replied.

"We call this the Haliç," said the young man. "The Golden Horn. And there on the north side is the Galata Tower. Your Genoese countrymen built it about a hundred and fifty years ago. Mind you, they called it the Christea Turris. But they would, wouldn't they? Are you from Genoa yourself?"

"I'm a Florentine."

"Ah well, can't be helped."

"It's a good city."

"*Affedersiniz.* I am not familiar enough with your part of the world. Though many of your countrymen live here still. There've been Italians here for centuries. Your famous Marco Polo—his father, Niccolò, was trading here well over two hundred years ago, with his brother." The young man smiled, watching Ezio's face. Then he turned his attention back to the Galata Tower. "There might be a way of getting you to the top. The security people might be persuaded. You get the most breathtaking view of the city from there."

"That would be—most rewarding."

The young man looked at him. "You've probably heard of another famous countryman of yours, still living, I believe. Leonardo da Vinci?"

"The name stirs some memories."

"Less than a decade ago, *Sayin* da Vinci *bey* was asked by our sultan to build a bridge across the Horn."

Ezio smiled, remembering that Leonardo had once mentioned it to him in passing. He could imagine his friend's enthusiasm for such a project. "What became of it?" he asked. "I see no bridge here now."

The young man spread his hands. "I'm told the design was beautiful, but, unfortunately, the plan never came to pass. Too ambitious, the sultan felt, at last."

"*Non mi sorprende,*" Ezio said, half to himself. Then he pointed to another tower. "Is that a lighthouse?"

The young man followed his gaze toward a small islet aft of them. "Yes. A very old one. Eleven centuries or more. It's called the Kiz Kulesi—how's your Turkish?"

"Weak."

"Then I'll translate. You'd call it the Maiden Tower. We called it after the daughter of a sultan who died there of a snakebite."

"Why was she living in a lighthouse?"

The young man smiled. "The plan was, to avoid snakes," he said. "Look, now you can see the Aqueduct of Valens. See that double row of arches? Those Romans certainly could build. I used to love climbing it, as a child."

"Quite a climb."

"You almost look as if you'd like to try it!"

Ezio smiled. "You never know," he said.

The young man opened his mouth to say something but changed his mind and shut it again. His expression as he looked at Ezio was not unkind. And Ezio knew exactly what he was thinking: an old man trying to escape the years.

"Where have you come from?" asked Ezio.

The young man looked dismissive. "Oh—the Holy Land," he said. "That is, *our* Holy Land. Mecca and Medina. Every good Muslim's supposed to make the trip once in his lifetime."

"You've got it over with early."

"You could say that."

They watched the city pass by in silence as they rode up the Horn to their anchorage. "There isn't a city in Europe with a skyline like this," Ezio said.

"Ah, but this side *is* in Europe," replied the young man. "Over there"—he gestured east across the Bosphorus—"*that* side's Asia."

"There are some borders even the Ottomans cannot move," Ezio observed.

"Very few," the young man replied quickly, and Ezio thought he sounded defensive. Then he changed the subject. "You say you're an Italian—from Florence," he went on. "But your clothes belie that. And—forgive me— you look as if you've been in them rather a long time. Have you been traveling long?"

"*Sì, da molto tempo.* I left *Roma* twelve months ago, looking for . . . inspiration. And that search has brought me here."

The young man glanced at the book in Ezio's hand but said nothing. Ezio himself didn't want to reveal more of his purpose. He leaned on the rail and looked at the city walls, and the other ships, from all the countries in the world, crowded at moorings, as their baghlah slowly passed them.

"When I was a child, my father told me stories of the fall of Constantinople," Ezio said at last. "It happened six years before I was born."

The young man carefully packed his astrolabe into a leather box slung from a belt round his shoulder. "We call the city Kostantiniyye."

"Doesn't it amount to the same thing?"

"We run it now. But you're right. Kostantiniyye, Byzantium, Nea Roma, the Red Apple—what real difference does it make? They say Mehmed wanted to rechristen it Islam-bul—*Where Islam Flourishes*—but that derivation's just another legend. Still, people are even using that name. Though of course, the educated among us know that it should be Istan-bol—*To the City*." The young man paused. "What stories did your father tell? Brave Christians being beaten down by wicked Turks?"

"No. Not at all."

The young man sighed. "I suppose the moral of any story matches the temper of the man who tells it."

Ezio pulled himself erect. Most of his muscles had recovered during the long voyage, but there was still an ache in his side. "That we can agree on," he said.

The young man smiled, warmly and genuinely. "*Güzel!* I am glad! Kostantiniyye is a city for all kinds and all creeds. Even the Byzantines who remain. And students like me, or . . . travelers like you."

Their conversation was interrupted by a young Seljuk married couple, who were walking along the deck past them. Ezio and the young man paused to eavesdrop on their conversation—Ezio, because any information he could glean about the city would be of interest to him.

"My father cannot cope with all this crime," the husband was saying. "He'll have to shut up shop if it gets any worse."

"It will pass," his wife replied. "Maybe when the sultan returns."

"Hah!" rejoined the man sarcastically. "Bayezid is weak. He turns a blind eye to the Byzantine upstarts, and look what the result is—*kargasa!*"

His wife shushed him. "You should not say such things!"

"Why not? I tell only the truth. My father is an honest man, and thieves are robbing him blind."

Ezio interrupted them. "Excuse me—I couldn't help overhearing—"

The man's wife shot her husband a look: *You see?*

But the man turned to Ezio and addressed him. "*Affedersiniz, efendim.* I can see you are a traveler. If you are staying in the city, please visit my father's shop. His carpets are the best in all the empire, and he will give you a good price." He paused. "My father is a good man, but thieves have all but destroyed his business."

The husband would have said more, but his wife hastily dragged him away.

Ezio exchanged a look with his companion, who had just accepted a glass of *sharbat* brought to him by what looked like a valet. He raised his glass. "Would you care for one? It's very refreshing, and it will be a while yet before we dock."

"That would be excellent."

The young man nodded at his servant, who withdrew. In the meantime, a group of Ottoman soldiers passed by, on their way home from a tour of duty in the Dodecanese, and talking of the city they were returning to.

Ezio nodded to them and joined them for a moment, while the young man turned his face away and stood aloof, making notes in his little ivory-bound book.

"What I want to know is, what are these Byzantine thugs holding out for?" one of the soldiers asked. "They had their chance once. They nearly destroyed this city."

"When Sultan Mehmed rode in, there were fewer than forty thousand people living here, and living in squalor," put in another.

"Aynen oyle!" said a third. "Exactly so! And now look at the city. Three hundred thousand inhabitants, and flourishing again for the first time in centuries. We have done our part."

"We made this city strong again. We rebuilt it!" said the second soldier.

"Yes, but the Byzantines don't see it that way," rejoined the first. "They just cause trouble, every chance they get."

"How may I recognize them?" Ezio asked.

"Just stay clear of any mercenaries you see wearing a rough, reddish garb," said the first soldier. "They are Byzantines. And they do not play nice."

The soldiers moved off then, called by an NCO to ready themselves for disembarking. Ezio's young man was standing at his elbow. At the same moment, his valet reappeared with Ezio's *sharbat*.

"So you see," said the young man. "For all its beauty, Kostantiniyye is not, after all, the most perfect place in the world."

"Is anywhere?" Ezio replied.

SEVENTEEN

Their ship had docked, and passengers and crew scrambled about, getting in each other's way, as mooring ropes were thrown to men on the quayside and gangplanks were lowered.

Ezio had returned to his cabin to collect his saddlebags—all that he carried. He'd know how to get what he needed once he was ashore. His young companion's servant had arranged three leather-bound trunks on the deck, and they awaited porters to carry them ashore. Ezio and his new friend prepared to take leave of one another.

The young man sighed. "I have so much work to return to—and yet it is good to be home."

"You are far too young to be worried about work, *ragazzo*!"

Ezio's eye was distracted by the appearance of the red-headed woman in green. She was fussing over a large parcel, which looked heavy. The young man followed his gaze.

"When I was your age, my interests were . . . were mainly . . ." Ezio trailed off, watching the woman. Watching the way she moved in her dress. She looked up, and he thought he'd caught her eye. *"Salve!"* he said.

But she hadn't noticed him after all, and Ezio turned back to his companion, who'd been watching him with amusement.

"Incredible," said the young man. "I'm surprised you got anything done at all."

"So was my mother," Ezio smiled back, a little ruefully.

Finally, the gates in the gunwale were opened, and the waiting crowd of passengers surged forward.

"It was a pleasure to have made your acquaintance, *beyefendi*," said the young man, bowing to Ezio. "I hope you will find something to hold your interest while you are here."

"I have faith that I will."

The young man moved away, but Ezio lingered, watching the woman struggling to lift the parcel—which she was unwilling to entrust to any porter—as she started to disembark.

He was about to step forward to assist when he saw that the young man had beaten him to it.

"My I be of some assistance, my lady?" he asked her.

The woman looked at the young man and smiled. Ezio thought that smile was more killing than any crossbow bolt. But it wasn't aimed at him. "Thank you, dear boy," she said, and the young man, waving his valet aside, personally hefted the package onto his shoulder, following her down the companionway to the quay.

"A scholar *and* a gentleman," Ezio called to him. "You are full of surprises."

The young man turned back and smiled again. "Very few, my friend. Very few." He raised a hand. "*Allaha ismarladik!* May God bless you!"

Ezio watched as the woman, followed by the young man, was swallowed up by the crowd. As he watched, he noticed a man standing slightly apart, looking at him. A tough man in his midthirties, in a white surcoat with a red sash, and dark trousers tucked into yellow boots. Long dark hair and beard, and four throwing knives in a scabbard attached high on his left shoulder. He also wore a scimitar, and his right forearm carried a triple-plated steel guard. As Ezio tensed and looked more closely, he thought, but was not sure, that he could detect the harness of a hidden-blade just beneath the man's right hand. The surcoat was hooded, but the hood was down, and the man's unruly hair was kept in check by a broad yellow bandana.

Ezio moved slowly down the gangplank to the quay. And the man approached.

When they were within two paces of each other, the man stopped, smiled cautiously, and bowed deeply.

"Welcome, Brother! Unless the legend is a lie, you are the man I have always longed to meet. Renowned Master and Mentor—Ezio Auditore da . . ." He broke off and his dignity deserted him. "Lah, lah-lah!" he finished.

"Prego?" Ezio was amused.

"Forgive me, I have a hard time getting my tongue round Italian."

"I am Ezio da Firenze. The city of my birth."

"Which would make me . . . Yusuf Tazim *da* Istanbul! I like that!"

"Istanbul. Ah—so that is what *you* call this city."

"It's a favorite with the locals. Come sir—let me take your pack—"

"No, thank you—"

"As you wish. Welcome, Mentor! I am glad you have arrived at last. I will show you the city."

"How did you know to expect me?"

"Your sister wrote from Rome to alert the Brotherhood here. And we had word from a spy in place at Masyaf of your exploits. So we have watched the docks for weeks in the hope and expectation of your arrival." Yusuf could see that Ezio remained suspicious. He looked quizzical. "Your sister *Claudia* wrote—you see? I know her name! And I can show you the letter. I have it with me. I knew you would not be a man to take anything at its face value."

"I see you wear a hidden-blade."

"Who else but a member of the Brotherhood would have access to one?"

Ezio relaxed, slightly. Yusuf's demeanor was suddenly solemn. "Come."

He put a hand on Ezio's shoulder and guided him through the teeming throng. The crowded lanes he led him down, each side filled with stalls selling all manner of goods under a kaleidoscope of colored awnings, were filled, it seemed, with people of every nation and race on earth. Christians, Jews, and Muslims were busy bartering with each other, Turkish street cries mingled with others in Greek, Frankish, and Arabic. As for Italian, Ezio had recognized the accents of Venice, Genoa, and Florence before he'd walked one block. And there were other languages he half recognized or could only guess at—Armenian, Bulgarian, Serbian, and Persian. And a guttural language he did not recognize at all, spoken by tall, fair-skinned men, who wore their red hair and beards wild and long.

"Welcome to the Galata District." Yusuf beamed. "For centuries, it has been a home to orphans from Europe and Asia alike. You won't find more diversity anywhere else in the city. And for that very good reason, we Assassins have our headquarters here."

"Show me."

Yusuf nodded eagerly. "*Kesinlikle*, Mentor. At once! The Brotherhood here is impatient to meet the man who put the Borgia out to grass!" He laughed.

"Does everyone in the city already know I'm here?"

"I sent a boy ahead as soon as I spotted you. And in any case, your Holy Land tussle with the Templars did not go unnoticed. We didn't need our spy for that!"

Ezio looked reflective. "When I first set out, violence was far from my mind. I sought merely wisdom." He looked at his new lieutenant. "The contents of Altaïr's library."

Yusuf laughed again though less certainly. "Not realizing that it's been sealed shut for two-and-a-half centuries?"

Ezio laughed a little himself. "No. I assumed as much. But I admit that I never quite expected to find Templars guarding it."

Yusuf now became serious. They were reaching less populous streets, and they relaxed their pace. "It is very troubling. Five years ago, Templar influence here was minimal. Just a small faction, with dreams of restoring the throne to Byzantium."

They'd reached a small square, and Yusuf drew Ezio to one side to point out a knot of four men crowded in a dark corner. They were dressed in dull grey armor over rough red woolen tunics and jerkins.

"There's a group of them now," Yusuf said, lowering his voice. "Don't look in their direction." He glanced around. "They're growing in number, day by day. And they know what we all know, that Sultan Bayezid is on his way out. They're watching, waiting for their moment. I believe they may try something dramatic."

"But is there no heir to the Ottoman throne?" Ezio asked, surprised.

"That's the trouble—there are two of them. Two angry sons. It's a familiar pattern with these royals. When the sultan coughs, the princes draw their swords."

Ezio pondered this, remembering what the young man on the ship had told him. "Between the Templars and the Ottomans, you must be kept busy," he said.

"Ezio, *efendim*, I tell you in truth that I barely have time to polish my blade!"

Just then, a shot rang out, and a bullet embedded itself in the wall inches to the left of Yusuf's head.

Eighteen

Yusuf dived behind a row of spice barrels, with Ezio close behind him.

"Talk of the devil, and there he is!" Yusuf said, tight-lipped, as he raised his head just enough to see the gun-man reloading across the square.

"Looks like our Byzantine friends over there didn't take kindly to being stared at."

"I'll take care of the guy with the musket," said Yusuf, measuring the distance between himself and his target as he reached back and plucked one of his throwing knives from the scabbard at his back. In a clean move-ment he threw it and it hurtled across the square, rotat-ing three times before it found its mark, burying itself deep in the man's throat, just as he raised his gun to fire again. Meanwhile, his friends were already sprinting toward them, swords drawn.

"Nowhere to run," said Ezio, drawing his own scimitar.

"Baptism of fire for you," said Yusuf. "And you've only just arrived. *Çok üzüldüm.*"

"Don't think about it," replied Ezio, amused. He'd picked up just enough Turkish to know that his companion in arms was saying sorry.

Yusuf drew his own sword, and together they leapt from their hiding place to confront the oncoming foe. They were more lightly clad than their three opponents, which left them worse protected but more mobile. Ezio quickly realized, as he joined with the first Byzantine, that he was up against a highly trained fighter. And he had yet to get used to using a scimitar.

Yusuf kept up his banter as they fought. But then he was used to this enemy, and a good fifteen years Ezio's junior. "The whole city stirs to welcome you—first the regents, like me—and now, the rats!"

Ezio concentrated on the swordplay. It went against him badly at first, but he quickly attuned himself to the light, flexible sword he was using and found its curved blade improved the swing incredibly. Once or twice, Yusuf, keeping an eye on his Mentor, shouted helpful instructions, and ended up casting him an admiring sidelong glance.

"*Inanilmaz!* A master at work!"

But he'd allowed his attention to falter for a second too long, and one of the Byzantines was able to slice through the material of his left sleeve and gash his forearm. As he fell back involuntarily and his assailant pressed his advantage, Ezio shoved his own opponent violently aside and went to his friend's aid, getting between Yusuf and the Byzantine and warding off with his left-arm bracer what would have been a fatal follow-up blow. This move wrong-footed the Byzantine just long enough for Yusuf to regain his balance and, in turn, fend off another mercenary who was closing in on Ezio's back, dealing the attacker a mortal blow at the same time as Ezio finished off the second man. The last remaining Byzantine, a big man with a jaw like a rock face, looked doubtful for the first time.

"Tesekkür ederim," said Yusuf, breathing heavily.

"Bir sey degil."

"Is there no end to your talents?"

"Well, at least I learned 'thank you' and 'you're welcome' on board that baghlah."

"Look out!"

The big Byzantine was bearing down on them, roaring, a big sword in one hand and a mace in the other.

"By Allah, I thought he'd run away," said Yusuf, side-stepping and tripping him up, so that, carried by the weight of his own momentum, he careered forward and crashed heavily into one of the spice barrels, falling headlong into a fragrant heap of yellow powder, where he lay immobile.

Ezio, after looking around, wiped his sword clean and sheathed it. Yusuf followed suit.

"You have a curious technique, Mentor. All feint and no fight. It seems. But when you strike . . ."

"I think like a mongoose—my enemy is the cobra."

"Striking expression."

"I try."

Yusuf glanced around again. "We'd better go. I think that's enough fun for one day."

The words were scarcely out of his mouth when another squad of Byzantine mercenaries, attracted by the sound of the fight, came boiling into the square.

Ezio was instantly on the alert, whipping his sword out again.

But then the other side of the square filled with more troops, wearing a different uniform—blue tunics and dark, conical felt hats.

"Hang on—wait!" Yusuf cried, as the new arrivals turned to attack the mercenaries, quickly causing them to retreat and pursuing them out of sight, out of the square.

"They were Ottoman regular troops," Yusuf said in response to Ezio's questioning look. "Not Janissaries— they are the elite regiment, and you'll know them when you see them. But all Ottoman soldiers have a special loathing for these Byzantine thugs, and that is to the advantage of the Assassins."

"How big an advantage?"

Yusuf spread his hands. "Oh, just a little one. They'll still kill you if you look at them in a way they don't like, same as the Byzantines. The difference is, the Ottomans will feel bad about it afterward."

"How touching."

Yusuf grinned. "It's not so bad, really. For the first

time in many decades, we Assassins have a strong presence here. It wasn't always that way. Under the Byzantine emperors, we were hunted down and killed on the spot."

"You'd better tell me about that," said Ezio, as they once again set off toward the Brotherhood's headquarters.

Yusuf scratched his chin. "Well, the old emperor, Constantine—the eleventh with that name—only had a three-year reign. Our sultan Mehmed saw to that. But by all accounts, Constantine wasn't too bad himself. He was the very last Roman emperor in a line that went back a millennium."

"Spare me the history lesson," Ezio interrupted. "I want to know what we're up against now."

"Thing is, by the time Mehmed took this city, there was almost nothing left of it—or of the old Byzantine Empire. They even say Constantine was so broke he had to replace the jewels in his robes with glass copies."

"My heart bleeds for him."

"He was a brave man. He refused the offer of his life in exchange for surrendering the city, and he went down fighting. But his spirit wasn't shared by two of his nephews. One of them has been dead a few years now, but the other . . ." Yusuf trailed off, thoughtfully.

"He's against us?"

"Oh, you can bet on that. And he's against the Ottomans. Well, the rulers, anyway."

"Where is he now?"

Yusuf looked vague. "Who knows? In exile, somewhere? But if he's still alive, he'll be plotting something."

He paused. "They say he was in pretty thick with Rodrigo Borgia at one time."

Ezio stiffened at the name. "The Spaniard?"

"The very same. The one you finally snuffed out."

"It was his own son that did the deed."

"Well, they never were exactly the Holy Family, were they?"

"Go on."

"Rodrigo was also close to a Seljuk called Cem. It was all very hush-hush, and even we Assassins didn't know about it until much later."

Ezio nodded. He had heard the stories. "If I remember rightly, Cem was a bit of an adventurer."

"He was one of the present sultan's brothers, but he had his eye on the throne for himself, so Bayezid threw him out. He ended up kind of under house arrest in Italy, and he and Rodrigo became friends."

"I remember," Ezio said, taking up the story. "Rodrigo thought he could use Cem's ambitions to take Constantinople for himself. But the Brotherhood managed to assassinate Cem in Capua, about fifteen years ago. And that put an end to that little plan."

"Not that we got much thanks for it."

"Our task is not wrought in order to receive thanks."

Yusuf bowed his head. "I am schooled, Mentor. But it was a pretty neat coup, you must admit."

Ezio was silent, so, after a moment, Yusuf continued: "The two nephews I mentioned were the sons of another of Bayezid's brothers, Tomas. They'd been exiled, too, with their father."

"Why?"

"Would you believe it—Tomas was after the Ottoman throne as well. Sound familiar?"

"The name of this family wouldn't be Borgia, would it?"

Yusuf laughed. "It's Palaiologos. But you're right—it almost amounts to the same thing. After Cem died, the nephews both went to ground in Europe. One stayed there, trying to raise an army to take Constantinople himself—he failed, of course, and died, like I said, seven or eight years ago, without an heir, and penniless. But the other—well, he came back, renounced any imperial ambition, was forgiven, and actually joined the navy for a time. Then he seemed to settle down to a life of luxury and womanizing."

"But now he's disappeared?"

"He's certainly out of sight."

"And we don't know his name?"

"He goes by many names—but we have been unable to pin him down."

"But he is plotting something."

"Yes. And he has Templar connections."

"A man to be watched."

"If he surfaces, we'll know about it."

"How old is he?"

"It's said he was born in the year of Mehmed's conquest, which would make him just a handful of years older than you."

"Still enough kick in him then."

Yusuf looked at him. "If you are anything to go by,

plenty." He looked around him. Their walk had taken them deep into the heart of the city. "We're almost there," he said. "This way."

They made another turn—into a narrow street, dim, cool, and shadowy despite the sunshine, which tried, and failed, to penetrate the narrow space between the buildings on either side. Yusuf paused at a small, unimpressive-looking green-painted door and raised the brass knocker on it. He tapped out a code, so softly that Ezio wondered that anyone within would hear. But within seconds, the door was swung open by a broad-shouldered, narrow-hipped girl who bore the Assassins' emblem on the buckle of her tunic belt.

Ezio found himself in a spacious courtyard, green vines clinging to the yellow walls. Assembled there was a small group of young men and women. They gazed at Ezio in awe as Yusuf, with a theatrical gesture, turned to him and said, "Mentor—say hello to your extended family."

Ezio stepped forward. "*Salute a voi, Assassini.* It is an honor to find such fast friends so far from home." To his horror, he found that he was moved to tears. Maybe the tensions of the past few hours were catching up with him; and he was still tired after his journey.

Yusuf turned to his fellow members of the Constantinople Chapter of the Assassin Brotherhood. "You see, friends? Our Mentor is not afraid to weep openly in front of his pupils."

Ezio wiped his cheeks with a gloved hand and smiled. "Do not worry—I will not make a habit of it."

"The Mentor has not been in our city more than a matter of hours, and already there is news," Yusuf went on, his face serious. "We were attacked on the way here. It seems the mercenaries are on the move once more. So"—he indicated three men and two women—"you— Dogan, Kasim, Heyreddin; and you—Evraniki and Irini—I want you to make a sweep of the area—now!"

The five silently rose, bowing to Ezio as they took their leave.

"The rest of you—back to work," Yusuf commanded, and the remaining Assassins dispersed.

Left alone, Yusuf turned to Ezio, a look of concern on his face. "My Mentor. Your weapons and your armor look in need of renewal—and your clothes—forgive me—are in a pitiful state. We will help you. But we have very little money."

Ezio smiled. "Have no fear. I need none. And I prefer to look after myself. It is time to explore the city alone, to get the feeling of it into my blood."

"Will you not rest first? Take some refreshment?"

"The time for rest is when the task is done." Ezio paused. He unslung his bags and withdrew the broken hidden-blade. "Is there a blacksmith or an armorer skilled and trustworthy enough to repair this?"

Yusuf examined the damage, then slowly, regretfully, shook his head. "This, I know, is one of the original blades, crafted from Altaïr's instructions in the Codex your father collected; and what you ask may be impossible to achieve. But if we cannot get it done, we will make sure you do not go out underarmed. But leave your weapons with me—those you do not need to take with you now—and I will have them cleaned and honed. And there will be fresh clothes ready for you on your return."

"I am grateful." Ezio made for the door. As he approached it, the young blond doorkeeper lowered her eyes modestly.

"Azize will be your guide, if you wish her to go with you, Mentor," Yusuf suggested.

Ezio turned. "No. I go alone."

NINETEEN

In truth, Ezio sought to be alone. He needed to collect his thoughts. He went to a taverna in the Genoese quarter, where wine was available, and refreshed himself with a bottle of Pigato and a simple *maccaroin in broddo*. He spent the rest of the afternoon thoroughly acquainting himself with the Galata District and avoided trouble, melting into the crowd whenever he encountered either Ottoman patrols or bands of Byzantine mercenaries. He looked just like many another travel-stained pilgrims wandering the colorful, messy, chaotic, exciting streets of the city.

Once he was satisfied, he returned to headquarters, just as the first lamps were being lit in the dark interiors of the shops and they were laying tables in the lokantas. Yusuf and some of his people were waiting for him.

The Turk immediately came up to him, looking pleased with himself. "Praise the heavens! Mentor! I am glad to see you again—and safe. We feared we had lost you to the vices of the big city!"

"You are melodramatic," said Ezio, smiling. "And as for vices, I am content with my own, *grazie*."

"I hope you will approve of the arrangements we have made in your absence."

Yusuf led Ezio to an inner chamber, where a complete new outfit had been laid out for him. Next to it, neatly arranged on an oak table, lay his weapons, sharpened, oiled, and polished, gleaming as new. A crossbow had been added to the set.

"We have put the broken blade in a place of safety," said Yusuf. "But we noticed that you have no hookblade, so we have organized one for you."

"Hookblade?"

"Yes. Look." Yusuf drew back his sleeve to reveal what Ezio had first taken to be a hidden-blade. But when Yusuf activated it, and it sprang forth, he saw that it was a more complex variant. The telescopic blade of the new weapon ended in a curved hook of well-tempered steel.

"Fascinating," said Ezio.

"You've never seen one before? I grew up using these."

"Show me."

Yusuf took a new hookblade from one of the Assassins in attendance, who'd held it in readiness, and tossed it over to Ezio. Transferring his good hidden-blade from his right wrist to his left, under the bracer, Ezio strapped the hookblade to his right. He felt its unfamiliar weight and practiced releasing and retracting it. He wished Leonardo had been there to see it.

"You'd better give me a demonstration."

"Immediately, if you are ready."

"As I'll ever be."

"Then follow me and watch what I do closely."

They went outside and down the street in the light of late afternoon to a deserted space between a group of tall brick buildings. Yusuf selected one, whose high walls were decorated with projecting horizontal runs of tiled brick at intervals of some ten feet. Yusuf set off toward the building at a run, leaping, when he reached it, onto a couple of water barrels placed close to it, then, springing upward from them, he released his hookblade and used it to grip the first projecting run of tiles, pulling himself up with the hookblade and using his momentum to hook onto the run above, and so on until he was standing on the roof of the building. The whole operation took less than a few seconds.

Taking a deep breath, Ezio followed suit. He managed the first two operations without difficulty, and even found the experience exhilarating, but he almost missed his hold on the third tier and swung dangerously outward for a moment, until he corrected himself without losing momentum and found himself soon afterward on the roof next to Yusuf.

"Don't stop to think," Yusuf told him. "Use your instincts and let the hook do the work. I can already see that after another couple of climbs like that, you'll have mastered it. You're a quick learner, Mentor."

"I have had to be."

Yusuf smiled. He extended his own blade again and showed Ezio the detail. "The standard Ottoman hook-blade has two parts, you see—the hook and the blade, so that you can use one or the other independently. An elegant design, no?"

"A pity I didn't have one of these in the past."

"Perhaps then you had no need of one. Come!"

He bounded over the rooftops, Ezio following, remembering the distant days when he had chased after his brother Federico across the rooftops of Florence. Yusuf led him to places where he could practice some more, out of sight of prying eyes, and once Ezio had accomplished, with increasing confidence, another three climbs, Yusuf turned to him and said, a glint in his eye: "There's still enough light left in the day. How about a bigger challenge?"

"Va bene." Ezio grinned. "Let's go."

Yusuf took off, running again, through the emptying streets, until they reached the foot of the Galata Tower. "They don't post guards in peacetime until the torches are lit on the parapets. We won't be disturbed. Let's go."

Ezio looked up the great height of the tower and swallowed hard.

"You'll be fine. Follow my lead, take a run at it, and let yourself go. Just throw yourself into it. And—again—let the hook do all the hard work. There are plenty of nooks and crannies in the stonework—you'll be spoiled for choice about where to hook in."

With a carefree laugh of encouragement, Yusuf set

off. His skillful use of the blade made it look as if he were walking—running, even—straight up the wall of the tower. Moments later, Ezio, panting but triumphant, joined him on the roof, looking around him. As the young man on the ship had said, the views across the city were stunning. And Ezio hadn't had to wait for permission from some bureaucrat to see them. He identified all the landmarks the young man had introduced him to from the deck of the baghlah, using the opportunity to familiarize himself further with the city's layout. But another part of his mind just drank in its beauty in the red-gold light of the setting sun, the light reminding him of the color of the hair of that beautiful woman who'd been his fellow passenger and who'd looked right through him.

"Welcome to Istanbul, Mentor," said Yusuf, watching his face. "The Crossroads of the World."

"I can see now why they call it that."

"Many generations of men have ruled this city, but they have never subdued her. Whatever yoke is placed on her neck, whatever neglect or pillage is visited on her, she always bounces back."

"It seems a fine place to call home."

"It is."

Yusuf stepped to the edge of the tower after another minute or two, looked down, then turned to Ezio again. "Race you to the bottom?" he asked, and, without waiting for a reply, threw himself from the parapet in an astounding Leap of Faith.

Ezio watched him plummet, like a hawk stooping,

and land safely in a hay wain he'd already singled out, 175 feet below. He sighed, pausing a moment longer to stare at the city spread out beneath him, in wonder. The Great City. The First City. The heiress of Ancient Rome. Constantinople was a thousand years old and had been home to hundreds of thousands of citizens at a time, in the not-too-distant past, when Rome and Florence were mere villages by comparison. She had been plundered and ravaged, and he knew the legendary beauty of the past was gone forever; but she had always awed her attackers and those who sought to reduce her; and, as Yusuf had said, she had never truly been subdued.

Ezio looked around one last time, scanning the whole horizon with his keen eyes. He fought down the deep sadness that filled his heart.

Then, in turn, he made his own Leap of Faith.

TWENTY

The following morning, Ezio and Yusuf sat in the courtyard of the Assassin headquarters, poring over plans
spread on a table, charting their next move. There was
no doubt in their minds that couriers from the Templars
at Masyaf would very soon arrive in the city, if they had
not done so already, and that a concerted Templar attack
must be anticipated.

"It's like a hydra, the Templar organization." Ezio
brooded. "Cut one head off, and two grow back."

"Not in Rome, Mentor. You've seen to that."

Ezio was silent. With his thumb, he tried the edge of
the hookblade he was oiling. "I am certainly impressed
by this weapon, Yusuf. My brothers in Rome would
profit from having them as part of their equipment."

"It's not a hard design to copy," Yusuf replied. "Just give credit where it's due."

"I need more practice," Ezio said, little realizing that he'd get it, soon enough, for at the moment, the street door burst open before Azize had time to reach it, and Kasim, one of Yusuf's lieutenants, rushed in, his eyes wild.

"Yusuf *bey*—come quickly!"

Yusuf was on his feet in an instant. "What's going on?"

"An attack on two fronts! Our Dens in Galata and at the Grand Bazaar."

"It never stops," Yusuf said, angrily. "Every day, the same bad news." He turned to Ezio. "Could this be the big attack you fear?"

"I have no way of knowing, but it must be dealt with."

"Of course. How is your appetite for swordplay?"

"I think you know the answer to that. I do what I must."

"Good man! It's time to put your hookblade to some real use! Let's go!"

TWENTY-ONE

In no time at all, they were sprinting across the rooftops in the direction of the Galata Den. As they grew close, they descended to the street in order to be less conspicuous to Byzantine crossbowmen. But they found their way blocked by a unit of heavily armed mercenaries, who ordered them, menacingly, to turn back. They pretended to retreat a few paces, conferring together.

"Use your hookblade, Mentor," said Yusuf. "There's a sure way to get past these thugs with the maximum of speed and the minimum of fuss."

"Sounds good to me."

"Watch. We call it a hook-and-roll."

Without more ado, Yusuf turned back to the line of men spread out across the street, facing them. He selected

one and ran toward him at such great speed that, before
the man or any of his companions could react, he leapt
into the air immediately in front of his target, projecting
his body forward with his hookblade unleashed and his
right arm plunging down, ready to stick the hook in the
back of the man's belt. Following through, Yusuf did a
somersault over the man, releasing his blade as he did so,
and carried on at speed away from the dumfounded mercenaries. Before they had time fully to regroup, Ezio followed Yusuf's lead, managing as he somersaulted over
his man to grab him by the neck and wrestle him to the
ground, landed some feet behind him, and ran on to join
his companion.

But there were more guards ahead to deal with, and in
doing so, Ezio picked up another technique from his
Seljuk friend. This time, Yusuf swung the hook low, stooping as he approached his target, and wrapped his weapon
round one of his opponent's ankles, felling him as he
swept past. Once again, Ezio copied the moves, and had
soon caught up with the leader of the Istanbul Assassins.

"And that's what we call a hook-and-run." Yusuf grinned. "But I can see you're a natural. Excellent work."

"I almost stumbled back there. Need to improve."

"You'll get plenty of practice."

"Look out, here come more of them!"

They were at the intersection of four streets, empty
now that the fighting had caused the ordinary citizens to
flee inside the buildings and shut the doors behind them.
But they were cornered—large units of Byzantines were
thundering toward them from each quarter.

"What now?" said Ezio, drawing his sword and releasing his left-hand hidden-blade.

"Put those away, Mentor. When he tires of running, an Assassin around here takes to the air."

Ezio quickly followed Yusuf as he scaled the nearest wall, using his hook to aid him, with increasing skill. Once on the rooftops again, Ezio noticed that, in this area, many were topped with stout vertical wooden posts, from which tarred ropes, stretched taut, led upward and downward to other posts on other rooftops, connected by a series of pulleys and blocks and tackle. Such a post stood on their roof, next to where they were standing.

"We introduced this system to transport goods about, from warehouse to warehouse, from warehouse to shop," explained Yusuf. "You can find it in various districts all over the city. It's a lot quicker than using the streets, which are too narrow and usually crowded. And it's a lot quicker for us, too."

Ezio looked down below, to where the Byzantines were trying to break into the building which they were standing on. Too heavily armored to climb, they'd decided to come at them from the interior.

"We'd better hurry."

"You use your hookblade for this, too," said Yusuf. "Just hook it to a rope, hang on tight, and let go—of course, it only works downhill!"

"I'm beginning to see why you developed this weapon—it's perfect for Constantinople."

"You can say that again." Yusuf cast a glance down to

the street below in his turn. "But you're right—we must make haste." Briefly, he scanned the surrounding roof-tops. About three hundred feet away, on the roof of a building downhill from where they were, he spotted a Byzantine scout, his back to them, keeping a lookout over the city, which spread itself below him.

"See that guy?" Yusuf said.

"Yes."

"And there's another, just over there, to the left—on a connecting roof."

"Got him."

"We're going to take them out." Yusuf extended his hookblade and notched it over the rope. He raised a warning hand as Ezio was about to do the same. "Do not follow me immediately. Allow me to show you."

"I am glad to learn the customs of the country."

"We call this a zipline. Watch!"

Yusuf waited until the second scout was looking in another direction, then let the rope take his weight. It strained slightly, but held. Then he swung his body clear, and in a moment he was sailing silently down the rope toward the unsuspecting first scout. At the last moment, he unhooked his blade and dropped the last few feet onto his target, swinging the blade round to slice into the man's side. He caught the scout's falling body and lowered it gently to the ground before stepping quickly behind the cover of a small outbuilding on the roof. From there, he let out a strangled cry.

This alerted the second scout, who turned quickly to look in the direction from which the sound had come.

"Help, comrade! Assassins!" Yusuf called, using Greek, in an anguished voice.

"Stand fast! I'm coming!" the second scout called back, racing across the roof to the aid of his fellow.

At that moment, Yusuf beckoned to Ezio, who rocketed down the rope in his turn, in time to drop fatally onto the second scout, by that time kneeling next to the body of his fallen companion.

Yusuf joined him by the two bodies. "You didn't even break a sweat," Yusuf said, chuckling. Then he immediately became serious, and continued, "I can see you can look after yourself, so I think it's time we split up. I'd better head to the Bazaar and see what's happening at our Den there. You go on to Galata, to help them there."

"Tell me the way."

Yusuf pointed across the rooftops. "You see the tower?"

"Yes."

"The Den's right by it. I can't be in two places at once, but now you're here, I don't have to be. Thank Allah you came, Mentor. Without your help . . ."

"You've done all right so far."

Yusuf took his hand. "*Haydi rastgele*—Ezio. Good luck!"

"Good luck to you, too."

Yusuf turned south while Ezio ran over the russet-colored tiles of the rooftops until he found another rope system. Sailing quickly and unopposed from holding post to holding post, and traveling a lot faster than he would have done on foot, he quickly made his way downward toward the tower's base, and his next battle.

TWENTY-TWO

Ezio arrived during a lull in the fighting and managed to slip into the Den without being seen. There, he was greeted by Dogan, one of the Assassin lieutenants he had briefly met earlier.

"Mentor, it is an honor. Is Yusuf not with you?"

"No—they've mounted another attack—on our Den by the Grand Bazaar. He's on his way there now." Ezio paused. "What is the situation here?"

Dogan wiped his brow. "We've beaten back the vanguard, but they're just fallen back to wait for reinforcements."

"Are your men ready for them?"

Dogan gave Ezio a wry smile, encouraged by the

Mentor's enthusiasm and confidence. "Now you're here, they are!"

"Where's the next attack likely to come from?"

"The north side. They think that's the weakest."

"Then we'd better make sure it's the strongest!"

Dogan redeployed his Assassins according to Ezio's instructions, and by the time the Templars launched their counterattack, they were ready for them. The fight was as fierce as it was short, leaving fifteen Templar mercenaries dead in the square near the tower where the Den was located. The Assassin troop counted two men and one woman wounded, but no fatalities. It had been a rout of the Templars.

"They will not be back soon," Dogan told Ezio when it was all over.

"Let's hope so. From my experience of the Templars, they do not like to be bested."

"Well, if they try it again around here, they'll have to learn to live with it."

Ezio smiled and clapped Dogan on the shoulder. "That's the kind of talk I like to hear!"

He made to take his leave.

"Where will you go now?" asked Dogan.

"I'm going to join Yusuf at the Den of the Grand Bazaar. Send word to me there if the Templars do regroup."

"In that unlikely event, you will be the first to know."

"And tend to your wounded. That sergeant of yours took a bad cut to the head."

"It is being attended to as we speak."

"Can I get there by using the zipline system?"

"Once you reach the south bank of the Horn. But you must cross that by ferry. It's the fastest way to the peninsula."

"Ferry?"

"There was to have been a bridge, but for some reason it was never built."

"Ah yes," said Ezio. "I remember somebody mentioning that." He put out his hand. *"Allaha ismarladik,"* he said.

"Güle güle." Dogan smiled back.

The Den Ezio needed to reach was located not far from the Bazaar, in the Imperial District, between the Bazaar itself and the ancient church of Haghia Sofia, now converted by the Ottomans into a mosque.

But the fighting Ezio reached was taking place a short distance to the southwest, close to the docks on the southern shores of the city. He stood for a moment on a rooftop, observing the battle, which was in full spate in the streets and on the quays below him. A rope from a wooden stake near him stretched down to a point near where he could see Yusuf, his back to the waters of the dock, in the thick of the fray. Yusuf was fending off a half dozen burly mercenaries, and his companions were too busy themselves to come to his aid. Ezio hooked onto the rope and swooped down, jumping from the rope at a height of twelve feet and spread-eagling himself, left-hand hidden-blade extended, to land on the backs of two of Yusuf's attackers, sending them sprawling. They were dead before they could react, and Ezio stood over them as the remaining four in their group turned to face him, giving Yusuf enough respite to edge round to their flank. Ezio kept his hookblade extended.

As the four Templar troopers fell roaring on Ezio, Yusuf rushed them from the side, his own hidden-blade brought quickly into play. One huge soldier was almost upon Ezio, having backed him up against a warehouse wall, when he remembered the hook-and-roll technique and used it to escape from, and fell, his opponent, stabbing the man's writhing body with his hidden-blade to deliver the coup de grace. Meanwhile, Yusuf had dispatched two of the others, while the survivor took to his heels.

Elsewhere, fierce fighting was simmering down as Yusuf's brigade got the better of the Templars, who finally fled, cursing, into the depths of the city to the north.

"Glad you arrived in time to meet my new playmates," said Yusuf, wiping and sheathing his sword, and retracting his hidden-blade, as Ezio did likewise. "You fought like a tiger, my friend, like a man late for his own— wedding."

"Do you not mean funeral?"

"You would not mind being late for that."

"Well, if we're talking about a wedding, I'm twenty-five years late already." Ezio pushed the familiar darkening mood aside and squared his shoulders. "Did I arrive in time to save the Bazaar Den?"

Yusuf shrugged regretfully. "Alas, no. We've only

managed to save our own skins. The Bazaar Den is taken. Unfortunately, I arrived too late to regain it. They were too well entrenched."

"Don't despair. The Galata Den is safe. The Assassins we used there can join us here."

Yusuf brightened. "With my 'army' doubled in size, we'll take the Bazaar back together! Come! This way!"

TWENTY-THREE

They made their way through the market streets and the massive, glittering maze of the souk itself, the splendid, frenetic, gold-and-red Grand Bazaar, with its myriad lanes of little shops selling everything from scents to spices to sheepskins to costly Persian carpets from Isfahan and Kabul, cedarwood furniture, swords and armor, brass and silver coffeepots with snaking spouts and elongated necks, tulip-shaped glasses for tea and larger, slender ones for *sharbat*—a cornucopia selling everything in the world a man could imagine or desire, amid a babel of traders' voices raised in at least a dozen different languages.

Once they'd passed out of the northeastern side, they came to streets nearer the Den. Here, the Templar presence was strong. The buildings were hung with their banners, and the merchants who did business there, Ezio could see, were not infrequently being harassed or otherwise bullied by Byzantine toughs.

"As you can see," Yusuf was telling him, "when the Templars take over a district, they like to flaunt it. It's a constant battle to keep them at bay; they like nothing better than to rub our noses in every victory they enjoy."

"But why does the sultan do nothing? This is his city!"

"Sultan Bayezid is far away. There aren't enough Ottoman resources for the governor here to keep matters in check. If it weren't for us . . ." Yusuf trailed off, then continued, following another train of thought. "The sultan is at war with his son, Selim, many leagues northwest of the city. He's been away for years, at least since the great earthquake in 1509, and even before that he was almost always absent. He is blind to all this turmoil."

"The earthquake?" Ezio remembered news of that reaching Rome. Over a hundred mosques had been reduced to rubble, along with a thousand other buildings, and ten thousand citizens had lost their lives.

"You should have seen it. We called it the Lesser Day of Judgment. The huge waves it caused in the Sea of Marmara almost brought down the southern walls. But the sultan's eyes remained closed, even to that warning."

"Ah, but your eyes are open, *sì*?"

"Like two full moons. Believe me."

They had reached a large open *karesi*, thronged with Templar mercenaries, who began to eye them suspiciously as they crossed the square.

"Too many to engage directly," Yusuf said. "We'd better use one of these."

He delved into the pouch at his side and produced a bomb.

"What's that—a smoke bomb?" Ezio said. "Hmn. I'm not confident that that will help us here."

Yusuf laughed. "Smoke bomb? Dear Ezio—Mentor— it's really high time you Italians joined the sixteenth century. These bombs do not obscure—they distract. Watch."

Ezio stood back as Yusuf threw the bomb some distance away from him. It exploded harmlessly, but sent a shower of small, apparently gold, coins into the air, which rained down over the mercenaries. Their attention was immediately distracted from Ezio and Yusuf as they hurried to pick up the coins, shouldering aside the civilians around who tried to join in.

"What was that?" asked Ezio in astonishment, as they continued on their way, now in no fear of molestation.

Yusuf smiled craftily. "That's what we call a Gold Bomb. It's filled with coins made of pyrite—they look exactly like gold coins but are very cheap to produce."

Ezio watched the troopers scatter, oblivious to anything but the Fool's Gold.

"You see?" said Yusuf. "They can't resist. But let's get a move on before they've picked them all up."

"You are full of surprises today."

"Crafting explosives is a new hobby of ours, one we've borrowed from the Chinese. We've taken to it with great passion."

"I'm obviously getting rusty. But a friend of mine

once made me some bombs, in Spain, long ago, so I know something of the subject. You'll have to teach me the new techniques."

"Gladly—but who is the Mentor here, Ezio? I'm beginning to wonder."

"That's enough of your cheek, Assassin!" Ezio grinned, clapping Yusuf on the shoulder.

A narrow street they'd been passing along gave way to another square, and there, again, in that Templar-infested district, was another large group of Byzantine mercenaries. They'd heard the commotion from the adjoining *karesi* and were looking restive. Yusuf drew a handful of small bombs from his pouch and handed them to Ezio. "Your turn," he said. "Make me proud. The wind's behind us, so we should be all right."

The Byzantines were already making for the two Assassins and drawing their swords. Ezio pulled the pins of the three bombs in his hands and threw them toward the oncoming mercenaries. They exploded on impact with the ground with little, harmless-sounding *pops*, and for a moment it looked as if nothing else had happened. But then the Templar troops hesitated and looked at each other, gagging and dabbing at their uniforms, which were covered with a stinking, viscous liquid. Quickly, they beat a retreat.

"There they go," said Yusuf. "It'll be days before their women will take them back into their beds."

"Another of your surprises?"

"Those were skunk-oil bombs. Very effective if you judge your moment and keep out of the prevailing wind!"

"Thanks for the warning."

"What warning?"

"Exactly."

"Hurry. We're nearly there."

They'd crossed the *karesi* into another street, broader this time but lined with what looked liked boarded-up shops. Yusuf paused at one of them and pushed cautiously at its door, which swung open. Beyond it was a small, plain courtyard, a few barrels and packing cases stacked up along the far wall. In the middle was an open trapdoor, with stone steps leading down from it. A tower rose from the rear left-hand corner of the courtyard.

"As I thought," said Yusuf. He turned to Ezio and spoke urgently. "This is one of our underground Dens. It looks deserted, I know, but below, the Templars will have it well guarded. Among their rabble there's a Templar captain. May I ask you to find him and kill him?"

"I'll get your hideout back for you."

"Good. When you've done so, climb that tower and set off the signal flare you'll find there. It's another one of our bombs, and it's a copy of the flares the Templars use to signal a retreat."

"And you?"

"It won't take those Templars in the square long to realize what's happened, so I'll go back and find a way of stopping them from following us here and trying to reinforce their friends. I've got a couple of phosphorus bombs clipped to my tunic belt. They should do the trick."

"So you *do* still use old-fashioned smoke screens?"

Yusuf nodded. "Yes, but these are pretty nasty, so—" He drew a scarf over his nose and mouth. "And before I go, there's one more little trick up my sleeve, which should bring the rabbits out of their hole—I wouldn't want you to go down to the Den and fight those thugs in semidarkness. Once they've surfaced, you should be able to pick them off without too much trouble." From his pouch, he produced a final bomb, and hefted it for a moment. "I'll set this off now, then be on my way. We've got to neutralize both groups of Templars simultaneously, or we'll be lost. Just cover your ears—this is a cherry bomb, and it's packed with sulfur, so it'll make a noise like a thunderclap. It'll bring them up all right, but I don't want you to burst your eardrums."

Ezio did as he was bidden, moving back to a strategic position on the shady side of the courtyard, with a good view of the trapdoor. He exchanged his left-hand hidden-blade for his adapted pistol harness, preferring to retain the hookblade for close combat. Yusuf, near the street, threw his cherry bomb to the far side of the courtyard, and disappeared.

There was a noise as loud as the Devil's Fart, and Ezio, though he'd covered his ears beneath his hood firmly, still had the aftershock in his head. He shook it to clear it, and as he did so, ten Templars, led by a ruddy-nosed captain, burst from the trapdoor into the sunlight, looking around them in panic. Ezio moved in swiftly and had cut three down before they'd had time to react. Using his hookblade, he was able to kill another three in the next minute of combat. Three more ran off, as they heard the sound of two more explosions, followed shortly afterward by the faint smell of smoke in the breeze.

"Perfect timing, Yusuf," murmured Ezio to himself.

The captain of the cohort stood and confronted Ezio. A brawny, walleyed man with well-used black shoulder armor over his dark red tunic, he held a heavy Damascus in his right hand and a wicked-looking curved dagger, with a barbed point, in his left.

"Rip and slit," said the captain in a hoarse voice. "I hook you in with the dagger and slit your throat with the sword. You're as good as dead, Assassin."

"It's really high time you Templars joined the sixteenth century," replied Ezio, raising his left arm and springing his pistol into his hand. He fired, thinking that at that range he really couldn't miss, even left-handed, and, sure enough, the ball sank into the bone straight between the captain's eyes.

The captain was still sinking to his knees as Ezio sprang across the courtyard, leapt onto one of the barrels for purchase, and used the hookblade to surge to the top of the tower.

The flare Yusuf had told him of had not been discovered or disturbed. There was a little mortar, and Ezio loaded the flare into it. A moment later, it streaked high into the sky, trailing a vivid streak of flame and violet smoke.

By the time he reached the foot of the tower again, Yusuf was waiting for him.

"No wonder you are our Mentor," said the Seljuk Assassin. "You could not have timed that better." He beamed in triumph. "The Templars are withdrawing on all fronts."

TWENTY-FOUR

The Bazaar Den was remarkably neat and tidy, given its recent occupation by the Templars.

"Any damage?" Ezio asked Yusuf, as his Turkish comrade stared at the ceiling.

"Not that I can see. Byzantine Templars may be bad hosts, but they are decent tenants. Once they capture a location, they like to keep it intact."

"Because they intend to stay?"

"Exactly!" Yusuf rubbed his hands. "We must take advantage of our little victories to prepare you further for the fight against our Greek friends," he said. "I've shown you how to use some of our bombs. But it'll be even better if you know how to make them."

"Is there someone here who can teach me?"

"Of course! The master himself! Piri Reis."

"Piri Reis is . . . one of us?"

"In a manner of speaking. He likes to keep himself aloof. But he's certainly on our side."

"I thought he was more of a mapmaker," said Ezio, remembering the map of Cyprus he'd been given by Ma'Mun.

"Mapmaker, seafarer, pirate—though these days he's rising swiftly through the ranks of the Ottoman Navy—he's a pretty good all-arounder. And he knows Istanbul—Kostantiniyye—like the back of his hand."

"Good—because there's something I'd like to ask him about the city that he may know. Apart from how to make bombs. When can I meet him?"

"No time like the present. And we don't have any to lose. Are you all right after that little skirmish? Need some rest?"

"No."

"Good! I'll take you to him now. His workroom isn't far from here."

Piri Reis—Admiral Piri—had a small set of second-story, open-plan rooms on the north side of the Grand Bazaar, whose tall windows threw a cold, clear light on the handful of map tables neatly arranged on the teak floors of a cramped studio. Equally neatly spread out on the tables were maps of a greater number and variety than Ezio had ever seen before, and, seated by them, a handful of assistants were diligently working in silence. The western and southern walls of the workroom were festooned with more maps, all neatly pinned up and squared-off to one another. Five large globes, one in each corner and one in the center of the room, completed the picture. The globes were also works in progress, and freshly inked-in areas showed the latest discoveries added.

The western wall was also covered with detailed technical drawings, expertly accomplished—but these were, as Ezio saw at a glance, designs for bombs. He was able to read enough, as he passed through the room toward where Piri sat, to see that the bomb drawings were divided into categories: Lethal, Tactical, Diversionary, and Special Casings. An alcove in the wall was big enough to contain a worktable, and behind it, arranged with precision, a number of metalworkers' tools were placed on shelves.

This was quite a contrast to the chaos in which Leonardo loved to work, Ezio thought, smiling to himself at the memory of his friend.

Yusuf and Ezio found Piri himself at work at a large drafting table directly under the windows. Six or seven years younger than Ezio, he was a tanned, weather-beaten, healthy, and robust figure of a man, wearing a blue silk turban, under which a strong face, currently bearing an expression of intense concentration, looked out at the work through piercing, clear grey eyes. His luxuriant brown beard was neatly trimmed, though worn long, covering the collar of the high-necked, silver brocade tunic he wore, with baggy blue trousers and plain wooden clogs.

He gave Ezio an appraising glance, which Ezio returned, as Yusuf made the introductions.

"What's your name again?" said Piri.

"Ezio. Ezio Auditore da Firenze."

"Ah yes. I thought for a moment Yusuf said 'Lothario.' Didn't hear the difference." He looked at Ezio, and Ezio could have sworn there was a twinkle in his eye. Had Ezio's reputation—in one department at least—preceded him?

He thought he was going to like this man.

"I have seen your work—your maps, anyway," Ezio began. "I had a copy of the one you made for Cyprus."

"Did you?" replied the sailor, gruffly. Clearly, he didn't like having his work interrupted. Or at least that was the impression he wanted to give.

"But it is another aspect of your expertise I have come to seek your advice about today."

"That was a good map, the one of Cyprus," said Piri, ignoring Ezio's remark. "But I've improved it since. Show me yours."

Ezio hesitated. "I don't have it anymore," he confessed. "I gave it—to a friend of mine."

Piri looked up. "Very generous of you," he said. "Do you know what my maps are worth?"

"Indeed. But I owed that man my life." Ezio hesitated again. "He's a seaman, like yourself."

"Hmn. What's his name? I might have heard of him."

"He's a Mamluk. Goes by the name of Al-Scarab."

Piri suddenly beamed. "That old rogue! Well, I hope he puts it to good use. At least he knows better than to try anything on us."

Then he turned his eye on Yusuf. "Yusuf! What are

you doing still standing there? Don't you have anything better to do? Take yourself off and leave your friend with me. I'll see that he has everything he needs. Any friend of Al-Scarab is a friend of mine!"

Yusuf grinned and took his leave. "I knew I'd be leaving you in safe hands," he said as he left.

When they were alone, Piri became more serious. "I know who you are, Ezio, and I have a pretty good idea why you are here. Will you take some refreshment? There's coffee, if you like it."

"I have acquired a taste for it at last."

"Good!" Piri clapped his hands at one of his assistants, who nodded and went to the back of the workshop, to return soon afterward with a brass tray holding a serpentine pot, with minute cups, and a dish of soft amber-colored sweetmeats, which Ezio had never tasted before.

"I remember Al-Scarab from my own privateering days," Piri said. "We fought side by side at both battles of Lepanto a dozen years ago or so, under the flag of my uncle Kemal. No doubt you've heard of him?"

"Yes."

"The Spaniards fought us like tigers, but I didn't think so much of the Genoese or the Venetians. You're a Florentine, yourself, aren't you?"

"Yes."

"So you're a landlubber."

"My family were bankers."

"On the surface, yes! But something far more noble underneath."

"As you know, banking does not run in my blood as seafaring does in yours."

Piri laughed. "Well said!" He sipped his coffee, wincing as he burned his lips. Then he eased himself off his stool and stretched his shoulders, laying down his pen. "And that's quite enough small talk. I see you're already looking at the drawings I'm working on. Make any sense of them?"

"I can see they're not maps."

"Is it maps you're after?"

"Yes and no. There is one thing I want to ask you—about the city—before I talk about anything else."

Piri spread his hands. "Go ahead."

Ezio took Niccolò Polo's book, *The Secret Crusade*, out of his side wallet, and showed it to Piri.

"Interesting," said the seaman. "Of course I know all about the Polos. Read Marco's book. Exaggerates a bit, if you ask me."

"I took this from a Templar at Masyaf. Yusuf knows of it and of its contents."

"Masyaf? So you have been there."

"It mentions the five keys to Altaïr's library. From my reading of it, I see that Altaïr entrusted the keys to Niccolò, and that he brought them here and concealed them."

"And the Templars know this? So it's a race against time."

Ezio nodded. "They've already found one, hidden in the cellars of the Topkapi Palace. I need to recover it and find the other four."

"So—where will you begin?"

"Do you know the location of the Polos' old trading post here?"

Piri looked at him. "I can tell you exactly where it was. Come over here." He led the way to where a large, immensely detailed map of Constantinople hung on the wall in a plain gold frame. He peered at it for an instant, then tapped a spot with his index finger. "It's there. Just to the west of Haghia Sofia. No distance from here. Why? Is there a connection?"

"I have a hunch I need to follow."

Piri looked at him. "That is a valuable book," he said, slowly.

"Yes. Very valuable, if I'm right."

"Well, just make sure it doesn't fall into the wrong hands."

He was silent for a long moment, thinking. "Be careful when you find the Polos' old trading post," he said. "You may find more than you bargain for there."

"Does that remark beg a question?"

"If it does, it is a question to which I have no answer. I just ask you to be wary, my friend."

Ezio hesitated before taking Piri further into his confidence. "I think my quest will start in that place. I am sure there must be something hidden there that will give me my first clue."

"It is possible," Piri said, giving nothing away. "But heed my warning."

Then he brightened, rubbing his hands vigorously, as if to chase away demons. "And now that we've settled that matter, what else can I help you with?"

"I'm sure you've guessed. I am here on an Assassin mission, perhaps the most important ever, and Yusuf tells me you would be prepared to show me how to make bombs. The special ones you've developed here."

"Ach, that Yusuf has a big mouth." But Piri looked serious again. "I cannot compromise my position, Ezio. I am Senior Navigator in the Sultan's Navy, and this is my current project." He waved his hands at the maps. Then he winked. "The bombs are a sideline. But I like to help my true friends in a just cause."

"You may rely on my discretion. As I hope I may on yours."

"Good. Follow me."

So saying, Piri led the way to the spacious alcove on the west wall. "The bombs are actually part of a naval research project, too," he continued. "Through my soldiering, I have gained an appreciation for artillery and explosives. And that has served the Assassins well. It gives us an edge."

He waved his hand at the technical drawings. "I have developed many kinds of bombs, and some are reserved for the use of your Brotherhood alone. As you can see, they are divided into four main categories. Of course, they are expensive, but the Brotherhood has always understood that."

"Yusuf told me the Assassins here are short of funds."

"Most good causes usually are," replied Piri. "But Yusuf is also resourceful. I gather you know how to use these weapons?"

"I had a crash course."

Piri looked at him levelly. "Good. Well, as Yusuf

evidently promised you, if you want to craft your own bombs, I can show you."

He went round the table and picked up two pieces of strange-looking metal lying on it. Ezio, leaning forward curiously, reached for a third.

"Ah ah ah! Don't touch that!" warned Piri. "One wrong move and BANG! The building comes down."

"Are you serious?"

Piri laughed. "The look on your face! Look, I'll show you."

For the next few hours, Piri Reis took Ezio through every basic step involved in constructing each kind of bomb and the materials involved.

Ezio learned that each bomb contained the fundamental ingredient of gunpowder, but that not all were designed to be lethal. He'd already had experience of lethal explosives when attacking Cesare Borgia's fleet in Valencia four years earlier, and Yusuf had shown him how to use diversionary bombs which created smoke screens, thunderclaps, appalling odors, and apparent pennies from heaven. Piri now demonstrated other applications. Among the bombs with lethal effect were those using coal dust, which added a heavy blasting power to the gunpowder, and fragmentation bombs whose shrapnel killed messily over a wide range. Bombs containing sachets of lambs' blood spattered their opponents with it, causing them to think they had been wounded, and panicking them. Another type of nonlethal explosive, useful in delaying pursuers, was the caltrop bomb, which showered numbers of twisted-together nails in the path of an oncoming enemy.

Perhaps the most unpleasant were the bombs that used either datura powder or deadly nightshade.

"Datura and deadly nightshade are two of what we call the witches' weeds, along with henbane and mandrake," Piri explained, his face grave. "I do not like to use them except in cases of great extremity and danger. When exploded in the midst of an enemy, datura causes delirium, deranging the brain, and death. It is perhaps the worst of all. Deadly nightshade produces a poison gas, which is equally lethal."

"The Templars would not hesitate to use them against us if they could."

"That is one of the moral paradoxes mankind will wrestle with until the day he becomes truly civilized," replied Piri. "Is it evil to use evil to combat evil? Is agreeing with that argument merely a simple justification for something none of us should really do?"

"For now," said Ezio, "there is not leisure to ponder such questions."

"You'll find the ingredients for these bombs in locations about the city, which Yusuf will tell you of," said Piri. "So keep your eyes open and your nose to the ground as you roam the streets."

Ezio rose to take his leave. Piri extended a walnut brown hand. "Come back whenever you need more help."

"Ezio shook hands and was unsurprised at the firmness of the grasp.

"I hope we will meet again."

"Oh," said Piri with an enigmatic smile. "I have no doubt of it."

TWENTY-FIVE

Following Piri Reis's instructions, Ezio made his way through the Bazaar once more, ignoring the insistent blandishments of the traders there, until he reached the quarter west of the enormous bulk of Haghia Sofia. He almost got lost in the labyrinth of streets and alleyways around it but came at last to the spot which, he was sure, Piri had indicated on his map.

A bookshop. And a Venetian name over the door.

He entered and, to his surprise and barely suppressed delight, found himself face-to-face with the young woman he had encountered on his voyage to Constantinople. She greeted him warmly, but he saw immediately that he was merely being welcomed as a potential customer. There was no sign of recognition on her face.

"*Buon giorno! Merhaba!*" she said, switching automatically from Italian to Turkish. "Please come in."

She was busying herself among her stock and, in turning, knocked over a pile of books. Ezio saw at a glance that this shop was the antithesis of Piri Reis's well-ordered studio.

"Ah!" said the woman. "Excuse the clutter. I have not had time to tidy up since my trip."

"You sailed from Rhodes, *no*?"

She looked at him in surprise. "*Sì*. How did you know?"

"We were on the same ship." He bowed slightly. "My name is Auditore, Ezio."

"And I am Sofia Sartor. Have we met?"

Ezio smiled. "We have now. May I look around?"

"*Prego*. Most of my best volumes are in the back, by the way."

Under the pretext of looking at the books, stacked in apparent chaos on a maze of teetering wooden shelves, Ezio delved deeper into the dark confines of the shop.

"It's nice to meet another Italian in this district," Sofia said, following him. "Most of us keep to the Venetian District, and Galata."

"It's good to meet you, too. But I thought the war between Venice and the Ottoman Empire would have driven most Italians away. After all, it's only seven or eight years ago."

"But Venice kept control of her islands in the White Sea, and everyone came to an arrangement," she replied. "At least, for the moment."

"So you stayed?"

She shrugged. "I lived here with my parents when I was a girl. True, when the war was on, we were pushed out, but I always knew I would return." She hesitated. "Where are you from?"

"Florence."

"Ah."

"Is that a problem?"

"No, no. I have met some very nice Florentines."

"There's no need to sound so surprised."

"Forgive me. If you have any questions about the books, just ask."

"*Grazie.*"

"There's even more stock in the rear courtyard if you're interested." She looked a little rueful. "More than I seem to be able to sell, to be honest."

"What took you to Rhodes?"

"The Knights of Rhodes are uneasy. They know the Ottomans haven't given up the idea of taking the island over. They think it's only a question of time. Philippe Villiers de L'Isle-Adam was selling off part of their library. So it was a shopping trip, if you like. Not very successful, either. The prices they were asking!"

"De L'Isle-Adam is a good Grand Master and a brave man."

"Do you know him?"

"Only by repute."

The woman looked at him as he poked around. "Look, nice as it is to chat with you—are you sure I cannot help? You seem a bit lost."

Ezio decided to come clean. "I am not really looking to buy anything."

"Well," she replied, a touch crisply, "I'm not giving anything away free, *Messere.*"

"Forgive me. Just bear with me a little longer. I will make it up to you."

"How?"

"I'm working on that."

"Well, I must say—"

But Ezio silenced her with a gesture. He had man-handled one bookshelf from the back wall of the covered courtyard. The wall was thicker than the others, he could see that, and he'd noticed a crack in it that wasn't a crack at all.

It was part of a doorframe, artfully concealed.

"Dio mio!" exclaimed Sofia. "Who put that there?"

"Has anyone ever moved these bookshelves before?"

"Never. They've been in place since before my father took over the shop, and before that, it had been in disuse for years—decades, even."

"I see." Ezio brushed dust and debris accumulated over what looked like far more than decades away from the doorframe but found no handle or any other means of opening the door. Then he remembered the secret door that led to the vault back in Monteriggioni, at his uncle's fortress, and felt around for a hidden catch. Before long, the door swung open and inward. Within, steps the width of the wall led downward into blackness.

"This is incredible," said the woman, peering over

Ezio's shoulder. He smelled the soft scent of her hair, her skin.

"With your permission, I'll find out where it leads to," he said firmly.

"I'll fetch you some light. A candle."

She was back in moments, with a candle and a tinder-box. "Who are you, *Messere*?" she asked, looking into his eyes.

"Only the most interesting man in your life."

She smiled, quickly. "Ah! *Presuntuoso!*"

"Stay here. Let no one into the shop. I'll be back before you know it."

Leaving her, he descended the steps, from whose foot a tunnel led deep in the earth.

TWENTY-SIX

Ezio found himself in a system of underground cisterns. By the feeble light of the candle, he could make out barrel-vaulted roofs supported by row upon row of slender columns, decorated at their capitals with a variety of symbols, among which Ezio recognized eyes. At their bases, some of them, bizarrely, showed the inverted heads of monstrous Gorgons.

Ezio recognized the place he must be in—the Yerebatan Sarnici. The great system of cisterns built below Constantinople. In his book, Niccolò Polo mentioned it. It had been built as a water-filtration system by Justinian a thousand years earlier. But knowing that didn't make it feel any less creepy.

He was all but daunted at the vast, cavernous space

around him, which he judged, from the echoes the
sound his movements made, to be as great as a cathedral.
But he remembered that Niccolò had given some indication in *The Secret Crusade* of where one key might be
found. The directions had been deliberately obscure, but
Ezio decided to try to follow them, concentrating as he
forced his mind to remember the details.

It was hard to make no noise at all, moving through
the shallow water that covered the floor of the cistern,
but with practice, Ezio managed to reduce this to a minimum. Besides, any sound he made was soon drowned
out by the noise of the unsuspecting people he heard up
ahead. Evidently, he was not alone in his quest, and he
reminded himself that, before he got hold of the book, it
had been in the Templars' possession.

There were lights up ahead as well. Ezio doused his
candle and crept forward toward them. Soon, he made
out the forms of two Templar foot soldiers, sitting by a
small fire in a dark passage. Ezio drew closer. His Greek
was good enough to pick up most of what they were
saying.

The one who was speaking was in a bad mood and
not afraid to let it show. Indeed, he seemed on the edge
of hysteria. *"Ti distihìa!"* he was saying in aggrieved
tomes. "What misery! Do you know how long we've
been searching this filthy cistern?"

"I've been here a few weeks," replied his quieter
friend.

"That's nothing! Try thirteen *months*! Ever since our
Grand Master found that damned key!" He calmed

himself a little. "But he hasn't got a clue what he's doing. All he knows"—the soldier's tone became sarcastic—"is that they're 'somewhere in the city.'"

Hearing this, the other soldier grew more excited himself, sounding overwhelmed at the prospect ahead of them. "This is a very big city . . ."

"I know! That's what I said myself—under my breath."

They were interrupted by the arrival of a sergeant. "Get on with your work, you bums! You think you're paid to sit around on your arses all day?"

Grumbling, the men resumed their task. Ezio shadowed them, hoping to pick up more information. The men were joined by a handful of other soldiers, similarly begrimed and discontented.

But Ezio had to watch his step. Tired and disgruntled the soldiers might have been, but they were well trained, and vigilant.

"Petros!" one called to another. "Make sure we have enough torches for the excavation. I'm tired of stumbling around in the dark."

Ezio pricked up his ears at the word "excavation," but as he moved forward again, his sword scabbard scraped against one of the columns, and the vaulted roofs echoed and amplified the slight sound.

The man called Petros darted a look behind him. "There's someone down here with us!" he hissed. "Keep your eyes open and your hands steady."

The troops were instantly on the alert, urgently calling to one another in muted voices.

"Do you see anything?"

"Search every corner!"

Ezio retreated farther into the shadows and waited patiently for the panic to die down. At the same time, he made a mental note to be extra careful in the exaggerated acoustic.

Gradually, the guards resumed their search. As he watched, he could see that their actions seemed aimless and that they knew it. But he continued to watch, hoping to detect a pattern, listening to their desultory conversation as he did so.

"It stinks down here."

"What do you expect? It's a sewer."

"I could use a breath of air."

"Patience! Shift's up in three hours!"

"Keep it down, you!" barked the sergeant, approaching again. "And keep your ears open. The Lord Jesus knows why they picked you lot for a delicate mission like this."

Ezio moved forward, past the men, until he came upon a stone embankment, on which two junior officers were standing by a brazier. He listened in to their conversation.

"We're one step ahead of the Assassins, I know that much," one was saying to the other.

"The Grand Master has ordered that we make all haste. They may be closer than we think."

"He must have his reasons. What do these keys look like anyway?"

"Like the one we discovered beneath Topkapi. That's got to be the assumption."

The other lieutenant shook himself. "Eight hours of this filth. *Apistefto!*"

"I agree. I've never been so bored in all my life."

"Yeah. But we're bound to find the keys soon."

"In your dreams."

But the first lieutenant to speak had suddenly glanced round quickly. "What was that?"

"Probably a rat. The Savior knows, there are enough of them down here."

"All the shadows seem to move."

"It's just the firelight."

"Someone is out there. I can feel it."

"Watch yourself. You'll go mad."

Ezio inched past them, moving as slowly as he could despite wanting to rush, for he dared not let the water around his calves make so much as a ripple. At last he found himself well beyond the two officers and the rest of the Templars, feeling his way along the wall of a dank corridor, much lower and narrower than the pillared halls it led off.

Somehow, it felt right. As soon as the light and noise of the Templars had died out completely behind him, he felt secure enough to relight the candle and drew it from his side satchel along with the tinderbox, praying that he would drop neither as he juggled to strike a spark to light it.

At last he was ready. Pausing for a moment to ensure that he wasn't being followed, he continued along the corridor as it twisted and turned, and, to his consternation, divided into separate, alternative passageways. Occasionally, he took the wrong one and came up against a blank wall. Retracing his steps to find the right way again, he began to wonder if he were not in some kind of maze. Ever deeper and darker he went, praying he'd remember the way back, and that he could trust the bookshop owner, until he was rewarded by a dim glow ahead of him. No more than the glow of a firefly but enough to guide him.

He followed the passageway until it opened out into a small circular chamber, its domed roof all but lost in the shadows above. Half columns stood along the walls at regular intervals, and there was no sound but that of dripping water.

In the center of the chamber was a small stone stand, and on it rested a folded map. Ezio opened it and found it to be a plan of Constantinople, in infinite detail, with the Polo brothers' old trading post clearly marked at its center. Four lines divided up the map, and each demarcated section showed a landmark of the city.

Around the margins of the map the titles of twelve books were written, but of these twelve the titles of four were placed, one each, next to each divided section of the map. The four books had their titles illuminated in green, blue, red, and black.

Ezio carefully folded the map again and placed it in his satchel. Then he turned his attention to what was placed at the center of the stone stand.

It was a carved-stone disc, no more than four inches across. The disk was thin, tapering toward its outer edges, and made of a stone that might have been obsidian. It was pierced at its exact center by a precisely circular hole, half an inch in diameter. Its surface was covered with designs, some of which Ezio recognized from the Codex pages that had been in his father and uncle's collection. A sun whose rays ended in outstretched hands extending toward a world; strange humanoid creatures of indeterminate sex, with exaggerated eyes, lips, foreheads, and bellies; what looked like abstruse mathematical symbols and calculations.

From this, the lightning-bug glow emanated.

Carefully, almost reverently, Ezio took it in his hands. He had not experienced such a feeling of awe since he had last handled the Apple, and he already seemed to know what it was he was handling.

As he turned it over in his hands, its glow intensified.

Che succede? Ezio thought. What's happening . . . ?

As he watched, the glow became a sunburst, from which he had to shield his eyes, as the chamber exploded into a hurricane of light.

TWENTY-SEVEN

Somehow Ezio was there, and not there. But he couldn't be sure if was dreaming or had fallen into some kind of trance.

But he knew exactly when and where he was—it was centuries before his own birth—late in the twelfth century. The date of the year of Our Lord 1189 floated through his consciousness, as he walked—or drifted— through swirling clouds and crisscrossing rays of unearthly light, which parted at last to reveal—at a distance—a mighty fortress.

Ezio recognized the place at once: Masyaf. The clouds seem to bear him closer. There were the sounds of fierce battle. Ezio saw cavalrymen and infantry locked in mortal combat. Then the sounds of a horse's hooves, as it approached at full gallop. A young Assassin, dressed in white, cowled, riding furiously through the scene.

Ezio watched—and, as he watched, seemed to lose himself—his own personality . . . Something was happening which seemed half-recognized, half-remembered; a message from a past of which he knew nothing yet with which he was totally familiar . . .

The young man in white charged, with his sword drawn, through the gates, into the midst of the skirmish. Two burly Crusaders were about to deliver the coup de grace to a wounded Assassin. Leaning from the saddle, the young man felled the first soldier with a clean stroke before reining his horse in and leaping off his mount in a swirl of dust. The second Crusader had whirled around to confront him. In a second, the young man drew a throwing knife and aimed it at the Crusader, hurling it with deadly accuracy, so that it buried itself in the man's neck, just below the helmet. The man fell to his knees, then collapsed forward, on his face in the dirt.

The young man dashed over to the aid of his comrade, who had collapsed against a tree. The injured man's sword had slipped from his hand, and he leaned forward, his back against the tree trunk, grasping his ankle and grimacing.

"Where are you hurt?" asked the young man, urgently.

"Broken foot. You arrived in the nick of time."

The young man bent under his comrade and helped him to his feet, placing one of his arms round his shoulders and helping him to a bench against the wall of a stone outbuilding.

The injured Assassin looked up at him. "What is your name, brother?"

"Altaïr. Son of Umar."

The injured Assassin's face brightened in recognition. "Umar. A fine man, who died as he had lived—with honor."

A third Assassin was staggering toward them from the main part of the battle, bloodied and exhausted. "Altaïr!" he cried. "We have been betrayed! The enemy has overrun the castle!"

Altaïr Ibn-La'Ahad finished dressing his fallen comrade's wound. Patting him on the shoulder, he reassured him: "You'll live." Then he turned to address the newcomer. No friendly look was exchanged between them. "Grave news, Abbas. Where is Al Mualim?"

Abbas shook his head. "He was inside when the Crusaders broke through. We can do nothing for him now."

Altaïr didn't reply immediately but turned to face the castle, rising among its rocky crags a few hundred yards away. He was thinking.

"Altaïr!" Abbas interrupted him. "We must fall back!"

Altaïr turned back to him calmly. "Listen. When I close the castle gates, flank the Crusader units in the village and drive them into the canyon to the west."

"Same foolhardiness," growled Abbas angrily. "You don't stand a chance!"

"Abbas!" retorted Altaïr sternly. "Just—make no mistakes."

Remounting, he rode toward the castle. As he cantered along the familiar roadway, he was grieved at the scenes of destruction that met his eye. Villagers were straggling along the side of the path. One raised her head as she was passing, and cried: "Curse these Crusaders! May they fall beneath your sword, every one of them!"

"Leave prayers to the priests, my sister."

Altaïr spurred his horse on, his progress slowed by pockets of Crusaders engaged in looting, and preying upon those denizens of Masyaf attempting to regain the village from the beleaguered fortress. Three times he had to expend precious time and energy in defending his people from the depredations of these surly Franks, who styled themselves Soldiers of Christ. But the words of gratitude and encouragement rang in his ears as he rode on, and spurred his purpose:

"Bless you, Assassin!"

"I was certain I'd be killed! Thank you!"

"Drive these Crusaders back into the sea, once and for all!"

At last he reached the gate. It yawned open. Looking up, Altaïr could see a fellow Assassin frantically working at the winch mechanism on the gatehouse, some hundred feet above. A platoon of Assassin foot soldiers were grouped at the foot of one of the nearby towers.

"Why is the gate still open?" Altaïr called to him.

"Both winches are jammed. The castle is swarming with the enemy."

Altaïr looked into the courtyard of the castle to see a

group of Crusaders making for him. He addressed the lieutenant in charge of the platoon. "Hold this position."

Sheathing his sword and dismounting, he started to climb the outer wall of the gatehouse and, shortly afterward, arrived at the side of the comrade who was working to free the winches. Frantically, they worked on them, and their combined strength prevailed—at least, enough to free the gate partially, and it slipped down a few feet, juddering and groaning.

"Nearly there," said Altaïr, through gritted teeth. His muscles bulged as he and his fellow Assassin struggled to dislodge the cogs of the second winch. At last it gave, and the gate came crashing down on the melee between Assassins and Crusaders taking place below. The Assassins managed to leap clear, but the Crusaders' troop was divided by the falling gate, some inside the castle, others trapped outside.

Altaïr made his way down the stone steps that led from the top of the gatehouse to the central courtyard of Masyaf. The scattered bodies of Assassins attested to the fierce fighting that had only recently taken place there. As he looked around, scanning the ramparts and battlements, a door in the Great Keep opened, and from it emerged a group of people who made him draw in his breath sharply. A company of elite Crusader infantrymen surrounded the Mentor of the Brotherhood—Al Mualim. The old man was semiconscious. He was being dragged along by two brutal-looking troopers. With them was a figure with a dagger, whom Altaïr recognized.

A big, tough man with dark, unreadable eyes, and a deep, disfiguring scar on his chin. His thin hair was tied up in a black ribbon.

Haras.

Altaïr had long wondered where Haras's true loyalties had lain. An Assassin adept, he had never seemed satisfied with the rank assigned to him within the Brotherhood. He was a man who sought an easy route to the top rather than one that rewarded merit. Though a man with a well-deserved reputation as a fighter, chameleonlike, he had always managed to worm his way into other people's confidence by adapting his personality to suit theirs. His ambitions had clearly got the better of him, and, seeing an opportunity, he had traitorously thrown in his lot with the Crusaders. Now he even dressed in Crusader uniform.

"Stand back, Altaïr!" he cried. "Another step, and your Mentor dies!"

At the sound of the voice, Al Mualim rallied, stood proud, and raised his own voice. "Kill this wretch, Altaïr! I do not fear death!"

"You won't leave this place alive, traitor!" Altaïr called to Haras.

Haras laughed. "No. You misunderstand. I am no traitor." He took a helmet, which was hanging from his belt, and donned it. A Crusader helmet! Haras laughed again. "You see? *I could never betray those I never truly loved.*"

Haras started to walk toward Altaïr.

"Then you are doubly wretched," said Altaïr. "For you have been living a lie."

Things happened quickly then. Haras drew his sword and lunged toward Altaïr. At the same moment, Al Mualim managed to break free of his guards and, with a strength that belied his age, wrested the sword from one of them and cut him down. Profiting from Haras's momentary distraction, Altaïr unleashed his hidden-blade and struck at the traitor. But Haras squirmed out of the way and brought his own sword down in a cowardly stroke while Altaïr was off balance.

Altaïr rolled to one side, springing back to his feet quickly as a knot of Crusaders rushed to Haras's defense. Out of the corner of his eye, he could see Al Mualim fighting another group.

"Kill the bastard!" snarled Haras, stepping out of harm's way.

Altaïr tasted fury. He surged forward, slicing through the throats of two Crusader assailants. The others fell back in fear, leaving Haras isolated and petrified. Altaïr cornered him where two walls met. He had to make haste and finish the job, to go to his Mentor's assistance.

Haras, seeing Altaïr momentarily distracted, cut at him quickly, ripping the cloth of his tunic. Altaïr lashed back in retaliation and plunged his hidden-blade straight into the base of Haras's neck, just above the sternum. With a strangled cry, the traitor fell back, crashing against the wall. Altaïr stood over him.

Haras looked up as Altaïr's figure blocked the sun.

"You put too much faith in the hearts of men, Altaïr," he said, barely getting the words out as the blood bubbled from his chest. "The Templars know *what is true*. Humans are weak, base, and petty." He didn't know he could have been describing himself.

"No, Haras. Our Creed is evidence to the contrary. Try to return to it, even now, in your last hour. I beg you out of pity to redeem yourself."

"You will learn, Altaïr. And you will learn the hard way." Nevertheless, Haras paused in thought for a moment, and even as the light in his eyes slowly died, he fought for speech. "Perhaps I am not wise enough to understand, but I suspect the opposite of what you believe is true. I am at least too wise to believe such rubbish as you do."

Then his eyes became marble, and his body leaned to one side, a long, rattling sigh escaping from it as it relaxed in death.

The doubt he'd seeded in Altaïr's mind didn't take root immediately. There was too much to be done for there to be time for thought. The young man wheeled round and joined his Mentor, fighting shoulder to shoulder until the Crusader band was routed, either sprawled in the bloody dust or fled.

Around them, meanwhile, the signs were that the battle had turned in the Assassins' favor. The Crusader army was beating a retreat from the castle though the battle beyond it continued. Messengers soon arrived to confirm that.

Recovering from their exertions, Altaïr and Al Mualim

paused for a moment's respite under a tree by the side of the gate of the Great Keep.

"That man—that wretch, Haras—you offered him a last chance to salvage his dignity, to see the error of his ways. Why?"

Flattered that his Mentor should seek his opinion, Altaïr replied: "No man should pass from this world without knowing some kindness, some chance of redemption."

"But he shunned what you proffered him."

Altaïr shrugged mildly. "That was his right."

Al Mualim watched Altaïr's face closely for a moment, then smiled, and nodded. Together, they started to walk toward the castle gate. "Altaïr," Al Mualim began, "I have watched you grow from a boy to a man in a very short time—and I have to say that this fills me with as much sadness as pride. But one thing is certain: You fit Umar's shoes as if they had been made for you."

Altaïr raised his head. "I did not know him as a father. Only as an Assassin."

Al Mualim placed a hand on his shoulder. "You, too, were born into this Order—this Brotherhood." He paused. "Are there ever times when you—regret it?"

"Mentor—how can I regret the only life I have ever known?"

Al Mualim nodded sagely, looking up briefly to make a sign to an Assassin lookout perched high on the parapet wall. "You may find another way, in time, Altaïr. And if that time comes, it will be up to you to choose the path you prefer."

In response to Al Mualim's signal, the men in the gatehouse were winching up the castle gate again.

"Come, my boy," the old man said. "And ready your blade. This battle is not won yet."

Together, they strode toward the open gate, into the bright sunshine beyond.

Bright sunshine, a white light so strong, so all-encompassing, that Ezio was dazzled. He blinked to rid his eyes of the multicolored shapes that appeared before them, shaking his head vigorously to escape from whatever vision had him in its grip. He squeezed them tight shut.

When he opened them, his heartbeat had begun to settle to its normal rhythm, and he found himself once again in the subterranean chamber, the soft light returned. He found that he was still holding the stone disc in his hand, and now he was in no doubt at all about what it was.

He had found the first key.

He looked at his candle. He had seemed to be away for a long time, yet the flame burned steadily and had eaten up scarcely any tallow.

He stowed the key with the map in his pouch and turned to make his way back to the daylight, and to Sofia.

TWENTY-EIGHT

Excitedly, Sofia put down the book she'd been trying to read and ran over to him, but drawing the line at taking him in her arms. "Ezio! *Salve!* I'd thought you were gone forever!"

"So did I," said Ezio.

"Did you find anything?"

"Yes, I did. Something that may interest you."

They walked over to a large table, which Sofia cleared of books as Ezio produced the map he'd found and spread it out.

"*Dio mio*, how beautiful!" she exclaimed. "And look—there's my shop. In the middle."

"Yes. It's on a very important site. But look at the margins."

She produced a pair of eyeglasses and, bending over, examined the book titles closely.

"Rare books, these. And what are the symbols surrounding them?"

"That's what I hope to find out."

"Some of these books are really extremely rare. And a few of them haven't been seen for—well—more than a millennium! They must be worth a fortune!"

"Your shop is on the very site of the trading post once run by the Polo brothers—Niccolò and Maffeo. Niccolò hid these books around the city. This map should tell us where if we can find out how to interpret it."

She took off her glasses and looked at him, intrigued. "Hmmn. You are beginning to interest me. Vaguely."

Ezio smiled and leaned forward. He pointed to the map. "From what I can see, from among the twelve titles, I need to find these three first."

"What of the others?"

"That remains to be seen. They may be deliberate red herrings. But I am convinced that these are the ones to concentrate on. They may contain clues about the locations of the rest of *these*—"

He produced the round stone from his satchel. She donned her glasses again and peered at it. The she stood back, shaking her head. *"Molto curioso."*

"It's the key to a library."

"Doesn't look like a key."

"It's a very special library. Another has been found already—beneath Topkapi Palace. But, God willing, there is still time to find the others."

"Found—by whom?"

"Men who do not read."

Sofia grinned at that. But Ezio remained earnest. "Sofia—do you think you could try to decipher this map? Help me find these books?"

Sofia studied the map again for a few minutes, in silence. Then she straightened and looked at Ezio, smiling, a twinkle in her eye. "There are plenty of reference books in this shop. With their help, I think I can unravel this mystery. But on one condition."

"Yes?"

"May I borrow the books when you've finished with them?"

Ezio looked amused. "I daresay we can work something out."

He took his leave. She watched him go, then closed the shop for the day. Returning to the table, after collecting a number of tomes from the shelves nearby to help her, and a notebook and pens, she pulled up a chair and settled down at once to examining the map in earnest.

TWENTY-NINE

The next day, Ezio met Yusuf near the Hippodrome in the southeast quarter of the peninsula. He found him conferring with a group of younger associates over a map they were studying. The meeting broke up as Ezio arrived, and Yusuf folded up his map.

"Greetings, Mentor," he said. "If I'm not mistaken, there's a pleasant surprise in store. And if I'm not dead by this time tomorrow, we should have some good stories to trade."

"Is there a chance of your being dead?"

"We've had wind of a plan the Byzantines are hatching. Now that the young Prince Suleiman has returned from the *hajj*, they plan to infiltrate Topkapi Palace. They've chosen this evening to make their move."

"What's special about this evening?"

"There's an entertainment at the palace. A cultural event. An exhibition of paintings—people like the Bellini brothers—and Seljuk artists, too. And there'll be music."

"So what's our plan?"

Yusuf looked at him gravely. "My brother, this is not your fight. There is no need for you to ensnare yourself in Ottoman affairs."

"Topkapi concerns me. The Templars found one of the keys to Altaïr's library beneath it, and I'd like to know how."

"Ezio, our plan is to protect the prince, not interrogate him."

"Trust me, Yusuf. Just show me where to go."

Yusuf looked unconvinced, but said: "The rendezvous is at the main gate of the palace. We plan to disguise ourselves as musicians and walk right in with the authentic players."

"I'll meet you there."

"You'll need a costume. And an instrument."

"I used to play the lute."

"We'll see what we can do. And we'd better place you with the Italian musicians. You don't look Turkish enough to pass for one of us."

By dusk, Ezio, Yusuf, and his picked team of Assassins, all dressed in formal costumes, had assembled near the main gate.

"Do you like your getup?" asked Yusuf.

"It's fine. But the sleeves are cut tight. There was no room for any concealed weapon."

"You can't play a lute in loose sleeves. And that's what you are—a lute player. Isn't that what you wanted?"

"True."

"And we are armed. You mark any targets and leave it to us to take them out. Here's your instrument." He took a fine lute from one of his men and passed it to Ezio, who tried it, tentatively.

"By Allah, you'll have to make a better sound than that!" said Yusuf.

"It's been a long time."

"Are you sure you know how to play that thing?"

"I learned a few chords when I was young."

"Were you really ever young?"

"A long time ago."

Yusuf twitched at his own costume, a green-and-yellow satin number. "I feel ridiculous in this outfit. I look ridiculous!"

"You look just like all the other musicians, and that's the important thing. Now, come on—the orchestra's assembling."

They crossed over to where a number of Italian instrumentalists were milling about, impatient to gain entry to the palace. Yusuf and his men were equipped as Turkish musicians, with tanburs, ouds, kanuns, and kudüms, all instruments which, between them, they could play passably. Ezio watched them being ushered through a side entrance.

Ezio found it agreeable to be among his fellow

countrymen again, and dipped in and out of conversation with them.

"You're from Florence? Welcome! This should be a good gig," one told him.

"You call this a good gig?" a viol player chipped in. "You should try playing in France! They've got all the best people. I was there not six months ago and heard Josquin's *Qui Habitat*. It's the most beautiful chorale I've ever listened to. Do you know his work, Ezio?"

"A little."

"Josquin," said the first musician, a sackbut player. "Yes, he's a treasure. There's certainly no man in Italy to match his talent."

"Our time will come."

"I see you're a lutenist, Ezio," a man carrying a chitarra said to him. "I've been experimenting with alternative tunings lately. It's a wonderful way to spark new ideas. For example, I've been tuning my fourth string to a minor third. It gives a very somber sound. By the way, did you bring any extra strings with you? I must have broken six this month."

"Josquin's music's too experimental for me," said a citternist. "Believe me, polyphony will never catch on."

"Remind me," said the chitarra player, ignoring his colleague's remark. "I'd like to learn a few eastern tunings before we leave."

"Good idea. I must say this is a great place to work. The people here are so kind, too. Not like Verona. You can hardly cross the street there these days without getting mugged," a musician carrying a shawm put in.

"When do we go on?" Ezio asked.

"Soon enough," replied the cittern player. "Look, they're opening the gates now."

The man with the viol plucked critically at his strings, then looked pleased. "It's a splendid day for music, don't you think, Ezio?"

"I hope so," Ezio replied.

They made their way to the gate, where Ottoman officials were checking people through.

Unluckily, when Ezio's turn came, one of them stopped him.

"Play us a tune," he said. "I like the sound of a lute."

Ezio watched helplessly as his fellow musicians filed past. "*Perdonate, buon signore*, but I'm part of the entertainment for Prince Suleiman."

"Any old *gerzek* can carry an instrument around, and we don't remember you being part of this particular band. So play us a tune."

Taking a deep breath, Ezio started to pluck out a simple *ballata* he remembered learning when they still had the family palazzo in Florence. He twanged awfully.

"That's—forgive me—terrible!" said the official. "Or are you into some new experimental music?"

"You might as well be strumming a washboard, as strings, the racket you're making," said another, coming over, amused.

"You sound like a dying cat."

"I can't work under these circumstances," Ezio said huffily. "Give me a chance to get warmed up."

"All right! And get yourself in tune while you're at it."

Ezio willed himself to concentrate and tried again. After a few initial stumbles, this time he managed to make a fair fist of a straightforward old piece by Landini. It was quite moving, in the end, and the Ottoman officials actually applauded.

"Pekala," said the one who had first challenged him. "In you go, then, and bother the guests with that noise."

Once inside, Ezio found himself in the midst of a great throng. A wide marble courtyard, partially covered, like an atrium, glittered with light and color under the boughs of tamarinds. Guests were wandering about as servants made their way between them with trays loaded with sweetmeats and refreshing drinks. There were plenty of Ottoman gentry present, as well as diplomats and high-profile artists and businessmen from Italy, Serbia, the Peloponnese, Persia, and Armenia. It was hard to detect any possible Byzantine infiltrators in this sophisticated assembly.

Ezio decided that his best course of action would be to try to rejoin the Italian musical troupe he'd been talking with, but took his time about it, getting the lay of the land.

But the royal guards were vigilant, and before long, one of them accosted him.

"Excuse me, sir, are you lost?"

"No."

"Musician are you? Well, you're being paid to play, not to mingle!"

Ezio was furious but had to contain his anger in order

not to blow his cover. Fortunately for him, he was rescued by a group of wealthy-looking locals, four sleek men and four heartstoppingly beautiful women.

"Play us something," they entreated him, forming a circle round him.

Ezio ran through the Landini again, remembering some other pieces by that composer and praying that his audience wouldn't find them too old-fashioned. But they were entranced. And, as his confidence increased, Ezio was pleased that his musicianship also improved. He even dared to improvise a little. And to sing.

"Pek güzel," commented one of the men, as he finished a set.

"Indeed—quite beautiful," agreed his partner, in whose deep violet eyes Ezio would quite happily have died.

"Hmn. Technique's not quite what it might be," commented one of the other men.

"Oh, Murad, you are such a pedant. Think of the expression! That's the main thing."

"He plays almost as well as he dresses," said a second woman, eyeing him.

"A sound as beautiful as rainfall," said a third.

"Indeed, the Italian lute is every bit as lovely as our oud," conceded Murad, pulling his partner away from Ezio. "But now, alas, we must mingle."

"Tesekkür ederim, efendim," the women chirruped as they departed.

Ezio, his credentials confirmed, was left unmolested

by the guards from then on, and was able to make contact with Yusuf and his team.

"Brilliant, Mentor," said Yusuf, when they'd reconnected. "But don't be seen talking to us—it'll look suspicious. Try to make your way to the second courtyard—the inner one—through there. I'll join you."

"Good thinking," Ezio agreed. "But what may we expect there?"

"The inner circle. The entourage of the prince. And, if we are fortunate, Suleiman himself. But be on your guard, Mentor. There may be danger there, too."

THIRTY

It was considerably quieter in the second courtyard, but the decorations, the food and drink, and the quality of both music and art were just that little bit more splendid.

Ezio and Yusuf, keeping in the background, scanned the guests.

"I do not see Prince Suleiman," Yusuf said.

"Wait!" Ezio prompted him.

The orchestra struck up a fanfare, and the guests all turned expectantly toward a gateway in the center of the rear wall of the courtyard, draped with rich hangings. Costly silk Isfahan carpets were spread on the ground in front of it. Moments later, a small group of people emerged, clustered around the two men who led them—each clad in a suit of white silk, one wearing a turban with diamond pins, the other a turban with emeralds. Ezio's eyes were drawn to the younger of these, and his lips parted as he recognized him.

"The young man?" he asked his companion.

"That is Prince Suleiman," Yusuf told him. "Sultan Bayezid's grandson, and governor of Kefe. And he's only seventeen."

Ezio was amused. "I met him on the ship, on the way here. He told *me* he was a student."

"I've heard that he likes to travel incognito. It's also a security measure. He was returning from the *hajj*."

"Who is the other man? The one with emeralds in his turban?"

"His uncle, Prince Ahmet. The sultan's favored son. He is grooming himself for the succession as we speak."

As they watched, the two princes stood, as favored guests were presented to them. Then the princes accepted glasses of ruby-colored liquid.

"Wine?" asked Ezio.

"Cranberry juice."

"*Serefe! Sagliginiza!*" Ahmet said, raising his voice with his glass, toasting the assembly.

After the formal toasts, Yusuf and Ezio continued to watch, as both guests and hosts became more relaxed. Though as Suleiman in particular mingled, Ezio noticed that his guards were discreetly but continually attentive. These guards were tall, and none of them looked Turkish. They wore a distinctive uniform of white robes, and their headgear was a high, white, tapering cap, like that of a dervish. All, equally, wore mustaches. None was either clean-shaven or had a beard. Ezio knew enough about Ottoman custom to realize that this meant that they had the status of slaves. Were they some kind of private bodyguard?

Suddenly, Yusuf caught Ezio's arm. "Look! That man over there!"

A thin, pale young man with fine, light-colored hair and dark brown, expressionless eyes had sidled up close to Suleiman. He was expensively dressed and might have been a prosperous Serbian arms dealer, at any rate some-one important enough to have made it onto the guest list for the second courtyard. As Ezio quickly scanned the crowd, he saw four more elegantly dressed men, none of them Turks, by their looks, taking up what could only be backup positions and discreetly signaling to one another.

Before Yusuf or Ezio could react, the thin young man, already at Suleiman's elbow, had, with the speed of light, drawn a thin, curved janbiyah and was plunging it down toward the prince's chest. At the same instant, the closest guard to him noticed and sprang into the blade's path.

There was instantaneous chaos and confusion. Guests were pushed roughly aside as guards ran to assist both princes and their fallen comrade, while the five Templar would-be killers tried to make their escape through the crowd, now milling around in uproar and panic. The thin young man had vanished, but the guards had iden-tified his companions and were now pursuing them sys-tematically, the Byzantine plotters using the confused and disoriented guests as obstacles to put between them and their hunters. Exits were sealed, but the conspirators attempted to climb out of the courtyard. In the confusion, Prince Ahmet had disappeared, and Prince Suleiman had been left isolated. Ezio saw that he had drawn a small dagger but calmly stood his ground.

"Ezio!" Yusuf suddenly hissed. "Look there!"

Ezio followed the direction Yusuf was pointing in and saw that the thin young man had returned. Now, breaking out of the crowd behind the prince, he was closing on him, his weapon poised.

Ezio was far closer than Yusuf and realized that only he could save the prince in time. But he had no weapon himself! Then he looked down at the lute, which he was still holding in his hands, and, with a grunt of regret, made his decision and smashed it against a nearby column. It shattered but left him with a sharp shard of sprucewood in his hand.

In an instant, Ezio sprang forward and, seizing the Byzantine by his bony wrist and forcing him backward just as he was in the act of moving in for the kill, drove the shard four inches deep into the man's left eye. The Byzantine stopped as if he had been frozen in motion, then the janbiyah fell from his hand and clattered onto the marble floor. He himself crumpled to the ground immediately afterward.

The crowd fell silent, forming a circle around Ezio and Suleiman at a respectful distance. The guards tried to intervene, but Suleiman stayed them with a gesture.

The prince sheathed his own dagger and took a small

breath. Then he took a step toward Ezio—a signal honor from a prince, which the crowd acknowledged with a gasp.

"It is good to see you again, *mio bel menestrello*. Did I say that right?"

" 'My handsome minstrel.' Very good."

"It is a pity about your lute. So much more beautiful an instrument than a sword."

"You are right. But it does not save lives."

"Some would argue with that."

"Perhaps. In other circumstances." The two men exchanged a smile. "I hear you are a governor as well as a prince. Is there anything you do not do?"

"I do not talk to strangers." Suleiman bowed—a slight inclination of the head only. "I am Suleiman Osman."

"Auditore, Ezio . . ." Ezio bowed in his turn.

One of the white-clad guards approached then. A sergeant. "Forgive me, my prince. On behalf of your uncle, we must have your assurance that you are uninjured."

"Where is he?"

"He awaits you."

Suleiman looked at him coldly. "Tell him that, thanks to this man, I *am* uninjured. But *no thanks* to you! You! The Janissaries! The elite guard, and you fail me, a prince of the royal house, like this! Where is your captain?"

"Tarik Barleti is away—on an errand."

"On an *errand*? Do you really wish to show yourselves such amateurs in front of this stranger?" Suleiman drew himself up as the guard, a muscular giant who must have weighed all of three hundred pounds, trembled before him. "Clear this body away and send the guests home. Then summon Tarik to the Divan!"

Turning back to Ezio as the man scuttled off, Suleiman said: "This is embarrassing. The Janissaries are the bodyguard of the sultan."

"But not of his family?"

"On this occasion, it would appear not." Suleiman paused, giving Ezio an appraising look. "Now, I don't wish to impose on your time, but there is something I would like your opinion on. Something important."

Yusuf was signaling to Ezio from the edge of the crowd, now slowly dispersing.

"Allow me simply the time to change out of this costume," Ezio said, nodding discreetly to his friend.

"Very well. There's something I need to arrange first in any case. Meet me by the Divan when you are ready. My attendants will escort you."

He clapped his hands and departed the way he had come.

"That was quite a performance," Yusuf said, as they made their way out of the palace in the company of two of Suleiman's personal attendants. "But you've given us an introduction we would never have dreamed possible."

"The introduction," Ezio reminded him, "is mine."

THIRTY-ONE

Suleiman was already waiting when Ezio joined him outside the Divan—the council chamber—of the palace, a short time later. The young man was looking composed and alert.

"I have arranged a meeting with my uncle, Prince Ahmet, and Captain Tarik Barleti," he announced without preamble. "There is something I should explain first. The Janissaries are loyal to my grandfather, but they have become angry over his choice for the next sultan."

"Ahmet."

"Exactly. The Janissaries favor my father, Selim."

"Hmn," said Ezio, considering. "You are in a tough spot. But tell me—how do the Byzantines fit into this?"

Suleiman shook his head. "I was hoping you might be able to give me some guidance on that. Would you be willing to help me find out?"

"I am tracking them myself. As long as our interests do not conflict, it would be an honor to assist you."

Suleiman smiled enigmatically. "Then I must accept what I can get." He paused. "Listen. There is a hatch at the top of the tower you see over there. Go up and lift the hatch. You will be able to see and hear everything that is said in the Divan."

Ezio nodded and immediately took his leave, while Suleiman turned and entered the Divan himself.

By the time Ezio had reached his vantage point, the discussion in the council chamber below him had already begun and was already becoming heated. The three men involved sat or stood around a long table, covered with Bergama carpets. Behind the table, a tapestry depicting Bayezid, flanked by his sons, hung on the wall.

Ahmet, a vigorous man in his midforties, with short, dark brown hair and a full beard, currently bareheaded and changed into rich garments of red, green, and white, was in the middle of a tirade: "Heed my nephew, Tarik. Your incompetence borders on treason. To think that today your Janissaries were outshone by an Italian lute player! It is preposterous!"

Tarik Barleti, the lower half of his battle-scarred face lost in a grizzled beard, looked grim. "An inexcusable failing, *efendim*. I will conduct a full investigation."

Suleiman cut in. "It is *I* who will conduct the investigation, Tarik. For reasons that should be obvious."

Barleti nodded shortly. "*Evet, Sehzadem.* Clearly you have your father's wisdom."

Ahmet shot the captain a furious glance at that, while Suleiman retorted: "*And* his impatience." He turned to his uncle, his tone formal. "*Sehzad* Ahmet, I am at least relieved to see that you are safe."

"Likewise, Suleiman. May God protect you."

Suleiman, Ezio could see, was playing some kind of long game. As he watched, the young prince rose and summoned his attendants.

"I will take my leave of you now," he announced. "And I will make my report on this disgraceful incident very soon, you may be sure of that."

Accompanied by his retinue and guard, he strode from the Divan. Tarik Barleti was about to follow suit, but Prince Ahmet detained him.

"Tarik *bey*—a word?"

The soldier turned. Ahmet beckoned him to approach. His tone was cordial. Ezio had to strain to catch his words.

"What was the purpose of this attack, I wonder? To make me look weak? To make me appear an ineffective steward of this city?" He paused. "If that was your plan, my dear captain; if you had a hand in this mess, you have made a grave mistake! My father has chosen *me* as the next sultan, not my brother!"

Tarik did not answer immediately, his face expressionless, almost bored. At last, he said, "Prince Ahmet, I am not depraved enough to imagine the conspiracy you accuse me of."

Ahmet took a step back though his tone remained level and affable. "What have I done to earn such contempt from the Janissary Corps? What has my brother done for you that I have not?"

Tarik hesitated, then said: "May I speak freely?"

Ahmet spread his hands. "You'd better, I think."

Tarik faced him. "You are weak, Ahmet. Pensive in times of war and restless in times of peace. You lack passion for the traditions of the *ghazi*—the Holy Warriors—and you speak of fraternity in the company of infidels." He paused. "You would make a decent philosopher, Ahmet, but you will be a poor sultan."

Ahmet's face darkened. He snapped his fingers, and his own bodyguard came to attention behind him.

"You may show yourself out," he told the Janissary captain, and his voice was like ice.

Ezio was still watching, as, a few minutes later, Ahmet himself swept out of the Divan. A moment later, Ezio was joined by Prince Suleiman.

"Quite a family, eh?" said the prince. "Don't worry. I was listening, too."

Ezio looked worried. "Your uncle lacks sway over the very men he will soon command. Why did he not cut that man down where he stood, for such insolence?"

"Tarik is a hard man," replied the prince, spreading

his hands. "Capable, but ambitious. And he admires my father greatly."

"But he failed to safeguard this palace against a Byzantine attempt on your life in its inner sanctum! That alone is worthy of investigation."

"Precisely."

"So—where should we begin?"

Suleiman considered. Ezio watched him. *An old head on very young shoulders,* he thought, with renewed respect.

Suleiman said, "For now, we'll keep an eye on Tarik and his Janissaries. They spend much of their free time in and around the Bazaar. Can you handle that—you and your . . . associates?" He phrased the last words delicately.

At the back of Ezio's mind was the memory of Yusuf's admonition not to get involved in Ottoman politics, but somehow his own quest and this power struggle looked connected. He made his decision.

"From now on, Prince Suleiman, none of them will purchase so much as a handkerchief without our knowledge."

THIRTY-TWO

Having ensured that Yusuf and the Assassins of Constantinople were fully briefed in shadowing all movements of off-duty Janissaries in the Grand Bazaar, Ezio, accompanied by Azize, made his way down to the southern docks of the city to collect bomb-making materials from a list compiled for him by Piri Reis.

He had completed his purchases and dispatched them, with Azize, to the Assassins' headquarters in the city, when he noticed Sofia in the crowd thronging the quays. She was talking to a man who looked as if he might be an Italian, a man of about his own age. As he drew closer, he not only saw that she was looking more than a little discomfited but recognized who she was talking to. Ezio was amused, but also not a little discomfited himself.

The man's unexpected appearance evoked a number of memories and a number of conflicting emotions.

Without revealing his presence, Ezio drew closer.

It was Duccio Dovizi. Decades earlier, Ezio had come close to breaking his right arm since Duccio had been two-timing Claudia, to whom he was engaged. The arm, Ezio noticed, still had a kink in it. Duccio himself had aged badly and looked haggard. But that clearly hadn't cramped his style. He was evidently smitten by Sofia and was pestering her for attention.

"*Mia cara*," he was saying to her, "the strings of Fate have drawn us together. Two Italians, lost and alone in the Orient. Do you not feel the *magnetismo*?"

Sofia, bored and annoyed, replied: "I feel many things, *Messere*—nausea, above all."

With a sense of déjà vu, Ezio thought it was time to make his move. "Is this man bothering you, Sofia?" he asked, approaching.

Duccio, fuming at this interruption, turned to face the newcomer. "Excuse me, *Messere*, but the lady and I are—"

He trailed off as he recognized Ezio. "Ah! *Il diavolo* in person!" His left hand went involuntarily to his right arm. "Stay back!"

"Duccio, what a pleasure to see you again."

Duccio didn't reply but stumbled away, tripping over the cobblestones as he did so, and crying, "Run, *buona donna*! Run for your life!"

They watched him disappear along the jetty. There was an awkward pause.

"Who was that?"

"A dog," Ezio told her. "He was engaged to my sister, many years ago."

"And what happened?"

"His *cazzo* was engaged to six others."

"You express yourself very candidly." Sofia sounded mildly surprised by Ezio's use of the word "dick" but not offended.

"Forgive me." He paused for a moment, then asked: "What brings you to these docks?"

"I took a break from the shop to collect a package, but the customs people here claim that the ship's papers are not in order. So, I wait."

Ezio glanced around the well-guarded harbor, getting a sense of its layout.

"It's such a bother," Sofia continued. "I could be here all day."

"Let me see what I can do," he said. "I know a few ways of bending the rules."

"Do you now? Well, I must say I admire your bravado."

"Leave it to me. I'll meet you back at your shop."

"Well then"—she rummaged in her bag—"here is the paperwork. The parcel is quite valuable. Please take care of it—if you manage to get it away from them."

"I will."

"Then—thank you." She smiled at him and made her way back toward the city.

Ezio watched her go for a moment, then made his way to the large wooden building that held the customs offices.

Inside, there was a long counter and, behind it, shelves containing a large number of packages and parcels. Near the front of one of the lower shelves closest to the counter he could see a wooden map tube with a label attached to it: SOFIA SARTOR.

"Perfetto," he said to himself.

"May I help you," said a portly official, coming up to him.

"Yes, if you please. I've come to collect that package over there." He pointed.

The clerk looked across. "Well, I'm afraid that's out of the question! All those parcels and packages have been impounded pending paperwork clearance."

"And how long will that take?"

"I wouldn't like to say."

"Hours?"

The clerk pursed his lips.

"Days?"

"That all depends. Of course, for a consideration . . . something might be arranged . . ."

"To hell with that!"

The clerk became less friendly. "Are you trying to impede me in my duties?" he barked. "Get out of the way, old man! And don't come back if you know what's good for you!"

Ezio swept him aside and bounded over the counter. He seized the wooden map tube and turned to leave. But the clerk was frantically blowing a whistle, and several of his colleagues, some of them members of the heavily armed dockyard guard, responded instantly.

"That man!" yelped the clerk. "He tried to bribe me, and when that failed, he resorted to violence!"

Ezio took a stand on the counter as the customs men surged forward to grab him. Swinging the weighty wooden map tube round, he cracked a few skulls with it and leapt over the heads of the rest of them, running toward the exit and leaving confusion in his wake.

"That's the only way to deal with petty officialdom," he said to himself, contentedly. He had disappeared into the twisting labyrinth of streets north of the docks before his pursuers had had time to collect themselves. Without Sofia's papers, which he still had safely stowed in his tunic, they'd never be able to trace her.

THIRTY-THREE

Toward noon, he entered the bookshop west of Haghia Sofia.

She looked up as he came in. The shelves were far more orderly now than they had been when he'd first visited. In the back room, he could see her worktable, with his map from the cisterns neatly laid out alongside a number of thick books of reference.

"*Salute*, Ezio," she said. "That was a lot quicker than I expected. Any luck?"

Ezio held up the wooden map tube and read from the label: "*Madamigella Sofia Sartor, libraia, Costantinopoli.* Is that you?"

He handed her the tube with a smile. She took it gladly, then examined it closely, her face turning sour.

"Oh, no! Look at the damage! Did they use this to fight off pirates, do you suppose?"

Ezio shrugged, a little sheepishly. Sofia opened the tube and withdrew the map within. She inspected it. "Well, so far, so good."

Taking it over to a table, she spread it out carefully. It was a copy of a map of the world.

"Isn't it beautiful?" she said.

"Indeed." Ezio stood next to her, and they both pored over it.

"It's a print of a map by Martin Waldseemüller. It's still quite new—he only published four years ago. And look—here on the left! The new lands *Navigatore* Vespucci discovered and wrote about only four or five years before the map was drawn."

"They work fast, these Germans," said Ezio. "I see he's named the new lands after Vespucci's Christian name—Amerigo."

"America!"

"Yes . . . Poor Cristoforo Colombo. History has a strange way of unfolding."

"What do you make of this body of water—here?" She pointed to the oceans on the far side of North and South America. Ezio leaned forward to look.

"A new ocean, perhaps? Most of the scholars I know claim the size of the globe has been underestimated."

Sofia sounded wistful. "It's incredible. The more we learn about the world, the less we seem to know."

Quite taken with the thought, they both fell silent for a moment. Ezio considered the new century they were in—the sixteenth. And only near its beginning. What would unfold during it, he could only guess; and he knew that, at his age, he would not see very much more of it.

More discoveries, and more wars, no doubt. But essentially the same play repeating itself—and the same actors, only with different costumes and different props for each generation that swallows up the last, each thinking that it would be the one to do better.

"Well, you honored your promise," said Sofia. "And here is mine fulfilled."

She led the way to the inner room and picked a piece of paper up from the table. "If I am correct, this should show you the location of the first book."

Ezio took the paper from her and read what was on it.

"I must admit," Sofia went on, "my head is swimming at the prospect of actually seeing these books. They contain knowledge the world has lost and should have again." She sat at the table and cupped her chin in her hands, daydreaming. "Perhaps I could have a few copies printed to distribute myself. A small run of fifty or so . . . That should be enough . . ."

Ezio smiled, then laughed.

"What's there to laugh about?"

"Forgive me. It is a joy to see someone with a passion so personal and so noble. It is . . . inspiring."

"Goodness," she replied, a little embarrassed. "Where is this coming from?"

Ezio held up the piece of paper. "I intend to go and

investigate this immediately," he said. "*Grazie*, Sofia—I will return soon."

"I'll look forward to that," she replied, watching him go with a mixture of puzzlement and concern.

What a mysterious man, she thought, as the door closed after him, and she returned to the Waldseemüller map, and her own dreams of the future.

THIRTY-FOUR

Sofia's calculations had been correct. Hidden behind a wooden panel in an old, deserted building in the Constantine District of the city, Ezio found the book he was looking for.

It was an ancient but well-preserved copy of *On Nature*, the poem written over two thousand years earlier by the Greek philosopher Empedocles, outlining the sum of his thoughts.

Ezio lifted the book from its hiding place and blew the dust from the small volume. Then he opened it to a blank page at its front.

As he watched, the page began to glow, and within the glow, a map of Constantinople revealed itself. As he looked closer, and concentrated, he discerned a pinpoint on the map. It showed the Maiden Tower, the lighthouse on the far side of the Bosphorus, and, as Ezio peered closer still, a precise spot there, within the cellars built into its foundations.

If all went well, this would be the location of the second key to Altaïr's library at Masyaf.

He made his way in haste through the teeming city to the Maiden Tower. Slipping past the Ottoman guards and crossing over in a "borrowed" boat, he found a doorway from which steps led downward into the cellars. He held the book in his hand and found that it was guiding him. Guiding him through a maze of corridors lined with innumerable doorways. It didn't seem possible that there could be so many in such a relatively confined space. But at last he came to a door, identical to all the others but through whose cracks a faint light seemed to emanate. The door opened at his touch, and there, on a low stone plinth before him, a circular stone had been placed, slim as a discus and, like the first he had discovered, covered with strange symbols, as mysterious as the first set, but different. The form of a woman—a goddess, perhaps—who looked vaguely familiar, indentations that might either have been formulae, or possibly notches that might slot into pegs—maybe pegs within the keyholes in the library door at Masyaf.

As Ezio took the key in his hands, the light coming from it grew, and grew, and he braced himself to be transported—he knew not where—as it engulfed him, and whirled him back down centuries. Down 320 years. To the year of Our Lord 1191.

*   *   *

Masyaf.

Within the fortress, a time long ago.

Figures in a swirling mist. Emerging from it, a young man and an old. Evidence of a fight, which the old man—Al Mualim—had lost.

He lay on the ground; the young man knelt astride him.

His hand, losing its strength, let go of something, which rolled from his grasp and came to rest on the marble floor.

Ezio drew in a breath as he recognized the object—it was—surely—the Apple of Eden. But how?

And the young man—the victor—in white, his cowl drawn over his head. Altaïr.

"You held fire in your hand, old man," he was saying. "It should have been destroyed."

"Destroyed?" laughed Al Mualim. "The only thing capable of ending the Crusades and creating true peace? Never."

"Then I will destroy it."

The images faded, dissolved, like ghosts, only for another scene to replace them.

*   *   *

Within the Great Keep at Masyaf, Altaïr stood alone with one of his captains. Near them, laid out in honor on a stone bier, was the body of Al Mualim, peaceful in death.

"Is it truly over?" the Assassin captain was saying. "Is that sorcerer dead?"

Altaïr turned to look at the body. He spoke calmly, levelly. "He was no sorcerer. Just an ordinary man, in command of—illusions."

He turned back to his comrade. "Have you prepared the pyre?"

"I have." The man hesitated. "But, Altaïr, some of the men . . . they will not stand for such a thing. They are restive."

Altaïr bent over the bier. He stooped and took the old man's body in his arms. "Let me handle it."

He stood erect, his robes flowing about him. "Are you fit to travel?" he asked the captain.

"Well enough, yes."

"I have asked Malik Al-Sayf to ride to Jerusalem with the news of Al Mualim's death. Will you ride to Acre and do the same?"

"Of course."

"Then go, and God be with you."

The captain inclined his head and departed.

Bearing the dead Mentor's body in his arms, his successor strode out to confront his fellow members of the Brotherhood.

At his appearance, there was an immediate babel of voices, reflecting the bewilderment in their minds. Some asked themselves if they were dreaming. Others were aghast at this physical confirmation of Al Mualim's passing.

"Altaïr! Explain yourself!"

"How did it come to this?"

"What has happened?"

One Assassin shook his head. "My mind was clear, but my body . . . it would not move!"

In the midst of the confusion, Abbas appeared. Abbas. Altaïr's childhood friend. Now, that friendship was far less sure. Too much had happened between them.

"What has happened here?" asked Abbas, his voice reflecting his shock.

"Our Mentor has deceived us all," Altaïr replied. "The Templars corrupted him."

"Where is your proof of that?" Abbas responded, suspiciously.

"Walk with me, Abbas; and I will explain."

"And if I find your answers wanting?"

"Then I will talk until you are satisfied."

They made their way, Altaïr still bearing Al Mualim's body in his arms, toward the funeral pyre that had been prepared for it. Beside him, Abbas, unaware of their destination, remained testy, tense, and combative, unable to disguise his mistrust of Altaïr.

And Altaïr knew with what reason and regretted it. But he would do his best.

"Do you remember, Abbas, the artifact we recovered from the Templar Robert de Sable, in Solomon's Temple?"

"You mean the artifact *you* were sent to retrieve but *others* actually delivered?"

Altaïr let that go. "Yes. It is a Templar tool. It is called the Apple of Eden. Among many other powers, it can conjure illusions and control the minds of men—and of the man who thinks *he* controls *it*. A deadly weapon."

Abbas shrugged. "Then better, surely, that we have it than the Templars."

Altaïr shook his head. "That makes no difference. It seems to corrupt all who wield it."

"And you believe that Al Mualim fell under its spell?"

Altaïr made a gesture of impatience. "I do. Today, he used the Apple in an attempt to enslave Masyaf. You saw that for yourself."

Abbas looked doubtful. "I do not know *what* I saw."

"Listen, Abbas. The Apple is safe in Al Mualim's study. When I am finished here, I will show you all I know."

They had arrived at the pyre, and Altaïr ascended the steps to it, placing the body of his late Mentor reverently at its top. As he did so, Abbas looked aghast. It was his first sight of the pyre.

"I cannot believe you really intend to go through with this!" he said in a shocked voice. Behind him, the assembled Brotherhood of the Assassins rippled like corn in a breeze.

"I must do what I must do," Altaïr replied.

"No!"

But Altaïr had already taken one of the torches that

stood ready lit by the pyre and thrust it into the base of the woodpile. "I must know that he *cannot return*."

"But this is not our way! To burn a man's body is forbidden!"

A voice from the crowd behind him cried out suddenly, in rage: "Defiler!"

Altaïr turned to face the restive crowd below him. "Hear me out! This corpse could be just another one of Al Mualim's *phantom* bodies. *I must be certain!*"

"Lies!" Abbas yelled. As the flames took hold on the pyre, he stepped in close to Altaïr's side, raising his voice so all could hear him. "All your life you have made a mockery of our Creed! You bend the rules to suit your whims while belittling and humiliating those around you!"

"Restrain Altaïr!" yelled an Assassin in the crowd.

"Did you not hear what he said?" a comrade next to him responded. "Al Mualim was bewitched!"

The first Assassin's reply was to fly out with his fists. A general fight ensued, which escalated as rapidly as the flames rose.

On the ledge next to Altaïr, Abbas pushed him violently down from it, into the midst of the melee.

As Abbas then made his way furiously back to the castle, Altaïr struggled to find his feet among his clashing fellow Assassins, standing with their swords drawn. "Brothers!" he shouted, striving to restore order. "Stop! Stay your blades!"

But the fight continued, and Altaïr, who had just risen to his feet in time to see Abbas returning to the fortress, was forced to struggle among his own men, disarming them where he could and exhorting them to desist. He did not know for how long he battled, but the strife was suddenly interrupted by a searing flash of light, which caused the combatants to stagger back, shielding their eyes.

The light came from the direction of the castle.

Altaïr's worst fears were realized.

There, on the parapet of a tall tower, stood Abbas, and the Apple was in his hand.

"What did I tell you, Altaïr?" Abbas yelled down to him.

"Abbas! Stop!"

"What did you think would happen when you murdered our beloved Mentor?"

"You loved Al Mualim less than anyone! You blamed him for all your misfortune, even your father's suicide!"

"My father was a *hero*!" Abbas screamed defiantly.

Altaïr ignored him and turned hastily to the Assassins grouped questioningly around him.

"Listen!" he told them. "This is not the time to quarrel over what's been done. We must decide—now!—what is to be done with *that weapon*!" He pointed to where Abbas was standing, holding the Apple aloft.

"Whatever this artifact is capable of, Altaïr," he cried, "you are not worthy to wield it!"

"No man *is*!" Altaïr hurled back.

But Abbas was already staring into the Apple's glow. The light, as he looked, intensified. Abbas seemed entranced. "It is beautiful, is it not?" he said, only just loudly enough to be heard.

Then a change came over him. His expression was transformed from a smile of amused triumph to a grimace of horror. He began to shake, violently, as the power of the Apple swept into him, taking him over. Assassins still sympathetic to him were running to his aid when the unearthly instrument he still held in his hand threw out an all-but-visible pulse wave, which threw them savagely to their knees as they clutched their heads in agony.

Altaïr raced toward Abbas, scaling the tower with supernatural speed, driven by desperation. *I have to get there in time!* As he approached his former friend, Abbas began to scream as if his very soul was being ripped out of him. Altaïr made one final leap forward, disabling his former friend and knocking him down. Abbas crumpled to the ground with a despairing cry, as the Apple tumbled from his grasp, sending a final violent shock wave out from the tower as it did so.

Then there was silence.

The Assassins spread out below gradually pulled themselves together and got to their feet. They looked at one another in wonderment. What had happened continued to resound in their bodies and their minds. They looked up to the ramparts. Neither Altaïr nor Abbas was visible.

"What was that?"

"Are they dead?"

And then Altaïr appeared alone on the parapet of the

tower. The wind blew his white robes about him. He raised his hand. In it, secure, was the Apple. It crackled and pulsated like a living thing, but it was under his control.

"Forgive me . . ." Abbas was gasping from the flagstone floor behind him. He could barely form the words. "I did not *know* . . ."

Altaïr turned his gaze back from the man to the Apple, resting in his hand. It sent curious sensations, like shocks, the length of his extended arm.

"Have you anything to teach us?" said Altaïr, addressing the Apple as if it were a sensate thing. "Or will you lead us all to ruin?"

The wind then seemed to blow up a dust storm—or was it the return of the swirling fumes of cloud that had heralded the vision? With it came the blinding light that had preceded it, growing and growing, until all else was blotted out. And then it dimmed once more, until there was just the gentle glow of the key in Ezio's hand.

Exhausted, Ezio lowered himself to the floor and rested his back against the stone wall of the chamber. Outside, dusk would be falling. He longed for rest but could afford none.

After a long moment, he raised himself again and, carefully stowing both the key and the copy of Empedocles in his satchel, made his way to the streets above.

THIRTY-FIVE

At dawn the next day, Ezio made his way to the Grand Bazaar. It was time he saw for himself what talk there might be among the Janissaries, and he was impatient to be on the trail of their captain, Tarik Barleti.

But it was impossible, once there, entirely to avoid the importunate traders, who were all past masters of the hard sell. And Ezio had to pass himself off as just another tourist for fear of arousing suspicion, either among Ottoman officials or Byzantine Templars.

"You see this rug!" A merchant accosted him, plucking at his sleeve and, as Ezio had found to be the case so often there, getting too close to him, invading his body space. "Your feet will love you more than your wife does!"

"I am not married."

"Ah," continued the merchant, seamlessly, "you are better off. Come! Just feel it!"

Ezio noticed a group of Janissaries standing not far away. "You have sold well today?" he asked the merchant.

The man spread his hands, nodding to his right at the Janissaries. "I have not sold a thing! The Janissaries confiscated most of my stock just because it was imported."

"Do you know Tarik Barleti, their captain?"

"Eh, he's around here somewhere, no doubt. An arrogant man, but—" The merchant was about to go on but interrupted himself, freezing up before reverting to his sales patter, his eyes focused not on Ezio but well beyond him. "You insult me, sir! I cannot take less than two hundred *akçe* for this! That is my final offer."

Ezio turned slightly and followed the man's gaze. Three Janissaries were approaching, not fifty feet away.

"When I find him, I will ask him about your rugs," Ezio promised the merchant quietly as he turned to go.

"You drive a hard bargain, stranger!" the merchant called after him. "Shall we compromise at one-eighty? One hundred eighty *akçe*, and we part as friends!"

But Ezio was no longer listening. He was following the group, shadowing them at a safe distance, hoping they might lead him to Tarik Barleti. They were not walking idly—they had the look of men going to some kind of appointment. But he had to be vigilant—not only to keep his quarry in sight but to avoid detection himself, and the crowded lanes of the souk both helped and hindered him in his task. The merchant had said the captain would be somewhere in the Bazaar, but the Bazaar was a big place—a confusing labyrinth of stalls and shops, a small city in itself.

But at length his patience paid off, and the men he was following arrived at a crossroads in the lanes which broadened out into a little square with a coffee shop on each corner. In front of one stood the big captain with the grizzled beard. The beard was as much a mark of his rank as his resplendent uniform. He was clearly no slave.

Ezio crept as close as he could, to hear what was being said.

"Are you ready?" he asked his men, and they nodded their assent. "This is an important meeting. Make sure I am not being followed."

They nodded again and split up, disappearing into the Bazaar in different directions. Ezio knew they would be looking for any sign of an Assassin in the crowds, and for one heartstopping moment one of the soldiers seemed to catch his eye, but then the moment passed, and the man was gone. Waiting as long as he dared, he set off in pursuit of the captain.

Barleti hadn't gone far before he came to another Janissary, a lieutenant, who to the casual eye would have just seemed to be window-shopping in front of an armorer's establishment. Ezio had already noticed that Janissaries were the only people not to be badgered by the traders.

"What news?" Barleti said as he drew level with the soldier.

"Manuel has agreed to meet you, Tarik. He's waiting by the Arsenal Gate."

Ezio pricked up his ears at the name.

"An eager old weasel, isn't he?" Tarik said flatly. "Come."

They set off, out of the Bazaar, and into the city streets. It was a long way to the Arsenal, which was situated on the north side of the Golden Horn, farther to the west, but they showed no sign of taking any kind of transport yet, and Ezio followed them on foot. A matter of a couple of miles—and he would have to be careful when they took the ferry across the Horn. But his task was made easier by the fact that the two men were engrossed in conversation, most of which Ezio managed to catch. It was not hard to blend in, in the streets of Constantinople, crowded with people from all over Europe and Asia.

"How did Manuel look? Was he nervous? Or cagey?" Tarik asked.

"He was his usual self. Impatient and discourteous."

"Hmn. I suppose he has earned that right. Have there been dispatches from the sultan?"

"The last news was a week ago. Bayezid's letter was short and full of sad tidings."

Tarik shook his head. "I could not imagine being at such odds with my own son."

THIRTY-SIX

Ezio followed the two Janissaries to a building close by the Arsenal Gate. Waiting for Tarik and his lieutenant was a large, plump, expensively dressed man in his late fifties, sporting a full grey beard and waxed mustaches. His feathered turban was encrusted with jewels, and there was a jeweled ring on each of his pudgy fingers. His companion was thinner, sparely built, and, to judge from his dress, hailed from Turkmenistan.

Ezio, having selected a suitable place to make himself invisible, hiding discreetly among the heavy branches of a tamarind tree that grew close by, paid close attention as preliminary greetings were exchanged and learned that the plump dandy was—as he'd suspected—Manuel Palaiologos. Given what he'd heard from Yusuf about

Manuel's ambitions, this meeting would be an interesting one to listen in on. Palaiologos's companion, also his bodyguard, as became apparent as the introductions were made, went by the name of Shahkulu.

Ezio had heard of him. Shahkulu was a rebel against the Ottoman rulers of his country, and the rumors were that he was fomenting revolution among his people. But he also had a reputation for extreme cruelty and banditry.

Yes, this meeting would indeed be interesting.

Once the niceties—always elaborate, in this country, Ezio had noticed—had been dealt with, Manuel gestured to Shahkulu, who entered the building behind them—a kind of guard post, now evidently deserted—and from it brought a small but heavy wooden chest, which he placed at Tarik's feet. The Janissary lieutenant opened it and began counting the gold coins with which it was filled.

"You may verify the amount, Tarik," Manuel said in a voice as plummy as his body, "but the money stays with me until I have seen the cargo for myself and ascertained its quality."

Tarik grunted. "Understood. You are a shrewd man, Manuel."

"Trust without cynicism is hollow," intoned Palaiologos, unctuously.

The Janissary had been counting fast. Soon afterward, he closed the chest. "The count is good, Tarik," he said. "It's all here."

"So," said Manuel to Tarik. "What now?"

"You will have access to the Arsenal. When you are

satisfied, the cargo will be delivered to a location of your choosing."

"Are your men prepared to travel?"

"Not a problem."

"Poi kalà." The Byzantine princeling relaxed a little. "Very good. I will have a map drawn up for you within a week."

They parted company then, and Ezio waited until the coast was clear before he climbed down from the tree and made his way with all possible haste to the Assassins' headquarters.

THIRTY-SEVEN

It was dusk when Ezio returned to the Arsenal and found Yusuf already there waiting for him.

"One of my men claims he saw a shipment of weapons brought in here earlier. So we got curious."

Ezio pondered this. It was as he had suspected. "Weapons." He paused. "I would like to see them for myself."

He scanned the outer walls of the Arsenal. They were well guarded. The main gate looked impregnable.

"Short of killing everyone in sight," Yusuf said, following his Mentor's thoughts, "I'm not sure how you will get inside."

The square behind them was still teeming with life—people hurrying home after work, coffee bars and restaurants opening their doors. Suddenly, their attention was drawn to an altercation that had broken out near the main gate in the Arsenal walls, between a trader and three Janissaries, who were harassing him.

"You have been warned twice," one of the Janissaries, a sergeant, was saying. "No merchants near the Arsenal walls!" He turned to his men. "Take this stuff away!"

The privates started to pick up the trader's crates of fruit and carry them away.

"Hypocrites!" the man grumbled. "If your men didn't buy my produce, I wouldn't be selling it here in the first place!"

The sergeant ignored him, and the soldiers went on with their work, but the trader hadn't finished. He went right up to the sergeant, and said, "You are worse than the Byzantines, you traitor!"

By way of reply, the Janissary sergeant whacked him with a hard fist. He collapsed, groaning, holding his bleeding nose.

"Hold your tongue, parasite!" growled the sergeant.

He turned away to supervise the continuing confiscation of the fruit, while a woman from the crowd rushed up to help the injured trader. Yusuf and Ezio watched as she helped him to his feet, staunching the blood from his face with a handkerchief.

"Even in times of peace," said Yusuf grimly, "the poor are always under siege."

Ezio was thoughtful, thinking of similar circumstances in Rome not so long ago. "Perhaps if we inspire them to vent their anger, that will help our cause."

Yusuf looked at him. "You mean—recruit these people? Incite them to rebel?"

"It need only be a demonstration. But, with enough of them on our side . . ."

The two men watched as the Janissaries, unimpeded, proceeded to carry off what was left of the man's stock, leaving his stall completely bare. They disappeared through a wicket in the main gate.

"Feigning solidarity to push your own agenda," said Yusuf with a hint of contempt. "What a gentleman!"

"It's not pretty, I know. But it will work, believe me."

"*Whatever* works." Yusuf shrugged. "And I see no other way of effecting a break-in here."

"Come—there's a big crowd here, and it looks as if that trader is pretty popular. Let's go and do some canvassing among the people."

For the next half hour and more, Ezio and Yusuf worked the crowd, hinting and persuading, cajoling and inspiring the ordinary working people around them, whom they found to be very open to the idea of putting an end to their oppression. All they had needed, it seemed, was someone to fire them up. Once a sufficient number had gathered into a mob, Ezio addressed them. The fruit trader stood by his side, defiant now. Yusuf had seen to it that most of the men and women had armed themselves in one way and another. The fruit trader held a large curved pruning knife.

"Fight with us, brothers," Ezio declaimed. "And avenge this injustice. The Janissaries are not above the law! Let's show them we won't stand for their tyranny."

"Yes!" several voices roared.

"It makes me sick to see the kind of abuse they hand out," Ezio continued. "Doesn't it you?"

"Yes!"

"Will you fight with us?"

"Yes!"

"Then—let's go!"

By then, a detachment of armed Janissaries had issued forth from the Arsenal Gate, which was firmly closed behind them. They took up positions in front of it, swords drawn, and faced the mob, whose mood had reached the boiling point. Undaunted by the soldiers' show of strength—indeed, incensed by it—the crowd, whose volume grew by the minute, surged forward toward the gate. Whenever a Janissary was rash enough to close with people in the front rank, he was overcome by the sheer weight of numbers and either hurled aside or crushed under advancing feet. Soon afterward, the crowd was milling about at the gate itself, with Ezio and Yusuf keeping just enough command to direct their improvised strike force to batter it open.

"Down with the Janissaries!" shouted a hundred voices.

"You are not above the law!" yelled a hundred more.

"Open the gate, you coward, before we tear it down!"

"That gate won't stay closed for long," said Ezio to Yusuf.

"The people are doing you a favor, Mentor. Return it and keep them safe from harm."

As Yusuf spoke, two detachments of Janissary reinforcements bore down on the crowd from right and left, having emerged from side gates in the north and south walls.

"This calls for close-quarters fighting," Ezio said, as, accompanied by Yusuf, he unleashed his hookblade and his hidden-blade, and threw himself into the fray.

Encouraged by the professional skills of the two Assassins, the men and women on each flank of the crowd turned bravely to face the Janissary counterattack. As for the Janissaries, they were taken aback to encounter such firm resistance from such an unexpected quarter, and they hesitated—fatally—and were repulsed. In the meantime, those working on the gate were rewarded to see the firm planks of its doors first groan, then give, then buckle, then crumble. With a mighty crack, the main crossbeam holding the gate shut from within snapped like matchwood, and the gate fell back, its doors hanging drunkenly from their massive iron hinges.

The crowd roared with one voice, like a great triumphant beast, and as they poured into the Arsenal, individual voices could be heard raised above the rest:

"Push through!"

"We're inside!"

"Justice or death!"

The defending Janissaries within were powerless to prevent the onrush but, with their greater discipline, managed to hold it in check as ferocious fighting broke out in the Arsenal's main quadrangle. Through it all, Ezio slipped like a wraith, into the inner confines of the fortress-like edifice.

THIRTY-EIGHT

Far from the shattered gate, deep within the western sector of the Arsenal, Ezio came at last to the place he was looking for. It was quiet there, for most of the fighting men in the Arsenal garrison were engaged in the quadrangle, and the handful of guards he did encounter, if he could not slip past them unnoticed, he swiftly dispatched. He would have to sharpen his hookblade once his work there was done.

He made his way down a long stone corridor, so narrow that no one could enter the chamber at its end with any hope of surprising those within. Ezio approached slowly, soft-footed, until he came to an iron ladder fixed to the wall near the chamber's entrance, which led to a gallery overlooking it. Strapping his sword scabbard to his leg so that it would not clatter, he climbed up, swiftly, and with as little noise as a flower makes when it opens. From his vantage point, he stared grimly at the scene taking place below him.

Manuel and Shahkulu stood in the middle of the chamber, surrounded by a jumble of large crates, some of them open. A small Janissary guard unit stood at attention just inside the door. If Ezio had tried to enter, he would have fallen victim to an ambush. Softly, he breathed a sigh of relief. His instincts and experience had saved him, this time.

Manuel paused in his examination of the contents of the crates. The angle of vision available to Ezio did not allow him to see what they were, though he could guess.

"Twenty years in this city, living like a cipher," Manuel was saying. "And now, at last, everything is falling into place."

Shahkulu replied, a note of menace in his voice: "When the Palaiologos line is restored, Manuel, do not forget who it was that helped you bring it back."

Manuel looked at him keenly, small eyes glittering coldly amid the folds of flesh. "Of course not, my friend! I would not dream of betraying a man of your influence. But you must be patient. Nova Roma was not built in a day!"

Shahkulu grunted noncommittally, and Manuel turned to the captain of his escort. "I am satisfied. Take me to my ship."

"Follow me. There is a passage to the west gate by which we can avoid the fighting," said the captain.

"I hope and expect you will soon have that under control."

"As we speak, Prince."

"If one single item here is damaged, the money stays with me. Tell Tarik that."

Ezio watched them go. When he was satisfied that he was alone, he descended to the chamber and made a quick inspection of the crates, lifting the lid of one that had been unsealed.

Rifles. One hundred or more.

"Merda!" Ezio breathed.

His thoughts were interrupted by a brazen clang— surely the west gate banging shut after Manuel's departure. Immediately afterward, the sound of boots on stone approaching. The Janissaries would be returning to reseal the opened crates. Ezio pressed himself against the wall, and, as the soldiers entered, cut them down. Five of them. If they'd been able to enter together, instead of one at a time, the story might have been different. But the narrow corridor had turned out to be his friend.

He passed back the way he had come. In the quadrangle, the battle was over, leaving the usual vile aftermath of combat. Ezio walked slowly past a sea of bodies, mostly still, some writhing in their last agonies, while the only sound was the keening of women as they knelt by the fallen, in the pitiless wind that blew through the yawning gateway.

With his head bowed, Ezio strode from the place. The price paid for the knowledge he had gained seemed very high indeed.

THIRTY-NINE

It was high time to return to Sofia's bookshop. He hurried there straightaway.

The shop was still open, and lights within burned brightly. When she saw Ezio enter, Sofia took off her eyeglasses and got up from the worktable in the inner room, where the map he'd discovered in Yerebatan was spread out, amid several open books.

"*Salute.*" She greeted him. Closing the door behind him and pulling down the blinds. "Time I closed for the day. Two customers all afternoon. I ask you. It's not worth staying open for the evening trade." Then she saw the expression on Ezio's face and led him to a chair, where he sat, heavily, as she fetched him a glass of wine.

"Grazie," he said gratefully, glad she didn't start asking questions.

Instead, she said, "I'm closing in on two more books—one near Tokapi *Saray*, and the other in the Bayezid District."

"Let's try the Bayezid first. The Topkapi will be a dead end. It was there that the Templars discovered the key they have."

"Ah—*sì*. They must have found it by chance, or by other means than ours."

"They had Niccolò's book."

"Then we must thank the Mother of God that you rescued it from them before they could use it further."

She returned to the map, seated herself before it, and resumed writing. Ezio leaned forward and, producing the copy of Empedocles, placed it on the table by her. The second key that he had found had already joined the first, under secure guard, at the Assassins' headquarters in Galata.

"What do you make of this?" he said.

She picked it up carefully, turning it over reverently in her hands. Her hands were delicate but not bony, and the fingers were long and slender.

Her jaw had dropped in wonder. "Oh, Ezio! *È incredibile!*"

"Worth something?"

"A copy of *On Nature* in this condition? In its original Coptic binding? It's fantastic!" She opened it carefully. The coded map within no longer glowed. In fact, Ezio could see that it was no longer visible.

"Amazing. This must be a third-century transcription of the original," Sofia was saying, enthusiastically. "I don't suppose there's another copy like this in existence."

But Ezio's eyes were restlessly scanning the room. Something had changed, and he could not yet put his finger on what it was. At last, his gaze came to rest on a boarded-up window. The glass was gone from its panes.

"Sofia," he said, concerned. "What happened here?"

Her voice took on a slight irritation though clearly overridden by her excitement. "Oh, that happens once or twice a year. People try to break in, thinking they will find money." She paused. "I do not keep much here, but this time they succeeded and made off with a portrait of some value. No more than three hours ago, when I was out of the shop for a short time." She looked sad. "A very good portrait of me, as it happens. I shall miss it, and not just for what it is worth. I'm certainly going to find a very safe place for *this*," she added, tapping the Empedocles.

Ezio was still suspicious that there might be more behind this painting theft than met the eye. He roamed through the room, looking for any clues it might afford him. Then he came to a decision. He was rested enough for the moment, and he owed this woman a favor. But there was more to it than that. He *wanted* to do whatever he could for her.

"You keep working," he said. "I will find your painting for you."

"Ezio, the thief could be anywhere by now."

"If the thief came for money, found none, and took

the portrait instead, he should still be in this district, close by, eager to get rid of it."

Sofia looked thoughtful. "There are a couple of streets near here where a number of art dealers do business . . ."

Ezio was already halfway to the door.

"Wait!" she called after him. "I have some business in that direction. I'll show you the way."

He waited as she locked the *On Nature* carefully in an ironclad chest by one wall, then followed her as she left the shop and locked the door firmly behind her.

"This way," she said. "But we part company at the first turning. I'll point you in the right direction from there."

They walked on in silence. A few dozen yards down the street, they came to a crossroads, and she halted.

"Down there," she said, pointing. Then she looked at him. There was something in her clear eyes that he hoped he wasn't imagining.

"If you happen to find it within the next couple of hours, please come and meet me by Valens' Aqueduct," she said. "There's a book fair I need to attend, but I'd be so glad to see you there."

"I will do my best."

She looked at him again, then away, quickly.

"I know you will," she said. "Thank you, Ezio."

FORTY

The picture dealers' quarter wasn't hard to find—a couple of narrow streets running parallel to one another, the little shops glowing in the lamplight that shone on the treasures they held.

Ezio passed slowly from one to another, looking at the people browsing the art more than the art itself, and before too long he saw a shifty-looking character in gaudy clothes coming out of one of the galleries, engrossed in counting out coins from a leather purse. Ezio approached him. The man was immediately on the defensive.

"What do you want?" he asked, nervously.

"Just made a sale, have you?"

The man drew himself up. "If it's any business of yours . . ."

"Portrait of a lady?"

The man took a swipe at Ezio and prepared to duck and run, but Ezio was a little too quick for him. He tripped him up and sent him sprawling. Coins scattered everywhere on the cobbles.

"Pick them up and give them to me," said Ezio.

"I have done nothing," snarled the man, obeying nevertheless. "You can't prove a damn thing!"

"I don't need to," Ezio snarled back. "I'll just keep hitting you until you talk."

The man's tone changed to a whine. "I found that painting. I mean—someone gave it to me."

Ezio whacked him. "Get your story straight before you lie to my face."

"God help me!" the man wailed.

"He has much better things to do than answer your prayers."

The man finished his task and handed the full purse meekly to Ezio, who pulled him upright and pinned him to a nearby wall. "I do not care how you got the painting," said Ezio. "Just tell me where it is."

"I sold it to a merchant here. For a lousy two hundred *açke*." The man's voice broke as he indicated the shop. "How else will I feed myself?"

"Next time, find a nicer way to be a *canaglia*."

Ezio let the man go, and he scampered off down the lane, cursing. Ezio watched him for a moment, then made his way into the gallery.

He looked carefully among the pictures and sculptures on sale. It wasn't hard to spot what he was after, as the gallery owner had just finished hanging it. It wasn't a large painting, but it was beautiful—a head-and-shoulders, three-quarter-profile portrait of Sofia, a few years younger, her hair in ringlets, wearing a necklace of jet and diamond stones, a black ribbon tied to the left front shoulder of her bronze satin dress. Ezio guessed it must have been done for the Sartor family when *Meister* Dürer was briefly resident in Venice.

The gallery owner, seeing him admiring it, came up to him. "That's for sale, of course, if you like the look of it." He stood back a little, sharing the treasure with his prospective client. "A luminous portrait. You see how lifelike she looks. Her beauty shines through!"

"How much do you want for it?"

The gallery owner hemmed and hawed. "Hard to put a price on the priceless, isn't it?" He paused. "But I can see you are a connoisseur. Shall we say . . . five hundred?"

"You paid two hundred."

The man held up his hands, aghast. "*Efendim!* As if I would take such advantage of a man like you! In any case—how do you know?"

"I've just had a word with the vendor. Not five minutes ago."

The gallery owner clearly saw that Ezio was not a man to be trifled with. "Ah! Indeed. But I have my overheads, you know . . ."

"You've only just hung it. I watched you."

The gallery owner looked distressed. "Very well . . . four hundred, then?"

Ezio glared.

"Three hundred? Two-fifty?"

Ezio placed the purse carefully in the man's hand. "Two hundred. There it is. Count it if you like."

"I'll have to wrap it."

"I hope you don't expect extra for that."

Grumbling sotto voce, the man unhooked the picture and wrapped it carefully in cotton sheeting, which he drew from a bolt by the shop counter. Then he passed it to Ezio. "A pleasure doing business with you," he said, drily.

"Next time, don't be so eager to take stolen goods," said Ezio. "You might have had a customer who wanted the provenance on a painting as good as this one. Luckily for you, I'm prepared to overlook that."

"And why, might one ask?"

"I'm a friend of the sitter."

Flabbergasted, the gallery owner bowed him out of the shop, with as much haste as politeness permitted.

"A pleasure doing business with you, too," said Ezio, aridly, in parting.

FORTY-ONE

Unable to keep a rendezvous with Sofia that evening, Ezio sent her a note arranging to meet the following day at the Bayezid Mosque, where he would give her back the picture.

When he arrived, he found her already there, waiting for him. In the dappled sunlight, he thought her so beautiful that the portrait scarcely did her justice.

"It's a good likeness, don't you think?" she said, as he unwrapped it and handed it to her.

"I prefer the original."

She elbowed him playfully. *"Buffone,"* she said, as they began walking. "This was a gift from my father when we were in Venice for my twenty-eighth birthday." She paused in reminiscence. "I had to sit for *Meister*

Albrecht Dürer for a full week. Can you imagine? Me sitting still for seven days? Doing nothing?"

"I cannot."

"Una tortura!"

They'd arrived at a nearby bench, on which she sat, as Ezio suppressed a laugh at the thought of her posing, trying not to move a muscle, for all that time. But the result had certainly been worth it—even though he really *did* prefer the original.

The laughter died on his lips as she produced a slip of paper; his expression immediately became serious, as did hers.

"One good turn . . ." she said. "I've found you another book location. And it's not far from here, actually."

She handed him the folded slip. He took it and read it.

"Grazie," he said. The woman was a genius. He nodded gravely to her and made to go, but she stopped him with a question.

"Ezio—what is this all about? You're not a scholar, that much is clear." She eyed his sword. "No offense, of course!" She paused. "Do you work for the Church?"

Ezio gave an amused laugh. "Not the Church, no. But I am a teacher . . . of a kind."

"What then?"

"I will explain one day, Sofia. When I can."

She nodded, disappointed, but not—as he could see—actually devastated. She had sense enough to wait.

FORTY-TWO

The decoded cipher led Ezio to an ancient edifice barely three blocks distant, in the center of the Bayezid District. It seemed once to have been a warehouse, currently in disuse, and looked securely shut, but the door, when he tried it, was unlocked. Cautiously, looking up and down the street for any sign of either Ottoman guards or Janissaries, he entered, following the instructions on the paper he held in his hand.

He climbed a staircase to the first floor and went down a corridor, at the end of which he found a small room, an office, covered in dust; but its shelves were still full of ledgers, and on the desk lay a pen set and a paper knife. He examined the room carefully, but its walls seemed to hold no clue at all about what he sought, until at last his keen eyes noticed a discrepancy in the tilework that surrounded the fireplace.

He explored this with his fingers, delicately, finding that one tile moved under his touch. Using the paper knife from the desk, he dislodged it, listening all the time for the sound of any movement from below— though he was certain no one had noticed him enter the building.

The tile came away after only a moment's work, revealing behind it a wooden panel, which he removed, seeing in the faint light behind it a book, which he with-drew carefully. A small, very old, book. He peered at the title on its spine: the version of Aesop's *Fables* put into verse by Socrates while he was under sentence of death.

He blew the dust from it and expectantly opened it to a blank page at the front. There, as he had hoped, a map of Constantinople revealed itself. He scanned it care-fully, patiently, concentrating. And as the page glowed with an unearthly light, he could see that the Galata Tower was pinpointed on it. Stowing the book carefully in his belt wallet, he left the building and made his way north through the city, taking the ferry across the Golden Horn to a quay near the foot of the tower.

He had to use all his blending-in skills to get past the guards but, once inside, was guided by the book, which took him up a winding stone staircase to a landing between floors.

It appeared to contain nothing beyond its bare stone walls.

Ezio double-checked with the book and verified that

he was in the right place. He searched the walls with his hands, feeling for any giveaway crevice that might indicate a hidden aperture, tensing at the sound of the slightest footfall on the stairway, but none approached. At last he found a gap between the stonework that was not filled with mortar, and followed it with his fingers, disclosing what was a very narrow, concealed doorway.

A little more research led him to push gently against the surrounding stones until he found one about three feet from the floor that gave slightly, allowing the door to swing back, revealing, within the depth of the tower's wall, a small room, scarcely big enough to enter. Inside, on a narrow column, rested another circular stone key—his third. He squeezed into the space to retrieve it, and as he did so, it began to glow, its light increasing fast, as the room in turn seemed to grow in volume, and Ezio felt himself transported to another time, another place.

As the light was reduced to a normal brightness, the brightness of sunshine, Ezio saw Masyaf again. But time had moved on. In his heart, Ezio knew that many years had passed. He had no idea whether or not he was dreaming. It seemed to be a dream, as he was not part of it; but at the same time, somehow, he was involved, and as well as having the feeling of dreaming, the experience was also, in some way Ezio could not define, like a memory.

Disembodied, at one with the scene that presented itself to him, yet no part of it, he watched, and waited . . .

And there again was the young man in white, though no longer young; whole decades must have passed.

And his look was troubled . . .

FORTY-THREE

Altaïr, now in his sixties, but still a lean and vigorous man, sat on a stone bench outside a dwelling in the village of Masyaf, thinking. He was no stranger to adversity, and disaster seemed, once again, poised to strike. But he had kept the great, terrible artifact safe through it all. How much longer would his strength hold, to do so? How much longer would his back refuse to buckle under the blows Destiny rained on it?

His ponderings were interrupted—and the interruption was not unwelcome—by the appearance of his wife, Maria Thorpe, the Englishwoman who had once—long ago—been his enemy, a woman who had longed to be counted among the Company of the Templars.

Time and chance had changed all that. By then, after a long exile, they had returned to Masyaf. And they faced Fate together.

She joined him on the bench, sensing his lowered spirits. He told her his news.

"The Templars have retaken their Archive on Cyprus. Abbas Sofian sent no reinforcements to aid the defenders. It was a massacre."

Maria's lips parted in an expression of surprise and dismay. "How could God have permitted this?"

"Maria, listen to me. When we left Masyaf ten long years ago, our Order was strong. But since then, all our progress—all that we built—has been undone, dismantled."

Her face was a mask of quiet fury. "Abbas must answer for this."

"Answer to whom?" replied Altaïr, angrily. "The Assassins obey only *his* command now."

She placed a hand on his arm. "Resist your desire for revenge, Altaïr. If you speak the truth, they will see the error of their ways."

"Abbas executed our youngest *son*, Maria! He deserves to *die*!"

"Yes. But if you cannot win back the Brotherhood by honorable means, its foundation will crumble."

Altaïr didn't reply for a moment but sat silently, brooding, the subject of some deep inner struggle. But at last he looked up, and his face had cleared.

"You are right, Maria," he said, calmly. "Thirty years

ago, I let passion overtake my reason. I was headstrong and ambitious, and I caused a rift within the Brotherhood that has never fully healed."

He rose, and Maria rose with him. Slowly, immersed in conversation, they walked through the dusty village.

"Speak reasonably, Altaïr, and reasonable men will listen," she encouraged him.

"Some will, perhaps. But not Abbas." Altaïr shook his head. "I should have expelled him thirty years ago when he tried to steal the Apple."

"But my dear, you earned the respect of the other Assassins because you were merciful—you let him stay."

He smiled at her slyly. "How do you know all this? You weren't even there."

She returned his smile. "I married a master storyteller," she replied, lightly.

As they walked, they came into view of the massive hulk of the castle. But there was an air of neglect hanging over it, of desolation, even.

"Look at this place," growled Altaïr. "Masyaf is a shadow of its former self."

"We have been away a long time," Maria reminded him, gently.

"But not in hiding," he said, testily. "The threat from the Mongols—the Storm from the East, the hordes led by Khan Genghis—demanded our attention, and we rode to meet it. What man here can say the same?"

They walked on. A little later, Maria broke their silence by saying, "Where is our eldest son? Does Darim know that his brother is dead?"

"I sent Darim a message four days ago. With luck, it will have reached him by now."

"Then we may see him soon."

"If God wills it." Altaïr paused. "You know, when I think of Abbas, I almost pity him. He wears his great grudge against us like a cloak."

"His wound is deep, my darling. Perhaps . . . perhaps it will help him to hear the truth."

But Altaïr shook his head. "It will not matter, not with him. A wounded heart sees all wisdom as the point of a knife." He paused again, looking around him, at the handful of villagers who passed them with their eyes either lowered or averted. "As I walk through this village, I sense great fear in the people, not love."

"Abbas has taken this place apart and robbed it of all joy."

Altaïr stopped in his tracks and looked gravely at his wife. He searched her face, lined now, but still beautiful, and the eyes still clear, though he fancied he saw reflected in them all they had been through together. "We may be walking to our doom, Maria."

She took his hand. "We may. But we walk together."

FORTY-FOUR

Maria and Altaïr had reached the confines of the castle and began to encounter Assassins—members of the Brotherhood—who knew them. But the meetings were far from friendly.

One approached them and made to pass by without acknowledgment, but Altaïr stopped him.

"Brother. Speak with us a moment."

Unwillingly, the Assassin turned. But his expression was stern. "For what reason should I speak with you? So that you can twist my mind into knots with that devilish artifact of yours?"

And he hurried away, refusing to talk any further.

But hard on his heels came another Assassin. He, too,

however, clearly wished to avoid any contact with the former Mentor and his wife.

"Are you well, brother?" asked Altaïr, accosting him, and there was something challenging in his tone.

"Who is asking?" he replied, rudely.

"Do you not recognize me? I am Altaïr."

He looked at him levelly. "That name has a hollow sound, and you—you are a cipher, nothing more. I would learn more talking to the wind."

They made their way unchallenged to the castle gardens. Once there, they knew why they had been allowed to penetrate so far. Suddenly, they were surrounded by dark-clad Assassins, loyal to their usurping Mentor, Abbas, and they stood ready to strike at any moment. Then, on a rampart above them, Abbas himself appeared, sneeringly in control.

"Let them speak," he ordered in an imperious voice. To Altaïr and Maria, he said: "Why have you come here? Why have you returned, unwelcome as you are, to this place? To defile it further?"

"We seek the truth about our son's death," replied Altaïr in a calm, clear voice. "Why was Sef killed?"

"Is it the truth you want or an excuse for revenge?" Abbas responded.

"If the truth gives us an excuse, we will act on it," Maria threw back at him.

This retort gave Abbas pause, but after a moment's reflection he said, in a lower tone: "Surrender the Apple, Altaïr, and I will tell you why your son was put to death."

Altaïr nodded, as if at a secret insight, and, turning, prepared himself to address the assembled Brotherhood of Assassins. He raised his voice commandingly.

"Ah, the truth is out already! Abbas wants the Apple for himself. Not to open your minds—but to control them!"

Abbas was quick to reply. "You have held that artifact for thirty years, Altaïr, reveling in its power and hoarding its secrets. It has corrupted you!"

Altaïr looked around at the sea of faces, most set against him, some—a few—showing signs of doubt. His mind worked quickly as he concocted a plan, which might just work.

"Very well, Abbas," he said. "Take it."

And he took the Apple from the pouch at his side and held it up high.

"What—?" said Maria, taken aback.

Abbas's eyes flashed at the sight of the Apple, but he hesitated before signaling to his bodyguard to go and take it from Altaïr's gaunt hand.

The bodyguard came close. When he was standing next to Altaïr, a demon possessed him. An amused expression on his face, he leaned in to the former Mentor, and whispered in his ear: "It was I who executed your son Sef. Just before I killed him, I told him that it was you yourself who had ordered his death."

He did not see the flash of lightning in Altaïr's eyes. He blundered on, pleased with himself, and, scarcely restraining a laugh, said: "Sef died believing you had betrayed him."

Altaïr turned burning eyes on him then. In his hand, the Apple exploded with the light of a bursting star.

"Ahhhh!" screamed the bodyguard in pain. His whole body writhed uncontrollably. His hands went to his head, scrabbling at his temples. It looked as if he were trying to tear his head from his body in an attempt to stop the agony.

"Altaïr!" cried Maria.

But Altaïr was deaf to her. His eyes were black with fury as, driven by an unseen force, the bodyguard, even as he tried to resist his own impulses, pulled a long knife from his belt and, with hands trembling as they tried to oppose the power which drove them, raised it, ready to plunge it into his own throat.

Maria seized her husband's arm, shaking him, and crying again, "Altaïr! No!"

Her words had their effect at last. An instant later, visibly shaken, Altaïr broke free of the trance that had gripped him. His eyes became normal again, and the Apple withdrew its light, becoming dark and dull, inert in his hand.

But the bodyguard, freed of the force which had held him in its grasp, shook himself like a dog, looked around madly, in anger and fear, and with a terrible oath, threw himself on Maria, striking his knife deep into her back.

Then he drew back, leaving the knife buried where he had driven it. Maria stood, a faint cry forming on her lips. The entire company of Assassins stood as if turned to stone. Abbas himself was silent, his mouth open, but no sound came forth.

It was Altaïr who moved. To the bodyguard, it seemed

as if his former Mentor unleashed his hidden-blade with appalling slowness. The blade snicked out and the sound it made might have been as loud as a rock snapping in the heat of the sun. The bodyguard saw the blade coming toward him, toward his face, saw it approach inch by inch, second by second, as it seemed to him. But then the speed was sudden and ferocious as he felt it split his face open between the eyes. There was an explosion in his head, and then, nothing.

Altaïr stood for a fraction of a second as the bodyguard fell to the ground, blood shooting from his head between the shattered eyes, then caught his wife as she began to collapse, and lowered her gently to the earth which would soon, he knew, receive her. A ball of ice grew in his heart as he bent over her, his face so close to hers that they seemed like lovers about to kiss.

They were caught in a silence that wrapped itself around them like armor. She was trying to speak. He strained to hear her.

"Altaïr. My love. Strength."

"Maria . . ." His voice was no more than an anguished whisper.

Then, appallingly, the sounds and the dust and the smells rose up violently around him again, smashing through the protecting armor, and above it all the shrieking voice of Abbas:

"He is possessed! Kill him!"

Altaïr rose and, drawing himself to his full height, backed slowly away.

"Take the Apple!" screamed Abbas. "Now!"

FORTY-FIVE

Altaïr fled before they could react—fled from the castle, through its gaping portal, down the escarpment, and into the sparse wood that bounded the area between fortress and village on the northern side. And there, in a clearing, as if by a miracle, he was brought short by an encounter with another man, like him, but a generation younger.

"Father!" exclaimed the newcomer. "I came as soon as I'd read your message. What has happened? Am I too late?"

From the castle behind them, horns were crying out the alarm.

"Darim! My son! Turn back!"

Darim looked past his father, over his shoulder. There,

on the ridges beyond the wood, he could see bands of Assassins assembling, getting ready to hunt them down. "Have they all gone mad?"

"Darim—I still have the Apple. We have to go. Abbas must not get his hands on it."

For answer, Darim unslung his pack and drew a scabbard of throwing knives from it before placing it on the ground. "There are more knives in there, take them if you need them."

The Assassins loyal to Abbas had seen them by then, and some were heading toward them while others fanned out to outflank them.

"They'll try to ambush us," said Altaïr grimly. "Keep a good stock of knives with you. We must be prepared."

They made their way through the wood, going ever deeper.

It was a perilous passage. Often, they had to take cover as they spotted groups of Assassins who'd got ahead of them or who tried to take them from the side, or obliquely, from behind.

"Stay close!" Darim said. "We go together."

"We'll try to work our way around. There are horses in the village. Once we've got mounts, we'll try to make for the coast."

Up until then, Darim had been too preoccupied with their immediate danger to think of anything else, but now he said, "Where is Mother?"

Altaïr shook his head, sadly. "She is gone, Darim. I am sorry."

Darim took a breath. "What? How?"

"Later. Time for talk later. Now we have to get clear. We have to fight."

"But they are our Brothers. Our fellow Assassins. Surely we can talk—persuade them."

"Forget reason, Darim. They have been poisoned by lies."

There was silence between them. Then Darim said, "Was it Abbas who killed my brother?"

"He killed your brother. He killed our great comrade, Malik Al-Sayf. And countless others," replied Altaïr, bleakly.

Darim bowed his head. "He is a madman. Without remorse. Without conscience."

"A madman with an army."

"He will die," said Darim, coldly. "One day, he will pay."

They reached the outskirts of the village and were lucky to make their way to the stables unmolested, for the village itself was teeming with Assassin warriors. Hastily, they saddled up and mounted. As they rode away, they could hear Abbas's voice, bellowing like a beast in pain as he stood atop a small tower in the village square. "I will have the Apple, Altaïr! And I will have your HEAD, for all the dishonor you have brought upon my family! You cannot run forever! Not from us, and not from your lies!"

His voice faded into the distance as they galloped away.

*   *   *

Five miles down the road, they reined in. They had not—as yet—been pursued. They had gained time. But Darim, riding behind him, noticed that his father sat slumped in the saddle, exhausted and anguished. He spurred his horse closer and looked into Altaïr's face with concern.

Altaïr sat low, hunched, on the verge of tears.

"Maria. My love . . ." Darim heard him murmur.

"Come, Father," he said. "We must ride on."

Making a supreme effort, Altaïr kicked his horse into a gallop, and the two of them sped away, specks disappearing into the forbidding landscape.

FORTY-SIX

Having deposited the new key with the others in the safety of the Assassins' Constantinople headquarters, and having delivered the copy of the Socrates *Fables* to a grateful and marveling Sofia, Ezio decided that it was time to make a report to Prince Suleiman on what he had discovered at the Arsenal.

He'd had some indication of where to find him and made his way to a fashionable park near the Bayezid Mosque, where he found Suleiman and his uncle Ahmet seated in the shade of an oriental plane, the sunshine intensifying the bright green of its broad leaves.

A Janissary guard detail stood around them at a discreet distance while they played chess. Ezio took up a position where he could watch, unobserved. He wanted to speak with the prince alone. But he was interested in chess—its strategies had taught him many skills to be applied elsewhere—and he watched the progress of the game with interest.

The two players seemed pretty equally matched. After a while, Suleiman, having pondered a move of his uncle's that put his king in danger, responded by castling.

"That's not a legal move," said Prince Ahmet, in surprise.

"It is a European variation—*arrocco*."

"It's interesting, but not exactly fair, when you play by different rules from your opponent."

"You may think differently when you are sultan," replied Suleiman, flatly.

Ahmet looked as if he had been slapped but said nothing. Suleiman picked up his king. "Shall I take it back?" he asked.

In response, Ahmet rose to his feet. "Suleiman," he said, "I know it has been hard on you, watching your father and me quarrel over Bayezid's throne."

The young man shrugged. "Grandfather has chosen you, and his word is law—*kanun*. What is there to argue about?"

Prince Ahmet looked at his nephew in grudging admiration. "Your father and I were close once, but his cruelty and ambition have—"

"I have heard the rumors, Uncle," Suleiman cut in, hotly.

Embarrassed, Ahmet looked away across the park for a moment before returning his gaze to the chessboard.

"Well," he said finally, "I have a meeting with the council of viziers shortly. Shall we continue another time?"

"Whenever you wish." Suleiman was cordial.

He rose and bowed to his uncle, who bowed in return, before leaving with his bodyguard. Ezio waited a moment, watching Suleiman as he sat down again, contemplating the chessboard in his turn.

Then he moved forward.

Suleiman saw him approach and gestured to his guards not to hinder his visitor.

"Ezio," he said.

Ezio came straight to the point. "Tarik has been selling guns to a local miser—Manuel Palaiologos."

Suleiman's face darkened. He clenched his fist. "Palaiologos. That is a sad sound in my ears." Once again, he rose to his feet. "The last Byzantine emperor was Constantine Palaiologos. If this heir of his is arming a militia of some kind, there will be conflict, and it will escalate. All this at a time when my father and grandfather are at odds with one another." He trailed off and grew thoughtful. Ezio imagined that he must be brooding over one of the hardest decisions he'd ever had to make in his short life.

"Tarik knows where the rifles are headed," Ezio said. "If I find him first, I can follow the weapons straight to the Byzantines."

Suleiman looked at him. "Tarik will be with his Janissaries, at their barracks. So, if you want to get close, you will have to 'become' a Janissary yourself."

Ezio smiled. "Not a problem," he said.

"Güzel," said Suleiman. "Excellent." He thought some more, and it was clear that the decision he was coming to caused him distress; but once he'd made it, he was firm. "Get the information you need—then kill him."

Ezio raised an eyebrow. This was a side of Suleiman he had not seen before. "Are you sure, Suleiman? You told me Tarik and your father were close friends."

Suleiman swallowed hard, then looked defiant: "This is true. But such naked treason against my grandfather deserves death."

Ezio looked at him for a moment, then said: "Understood."

There was nothing more to discuss. Ezio took his leave. When he looked back, Suleiman was studying the chessboard again.

FORTY-SEVEN

With a little help from Yusuf's Assassins, Ezio was able to isolate and corner an unsuspecting off-duty Janissary in the Bazaar and relieve him of his uniform. But it was not without a price. The Janissary put up stiff resistance and badly wounded two Assassins before he was overcome; but not before he himself had sustained a mortal wound. It was necessary for Ezio, with Azize's help, to wash the bloodstains thoroughly from the white garments before he put them on. But then he could pass for a Janissary guard without any question, provided he was careful to keep his beard covered with a white scarf, exposing only his mustache.

As he made his way to the barracks, he was amused

and, at the same time, disconcerted at the response he evoked among the local population, both male and female, Ottomans and Byzantines alike, though the reactions were the same mixture among all the nationalities he encountered. Some were apparently admiring, even ingratiating. Others were subtly dismissive, and yet more reacted with fear and uncertainty. It was clear enough that the Janissaries were at best tolerated, at worst loathed. There was not a hint of genuine affection or regard. But from what he could gather, the greatest disdain seemed to be leveled specifically at the Janissaries belonging to Tarik's barracks. Ezio stored this experience in his memory, certain that it would prove useful at some future date, but for the moment he concentrated on his goal.

He was relieved that his uniform allowed him to pass unhindered and uncontested as he made his way to the barracks, the more so as he was soon to discover that the Assassins' killing of the Janissary had already been discovered. As he drew close to his destination, he passed a square where a Seljuk herald was announcing the man's death to a crowd of interested onlookers.

"Dark tidings, citizens of Kostantiniyye," the herald was proclaiming. "A servant of our sultan has fallen at the hands of a criminal and been stripped of his garments." He looked round and raised his voice a notch. "Be on the lookout for any suspicious activity."

Ezio crossed the square as discreetly as possible, but eyes inevitably fell on him. He prayed that he would be able to enter the barracks unchallenged. If they knew about the murder and that the man had been killed for his uniform, they would tighten security faster than a man could say "knife."

"Woe betide the murderer who took the life of a beloved Janissary," the herald continued to intone. "This enemy of civilization must be found and brought to justice! If you see something, say something!" He glared around at the crowd impressively and shook his scroll for additional effect, before going on: "Citizens, beware! A killer stalks our streets, a man without conscience, targeting the servants of our sultan. The Janissaries have dedicated their lives to the protection of the empire. Return the favor they have done us and find this killer before he strikes again!"

The postern gate of the Janissary Garrison stood open, though flanked by a double guard. But they came to attention as Ezio arrived, and he realized that he had had the luck to waylay a senior NCO or junior officer— for the dress he wore clearly commanded respect, though to an uninitiated eye, the Janissaries' uniforms looked virtually indistinguishable between officers and men.

He entered the compound without difficulty, but no sooner had he done so than he began to pick up snippets of conversation regarding the killing.

"*Kardeslerim*, one of our own was found murdered and stripped of his garments not an hour ago, and his body, they say, was dumped on a dunghill like so much rubbish," one said to a couple of his brother soldiers, who murmured angrily at the news. "Keep a close watch on these streets as you move through them," the first to speak continued. "Someone is planning to strike, using our uniform as cover. We must be constantly on our guard until the culprit is caught."

"And disemboweled," added another.

Ezio decided to be as cautious as possible for as long as he was in the compound. Keeping his head down, he moved around the barracks, familiarizing himself with them, and, as he did so, eavesdropping on various conversations. What he heard was most revealing and of great value.

"Selim understands our plight. The Byzantines, the Mamluks, the Safavid—only he has the courage to face the threats those peoples represent for us," said one soldier.

"You speak the truth. Selim is a warrior. Like Osman and Mehmed before him," another replied.

"So—why has our sultan Bayezid chosen a pussycat over a lion?"

"Prince Ahmet shares the sultan's calm temperament. That's why. They are too much alike, I fear."

A third soldier joined the conversation. "Sultan Bayezid is a good man, and a kind ruler . . . But he has lost the fire that made him great."

"I disagree," said a fourth. "He is still a fighter. Look at the army he has raised against Selim."

"That's just further evidence of his decline! To take up arms against his own son? It's shameful."

"Do not bend the truth to match the contours of your passion, *efendim*," the fourth man rebuked him. "It was Selim, after all, who attacked our sultan first."

"*Evet, evet.* But Selim did so for the glory of the empire, not for himself."

"Speaking of the war, is there any news from the north?" a fifth soldier chimed in.

"I hear that Selim's forces have fallen back to Varna," said a sixth. "Heavy losses, I am told."

"Incredible, isn't it? I pray for a swift conclusion."

"Yes, but in which direction?"

"I cannot say. My heart sides with our sultan, but my head hopes for Selim."

"And what of Selim's young son, Prince Suleiman?" a seventh Janissary put in. "Have you met him?"

"Not personally," an eighth replied; "But I have seen him. I know he is a remarkable boy."

"Hardly a boy—a capable young man. With a magnificent mind."

"Does he take after his father?"

The seventh Janissary shrugged. "Perhaps. Though I suspect he is another sort of man altogether."

Two more Janissaries came up and joined the conversation as Ezio lingered at its edge. One of them was clearly a bit of a joker. "Why does Prince Ahmet linger in this city?" he asked wryly. "He knows he is not wanted."

"He's like a moth hovering around an open flame. Waiting for his father to perish, so that he may take the throne."

"Did you hear," said the joker, "that he offered Tarik a bribe in return for our loyalty?"

"God damn him for that. What did Tarik do?"

The other guard laughed. "He spent half the money on horse feed and sent the rest to Selim!"

FORTY-EIGHT

Several ornate tents were pitched within the broad compound, protected by the high walls that surrounded it. Leaving the Janissary soldiers, Ezio moved on among them, getting ever closer to the center, where he guessed Tarik's quarters would be found. Sure enough, as he approached, he heard the familiar tones of Tarik's voice as he spoke to a courier who had just come up, joining Tarik, who was in the company of a third Janissary, evidently an adjutant.

"Tarik *bey*," said the courier. "A letter for you."

Tarik took the letter without comment, broke the seal, and read it. He was laughing in a satisfied manner even before he had reached the end. "Perfect," he said, folding the paper and putting it in his tunic. "The rifles

have arrived in Cappadocia, at the garrison of Manuel
Palaiologos's army."

"And our men, are they still with him?" asked the
adjutant.

"*Evet*. They will contact us when the Byzantines break
camp. Then we will meet them when they reach Bursa."

The adjutant smiled. "Then everything is falling into
place, *efendim*."

"Yes, Chagatai," Tarik replied. "For once."

He waved the men away and started to walk away,
among the tents. Keeping at a safe distance, Ezio shadowed him. But he could not remain completely unnoticed and was glad of the little Turkish he had already
picked up since his arrival in Constantinople, as guards
either came to attention or soldiers of similar rank to his
own greeted him. But it was not all plain sailing. Once
or twice he lost his trail and noticed suspicious looks
directed at him before he picked it up again; and once he
faced a direct challenge. Two guards blocked his way:

"What regiment are you from, *efendim*?" the first
asked him, politely enough, though with just enough
edge to his voice to make Ezio wary.

Before Ezio could reply, the second cut in: "I do not
believe I know you. I do not see your imperial insignia.
Are you cavalry?"

"When did you get in?" asked the first, his voice
openly unfriendly now.

"Where is your captain?"

Ezio's Turkish wasn't up to this. And he saw that, in
any case, their suspicions were more than aroused. Swiftly,

he unleashed his hookblade and tripped one up with it, sending him crashing into the other. Then he ran, darting between tents, jumping guy ropes and still keeping one eye on the now-distant Tarik.

There was shouting behind him:

"Imposter!"

"Deceiver! You will die!"

"Stop him!"

"It's the outlaw who killed Nazar! Grab him!"

But the compound was very large, and Ezio took full advantage of the fact that, in their uniforms and with their almost identical mustaches, one Janissary looked very like another. Leaving confusion in his wake, he soon picked up Tarik's trail again and located him in a quiet corner of the barracks, where the senior officers' map-rooms were to be found.

Ezio watched as Tarik entered one of the map-rooms; he glanced around to ensure that the man was alone and that he himself had thrown off the last traces of pursuit, and followed Tarik in. He closed and bolted the door behind him.

Ezio had already collected all the information he believed he needed. He knew that Tarik planned to rendezvous with Manuel at Bursa, and he knew that the arms shipment had arrived at Manuel's garrison in Cappadocia. So when Tarik immediately drew his sword and flung himself at him, he did not need to ask questions first. He stepped neatly aside to his left as Tarik thrust with his sword, then unleashed his left-hand hidden-blade and plunged it into the right-hand side of the Janissary captain's back, ripping through the kidney as he cut in hard with the blade before withdrawing it.

Tarik crashed forward onto a map table, scattering the charts that covered it and drenching those that remained with blood. He caught his breath and, drawing on his last reserves of strength, heaved himself up on his right elbow and half turned to look at his attacker.

"Your villainy is finished, soldier," said Ezio, harshly.

But Tarik seemed resigned, almost amused. Ezio was suddenly seized by doubt.

"Ah, what bitter irony," said Tarik. "Is this the result of Suleiman's investigation?"

"You collude with the sultan's enemies," said Ezio, his confidence ebbing. "What did you expect would come of such treachery?"

Tarik gave him a regretful smile. "I blame myself." He paused, his breathing painful, as blood flowed steadily from his unstaunched side. "Not for treason, but hubris." He looked at Ezio, who had drawn closer to catch his voice, which had now sunk to little more than a whisper. "I was preparing an ambush. Preparing to strike the Byzantine Templars at the precise moment they felt safest."

"What proof do you have of this?"

"Look. Here."

Painfully, Tarik pulled a map from his belt with his left hand. "Take it," he said.

Ezio did so.

"This will lead you to the Byzantines in Cappadocia," Tarik continued. "Destroy them if you can."

Ezio's voice had sunk to a whisper, too. "You have done well, Tarik. Forgive me."

"There is no blame," Tarik replied, struggling with the effort of speaking at all. But he forced himself to go on, knowing that his next words would be his last. "Protect my homeland. *Allah ashkina!* In God's name, redeem the honor we have lost in this fight."

Ezio put Tarik's arm over his shoulder and lifted him onto the table, where he hastily tore the scarf from his neck and tied it as tightly as he could around the wound he had made.

But he was already too late.

"*Requiescat in Pace,*" said Ezio, sadly.

Outside, he heard the hue and cry for him taken up once more, and close by. There was no time to repine over his mistake. Hastily, he tore off the uniform until he was stripped down to the simple grey tunic and hose he wore underneath. The map-room was close to the barracks wall. With the help of his hookblade, he knew the wall would be climbable.

It was time to go.

FORTY-NINE

Ezio regained Assassin headquarters, changed, and returned to Topkapi Sarayi with a heavy heart. The guards had clearly been given orders to let him pass, and he was ushered into a private antechamber, where, after a few minutes had passed, Suleiman came to meet him. The young prince seemed surprised to see him—and agitated.

Ezio forestalled the question in his eyes. "Tarik was no traitor, Suleiman. He, too, was tracking the Byzantines."

"What?" Suleiman's distress was evident. "So, did you—?"

Ezio nodded, gravely.

Suleiman sat down heavily. He looked ill. "God

forgive me," he said, quietly. "I should not have been so quick to judge."

"Prince, he was loyal to your grandfather to the end; and through his efforts, we have the means to save your city." Ezio briefly explained what he had found out, told him what he had learned from listening to the Janissaries, and showed him the map Tarik had given him.

"Ah, Tarik," whispered Suleiman. "He should not have been so secretive, Ezio. What a terrible way to do a good thing."

"The weapons have been taken to Cappadocia. We must act immediately. Can you get me there?"

Suleiman snapped out of his reverie. "What—? Get you there? Yes, of course. I will arrange a ship to take you to Mersin—you can travel inland from there."

They were interrupted by the arrival of Prince Ahmet. Fortunately, he called out to Suleiman in an impatient voice before he arrived, so Ezio had time to withdraw to a corner of the room, where he would be less conspicuous.

Ahmet entered the room and wasted no time at all in coming to the point. "Suleiman, I have been set up and made to look like a traitor! Do you remember Tarik, the Janissary?"

"The man you quarreled with?"

Ahmet showed signs of getting seriously angry. "He has been murdered. It is no secret that he and I were at odds. Now the Janissaries will be quick to accuse me of the crime."

"This is terrible news, Uncle."

"It is indeed. When word of this reaches my father, he will banish me from the city!"

Suleiman could not suppress a nervous glance over his uncle's shoulder at Ezio. Ahmet noticed this and spun round. His manner immediately became more reserved. "Ah. Forgive me, nephew. I was not aware that you had a guest."

Suleiman hesitated, then said: "This is . . . Marcello. One of my European advisers in Kefe."

Ezio bowed low. *"Buona sera."*

Ahmet made an impatient gesture. "Marcello, my nephew and I have a private matter to discuss," he said, sternly.

"Of course. Please excuse me." Ezio bowed again, even lower, and backed his way to the door, exchanging a quick glance at Suleiman, who, he prayed, would get them out of this. Luckily, the young prince picked up his cue perfectly and said to Ezio in a clipped, official voice:

"You know your orders. As I've said, there will be a ship waiting for you when you are ready to leave."

"Grazie, mio principe," Ezio replied. He left the room then but lingered just outside it, wishing to hear how the conversation would end. What he heard did not convince him that he was out of the woods at all:

"We will track down the perpetrator of this crime, Uncle," Suleiman was saying. "Have patience."

Ezio mulled that over. Could matters be that dire? But he didn't know Suleiman that well. And what was it

Yusuf had warned about? Against meddling in Ottoman politics?

His mood was grim as he left the palace. There was one place he needed to be. One place where he could relax—as he badly needed to—and collect his thoughts.

FIFTY

So now we entered on that hidden path,
my lord and I, to move once more towards
a shining world. We did not care to rest.
We climbed, he going first and I behind,
until through some small aperture I saw
the lovely things the skies above us bear.
Now we came out, and once more saw the stars.

Ezio had started rereading Dante's *Inferno* at Sofia's suggestion several days earlier. He had read it before, as a student, but never really taken it in, since his mind was preoccupied with other matters in those days, but now it seemed like a revelation. But, having finally finished it, he put the book down with a sigh of pleasure. He looked across at Sofia, her glasses perched on her nose as she sat, head down, glancing from the original map to her reference books, to a notebook she was writing in. He gazed at her as she worked but did not interrupt, so deeply engaged did she seem in the task at hand. Instead, he reached for the book again. Perhaps he should make a start on the *Purgatorio*.

But just then, Sofia lifted her eyes from her work. She smiled at him.

"Enjoying the poem?"

He smiled back, placed the book on the table by his chair, and rose. "Who were these men he condemned to hell?"

"Political opponents, men who wronged him. Dante Alghieri's pen cuts deeply, no?"

"*Sì,*" Ezio replied, thoughtfully. "It is a subtle way to seek revenge."

He didn't want to return to reality, but the urgency of the journey he soon had to make pressed upon him. Still, there was nothing he could do until he had word from Suleiman. Provided that he could trust the prince. But his thoughts had calmed. How could it profit Suleiman to betray him? He resumed his seat, picked up *The Divine Comedy* again, and turned to the place where he had left off.

She interrupted him. "Ezio," she began, hesitantly, "I plan to make a trip to Adrianopolis in a few weeks, to visit a new printing press there."

Ezio noticed the shy tone of her voice and wondered if she had picked up the softness that had crept into his whenever he spoke to her. Had she realized how great his . . . affection for her had become? Overcompensating, he was deliberately nonchalant when he replied, "That should be fun."

She was still diffident. "It is a five- or six-day ride from here, and I will need an escort . . ."

"Prego?"

She was instantly embarrassed. "I'm sorry. You are a busy man."

It was his turn to be embarrassed. "Sofia, I would love to accompany you, but my time is running short—"

"That is true for all of us."

He didn't know how to respond to that, taking its meaning several ways, and remained silent. He was thinking of the twenty-year age gap between them.

Sofia looked down at the map for a moment, then back up. "Well, I could try to finish this last cipher now, but I need to run an errand before sundown. Can you wait a day?"

"What do you need?"

She looked away and back again. "It's silly, but . . . a bouquet of fresh flowers. White tulips, specifically."

He got up. "I'll get you the flowers. *Nessun problema.*"

"Are you sure?"

"It will be a nice change of pace."

She smiled warmly. "*Bene!* Look—meet me in the park just to the east of Haghia Sofia. We will trade: flowers for . . . information!"

FIFTY-ONE

The Flower Market was a blaze of color and pleasant scents, and there wasn't a Janissary in sight. Ezio made his way through it anxiously, as nowhere in all this cornucopia had he yet been able to find any of the flowers he sought.

"You look like a man with money to spend," said a flower seller, as Ezio approached his stall. "What do need, my friend?"

"I'm looking for tulips. White ones, if you have them."

The flower seller looked doubtful. "Ah. Tulips. Forgive me, but I am fresh out. Something else, perhaps?"

Ezio shook his head. "It's not my call, unfortunately."

The flower seller thought about the problem for a

moment, then leaned forward. He spoke confidentially. "OK, just for you, here is my secret. Many of the white tulips I sell, I pick myself near the hippodrome. Not a word of a lie. You go and see for yourself."

Ezio smiled, took out his wallet, and tipped the flower seller generously. *"Grazie."*

Busily, a man in haste, he made his way through the sun-warmed streets to the hippodrome, and, sure enough, in the grass along one side of the racetrack, he found white tulips growing in abundance. Happily, he bent down and, unleashing his hidden-blade, cut as many as he hoped Sofia would want.

FIFTY-TWO

The Imperial Park to the east of Haghia Sofia was laid out in formal gardens, interspersed with verdant lawns dotted with white marble benches and arbors ideal for private meetings, and in one of them he soon found Sofia.

She had laid out a little picnic, and Ezio could see at a glance that it wasn't local food and drink. She'd managed somehow to organize a lunch that brought together some of the specialties of both their hometowns, so there was *moleche* and *rixoto de gò* from Venice, and *panzanella* and *salame toscano* from Florence. She'd also provided figs from Tuscolo and olives from Piceno, and there was a dish of macaroni and turbot. The wine she'd brought was a Frescobaldi. A wicker hamper stood by the neat white cloth she'd laid.

"What is this?" he said, marveling.

"A gift. Sit."

Ezio bowed, handing her the flowers, and did as he was bidden.

"These are beautiful—thank you," she said, accepting the huge bouquet of tulips he had cut for her.

"So is this," he replied. "And don't think I don't appreciate the trouble you've been to."

"I wanted to thank you for letting me play a small role in your adventure."

"I would scarcely have called it small, but a 'small' role is quite enough for this adventure, believe me."

She laughed quietly. "You are a mystery, Ezio Auditore."

He looked worried. "I'm sorry—I do not mean to be."

She laughed again. "It's fine!" She paused, then added: "It's attractive."

Ezio didn't know how to respond to that, so he concentrated on the food. "This looks delicious."

"Why, thank you."

Ezio smiled. He didn't want to break the mood, but a shadow had fallen over his thoughts. He mustn't celebrate—or hope for anything—prematurely. He looked at her more seriously, and she immediately caught his frame of mind.

"Any luck with the final code?" he asked, as casually as he could.

"Ah, the code," she replied, still a little playful, and Ezio was relieved. "Yes, I've solved it. A few hours ago.

But you'll have to be patient. You will get it soon enough."

And she looked at him then in a way that broke down any defenses Ezio had left.

FIFTY-THREE

The last book was located in a place more difficult to get to. Niccolò Polo had managed to conceal it high on the front façade of the mosque of Haghia Sofia itself, above the great curved arch that stood before the principal dome of the former basilica.

Ezio chose to complete his mission in the wee hours before dawn, as then there would be the smallest number of people about. He reached the building unchallenged and carefully made his way to the exonarthex, looking up at the cliff of stone he had to climb. There were few crevices for his hookblade to get a grip, but after several unsuccessful attempts, he managed to climb to the spot Sofia had pinpointed. There, he found a weathered wooden panel, overhung with cobwebs.

He managed to belay himself to some nearby pipe-work which, after testing it, he found solid enough to take his weight, and he used the hookblade again to pry the panel open. The wooden board fell away, falling to the ground beneath with what to Ezio's ears was a deafening, echoing clatter, and he hung there in the grey light of false dawn silently, praying that no one had been alerted by the noise. But after he had waited for three whole minutes, and there was no reaction, he reached into the cavity the board had concealed and from it drew the book he sought.

Once back on the ground, he sped away and found a quiet spot in the very park where he had dined with Sofia only the day before, and there examined his find. The book was a copy of Luitpold of Cremona's *Mission to Constantinople*. He allowed himself to imagine for a moment Sofia's pleasure at the sight of such a rarity, before turning to its front.

The blank pages glowed about as brightly as the thin streaks of dawnlight he could see away to the east across the Bosphorus. And a map of the city appeared, which, as he watched hopefully, resolved itself into focus, and on it appeared another light, brighter than the rest, clearly marking the Forum of the Ox.

Following the trail indicated in the book, Ezio made his way to the Forum, away in the west of the city, past the Second and Third Hills, and about midway between the Aqueduct of Valens to the north and the Harbor of Theodosius to the south. It was quite a walk, but when he arrived, it was still too early for anyone to be about.

Ezio scanned the huge, deserted square for some kind of clue, but the marked spot in the book gleamed sharply, and he remembered the system of subterranean cisterns beneath the city. He concentrated his search and located, after a little time, a manhole, from which stone steps descended into the bowels of the earth.

Ezio closed the book and stowed it safely in his satchel. He replaced his hookblade with his pistol, checked his hidden-blade, and warily made his way downward.

He soon found himself in a vaulted cavern, on a stone embankment by which an underground river ran. Lit torches stood in sconces on the walls, and, as he crept quietly through a narrow, damp corridor, he heard, above the sound of rushing water, voices echoing, raised above the din the river made. Following the sound of them, he came upon two Byzantine Templars.

"What have you found?" one said. "Another key?"

"A door of some kind," his comrade answered. "Bricked up with hard stone."

Edging closer, rounding a corner, Ezio saw a number of soldiers a short distance away, standing on an old pier that jutted into the river. One of them was rolling a barrel off one of two waiting rafts.

"That sounds promising," the first of the nearer Templars said. "The first key was found behind a similar door."

"Is that so? And how did they open that door?"

"They didn't. The earthquake did."

On a signal from the men closer to Ezio, the other soldiers came up with the barrel, which they proceeded to lodge in place against the door. Ezio could now see that the opening was sealed with close-fitting blocks of some hard black stone, cut by a master mason.

"The earthquake! That was helpful," said the second Templar. "And all we have is a few barrels of gunpowder."

"This one should be big enough for the job," replied the first.

Ezio's eyes narrowed. He quietly released his gun and pulled back the hammer.

"If it isn't, we'll just get more," the first Templar continued.

Ezio raised his arm and took aim, but the barrel of the gun caught the light of a torch as he did so and glinted, the unusual flash of light catching the eye of one of the soldiers.

"What?" he snapped.

He saw the gun and leapt in front of the barrel at the same moment that Ezio fired. The ball struck him, and he fell dead instantly.

Ezio swore to himself.

But the soldiers were onto him.

"It's the Assassin! Let's get out of here!"

Ezio tried to reload, but the soldiers were already making their way back toward the rafts. He followed them, desperate to stop them before they could raise the alarm. But as he reached the pier, they were already pushing off. By the time Ezio had leapt onto the second raft and was struggling to loose its moorings, the soldiers were in midstream, floating away.

He had cast off and was in pursuit when the thought

struck him—were they scared of him, or were they leading him on? Well, it was too late now. He'd have to play this to the end.

As his raft was lighter, the current began to carry him closer. The soldiers seemed to be in a panic, but that didn't stop them from priming bombs and loading muskets.

"We have gunpowder aboard, we should use it!" one cried.

"We'll blast him out of the water," said another, throwing a bomb, which exploded as it hit the water barely a foot ahead of Ezio's prow.

"Give me some room," yelled another soldier, trying to steady himself to take aim with his musket.

"Shoot him!"

"What do you think I'm trying to do?"

"Just kill the bastard!"

They careered on downstream. Ezio had managed by then to grasp the tiller of his raft and bring it under control, all the while having to duck and dive to avoid the musket balls that cannoned toward him, though the pitch and roll of their raft made it all but impossible for the soldiers to take serious aim. Then one of the barrels aboard worked free of its ropes and rolled around the deck, knocking two soldiers into the torrent—one of them their tillerman. The raft bucked wildly, throwing another man into the black water, then smashed into the side of the embankment. The survivors scrambled to the bank. Ezio looked up to the high vault, which ran perhaps twenty feet above the river. In the gloom, he could see that a taut rope had been slung the length of the roof, and no doubt barges or rafts were often hooked to it to guide them down the river. You'd only need one person aboard with a pole to unhook and rehook round each of the eyelets to which the rope was affixed at regular intervals.

And Ezio could see that the rope, following the river's downhill course, sloped gradually downward, too. Just enough for what he had planned.

Bracing himself, Ezio steered his own raft for the embankment, and as it smashed into the one he'd been pursuing, he leapt from it onto the stone pathway at the river's side.

By that time, the surviving soldiers were already some way ahead of him, running for their lives—or to summon reinforcements. Ezio had no time to waste.

Working fast, he swapped his gun for his hookblade, scrambled up the side wall of the cavern, and threw himself toward the rope over the river. He had just enough momentum to catch it with his hookblade, and soon he was shooting downstream over the water, far faster than the soldiers could run though he had to unhook and rehook with split-second timing at each eyelet in the roof to avoid falling into the roaring torrent beneath.

As he caught up with the soldiers, he reversed his first maneuver and unhooked at the crucial moment, throwing his body sideways so that he landed on the embankment just ahead of the Templars. They stopped dead, panting, facing him.

"He is a madman," said the first Templar.

"This is no man—this is a demon," a second cried.

"Let's see if demons bleed," bellowed a braver comrade, coming at Ezio, his sword whirling in his hand.

Ezio performed a hook-and-roll over his back and pitched him, while he was still off balance, into the river. Three soldiers remained. The fight had all but gone out of them, but Ezio knew he could not afford to be merciful. The ensuing clash was short and bloody, and left Ezio nursing a gashed left arm; and three corpses lay before him.

Gulping air, he made his way back to the sealed door. They had come a long way downriver, and it took him a good ten minutes to regain the jetty where the rafts had originally been moored. But at least he knew that he need be in no immediate fear of pursuit; and the barrel of gunpowder was still lodged where the Templar soldiers had placed it.

Replacing his hookblade with his pistol once more, Ezio loaded it, chose a position upstream, from where he could take cover behind a projecting buttress, took careful aim, and fired.

There was the crack of the pistol and the hiss of the ball as it shot toward the barrel, even the thud as it struck home, but then there was, for what seemed an eternity, silence.

Nothing happened.

But then . . .

The explosion in those confines was like a thunderclap, and Ezio was deafened, thinking, as tiny stones rained down all around him, that he might have brought the roof in, that he might have irreparably damaged whatever was behind the door. But when the dust settled, he could see that for all the force of the explosion, the sealed entrance was still only partially breached.

Enough, however, for him to look within it and see the familiar plinth, on which, to his intense relief, the circular obsidian key, partner to the others he had collected, rested undamaged. But he had no time to relax. Even as he reached for it, he noticed, emanating from it, the glow that he had experienced with the others. As it grew in intensity, he tried, this time, to resist its power. He felt undermined, unsettled by the strange visions that succeeded the blinding light he had come to expect.

But it was no use, and he felt himself once more surrendering to a power far greater than his own.

FIFTY-FOUR

To Ezio, it appeared that twenty long years had passed. The landscape was one he knew, and there, rising from it like a giant claw, stood the by-now-familiar castle of Masyaf. Not far from its gate, a group of three Assassins sat near a blazing campfire . . .

The Assassins' faces were those of people whose better dreams have gone dark. When they spoke, their voices were quiet, weary.

"They say he screams in his sleep, calling out for his father. Ahmad Sofian," said one of them.

One of the men scoffed bitterly. "So, Cemal, he calls out for his daddy, does he? What a miserable man Abbas is."

They had their faces to the fire and did not at first

notice the old, cowled man in white robes who was approaching through the darkness.

"It is not our place to judge, Teragani," said the second man, coldly.

"It certainly is, Tazim," Cemal cut in. "If our Mentor has gone mad, I want to know about it."

The old man had come close, and they became aware of him.

"Hush, Cemal," said Tazim. Turning to greet the newcomer, he said, *"Masa'il kher."*

The old man's voice was as dry as a dead leaf. "Water," he said.

Teragani stood and passed him a small gourd which he had dipped in a water jar next to him.

"Sit. Drink," said Cemal.

"Many thanks," said the old man.

The others watched him as he drank quietly.

"What brings you here, old man?" asked Tazim, after their guest had drunk his fill.

The stranger thought for a moment before he spoke. Then he said, "Pity Abbas, but do not mock him. He has lived as an orphan most of his life and been shamed by his family's legacy."

Tazim looked shocked at this statement, but Teragani smiled quietly. He stole a glance at the old man's hand and saw that his left-hand ring finger was missing. So, unless it was an extraordinary coincidence, the man was an Assassin. Teragani looked covertly at the lined, gaunt face. There was something familiar about it . . .

"Abbas is desperate for power because he is power-*less*," the old man continued.

"But he is our Mentor!" Tazim cried. "And, unlike Al Mualim or Altaïr Ibn-La'Ahad, he never betrayed us!"

"Nonsense," Teragani said. "Altaïr was no traitor." He looked at the old man keenly. "Altaïr was driven out—unjustly."

"You don't know what you speak of!" stormed Tazim, and, rising, he strode off into the darkness.

The old man looked at Teragani and Cemal from beneath his cowl but said nothing. Teragani looked at the face again. Most of it was shaded by the hood, but the eyes could not be hidden. And Teragani had noticed that the man's right cuff just failed to conceal the harness of a hidden-blade.

The Assassin spoke tentatively. "Is it . . . Is it—you?" He paused. "I heard rumors, but I did not believe them."

The old man gave the ghost of a smile. "I wonder if I might speak with Abbas myself. It has been a long time."

Cemal and Teragani looked at each other. Cemal drew in a long breath. He took the old man's gourd from him and refilled it, handing it back to him with reverence. He spoke awkwardly. "That would be impossible. Abbas employs rogue *Fedayeen* to keep us from the inner sanctum of the castle, these days."

"Less than half the fighters here are true Assassins now," added Teragani. He paused, then said: "Altaïr."

The old man smiled and nodded, almost imperceptibly. "But I can see that the true Assassins remain just that—*true*," he said.

"You have been away a long time, Mentor. Where did you go?"

"I traveled. Studied. Studied deeply. Rested. Recovered from my losses, learned to live with them. In short, I did what anyone in my position would have done." He paused, and his tone altered slightly as he went on: "I also visited our Brothers at Alamut."

"Alamut? How do they fare?"

Altaïr shook his head. "It is over for them now. The Mongols under Khan Hulagu overran them and took the fortress. They destroyed the library. The Mongols range ever westward like a plague of locusts. Our only hope for now is to reaffirm our presence here and in the west. We must be strong here. But perhaps our bases from now on should be among the people, not in fortresses like Masyaf."

"Is it really you?" asked Cemal.

"Hush!" Teragani interrupted. "We do not want to get him killed."

Cemal suddenly tensed. "Tazim!" he said, suddenly worried.

Teragani grinned. "Tazim is more bark than bite. He likes an argument for its own sake more than anything else in the world. And he has been as dispirited as us, which hasn't helped his mood. Besides, he left before this little play reached its denouement!" He turned to Altaïr, all trace of his former despondency gone. "We clearly have work to do."

"So," said the old man, "where do I begin?"

Cemal looked again at Teragani. They both rose and

pulled their hoods up over their heads. "With us, Altaïr," he said.

Altaïr smiled and rose in his turn. He got up like an old man, but once he was on his feet, he stood firm.

FIFTY-FIVE

They walked toward the castle together.

"You say these men are cruel," said Altaïr. "Has any man raised his blade against an innocent?"

"Alas, yes," Cemal replied. "Brutality seems to be their sole source of pleasure."

"Then they must die, for they have compromised the Order," said Altaïr. "But those who still live by the creed must be spared."

"You can put your trust in us," said Cemal.

"I am sure of it. Now—leave me. I wish to reconnoiter alone, and it is not as if I am unfamiliar with this place."

"We will remain within call."

Altaïr nodded and turned to face the castle gates as his two companions fell back. He approached the entrance, keeping to the shadows, and passed the sentries without difficulty, thinking with regret that no true Assassin sentries would have let him slip by so easily. He hugged the walls of the outer bailey, skirting them until he was able to cross to a torchlit guard post not far from the gates of the inner, where he saw two captains engaged in conversation. Altaïr paused to listen to them. After a few words had been exchanged, he knew them to be men loyal to Abbas. Abbas! Why, thought Altaïr, had he shown the man mercy? What suffering might have been avoided if he had not! But then, perhaps, after all, mercy had been Abbas's due, whatever the cost of it.

"You've heard the stories going around the village?" said the first officer.

"About Abbas and his nightmares?"

"No, no—" the first man dropped his voice. "About Altaïr."

"Altaïr? What?"

"People are saying that an old Assassin saved the life of a merchant, down in the valley. They say he fought with a hidden-blade."

The second officer shook his head, dismissively. "Rumors. I don't believe a word of it."

"True or not, say nothing to Abbas. He is sick with suspicion."

"If Altaïr is anywhere in these parts, we should act first—seek him out and kill him, like the vile old cur he is. He will only spread discontent like he did before, making each man responsible for his decisions. Under-mining the authority that has made Abbas great."

"An iron fist. That is all anyone understands."

"You are right. No order without control."

Altaïr had taken his time to assess the situation. He knew that Cemal and Teragani were somewhere in the shadows behind him. The two officers seemed to be all that stood between him and the inner bailey, and their speech had proved them to be sworn to Abbas's doctrines—doctrines that had far more to do with Templar thinking than that of true Assassins.

He coughed, very gently, and moved into the pool of light.

The two officers turned on him.

"Who the hell are you?"

"Clear out, old man, if you know what's good for you."

The first to speak laughed harshly. "Why don't we just cut him down where he stands? The pigs will be glad of the extra meal."

Altaïr did not speak. Instead, he extended his left hand, palm toward them, so that they could see that his ring finger was missing.

They took a step back, simultaneously drawing their scimitars. "The usurper returns!" barked the second captain.

"Who'd have thought it? After so long."

"What brings you back?"

"A dog returning to its vomit."

"You talk too much," said Altaïr. With the economical

movements an old man must learn, but with none of an old man's slowness, he unleashed his hidden-blade as he stepped forward and lunged—once, twice—with deadly accuracy.

He moved on toward the gates of the inner bailey, still wary, and his caution paid off. He saw a third captain standing by them and was just in time to duck out of sight before the man could notice him. As he watched, he heard a faint yell behind him, and, from the darkness, a young Assassin came sprinting toward the officer. He whispered something to him, and the captain's eyes went wide in surprise and anger. Clearly, the bodies of the corrupt Assassins Altaïr had just dispatched had already been discovered, and his own presence would doubtless no longer be a secret. Swiftly, Altaïr exchanged his hidden-blade for the spring-loaded pistol, which he had developed from designs during his studies in the East.

"Send him a message, quickly!" the captain was ordering his young henchman. He raised his voice. "Assassins of the Brotherhood of Abbas! To me!"

Altaïr had stood, quietly weighing his options, when from close to his elbow a friendly voice said: "Mentor!"

He turned to see Cemal and Tergani. With them were half a dozen fellow Assassins.

"We could not prevent the discovery of those captains you killed—two of the cruelest in the band, who would never has risen to rank under anyone save Abbas," Cemal explained quickly. "But we have brought reinforcements. And this is only a start."

"Welcome." Altaïr smiled.

Cemal smiled back. Behind him, the little detachment of true Assassins raised their hoods, almost in unison.

"We'd better shut him up," said Teragani, nodding toward the blustering third captain.

"Allow me," said Altaïr. "I need the exercise."

He stepped forward to confront the rogue Assassin officer. By then, a number of the man's own renegade soldiers had rushed to his aid.

"There he is!" yelled the captain. "Kill him! Kill all the traitors!"

"Think before you act," said Altaïr. "Every action has its consequences."

"You pathetic miser! Stand down or die!"

"You could have been spared, friend," said Altaïr, as his supporters stepped out of the shadows.

"I am not your friend, old man," retorted the captain, and rushed Altaïr, slicing at him with his sword before the old Mentor seemed fully ready.

But he was ready. The conflict was short and bloody. At the end of it, the captain and most of his men lay dead under the gates.

"Follow me to the castle keep," cried Altaïr. "And spill no more blood if you can help it. Remember the true Code."

But now, at the portal to the inner bailey, another captain stood, in his black and dark grey robes, the Assassin emblem glinting on his belt in the torchlight. He was an older man, of perhaps some fifty summers.

"Altaïr Ibn-La'Ahad," he said in a firm voice that

knew no fear. "Two decades have passed since we last saw you within these walls. Two decades which, I see, have been kinder to your face than they have been to our decrepit Order." He paused. "Abbas used to tell us stories . . . About Altaïr the arrogant. Altaïr the deceiver. Altaïr the betrayer. But I never believed these tales. And now I see here, standing before me, Altaïr the Master. And I am humbled."

He stepped forward and extended his arm in friendship. Altaïr took it in a firm grasp, hand gripping wrist, in a Roman handshake. A number of Assassin guards, clearly his men, ranged themselves behind him.

"We could use your wisdom, great Master. Now, more than ever."

He stood back and addressed his troops: "Our Mentor is returned!"

The soldiers sheathed their drawn weapons and raised their hoods. Joining forces with Altaïr's existing group of loyal Assassins, they made their way toward the dark-towered keep of Masyaf.

FIFTY-SIX

But hardly were they within the confines of the inner bailey than Abbas himself appeared, behind a detachment of rogue Assassins. Abbas, recognizable still, but an old man, too, with sunken eyes and hollow cheeks—a haunted, frightened, driven man.

"Kill him!" bellowed Abbas. "Kill him now!"

His men hesitated.

"What are you waiting for?" Abbas screamed at them, his voice cracking as it strained.

But they were frozen with indecision, looking at their fellows standing against them and at each other.

"You fools! He has bewitched you!"

Still nothing. Abbas looked at them, spat, and disappeared within the keep.

There was still a standoff, as Assassin confronted Assassin. In the tense silence, Altaïr raised his left hand—the one maimed at his initiation into the Brotherhood.

"There is no witchcraft here," he said simply. "Nor sorcery. Do as your conscience bids. But death has stalked here too long. And we have too many *real* enemies—we can't afford to turn against each *other*."

One of Abbas's reluctant defenders doffed her cowl and stepped forward, kneeling before Altaïr. "Mentor," she said.

Another quickly joined her. "Welcome home," she added.

Then a third: "I fight for you. For the Order."

The others quickly followed the example of the three women Assassins, greeting Altaïr as a long-lost brother, embracing their former opponents in fellowship again. Only a handful still spat insults and retreated after Abbas into the keep.

Altaïr, at the head of his troop, led the way into the keep itself. They stopped in the great hall, looking up to where Abbas stood at the head of the central staircase. He was flanked by rogue Assassins loyal to him, and spearmen and archers ranged the gallery.

Altaïr regarded them calmly. Under his gaze, the rogue Assassins wavered. But they did not break.

"Tell your men to stand down, Abbas," he commanded.

"Never! I am defending Masyaf! Would you not do the same?"

"Abbas, you corrupted everything we stand for and

lost everything we gained. All of it sacrificed on the altar of your own spite."

"As you," Abbas spat back. "You have wasted your life staring into that accursed Apple, dreaming only of your own glory."

Altaïr took a step forward. As he did so, two of Abbas's spearmen stepped forward, brandishing their arms.

"Abbas—it is true that I have learned many things from the Apple. About life and death, and about the past and the future." He paused. "I regret this, my old comrade, but I see that I have no choice but to demonstrate to you one of the things I have learned. Nothing else will stop you, I see. And you will never change now and see the light that is still available to you."

"Kill the traitors!" Abbas shouted in reply. "Kill every one of them and throw their bodies onto the dung-hill!"

Abbas's men bristled, but held off their attack. Altaïr knew that there was no turning back now. He raised his gun arm, unleashed the pistol from its harness, and, as it sprang into his grip, aimed and fired at the man who, seven decades earlier, had, for a short time, been his best friend.

Abbas staggered under the blow of the ball as it struck him, a look of disbelief and surprise on his wizened features. He gasped and swayed, reaching out wildly for support, but no one came to his aid.

And then he fell, crashing over and over down the long stone staircase, to come to rest at Altaïr's feet. His legs had broken in the fall and stuck out at crazy angles from his body.

But he was not dead. Not yet. He managed to raise himself painfully, high enough to hold his head up, and look Altaïr in the eye.

"I can never forgive you, Altaïr," he managed to croak. "For the lies you told about my family, my father. For the humiliation I suffered."

Altaïr looked down at him, but there was only regret in his eyes. "They were not lies, Abbas. I was ten years old when your father came to my room, to see me. He was in tears, begging to be forgiven for betraying *my* family." Altaïr paused. "Then he cut his own throat."

Abbas held his enemy's eye but did not speak. The pain in his face was that of a man confronting a truth he could not bear.

"I watched his life ebb away at my feet," Altaïr went on. "I shall never forget that image."

Abbas moaned in agony. "No!"

"But he was not a coward, Abbas. He reclaimed his honor."

Abbas knew he had not much longer to live. The light in his eyes was already fading as he said: "I hope there is another life after this. At least then I shall see him, and know the truth of his final days . . ."

He coughed, the movement racking his body, and when his breath came again as he strove to speak, the rattle was already in it. But when he found his voice, it was firm, and it was unrepentant.

"And when it is your time, O Altaïr, then, then we will find you. And then there will be no doubts."

Abbas's arms collapsed, and his body slumped to the stone floor.

Altaïr stood over him in the silence that surrounded them, his head bowed. There was no movement but that of the shadows stirred by the flickering torchlight.

FIFTY-SEVEN

When Ezio came to himself, he feared that the dawn would have broken, but he saw only the palest shades of red in the sky to the east, and the sun had not yet even breached the low brown hills of Asia, which lay in the distance beyond the city.

Weary, worn-out by his experience, he made his way first to the Assassins' headquarters, to give the key into the safekeeping of Azize. Then, his legs aching under him, he made his way almost instinctively to Sofia's shop. It would be early still, but he'd ring the bell until she awoke in her apartment above it, and he hoped she'd be pleased to see him—or at least, the new addition to her library. But he was frankly too tired to care whether she'd be excited or not. He just wanted to lie down and sleep. Later on, he knew, he had a rendezvous with Yusuf at the Spice Market, and he had to be fresh for that.

He was also impatient for news of his ship—the one that would take him to Mersin, from whence he'd journey north into Cappadocia. And that journey, he knew, would require all the strength he could summon up.

The Spice Market was already crowded by the time Ezio reached it, though he had contented himself with a mere two hours' rest. Ezio shouldered his way through the people milling around the stalls until, a few yards ahead of him, he saw a thief in the act of grabbing a large, stiff bag of spices, giving the elderly trader who tried to stop him a vicious shove as he made his getaway.

By luck, the thief ran in Ezio's direction, snaking his way through the mob with extraordinary agility. But as he came abreast of Ezio, the Assassin tripped him up neatly with his hookblade. The thief dropped the sack as he fell and glared up at Ezio, but one look from his attacker made him drop any thought of retaliation, and, picking himself up, he vanished into the crowd as fast as a rat into its hole.

"Thank you, *efendim*," said the grateful trader, as Ezio handed his bag back to him. "Saffron. You have spared me a great loss. Perhaps you will accept . . . ?"

But Ezio had spotted Yusuf in the crowd, and, after shaking his head and smiling briefly at the trader, he made his way over to his lieutenant.

"What news?" he said as he reached him.

"We have had word—very discreetly—that your ship

is ready to sail," said Yusuf. "I did not know that you planned to leave us."

"Is nothing I do a secret?" Ezio answered, laughing lightly but glad to hear that Suleiman had kept his word.

"The young prince's spies are almost as good as our own," replied Yusuf. "I expect he sent word to me because he knew you were . . . otherwise engaged."

Ezio thought back to the two hours he had spent with Sofia and was glad that he had managed to have them since now he did not know when he would see her again—*if* he would see her again. And still he had not dared tell her of the feelings that were growing within him and would no longer be denied. Could it really be that his long wait for love was finally coming to an end? If it was, it would have certainly been worth it.

But he had other, more immediate things on his mind.

"We had hoped to have had your broken hidden-blade repaired by now," Yusuf went on. "But the only armorer skilled enough to do the work is in Salonica and will not return until next month."

"Keep the blade, and when it is repaired, add it to your own armory," said Ezio. "In exchange for my hook-blade. It is more than a fair trade."

"I am glad you appreciate its qualities. I just watched you deal with that thief, and I think you have more than mastered its use."

"I could not have done without it."

The two men grinned at each other, but then Ezio's expression became serious. "I hope, though, that my intended voyage is not common knowledge."

Yusuf gave a little laugh. "Not to worry, brother. The captain of your ship is a friend, and already known to you."

"Who, then?"

"Piri Reis. You are honored." Yusuf paused, troubled now. "But neither of you is going anywhere just yet."

"What do you mean?"

"The Janissaries have raised the chain across the mouth of the Golden Horn and ordered a full blockade until you are caught." Yusuf paused. "Until that chain is down, nothing sails in or out."

Ezio felt rather proud. "You mean they raised the chain for me?"

Yusuf was amused. "We will celebrate later. Here—I have something for you."

Drawing Ezio into a discreet alcove, he produced a bomb and carefully handed it over. "Treat this with respect. It has fifty times the kick of our usual bombs."

"Thank you. And you had better gather your people. This will attract some attention."

"Here are two smoke bombs. You may find them useful, too."

"*Bene*. I know what to do."

"I'm sure. The suspense is palpable," joked Yusuf.

"I'll take the tower on the south bank. It's closer."

"I'll join you at the quay and point your ship out to you. *Sinav icin iyi sanslar!*"

Ezio grinned. "Good luck to you, too, my friend."

Yusuf was about to go when Ezio stopped him.

"Yusuf, wait. *Un favore*."

"Yes?"

"There is a woman running a bookshop at the old Polo trading post . . . Sofia. Look out for her. She is a remarkable lady."

Yusuf gave him a keen look, then said, seriously. "You have my word."

"Thank you. And now—we have work to do."

"The sooner the better!"

Placing the bomb carefully in his side pouch, and hooking the smoke bombs onto his belt, Ezio swapped his left-hand hidden-blade for his pistol and immediately hastened north toward the tower opposite Galata, on the south side of the Horn. The great chain was suspended between the two banks.

There, Yusuf joined him. "My archers are in place. They'll cover your escape," he said. "Now—look—there, in the outer harbor. The red dhow with the furled white sail and the silver pennant? That is Piri's ship. It is crewed and ready. He is waiting for you."

There was an open area around the tower, surrounded by ramparts and two smaller watchtowers from the tops of which taut haulage ropes led down to jetties and the western and eastern extremities of the area. At the outer point of one of them, Ezio noticed a weapon emplacement. A massive squitatoria, a flamethrower for Greek fire, stood primed, heated, and ready for action, manned by a crew of three.

Around the tower itself stood a number of Ottoman

guards. Ezio would have to put all of them out of commission before he'd be able to place the bomb, and he
thanked Yusuf silently for the smoke bombs. There was
nowhere to take cover, so he moved in boldly and quickly
for a frontal attack.

As soon as the guards saw him, a hue and cry was
raised, and they massed to fall on him. He stood his
ground, letting them approach but drawing his scarf
closely over his nose and mouth and pulling his hood
low over his eyes.

As soon as they were within range, he pulled the
pins on both bombs and threw them to the right and left
among the guards. They detonated instantly, and dense
grey smoke billowed out, encompassing the guards in a
moment. Diving into the confusion, Ezio, eyes narrowed
against the acrid fumes, drew his scimitar and with it cut
down all the defenseless soldiers as they staggered about,
disoriented by the unexpected fog that suddenly surrounded them. He had to act quickly, for the light wind
blowing in from the Bosphorus would soon disperse the
smoke, but he succeeded, and placed the bomb on a
ledge at the base of the tower, just beneath the first
huge links of the chain, which rose above his head to
the winch room inside. Then he took a good few steps
back toward the water's edge and from there unleashed
his pistol and fired at the bomb, igniting it, then instantly diving for cover behind a large iron bollard on
the quay.

The explosion was immense. Grime and stones were

thrown everywhere as the colossal chains snapped free of the tower and whiplashed over Ezio's head into the water, snapping ships' masts as they flew past. As Ezio watched, the tower itself shifted on its base. It shifted again, seeming to settle; but then it imploded, collapsing in a mass of broken brick and dust.

Moments later, a platoon of Janissaries rushed into the square, heading straight for Ezio, who by then had broken cover. He dodged past them and used his hookblade to scale the eastern watchtower, knocking out the guard at its top when he reached it and hooking himself to the rope leading from it down to the jetty on which the squitatoria was placed. As he prepared to effect a zipline, he saw the Janissaries fitting arrows to their bows, but before they had time to take aim and fire, they themselves were cut down by a hail of arrows that rained down on them from Assassin bows. More Assassins rushed into the area around the ruined tower, skipping lightly over the debris to engage with the Janissaries who'd survived the first onslaught.

Among them was Yusuf. Looking up, he yelled to Ezio, "Remember—the red dhow! And the ships between you and it are armed—they'll stop you from sailing if they can."

"I'll take care of them," Ezio called back, grimly.

"And we'll clear the docks!"

Ezio let the rope take his weight on the hookblade and kicked off from the watchtower, zooming down to the flamethrower emplacement and leaping off just before he reached it, throwing himself at the nearest of the crew, who were preparing to turn their weapon on the Assassins fighting by the tower. The first he knocked into the water, where the man was crushed between the shifting hulls of two moored barges. The others he swiftly dispatched with his hookblade.

He scanned the flamethrower, quickly acquainting himself with its mechanism. It was on a swivel base, operated by a crank at the left-hand side. The cannon itself was made of brass, its mouth in the shape of a lion's head, from which the end of the bronze tube within projected slightly. On its edge it was a flint that could be sparked by the trigger mechanism, which also released the pressurized oil vapor that would be shot from the heated vat in the base of the weapon.

He heard a voice coming to him from the melee near the broken tower. It was Yusuf. "That's it! Get the ships with Greek fire," he was yelling. "I like the way you think, Ezio!"

Across the Horn, on the north bank, the Ottoman Guard were bringing up two cannon, which they trained on the Assassins fighting near Ezio. Soon afterward, as Ezio was cranking round and training the flamethrower on the nearest ships, he saw the puffs of smoke from the cannon mouths, then heard the *crump* of their detonations. The first cannonball fell into the water, short of where he was, but the second smashed into the jetty, making it lurch dangerously.

But it did not collapse.

Ezio steadied himself and pressed the trigger. With a loud roar, a long tongue of flame instantly shot forth, and he played it across the yards and decks of the three ships riding between him and Piri's dhow. The fire he'd set sprang up in a moment. Ezio kept pressing the trigger until all the oil in the tank was used up, then, abandoning the weapon, he leapt down onto one of the barges riding beneath the jetty, sprinting its length and vaulting from it to catch hold of the outer gunwale of the first burning ship, hauling himself up onto the deck with his hookblade and there managing to fight off two desperate sailors who came toward him with belaying pins. He scaled the foremast from the burning deck and was just in time to zipline down a yard and hurl himself from it onto the second ship in line before the mast behind him snapped in the fire and collapsed in a chaos of flame onto the deck of the ship he'd just left.

The second ship, too, was burning fiercely, and beginning to sink at the after end. He ran toward the prow, pushing aside a handful of panicking mariners, and ran along its bowsprit to leap from there to the third ship, less damaged than the first two, where the crew was preparing to turn their cannon onto the red dhow, now only twenty yards distant. To Ezio's alarm, he saw Piri shouting orders to make sail, and his sailors were letting out the sheets frantically, in order to catch the wind and get out of firing range.

Ezio raised his voice and called for aid from the Brotherhood, but when he looked around, he saw that a number of his fellow Assassins had already followed his perilous route and were right behind him, ready to pounce.

Between them, they set on the gun crews, and a fierce and bloody skirmish followed, leaving several Assassins and all the mariners on the blockade ship dead. On the red dhow, Piri had raised an arm to halt operations and was bellowing to Ezio to make haste though his voice was lost in the tumult over the cannon.

But at last, Ezio stood at the gunwale of the blockade ship. He used his crossbow to fire a line over to the dhow, which Piri's crew secured, then he ziplined across the choppy water.

Behind him, the surviving Assassins waved their farewell before taking to the doomed ship's boats and making for the shore.

Ezio saluted back, catching his breath and wheezing a little. He flexed his joints, which were just a little stiff. Then he was surrounded by a handful of Piri's men, who checked him over for wounds and conducted him to the wheelhouse, where Piri stood before the now-fully-unfurled foresail.

"You took your time," said Piri Reis with a broad grin that was not unmixed with concern.

"Yes. Sorry for the delay."

The men at the prow were already hauling up the anchors, and, moments later, the dhow picked up the wind and made its way, gingerly but unimpeded, past rows of burning blockade ships—the wind that carried them forward had also seen to it that the fire started by Ezio had spread, and the ships had been anchored too close together for safety.

"Lucky I was upwind of that lot," Piri said. "But I expect you noticed that from the beginning."

"Naturally," Ezio said.

"Well," said Piri, as the red dhow eased out of the Horn and into the Bosphorus, steering a southbound course. "This should be an interesting trip."

PART II

The sounds I heard brought back into my mind
the same impression that we often get
when organs play, accompanying a voice.
Now, yes, we hear the words; now, no we don't.

—DANTE, *PURGATORIO*

FIFTY-EIGHT

At Mersin, Ezio took his leave of the Turkish admiral. The sun sparkled on the sea.

"May Allah protect you, my friend," said the seafarer.

"My thanks, Piri Reis."

"I will await your return here. But I cannot stay forever."

"I know."

"Will you not take some of my men with you?"

"No—it is best that I travel alone."

"Then at least allow me to arrange a horse for you. You will travel faster, and more safely."

"I will be grateful for that."

"You are a brave man, Ezio Auditore, and a worthy follower of the great Mentor, Altaïr."

"You do me too much honor." Ezio looked inland, his face set. "If I have not returned within two courses of the moon . . ."

Piri Reis nodded, gravely. "Go with whichever God guides you," he said, as they shook hands in farewell.

The two-week voyage was followed by a further two-week trek north, first across the Taurus Mountains, then, after breaking his journey at Nigde, between the Taurus and the Melendiz ranges, on north again through the low brown hills to Derinkuyu, where Ezio knew Manuel Palaiologos's rebel army was massing.

He broke his journey again in the grim little village of Nadarim, within sight of the city that was his goal. The foulness of the place contrasted with the beautiful countryside in which it was situated. Few people were about, as it was just before dawn, and the few who were eyed Ezio warily as he rode into the central square, which was flanked on one side by a church.

There was no sign of any military activity, and Ezio, after having stabled his horse, decided to scale the church's bell tower, to get a better view of Derinkuyu itself.

He peered through the lightening sky with eagle eyes, scanning the low buildings that comprised the not-far-distant city, a few spires piercing its profile. But there was no obvious sign of any garrison there either.

But, as he knew, there could be a reason for that.

He descended again. The square was deserted, and

Ezio was immediately on his guard. His intention had been to ride on, but now he wondered if it would be safe to retrieve his horse. His suspicions mounted as he spied a figure lurking in the shadows of the neglected church walls. He decided to approach.

As he did so, the figure spun round to face him, brandishing a dagger. It was a young woman. Tough, wiry, tanned. Almost feral.

"Not so close, *adi herif*!" she growled.

Ezio raised his hands. "Who are you calling a pig?" he asked, calmly. He saw doubt flicker in her eyes.

"Who are you? One of Manuel's scum?"

"Easy, now. Tarik sent me."

The girl hesitated, then lowered her blade. "Who are you?"

"Auditore, Ezio."

She relaxed some more. "We had word from the young prince," she said. "As we had news of Tarik's end. A bad business, and just when he was so close. I am Dilara," she added. "Tarik's principal agent here. Why have they only sent you? Why not more? Did they not get my reports in Kostantiniyye?"

"I am enough." Ezio looked around. "Where are your people?"

Dilara spat. "Captured by Byzantines over a week ago. I was dressed to look like a slave and managed to escape. But the others . . ." She trailed off, shaking her head. Then darted him a glance. "Are you a capable fighter?"

"I like to think so."

"When you've made up your mind, come and find me. In the town, over there. I'll be waiting by the west gate to the underground city."

She flashed her teeth at him and whisked away, fast as a lizard.

FIFTY-NINE

Ezio equipped himself with his pistol on his left wrist, his hidden-blade on his right, and a brace of smoke bombs clipped to his belt. He kept the hookblade in his pack.

He found Dilara waiting at the appointed place two hours later. The gate she had mentioned was large, iron-bound, and shut.

She greeted him curtly and began without further preamble: "The Byzantines took my men into this cave system some days ago. From what I can tell, this gate is the least protected of the lot. Every so often, the soldiers bring refuse through here, but it is deserted most of the time."

"So—we sneak in, free your men, and lead them out through here?"

"Exactly . . ."

Ezio tried the door. It didn't budge. He turned to Dilara with a disappointed smirk, feeling sheepish.

"I was going on to say, after you unlock it from the inside," Dilara concluded, drily.

"Of course."

"Come with me."

She led the way to where they had sight of another, larger gate, made of a huge circular stone that could be rolled open and closed in a stone track. It opened as they watched. Soldiers emerged and formed ranks before marching off on patrol.

"The main entrance is there, at the foot of that hill. But it is well guarded."

"Wait here," said Ezio.

"Where are you going?"

"I need to get a feel for this place."

"You'll need a guide."

"Why?"

"It's a warren. You see those towers?"

"Yes."

"Ventilator shafts. And water conduits. There are eleven floors of the city, and they go down three hundred feet."

"I'll manage."

"You're an arrogant man."

"No. I am cautious. And I am not unprepared. I know this place was made by Phrygians fifteen hundred years ago, and I know a little of its geography."

"Then you'll also know what's down there: an underground river system at the very bottom, and above it, on ten more levels, churches, schools, shops, stores, stables even; and room for fifty thousand people."

"Big enough to conceal a garrison, in fact."

Dilara looked at him. "You'll need a guide," she repeated.

"I need somebody here."

"Then go with God," she said. "But be quick. As soon as the patrols have all come out, they'll roll the gate closed again. With luck, you'll be able to get in with the supply wagons over there. I'll wait by the west gate."

Ezio nodded and silently took his leave.

He blended in with the local Byzantine people, who seemed less than happy with the new military presence in their midst, and managed to pass through the gate, walking alongside an oxcart, without difficulty.

The torchlit interior illuminated yellowish beige walls of soft volcanic rock, besmirched with the soot of ages, and yet the air was fresh. The streets—if you could call the broad, grimy corridors that—were alive with soldiers and citizens, jostling one another as they went about their business, and Ezio made his way among them, penetrating ever deeper into the underground city's interior.

At last, on the second level belowground, he came upon a spacious hall, with a barrel-vaulted roof and decorated with faded frescoes. He made his way along one of the galleries and looked down on the figures in the main room twenty feet below him. The acoustic was good, and he was easily able to hear what the two men there were saying to one another.

He had recognized them immediately. The portly figure of Manuel Palaiologos, and the gaunt one of Shahkulu. Near them, a group of guards stood at attention. Ezio noted a broad tunnel leading off westward—possibly a route to the west gate Dilara had shown him earlier.

"How soon before my soldiers are trained to use those guns?" Manuel was asking.

"A few weeks at most," replied the dour Türkmeni.

Manuel looked thoughtful. "The main Janissary force will know I have betrayed them by now. But do they have the resources for retribution?"

"Doubtful. The sultan's war with Selim commands most of their attention."

Manuel began to laugh—but his laugh quickly turned to coughing and gagging. "Ah!" he gasped. "What the hell is that smell? Have the ventilators been blocked?"

"Apologies, Manuel. Perhaps the wind has changed. Some of the Ottoman prisoners we took a week or so ago turned out to be . . . so fragile. We had to put them somewhere after they met with their unfortunate . . . accident."

Manuel was almost amused by this but also worried. "Shahkulu, try to moderate your anger. I know that the sultan humiliated your people. But there is no need to spit on men who are below us."

"Humiliated my people!" Shahkulu shouted. "He tried to crush us as if we were so many roaches! That is why I sided with Ismail of Persia and took the name

'Shahkulu'—servant of the Shah. Under that name, I will prevail against whatever the Seljuks try to throw against the Turkmen people, and those of us who follow the Safavid, and the law of Shia."

"Of course, of course—but nevertheless, get rid of the evidence," said Manuel, taking his leave, a scented handkerchief pressed to his nose.

Shahkulu sullenly watched him go, then snapped his fingers at the remaining bodyguards. "You three— gather the corpses and dump them outside on the western dunghill."

The sergeant of the guard looked nervous. "Shahkulu, I don't have the key to the west gate," he stammered.

Shahkulu exploded with rage. "Then find it, idiot!" he bellowed, storming off.

Left alone, the guards looked at one another.

"Who has the key? Any idea?" said the sergeant, testily. He didn't like being called an idiot in front of his men, and he didn't like their smirks, either.

"I think Nikolos has it," said one of them. "He's on leave today."

"Then he'll be at the market on Level Three," put in the other soldier.

"Stuffing his face, no doubt," groused the first man. "*Hristé mou!* I'd like to run Shahkulu through with a spear!"

"Hey, hey!" said the sergeant severely. "Keep that to yourself, *edáxi*?"

Ezio barely heard the last words. He was already on his way to the market, one floor below.

SIXTY

Apart from the fact that its hall was deep underground, the market was much as any other—stalls selling meat, vegetables, spices—whose odors were everywhere, and even denser than they would have been in the open air— clothes, shoes—whatever the people needed. And there were little tavernas and wine shops. Near one of them, in an open space, a drunken scrap had broken out— evidently over a light-skinned whore, a bony older woman who sat elegantly on a chair at one of the wine- shop tables, clearly enjoying the spectacle.

A circle had formed around the two men who were throwing punches at one another, the bystanders egging them on with ragged shouts of encouragement. Ezio joined the circle's outer edges:

"Give him one!"

"Hit him!"

"Kill the bastard!"

"Is that all you've got?"

"Blood! Blood!"

"Mangle him!"

Among the watchers, most of whom were as drunk as the brawlers, was a fat, red-faced soldier with a scruffy beard and a receding chin, holding a wineskin and roaring along with the rest of them. Ezio had already noticed the unclasped leather wallet on his belt and could see the bow of a large iron key protruding from it. He glanced around and saw the three guards from the painted hall approaching through the market on the far side.

No time to lose. He sidled up to the fat soldier from behind and plucked the key from the wallet just as his fellow soldiers hailed him by name.

Nikolos would have a lot of explaining to do, thought Ezio, as he made his way back to the Second Level and the tunnel from which the stench had emanated—the tunnel which, he guessed, led to the west gate.

SIXTY-ONE

"You took your time," said Dilara in a harsh whisper, as Ezio unlocked the west gate from the inside and let her in.

"You're welcome," muttered Ezio, grimly.

But Dilara then did exactly as Ezio had expected, and retched, her hand shooting to her face. *"Aman Allahim!* What is that?"

Ezio stepped back and indicated a pile of dead bodies, stacked in a broad niche just inside the doorway. "Not everyone was taken prisoner."

Dilara rushed forward toward the heap, but then stopped short, staring. "Poor men! God keep them!"

Her shoulders dropped as her spirits sank. She seemed a little more human, under the fierce façade she maintained. "That Türkmeni renegade Shahkulu did this, I know," she continued.

Ezio nodded.

"I'll kill him!"

And she ran off. "Wait!" Ezio called after her, but it was too late. She was already gone.

Ezio set off after her and found her at last in a secluded spot overlooking a small public square. He approached with care. She had her back to him and was staring at something happening in the square, still invisible to him.

"You aren't very good at cooperation," he said as he came up.

She didn't turn. "I'm here to rescue what remains of my men," she said coldly. "Not to make friends."

"You don't have to be friends to cooperate," said Ezio, drawing closer. "But it would help to know where your men were, and I can help you find them."

He was interrupted by an anguished scream and hurried up to join the Turkish spy. Her face had hardened.

"Right there," she said, pointing.

Ezio followed the direction of her finger and saw, in the square, a number of Ottoman prisoners seated on the ground, their hands bound. As they watched, one of them was thrown to the ground by Byzantine guards. There was a makeshift gallows nearby, and from it another Ottoman hung from his wrists, with his arms bent behind him. Near him stood Shahkulu, instantly recognizable despite the executioner's mask he wore. The man screamed as Shahkulu delivered blow after blow to his body.

"It's Janos," Dilara said to Ezio, turning to him at last. "We must help him!"

Ezio looked closely at what was going on. "I have a gun, but I can't use it," he said. "The body armor he's wearing is too thick for bullets." He paused. "I'll have to get in close."

"There's little time. This isn't an interrogation. Shahkulu is torturing Janos to death. And then there'll be another. And another . . ."

She winced at each blow and each scream.

They could hear the laughter and the taunts of Shahkulu's men.

"I think I can see how we can do this," said Ezio. He unhooked a smoke bomb from his belt. "When I throw this, you go around to the right. See if you can start cutting the bonds of your men under cover of the smoke from this bomb."

She nodded. "And Shahkulu?"

"Leave him to me."

"Just make sure you finish the rat."

Ezio pulled the pin from the bomb, waited a moment for the smoke to start to gush, and threw it toward the gallows with a careful aim. The Byzantines thought they had made sure of all the opposition and were not expecting an attack. They were taken completely by surprise.

In the confusion, Ezio and Dilara bounded down the slope and into the square, splitting to right and left. Ezio shot down the first guard to come at him and smashed another's jaw with the bracer on his left forearm. Then he unleashed his hidden-blade and moved in fast toward Shahkulu, who'd drawn a heavy scimitar and was standing his ground, twisting to the left and right, unsure of where the attack would come from. The moment his attention was diverted, Ezio leapt at him and plunged his blade into the top of his chest between the jawline of the mask and his body armor. Dark blood bubbled forth around his fist as he kept the blade where it was.

Shahkulu fell, Ezio holding on to him and falling with him, ending up kneeling over the man, whose struggles were losing their violence. His eyes closed.

"Men who make a fetish out of murder deserve no pity," Ezio said, his lips close to the man's ear.

But then Shahkulu's eyes sprang open in a manic stare, and a mailed fist shot to Ezio's throat, gripping it tightly. Shahkulu started to laugh crazily. As he did so, the blood pumped out faster from his wound, and Ezio rammed the blade in harder and twisted it viciously as he did so. With a last spasm, Shahkulu thrust Ezio from him, sending him sprawling in the dust. Then his back arched in his death agony, a rattle sounded in his throat, and he fell back, inert.

Ezio picked himself up and cleaned his blade on Shahkulu's cloak. Dilara had already cut some of her men free and Ezio was in time to see her throw herself on the back of the last, fleeing Byzantine survivor, bringing him down and slicing his throat open in one clean movement. She jumped back from the kill, landing like a cat, and turned to her rescued troops.

Ezio gave Shahkulu's body a kick, to be sure, this

time, that he was dead. Dilara was pulling her men to their feet.

"Bless you, Dilara," said Janos, as she cut him down.

"Can you walk?"

"I think so."

Ezio came up. "Was yours the detachment that brought the guns for Manuel?"

She nodded.

"Then they must be destroyed."

She nodded again. "But most of them don't actually work. The gunpowder's real enough though—we couldn't fake that."

"Bene," said Ezio. He looked at the Ottomans standing round him. "Get yourselves out of sight until you hear the explosions, then run!"

"Explosions?" said Dilara. "If you do that, all hell will break loose. You will panic the entire city."

"I'm counting on that," replied Ezio. "The explosions will destroy whatever good guns there are, and as for the panic, it can only help us."

Dilara considered this. "All right. I'll take my men to a place of safety. But what about you?"

"After the explosions have gone off, I'm going after Manuel Palaiologos."

SIXTY-TWO

There were great vaults in the underground city—vast man-made caverns where the gunpowder and arms caches for Manuel's army were stored. A system of block-and-tackle pulley systems for transporting powder kegs on taut ropeways from one place to another had been set up, and, as Ezio watched from a vantage point in a gallery he had reached on the Fifth Level, he saw groups of Byzantine civilians engaged in just such activity, under the watchful eye of Manuel's renegade troops. It was a perfect opportunity, and he thanked God that their security was so slack. They were obviously confident that they were under no threat of attack, and he had moved too fast to be overtaken by the discovery of Shahkulu's corpse and those of his fellow torturers.

He'd replaced his hidden-blade with his hookblade and reloaded his pistol. He got in among a group of workers and watched as a barrel was maneuvered down one of the ropes, between two sets of blocks and tackle. Around them, hundreds of barrels were piled on top of one another, and along the walls, wooden crates of muskets were ranged.

"Steady, now! Steady!" an overseer was shouting. "This is gunpowder, not millet!"

"Got it!" a man operating a winch called back.

Ezio surveyed his surroundings, planning. If he could manage to start one explosion in such a way that it would lead to a chain reaction along the three warehouse vaults he knew there to be . . .

It might just work.

As he roved between the halls, blending in with the workers, he listened carefully to their conversation, to test their mood. And in doing so, he discovered that not all Byzantines were villains. As usual, it was just the ones whose egos were too big, who were too hungry for power, who were to blame for everyone else's misfortune.

"It could be worse, you know," one woman was saying to a male fellow worker.

"Worse? Worse than this?"

"Better the turban of the Turk than the tiara of the Pope. At least the Ottomans have some respect for our Orthodox Church."

"Shh-h! If anyone heard you . . . !" warned another woman.

"She's crazy!" The man turned to the first woman. "Listen to yourself!"

"OK, so I'm crazy. And if you prefer forced labor, living underground like a mole, then fine!"

The man considered this. "Well, it's certainly true that I don't want to go to war. I just want to feed my family."

Another man, an overseer dressed in Templar uniform, had overheard this, and put in, not altogether unsympathetically: "No one wants war, friend—but what can we do? Look at us! Look how we live! Those Turks took our land. Do you think we should just roll over without a fight?"

"No, no," said the first man to speak. "I just—I don't know. I'm just tired of this. We're all so tired of fighting!"

Amen to that, thought Ezio, as he slipped away between two twenty-foot-high tiers of barrels.

Once he was alone, he broached a barrel at ground level with the point of his scimitar and, after collecting a stream of powder in a leather pouch, laid a trail down the aisle between the rows of barrels to the entrance of the second hall. He did the same thing there, and in the third hall, until the trail reached the arched door leading out of it. Then he waited patiently until all the ordinary workers had moved out of harm's way for the night.

Only the guards remained.

Ezio made sure his retreat was assured, took up a

position a few yards from the exit, unleashed his pistol, and fired into the nearest barrel. Then he turned and ran.

The titanic serial explosions that followed rocked the foundations of the underground city like an earthquake. Ceilings crumbled and fell behind him as he fled. Everywhere, there was smoke, dust, rubble, and chaos.

SIXTY-THREE

Ezio reached the great chamber on the Second Level at about the same time as Manuel, who stumbled in, surrounded by a large force of crack guards. Ezio concealed himself behind a buttress, watched, and waited. He was going to finish things tonight if he could. And he'd seen that Manuel was holding the missing Masyaf key—the one the Templars had unearthed beneath the Palace of Topkapi. If he had that with him, then the would-be next emperor of Byzantium must be planning his escape.

"What the hell is going on?" bellowed Manuel, half in anger, half in fear.

"Sabotage, Manuel," said a Templar captain at his elbow. "You need to take cover."

A crowd of bawling, panicky people had filled one end

of the chamber by then. Ezio watched Manuel as he stuffed the key into a satchel he had slung around his corpulent body, and elbowed the Templar officer aside. "Get out of my way," he snapped.

He clambered up onto a podium and addressed the crowd, which Ezio joined, edging through the throng, ever closer to his quarry as Manuel spoke.

"Citizens!" Manuel said in a high voice. "Soldiers! Compose yourselves. Do not give in to fear! We are the true shepherds of Constantinopolis. We are the lords of this land. We are Byzantines!" He paused for effect, but if he'd hoped for applause, there was none. So he plowed on. "*Kouráyo!* Have courage! Stand fast! Do not let anyone break your—"

He broke off, as he noticed Ezio approaching. Some sixth sense must have triggered an alarm within him, for he swore sharply to himself and jumped nimbly from the podium, hurrying away toward an exit at the back of the hall, yelling to his bodyguards as he did so, "Stop that man! The tall one in the peaked hood! Cut him down!"

Ezio thrust his way through the confused mob and started off in pursuit of Manuel, dodging and knocking down Templar guards as he did so. At last he was free of them and risked a glance behind him. They were as confused as the townsfolk, looking in every direction but the one in which he'd gone, shouting challenges, barking orders, and running off determinedly before checking themselves. Manuel himself had scuttled off too fast for any of his men to have had time to follow him. Only Ezio's sharp eyes had not let him out of his sight.

For such a portly person, Manuel could certainly move. Ezio rushed down a long, dimly lit corridor-street, pausing only to glance down side turnings to assure himself that his quarry had not turned off; then he caught a glimpse, far up ahead, of a shimmering silk robe catching the torchlight as Manuel scrambled up a narrow stone stairway cut into the rock, ascending to the First Level. The man who would be king was seeking the quickest way out, his munitions gone and his army in complete disarray.

Ezio stormed after him.

He cornered him at last in an empty house, carved out of the living rock on the First Level. Manuel turned to face him with a curious smile playing on his lascivious lips.

"Are you here for the Masyaf key?" he asked. "Is that it? Have you come to rob us of two years of effort—to recover what the Assassins threw away?"

Ezio did not reply but eyed him warily. There was no telling what tricks this man might still have up his sleeve.

"You wage a losing battle, Assassin!" Manuel continued, though something of desperation was creeping into his voice. "Our numbers are growing, and our influence is expanding. We are hidden in plain sight!"

Ezio made a step closer.

"Stop and think for a moment," Manuel said, holding up a beringed hand. "Think about the lives you have disrupted today—the anarchy you have sown here! You! You take advantage of a poor and displaced people, using us to further your own vain quest! But we fight for

dignity, Assassin! We fight to restore peace to this troubled land."

"Templars are always quick to talk of peace," Ezio
replied. "But very slow to concede power."

Manuel made a dismissive gesture. "That is because
power begets peace. Idiot! It cannot happen in reverse.
These people would drown without a firm hand to lift
them up and keep them in line!"

Ezio smiled. "And to think you are the monster I
came here to kill."

Manuel looked him in the eye, and Ezio had the dis-
quieting impression that the man was resigned to his
fate. There was a curious dignity about the plump, dan-
dified figure, with his flashing jewels and his beautifully
tended mustache. Ezio unleashed his blade and stabbed
Manuel deep in the chest, finding himself helping the
man down as he sank to his knees. But Manuel didn't
fall. He supported himself on the back of a stone bench
and looked at Ezio calmly. When he spoke, his voice
sounded exhausted.

"I should have been Constantine's successor. I had so
many plans. Do you know how long I waited?"

"Your dream dies with you, Manuel. Your empire has
gone."

Though clearly in pain, Manuel managed to sound
amused. "Ah, but I am not the only one with this vision,
Assassin. The dream of our Order is universal. Ottoman,
Byzantine . . . these are only labels, costumes and fa-
çades. Beneath these trappings, all Templars are part of
the same family."

Ezio found himself losing patience, and he was aware of time passing. He was not out of there himself, yet. "Enough prattling. I am here for the Masyaf key."

He stooped and took the satchel Manuel still had slung round his shoulder. Manuel suddenly looked much older than his fifty-eight years. "Then take it," he said in pained amusement. "Take it and seek your fortune. See if you get within a hundred leagues of the Masyaf Archive before one of us finishes you off."

Then his whole body stiffened, and he stretched his arms as if waking from sleep, before pitching forward into a blackness without dimension and without sound.

Ezio looked at the body for a moment, thinking his own thoughts, then rifled swiftly through Manuel's satchel. He took nothing but the key, which he transferred to his own side pouch, throwing the satchel down by Manuel's side.

Then he turned to go.

SIXTY-FOUR

The upper levels of the underground city had been sealed off by Templar and Byzantine troops, loyal to their officers and unsure of what might happen next. It would not be long before Manuel's body was discovered, and Ezio decided that his best—and perhaps his only—means of escape would be by way of the underground river system that occupied the Eleventh Level of the complex.

The lower levels of the Derinkuyu were like a hell on earth. Smoke and fumes filled the underground streets, and fires had broken out in pockets on levels both below and above the warehouses where Ezio had destroyed Manuel's armory and munitions dump. Fallen ceilings and walls had blocked many routes, and Ezio had to make frequent detours. Several times, as he passed piles of rubble, he could see protruding from the debris the limbs of those crushed by collapsing stonework. He tried, and failed, to close his mind to the consequences of what he had done. Soldiers and citizens alike wandered about in a kind of daze, scarves and handkerchiefs pressed to their faces, eyes streaming. Ezio, himself fighting to breathe at times, doggedly pressed on downward by a series of ramps, corridors, and stairways cut into the rock, until he reached the lowest level of all.

It was clearer here, and the dank smell of water in a confined space had begun to reach him even as he arrived at the Ninth Level.

Because of the tumult and confusion caused by the explosions, Ezio had been able to pass through the city unmolested, and he stood alone on a jetty by an artificial underground lake. Far away to what he imagined must be the south, for it was difficult to keep one's bearings down there, he saw a glimmer of light where the river feeding the lake led away from it again toward the open air. It had to be a long way away and far downhill from the site of Derinkuyu, but Ezio had no time to ponder this, because, setting off from another jetty perhaps twenty yards distant, he saw a raft, manned by a half dozen Byzantine sailors. But it was the passenger who really caught Ezio's attention. An elegant, bearded man standing on the after deck.

Prince Ahmet Osman.

Ahmet had seen Ezio, too, and directed his oarsmen to make their way toward him. When he came within speaking range, he called mockingly to the Assassin.

"Poor Manuel. The last of the Palaiologi."

Ezio was too surprised to speak for a moment. Then
he said: "News travels fast."

"The Assassins aren't the only ones with spies." He
shrugged. "But I should not have left Manuel in charge
of our Masyaf expedition. He was an arrogant man.
Impossible to keep in line."

"You disappoint me, Ahmet. Why the Templars?"

"Well, Ezio—or should I keep up the pretense and
continue to call you 'Marcello'?—it is like this: I am
tired of all the pointless blood feuds that have pitted
father against son and brother against brother. To
achieve true peace, mankind must think and move as one
body, with one master mind." He paused. "The secrets
in the Grand Temple will give us just that. And Altaïr
will lead us to it."

"You delude yourself! Altaïr's secrets are not for you!
And you will never find the Grand Temple!"

"We'll see."

Ezio noticed that Ahmet was looking past him, and,
turning, he saw a number of Byzantine troops edging
toward where he stood on the jetty.

"In any case, I am not interested in arguing morals
and ethics with you, Assassin. I am here for the Masyaf
keys."

Ezio smiled mockingly and produced the key he had
just taken from Manuel, holding it up. "Do you mean to
say there are more than just this one?"

"So I have heard," replied Ahmet, urbanely. "But perhaps I should ask someone who may be even better

informed than you. Sofia Sartor. Have I got the name right?"

Ezio was immediately troubled though he tried not to let it show. "She knows nothing! Leave her be!"

Ahmet smiled. "We shall see."

He motioned to his men, who started to steer the raft away.

"I will kill you if you touch her."

"I know you'll try, my dear Ezio. But I doubt if you'll succeed." He raised his voice, addressing the men onshore. "Kill him now and get the key. Then bring it to me immediately."

"Won't you stay and watch the show?" said Ezio, coldly.

"I have far too much respect for my own safety," replied Ahmet. "I know your reputation, and I've seen an example of your work here today. Cornered, as you are, I imagine you're doubly dangerous. Besides, I detest violence."

The raft sailed off, leaving Ezio to face the Byzantine troops ranged against him. He considered his options.

But there were no options.

He was at the end of the jetty, with no means of retreat, and there was no way he could make an escape by swimming. There must have been twenty or thirty of them. Some carried muskets that had escaped his destruction of the warehouses. The captain of the detachment came close.

"Give us the key, *kyrie*," he said sarcastically. "I do not believe you have a choice."

Musketeers flanking him raised their weapons.

Ezio looked at them. This time he knew he was beaten. He had his pistol, capable of two shots at most, his hidden-blade, and his scimitar. But at the very moment even he could make his quickest move, the muskets would send their balls straight through him. Perhaps they'd fire anyway. It would be the simplest way to get the key. Maybe he'd have time to hurl it into the lake before he fell.

Ezio could only pray that Yusuf would never let the other four keys fall into Templar hands and that Sofia would be spared needless torture, for he had kept her ignorant of their whereabouts for safety's sake.

But he had clearly not been careful enough.

Well, everyone's road had to end somewhere.

The captain raised his hand, and the musketeers' fingers curled around their triggers.

SIXTY-FIVE

The muskets fired. Ezio threw himself flat on the jetty.

Arrows from behind and above them fell on the Byzantine soldiers like rain. In seconds, all Prince Ahmet's soldiers lay dead or wounded by the lake's edge.

One ball had seared Ezio's hood, but otherwise he was unscathed, and he thanked God that age hadn't slowed his reactions. When he got to his feet, it was to see Dilara standing at the other end of the jetty. From vantage points at the top of the stairway that led down to it, her men were descending, and those who'd already reached ground level were moving among the Byzantines, checking the dead and tending the wounded.

"Can't leave you alone for a minute," said Dilara.

"So it would seem," said Ezio. "Thank you."

"Get what you came for?"

"Yes."

"Then we'd better get you out of here. You've raised hell, you know."

"Looks like it."

She shook her head. "It'll take them years to recover from this. If they recover at all. But there's enough kick left in them to send you flying if they find you. Come on!"

She started back up the stairs.

"Wait! Should I take a boat out of here?"

"Are you mad? They'll be waiting for you where the river comes out into the open. It's a narrow gorge. You'd be dead meat in a moment, and I don't want to see my work here wasted."

Ezio followed her obediently.

They climbed back up through several levels, then took a street winding away to the south. The smoke there had cleared somewhat, and the people who were about were too preoccupied with putting out fires to pay them much attention. Dilara set a very brisk pace, and, before long, they'd arrived at a gateway similar to the one Ezio had opened on the west side of the city. Dilara produced a key and opened the ironclad wooden door.

"I'm impressed," said Ezio.

"So you should be. Tell them in Kostantiniyye that they can rest easy that their people here are doing a good job."

Ezio squinted against the sunlight that poured in through the door, which seemed blinding after the dimness of the underground city. But he saw a road winding away to the south, with the dismal little village of Nadarim hunched in its path.

"Your horse is saddled and freshly fed and watered in the stables there. Food and drink in the saddlebags. You can pick her up without danger. The village has been liberated, and they've already started whitewashing the buildings—Allah knows it needed cheering up, and now it's broken free of its oppressors," said Dilara, her nostrils flaring in triumph. "But get out of here now. It won't be long before news reaches Ahmet of what's happened. He won't dare come back himself, of course, but you can be sure he'll send someone after you."

"Has he got anyone left?"

Dilara smiled—a little tightly, but she did smile. "Go on, go. You should be able to make Nigde by the end of the week. You'll be back in Mersin by the full moon if nobody cuts you down on the way."

"Ahead of schedule."

"Congratulations."

"What about you?"

"Our work here isn't finished. In any case, we don't move without a direct order from Kostantiniyye. Give my regards to Tarik."

Ezio looked at her in grim silence for a moment, then said, "I'll tell them at the Sublime Porte how much they owe to you."

"You do that. And now I've got to get back to my men and reorganize. Your little fireworks display wrecked our headquarters, among other things."

Ezio wanted to say something more, but she had already gone.

SIXTY-SIX

The journey back to the coast was fast and mercifully uneventful.

"You're early," said Piri Reis, when Ezio appeared at the foot of the gangplank of the red dhow.

"And it's good that I am. We must return to Kostantiniyye as soon as possible."

"Do you have the fifth key?"

Ezio smiled and patted the pouch at his side.

"It is well," said Piri, returning his smile. "And Manuel?"

"Manuel will trouble us no more."

"Better and better. They will make you a *sövalye* at this rate."

"But the battle is far from won. We must make haste."

"The ship has to be victualed, and we must wait for a favorable tide. But we can deal with one while we attend the other." Piri turned and issued terse orders to the ship's master, who had joined them. "The crew will have to be rounded up as well. We did not expect you to finish your business at Derinkuyu quite so fast."

"I was fortunate in having extraordinarily good assistance."

"I have heard of the chief of spies put in place there by the Sublime Porte. Her reputation goes always before her," said Piri.

"Then I have reason to thank the Ottoman government."

"Under Bayezid, the Sublime Porte has become a model of practical administration. It is fortunate that it continues to operate unhindered by the squabbles of the Royal Family."

"Speaking of them, I think we must keep a careful eye on Ahmet," Ezio said quietly. "I have discovered that he has some very undesirable friends."

"The Assassins should not meddle in Ottoman affairs."

"These friends of Ahmet's make those affairs ours, too."

Piri raised an eyebrow but said no more on the subject. "Your cabin is ready for you," he said. "No doubt you will wish to rest until we are ready to sail."

*   *   *

Once alone, Ezio divested himself of his equipment and cleaned and honed his arms. Then, when all was in readiness, he secured the cabin door, took out the fifth key, and placed it on the foldaway table, seating himself before it. He was curious to see whether it would behave in the same way as the others. He needed to know what more of Altaïr it might impart, especially as he had no means of telling whether it had performed any kind of mystical revelation to the Templars who had first discovered it. What knowledge might it already have imparted to them? Or had it some power to know, as it were, when to speak and when to be silent?

His mind was troubled, too, by thoughts of Sofia, and he was impatient to be back in Constantinople. To protect her and to ensure the safety of the other four keys. But for the moment he had to force himself to be patient, for he was at the mercy of the sea and the wind.

This key was similar to the others—the exact diameter and proportion of its fellows, decorated, as they were, with strange, indecipherable symbols and rutted with precise but mysterious grooves. He braced himself and reached out to touch it. It did not disappoint him. Soon, the soft light of the cabin seemed to sink into further gloom, and, by contrast, the glow that began to emanate from the obsidian disc grew greater and greater . . .

SIXTY-SEVEN

As he was drawn into the scene—at one with it, and yet not part of it at all, Ezio knew that ten more years had passed since last he was at Masyaf. He watched and, as he watched, was lost in the events that unfolded . . .

The men stood in the sunlit inner bailey of Masyaf, under the shade of a spreading cinnamon tree of great age.

Altaïr, his skin like paper and his gaunt frame so shrouded in his clothes that only his face and his long, pale hands were visible, stood with two stocky Venetians in their early thirties. The older of the two wore a crest on his sleeve—a blue shield on which, in yellow, was a jug surmounted by a single chevron, over which three pentangle stars were set in a row, the whole topped by a

silver helm. A little way beyond where they were standing, a large number of Assassin warriors were in the process of preparing for battle.

The Mentor touched the man's sleeve in a familiar,
friendly way. His movements were performed in the
careful and precise manner of the very old, but there was
nothing of the feebleness you might expect in a man of
ninety-one winters, especially one from whom life had
exacted so much. "Niccolò," said Altaïr. "We have long
held the Polo family—you and your brother here—close
to our hearts, though our time spent together was, I
know, brief enough. But I have faith that this Codex,
which I now place in your hands, will answer the many
questions you have yet to ask."

Altaïr gestured to an aide, who stepped forward to
place a leather-bound volume in Niccolò Polo's hands.

"Altaïr," said the Italian. "This gift is . . . invaluable.
Grazie."

Altaïr nodded in acknowledgment as the aide handed
him a small bag. "So," he said, turning back to the elder
Polo brother, "where will you go next?"

"Maffeo and I will return to Constantinople for a
time. We intend to establish a guild there before returning to Venice."

Altaïr smiled. "Your son Marco will be eager to hear
his father's wild stories."

"At three, he is a little young for such tales. But one
day soon, indeed, he will hear them."

They were interrupted by the arrival of Darim, who
came rushing through the inner gate toward them.

"Father! A vanguard of Hulagu's Mongols has broken through! The village is threatened!"

So soon? Altaïr stiffened. His tone when he spoke again to Niccolò was urgent. "Niccolò—your cargo and provisions are waiting for you by the village gate. We will escort you there. Then you must make all speed."

"Thank you, Mentor."

Altaïr then turned to two Assassins who had detached themselves from the larger group, all now in full readiness for the battle ahead and already riding out.

"Prepare the catapults," he ordered, "and watch for my signal."

They bowed their assent and ran off to do as he bid.

"Stay close," Altaïr commanded the Polo brothers.

"We must make our way to the village immediately, Father," Darim said. "I think you had better remain with Niccolò and Maffeo. I will clear the path ahead."

"Take care, Darim. And keep an eye on the trebuchets." Altaïr looked over to where the massive sling-mounted catapults were being pulled into place by their crews.

Darim smiled. "If they hit me, they will hit a dozen Mongols at the same time."

"Khan Hulagu is not an enemy to be trifled with."

"We are ready for him."

Altaïr turned to his guests. "Come," he said.

They mounted the horses that had been readied for them and rode out of the fortress at an easy pace, taking a route well clear of the main battle, which had been joined on the slopes of the nearby foothills.

"Will you hold them?" asked Niccolò, unable to disguise the nervousness in his voice.

"For as long as necessary," Altaïr reassured him, calmly. "I envy you your journey," he continued. "Byzantium is a splendid city."

Niccolò smiled—a bit tightly, for he was more than a little aware of the danger they were in, however little mind Altaïr seemed to be making of it. But he'd been in tough corners before, and he knew what Altaïr was trying to do—make light of it. He played the game: "You prefer the ancient name, I see. Have you ever been there?"

"Long ago. When you Venetians diverted the Frankish Crusaders to attack it instead of Jerusalem."

"Constantinople was Venice's greatest trade rival then. It was a great coup."

"It opened Europe to the east in more ways than one."

"The Mongols will never get that far," said Niccolò, but his voice was nervous.

Altaïr didn't pick him up on that. Instead, he said, "That little conflict in 1204 prevented me from bringing the Creed to Europe."

"Well, with luck—and patience—we will finish what you started."

"If you have the chance, the view from the top of Haghia Sofia is the best in the city."

"How does one get to the top?"

Altaïr smiled. "With training and patience." He paused. "I take it that, when you get away from here, you won't try the overland route there? That you'll be sailing to Byzantium?"

"Yes—as the saying goes. We'll ride to Latakia and get a ship there. The roads in Anatolia are fogged by memories of the Crusades."

"Ah," said Altaïr, "the deepest passions can be the most deadly."

"Do visit us if you are able, Altaïr. We will have plenty of space for you and your entourage."

"No," said Altaïr. "Thank you, but that is no country for old men, Niccolò. I will stay here, as I always must now."

"Well, should you change you mind, our door is always open."

Altaïr was watching the battle. The trebuchets had been brought into play and found their range. The stones they were hurling into the Mongol ranks were wreaking havoc.

A rider detached himself from the main body of Assassin cavalry and came toward them at a gallop. It was Darim.

"We will rest briefly at the village," said Altaïr to him as he rode up. "You seem to have the enemy in check."

"But for how long, Father?"

"I have every faith in you. After all, you are not a boy any longer."

"I am sixty-two years old."

"You make me feel quite ancient," Altaïr joked. But Darim could see the pallor on his cheeks and realized how tired his father really was.

"Of course, we will rest, and see our friends off properly."

They rode round to the village stables, and the Polo brothers made haste to transfer their belongings to the packhorses provided for them, together with the two fresh mounts for their journey westward to the coast. Altaïr, finally able to rest, slumped a little and leaned against Darim for support.

"Father—are you hurt?" asked Darim in a voice of concern.

He escorted him to a bench under a tree.

"Give me a moment," panted Altaïr, reluctant to give in to the pain he felt. He sat heavily and took a breath, looking back to the castle. An aged man, he thought, was nothing but a paltry thing, like a tattered cloak upon a stick; but he had at least let his soul clap its hands and sing.

"The end of an era," he whispered.

He looked at his son, and smiled.

Then he took the bag the aide had handed him earlier and removed its contents. Five obsidian discs, intricately carved. He stacked them neatly. "When I was very young," he said, "I was foolish enough to believe that our Creed would bring an end to these conflicts." He paused. "If only I had possessed the humility to say to myself, I have done enough for one life. I have done my part."

With an effort, he rose to his feet.

"Then again, there is no greater glory than fighting to find the truth."

He looked across the village, and beyond it, to the battle. Niccolò Polo came up. "We are ready," he said.

"A last favor, Niccolò," said Altaïr, giving him the stone discs. "Take these with you and guard them well. Hide them, if you must."

Niccolò gave him a quizzical look.

"What are these—artifacts?"

"They are indeed artifacts of a kind. They are keys, each one of them imbued with a message."

Niccolò examined one closely. He was puzzled. "A message—for whom?"

Altaïr took the key in his hand. "I wish I knew . . ."

He raised the key high. It began to glow. He closed his eyes, lost in concentration.

SIXTY-EIGHT

Ezio once more became aware of where he was. The light in the cabin resumed its normal comfortable dimness. He smelled the cedarwood of its walls and fittings, saw the dust motes in the sunlight coming through the porthole, and heard the sounds of running feet on the decks, the cries of the sailors, and the creak of the yards as the sails were hoisted.

They were under way.

Out at sea, they once saw the sail of a Barbary pirate, which made both Ezio and Piri think of their old friend Al-Scarab, but the pirate ship stood off and did not attack them. For most of the fifteen-day voyage they were alone on the wine-dark, mackerel-crowded water, and Ezio spent his time vainly attempting to decipher the symbols on the key, wishing Sofia were there to help him, worrying about her safety, and becoming increasingly impatient to reach their goal.

But at last, the day dawned when the domes, the cloud-capped towers, the walls, bell towers, and minarets of Constantinople appeared low on the horizon.

"We'll be there by midafternoon," said Piri Reis.

"The sooner the better."

The port was as crowded as ever, though it was a humid and oppressive day, and siesta time. There was a particularly dense mob around a herald, who stood on a podium at the shore end of the main quay. He was attended by a squad of Janissaries in their flowing white robes. While the red dhow was unloading, Ezio walked over to listen to what the man had to say.

"Citizens of the Empire, and travelers from foreign lands, take heed! By order of the Janissaries, new restrictions now apply to all who travel to and from the city. I hereby give notice that a reward of ten thousand *akçe* will be given without question to anyone who brings in information that leads to the immediate arrest of the Assassin Auditore, Ezio."

Ezio looked back to Piri Reis and exchanged a glance with him. Piri came over discreetly.

"Make your best way out of here," he said. "Have you your key with you?"

"Yes."

"Then take your weapons and go. I'll take care of the rest of your gear."

Nodding his thanks, Ezio slipped discreetly through the crowd and into the town.

He made his way by an indirect route to Sofia's shop, checking every so often that he had not been followed or recognized. When he was close, he started to feel both relief and pleasurable anticipation. But when he turned the corner of her street, he was brought up short. The shop door stood wide open, a small crowd was gathered nearby, and a group of Yusuf's Assassins, including Dogan and Kasim, stood on guard.

Ezio crossed to them quickly, his throat dry. "What is going on?" he asked Kasim.

"Inside," said Kasim, tersely. Ezio saw that there were tears in his eyes.

He entered the shop. Inside, it looked much as it had been when he last left it, but on reaching the inner courtyard, his heart all but stopped at the sight which confronted him.

Lying across a bench, facedown, lay Yusuf. The hilt of a dagger protruded between his shoulder blades.

"There was a note pinned to his back by the dagger," said Dogan, who had followed him in. It's addressed to you. Here it is." He handed Ezio a bloodstained sheet of parchment.

"Have you read it?"

Dogan nodded.

"When did this happen?"

"Today. Can't have been long ago because the flies haven't really gathered yet."

Ezio, caught between tears and rage, drew the dagger from Yusuf's back. There was no fresh blood to flow.

"You have earned your rest, brother," he said, softly. *"Requiescat in Pace."* Then he unfolded the sheet. Its message, from Ahmet, was short, but its contents made Ezio seethe with rage.

More Assassins had entered the courtyard now, and Ezio looked from one to the other.

"Where is Sofia?" he said, through his teeth.

"We don't know where he has taken her."

"Anyone else missing?"

"We cannot find Azize."

"Brothers! Sisters! It seems as if Ahmet wishes the whole city to rise against us while Yusuf's murderer watches and waits in the Arsenal, laughing. Fight with me, and let us show him what it means to cross the Assassins!"

SIXTY-NINE

They made their way en masse to the Arsenal and there, in no mood to trifle, made short and brutal work of the Janissary guard loyal to Ahmet, who stood watch. Ahmet could not have been expecting such a sudden surprise attack, or he had underestimated both the fury and the strength of the Assassins, whose power had grown steadily under Yusuf's command.

Either that, or Ahmet believed he still held the trump cards, for when Ezio cornered him, he showed little sign of alarm.

Ezio, swept along by his rage, only managed to stop himself from killing the Ottoman prince at the very last moment, throwing him to the floor and gripping him by the throat, but then driving his hidden-blade furiously into the tiles, inches from Ahmet's head. With Ahmet dead, he'd have no means of rescuing Sofia. That much had been clear from the note. But for an instant, blood had clouded Ezio's judgment.

His face was close to the prince's. Ezio smelled the scent of violets on his breath. Ahmet returned his livid gaze calmly.

"Where is she?" Ezio demanded sternly.

Ahmet gave a light laugh. "Such wrath!" he said.

"Where—is—she?"

"My dear Ezio, if you think you are in a position to dictate terms, you may as well kill me now and be done with it."

Ezio did not release his grip for a moment, nor did he retract the hidden-blade; but seconds later, reason got the better of him, and he stood up, flexing his wrist so that the blade shot back into its harness.

Ahmet sat up, rubbing his neck, but otherwise remained where he was, still with a laugh in his voice. It was almost as if the prince were playing an enjoyable game, Ezio thought with a mixture of frustration and contempt.

"I am sorry it had to come to this," said Ahmet. "Two men who should be friends, quarreling over—what? The keys to some dusty old archive."

He got to his feet, dusting himself off, and continued: "We both strive toward the same end, *Messer* Auditore. Only our methods differ. Do you not see that?" He paused. Ezio could guess what was coming next. He'd heard the Templars' rationale of their dictatorial ambitions too often before. "Peace. Stability. A world where men live without fear. People desire the truth, yes, but even when they have it, they refuse to look. How do you fight this kind of ignorance?"

The prince's voice had grown vehement. Ezio wondered if he actually believed what he was spouting. He countered: "Liberty can be messy, *Principe*; but it is priceless." To himself, he thought: *Tyranny is always better organized than freedom.*

"Of course," Ahmet replied, drily. "And when things fall apart, and the lights of civilization dim, Ezio Auditore can stand above the darkness, and say proudly: 'I stayed true to my Creed.'" Ahmet turned away, bringing himself under control. "I will open Altaïr's archive, I will penetrate his library, and I will find the Grand Temple. And, with the power that is hidden there, I will destroy the superstitions that keep men divided."

"Not in this life, Ahmet," Ezio replied, evenly.

Ahmet snorted impatiently and made to leave. Ezio didn't attempt to stop him. At the door, the prince turned to him once more. "Bring the keys to the Galata Tower," he said. "Do this, and Sofia Sartor will be spared." He paused. "And do not delay, Ezio. My brother's army will be here before too long. When it arrives, everything will change. And I need to be ready for that."

With that, Ahmet left. Ezio watched him go, signaling to his men not to hinder him.

His thoughts were interrupted by a polite cough behind him. He turned—and saw Prince Suleiman standing before him.

"How long have you been here?" he demanded.

"Long enough. Behind that arras. I heard your conversation. But then, I've had my dear uncle followed closely ever since he returned from his little trip abroad. In fact, I've been keeping an eye on him ever since he tried to have me killed—an attempt you so usefully foiled with your lute shard." He paused. "Nevertheless, I never expected to hear . . . all this."

"And what do you think?"

Suleiman pondered a moment before replying. Then he said, with a sigh, "He is a sincere man; but this Templar fantasy of his is dangerous. It flies in the face of reality." He paused. "Look, Ezio. I have not lived long, but I have lived long enough to know that the world is a tapestry of many colors and patterns. A just leader would celebrate this, not seek to unravel it."

"He fears the disorder that comes from differences."

"That is why we make laws to live by—a *kanun* that applies to all in equal measure."

They were interrupted by the arrival of a patrol of Janissary guards the Assassins outside had let pass, since this cohort was loyal to Suleiman. But when their lieutenant saw Ezio, he drew his scimitar.

"Stand back, my *prens*!" said the officer, making to arrest Ezio.

"Hold, soldier," said Suleiman. "This man is not our enemy."

The lieutenant wavered for a moment, then ordered his men out, muttering an apology.

Suleiman and Ezio smiled at one another.

"We have come a long way since that first voyage," said Suleiman.

"I was thinking, what a challenge it would be, to have a son like you."

"You are not dead yet, friend. Perhaps you will yet have a son worthy of you."

Suleiman had started to take his leave when a thought struck him. "Ezio, I know you will be under extreme pressure, but—spare my uncle, if you can."

"Would your father?"

Suleiman did not hesitate. "I hadn't thought about that—but, no."

SEVENTY

Ezio made his way to the Istanbul Assassins' headquarters at all possible speed. Once there, he took the four keys he'd already retrieved in the city and added the one he'd taken from Manuel in Derinkuyu to their number. Packing them safely in a shoulder satchel, he slung it round him. He strapped his hookblade to his right wrist and his pistol to his left, and, in case a quick escape from the top of the Tower should prove necessary, placed Leonardo's parachute in a backpack.

But before he went to the Tower, there was a quick duty he had to perform. He hastened to the Galata cemetery, where Yusuf's body had already been taken for burial. It was Dogan who had taken over as acting captain of the Istanbul Assassins, and he stepped forward to greet Ezio.

"Mentor."

"Mentor," said Irini, coming up in her turn to salute him.

Ezio addressed them briefly, standing by the coffin. "Now should be a time for remembrance and mourning, I know. But our enemies do not permit us that luxury." He turned to Dogan. "I know that Yusuf thought highly of you, and I find no reason to question his judgment. Do you have it in your heart to lead these men and women, and to maintain the dignity of our Brotherhood, as Yusuf did with such passion?"

"It would be an honor," Dogan replied.

"As it will continue to be an honor to work for our cause, and to support the Creed," said Evraniki, who stood beside him.

"*Bene,*" said Ezio. "I am glad." He stepped back and looked over the buildings that surrounded the cemetery, to where the Galata Tower stood. "Our enemy is close," he continued. "When the obsequies are done, take up your positions around the Tower and there await my command."

He hurried away. The sooner Sofia was safe, the better.

He came upon Ahmet, flanked by a single guard, on a rampart near the Tower's foot.

"Where is she?" he demanded.

Ahmet smiled that irritating smile of his, and replied. "I admire you, Ezio; but your bloodlust makes it hard for me to call you a friend."

"Bloodlust? That is a strange insult, coming from the man who ordered an attack on his own nephew."

Ahmet lost some of his sangfroid. "He was to be kidnapped, Assassin; not killed."

"I see. Kidnapped by the Byzantines, so that his uncle could rescue him, and be heralded a hero. Was that the plan?"

Ahmet shrugged. "More or less."

Then he nodded. At once half a dozen Templar soldiers appeared from nowhere and surrounded Ezio.

"Now, *Messer* Auditore—the keys, if you please."

Ahmet extended his hand.

But Ezio made a signal of his own. Behind the semicircle of Templars, a larger number of Assassins materialized, scimitars in their hands. "The girl first," said Ezio in a cold voice.

Ahmet chuckled. "She's all yours."

He made a gesture skyward. Ezio followed the direction of his arm and saw, atop the tower, a woman standing next to a guard, who was clearly poised to throw her over the edge. The woman was wearing a green dress, but her head was covered in a burlap sack. She was bound hand and foot.

"Sofia!" Ezio gasped involuntarily.

"Tell your men to back off!" snapped Ahmet.

Fuming, Ezio signaled the Assassins to do so. Then he threw Ahmet the satchel containing the keys. He caught it adroitly and checked its contents. Then he grinned. "As I said, she's all yours!"

With that, he disappeared from the rampart, his men

following. He boarded a waiting carriage, which sped off through the city, heading toward the North Gate.

Ezio had no time to watch him go. He took a running jump at the Tower and began his ascent.

Anxiety and anger speeded him, and in a matter of minutes he was on the topmost battlement, at the side of the woman. The guard backed away, toward the stairway which led downward.

Ezio leapt forward, wrenched the woman back from the edge of the Tower, and pulled the bag from her head.

It was Azize!

She'd been gagged to stop her crying out any warning, and now Ezio tore the scarf away from her mouth.

"Tesekkür, Mentor. Çok tesekkür ederim!" she gasped.

The guard cackled and rushed away down the stairs. He would meet a grim reception at the bottom.

Ezio was in the process of freeing Azize from her bonds when he was interrupted by a woman's scream. Turning to look, he saw, on another battlement, not far distant, that a temporary gallows had been erected. On the scaffold, a rope already round her neck, stood Sofia, poised on a stool. As he watched, a Byzantine soldier reached up and tightened the noose with rough hands.

Ezio gauged the distance between the top of the Galata Tower and the battlement he had to reach. Leaving Azize to free herself from the rest of her bonds, he unslung his backpack and swiftly assembled the parachute. A matter of seconds later he was flying through the air, guiding the chute with his weight toward the scaffold, where the Byzantines had kicked the stool from beneath Sofia's feet and tied off the rope. Still airborne, he unleashed his hookblade and used it to slice through the taut rope inches above Sofia's head. He landed an instant later and caught her falling body in his arms.

Uttering curses, the Byzantine guards made off. Assassins were racing through the streets between the Galata Tower and this battlement, but Ezio could see Byzantines coming toward them to block their approach. He would have to act alone.

But first he turned to Sofia, pulling the rope from her neck with frantic hands, feeling her breast rise and fall against his own.

"Are you hurt?" he asked, urgently.

She coughed and choked, getting her breath back. "No, not hurt. But very confused."

"I didn't mean to drag you into this. I am sorry."

"You aren't responsible for other men's actions," she said, hoarsely.

He gave her a moment to recover and looked at her. That she could be so rational at such a moment . . . ! "All this will be . . . behind us, soon. But first I must recover what they have taken. It is of primal importance!"

"I don't understand what's happening, Ezio. Who are these men?"

She was interrupted by a cannon's blast. Moments later, the battlement they were on shook with the impact of a twenty-pound ball. Sofia was knocked to the ground as shattered stonework flew.

Ezio pulled her to her feet and scanned the area beneath them. His eye lit on an empty carriage guarded by two regular Ottoman troops, who had taken cover immediately when the gunfire started.

He gauged the distance again. Would the parachute take both her weight and his? He'd have to risk it.

"Come!" he said, taking her in his arms tightly and leaping from the battlement.

For a terrible moment, it looked as if the parachute would snag on the crenellations, but it just cleared them, and they dropped—very fast, but still slowly enough to make a safe landing near the carriage. Ezio folded the chute and stuffed it into his pack, not bothering to unclip it, and the two of them made a dash for the carriage. Ezio hurled Sofia onto the driver's seat, smacked one of the horse's flanks, and leapt on after her. He seized the reins and drove away at breakneck speed, the Ottoman guards shouting vainly for him to stop as they pursued on foot.

Ezio drove hard, heading through the Galata District north, and out of the city.

SEVENTY-ONE

They were not far into the countryside when, as he'd hoped, Ezio saw Ahmet's carriage careering along the road ahead of them.

"Is that who you're after?" said Sofia, breathlessly.

Ezio crouched forward over the reins. "That's him. We're gaining on them! Hang on!"

Ahmet had seen them, too, and leaned out of his window, shouting. "Well, well! You have come to see me off, have you?"

The two men posted on the back outer seat of his carriage had turned round, trying to steady themselves as they aimed crossbows at Ezio and Sofia.

"Take them down!" ordered Ahmet. "NOW!"

But Ezio urged his horses forward and soon drew

abreast of Ahmet's carriage. In response, Ahmet's coachman swerved so that he crashed into his pursuer. Neither
vehicle capsized, but Ezio and Sofia were flung brutally
sideways. Sofia managed to hang on to the side of the
seat, but Ezio was thrown clear, having only just time to
seize a baggage rope that was attached to the top of the
carriage. He felt himself crash onto the roadway, then he
was being dragged along behind his own coach, now out
of control, though Sofia had caught the reins and strove
to pull the horses back from their frantic gallop.

This is becoming a habit, thought Ezio grimly to himself, and he tried to haul himself up the rope. But the
carriage took a turn, and he was thrown violently off the
track, narrowly missing a gnarled tree by the wayside.
He retained his grip, however, but realized he could get
no farther up the rope at that speed.

Gritting his teeth and holding on with one hand, he
reached back with the other to his pack and pulled out
the parachute. The force of the air driving past them
blew it open, and the clip that held it to his pack held.

Ezio felt himself being lifted aloft, sailing behind the
carriage, which had fallen again to the rear of Ahmet's,
now accelerating away from them. But Ezio found it
easier to maneuver himself down the rope even though
it was a struggle against the power of the flying wind. At
last, when he was close enough, he unleashed his hookblade and, reaching up behind him, cut the parachute
free, landing with a crash in the seat next to Sofia.

"Jesus really must smile on you," she said.

"You've brought the horses under control—few

people would have been able to do that," Ezio replied, catching his breath. "Perhaps he smiles on you, too." He noticed blood on her dress. "Are you hurt?"

"A scratch. When I hit the side of the seat."

"Stay strong!"

"I'm doing my best!"

"Do you want me to take the reins?"

"I daren't let go of them!"

They were gaining on Ahmet again.

"Your determination would be charming—if it were not also so infuriating!" he yelled at them. Evidently, he had lost none of his urbanity through the perils of the chase.

They were hammering toward a village where, as they could see, a platoon of Ottoman troops was stationed, guarding the road to the city. They had a barrier in place across the thoroughfare, but its arm was raised.

"Stop them!" Ahmet roared as his carriage passed the bewildered soldiers "They are trying to assassinate your prince!"

The soldiers hurried to lower the barrier's arm as Sofia charged toward them, smashing through the barrier and scattering soldiers like chickens in her wake.

"Sorry!" she cried, then proceeded to knock down a whole row of market stalls lining the main street.

"Oh!" she called. "Forgive me!"

"Sofia, you must be careful," Ezio said.

"I don't want one single crack out of you about women drivers," she snapped back, her teeth bared as their carriage clipped one of two poles supporting a

banner across the street, bringing it down on the heads
of the infuriated villagers storming in their wake.

"What are you doing?" said Ezio, his face white.

"What do you think I'm doing? Keeping us on track!"

Meanwhile, Ahmet's coachman had gained ground,
and the front coach was flying out of the village as Ahmet
urged his men on. Looking back, Ezio saw that a cavalry
patrol had set off in pursuit of them. The crossbowmen at
the back of Ahmet's carriage were bracing themselves to
try to fire again, and this time they succeeded in getting
a couple of shots off. One bolt grazed Sofia's shoulder.

"Aië!" she cried. "Ezio!"

"Hang on!" He ran his fingers over the slight wound,
touching the soft skin. Despite all that was going on, he
felt a tingle in his fingertips. A tingle he'd only felt once
before, during an experiment Leonardo had shown him,
when his friend was tinkering about with something
he'd called "electricity."

"It's a graze, nothing serious."

"It's one graze too many! I could have been killed!
What have you got me into?"

"I can't explain now!"

"Typical! Any excuse!"

Ezio turned in his seat and scanned the cavalrymen
riding behind. "Get rid of them!" Sofia implored him.

He unleashed his pistol, checked it, and took careful
aim at the front rider, bracing himself against the jolting
and bucking carriage. Now or never! He took a deep
breath, and fired.

The man flung up his arms as his horse swerved out

of control across the path of his followers, and there was a mighty snarl-up as several horses crashed into one another, stumbling and falling, and bringing their riders down, even as those coming on from behind were unable to veer, and cannoned into the turmoil themselves. In the complete chaos of yelling men, whinnying horses, and dust, the pursuit came to an abrupt halt.

"Glad you've made yourself useful at last!" said Sofia, as they sped away from the confusion behind them. But looking ahead, Ezio could see that the road led through a very narrow gorge between two high cliffs that reared on either side.

Ahmet's carriage just passed between them. But their own vehicle was wider. "Too narrow!" breathed Ezio.

"Brace yourself!" said Sofia, snapping the reins.

They flew into the gorge at top speed. The bare rock flashed past inches from Ezio's shoulder.

Then they were out the other side.

"Eeah!" Ezio gasped.

Sofia flashed him a triumphant grin.

They had just come close enough to hear Ahmet cursing his crossbowmen, who had managed to reload and fire again but whose bolts flew well wide.

"Incompetent *children*!" he was hollering. "What's the matter with you? Where did you learn to fight?"

After emerging from the gorge, the road wound to the west, and soon the glittering waters of the Black Sea were in view to the north, on their right.

"Shape up or throw yourselves into the ocean!" Ahmet was bellowing.

"Oh no," said Ezio, looking ahead.

"What?" asked Sofia. Then she saw what he'd seen, and in her turn, she said, "Oh, no."

Another village. And, beyond it, another Ottoman guard post. Another pole across the road.

"I must say you've got those horses under pretty good control," said Ezio, reloading his pistol with difficulty as the carriage bucked and jumped. "Most people would have lost them by now, and they'd have bolted. Not bad at all—for a Venetian."

"You should see me handle a gondola," said Sofia.

"Well, now's the time to put them through their paces again," said Ezio.

"Just watch me."

It was market day there, too, but as the two carriages shot toward them the crowd parted like the Red Sea did for Moses.

"Sorry!" cried Sofia as a fish stall collapsed in her wake. Then it was the turn of a pottery stand. Shards flew everywhere, and the air turned blue with the trader's oaths and imprecations.

Next thing, a live chicken landed squawking in Ezio's lap.

"Did we just buy this?" he asked.

"It's a drive-through."

"What?"

"Never mind."

The chicken struggled out of Ezio's grasp, pecking him for good measure, and half flew, half scrambled back to the relative safety of the ground.

"Look out! Up ahead!" Ezio shouted.

The guards had let Ahmet through, but they'd got their roadblock down behind him this time, and stood ready, pikes held out toward Sofia's horses. Unpleasant looks of anticipated triumph lit up their mean, swarthy faces.

"It's ridiculous," said Sofia.

"What is?"

"Well, look—they've got their roadblock in the middle of the road all right, but there's nothing but bare ground either side of it. Do they take us for fools?"

"Perhaps they are the fools," said Ezio, amused.

Then he had to grab hold of the seat fast as Sofia pulled hard on the left reins and dragged the horses in a tight turn, to gallop round the roadblock, leaving it to their right. Then she hauled hard right and regained the road thirty yards past the soldiers, some of whom hurled their pikes impotently after them.

"See any cavalry?" asked Sofia.

"Not this time."

"Good." She snapped the reins, and once again they began to close the gap between themselves and Ahmet.

But there was yet another village, a small one, up ahead.

"Not again!" said Sofia.

"I see it," said Ezio. "Try to close with him now!"

Sofia whipped up the horses, but, as they reached the hamlet, Ahmet's coachman craftily slowed. The soldiers on the backseat had replaced their crossbows with short-poled, vicious-looking halberds, whose axeheads gleamed in the sun. Despite her efforts to slow down, too, Sofia couldn't help drawing level, and Ahmet's coachman managed to veer and clip them again. This time, he succeeded in throwing their carriage off balance, and it began to topple. But the crash had had the same effect on Ahmet's vehicle.

At the moment of collision, Ezio threw himself off his seat, into the air, and landed on the roof of Ahmet's coach. He whipped out the hookblade and swung it violently at the two soldiers to his left, slicing into each of them and bringing them down before they could bring their halberds into play. The coachman had spurred his horses on again in an effort to right his carriage, while Sofia's had already capsized and crashed a short way behind them, in a cloud of dust. They were at the side of a sharp drop, and Ahmet's wheels went over it, taking his carriage down in turn.

Ezio, thrown clear, staggered to his feet and looked around, but the entire scene was obscured by choking dust. Confused cries came from somewhere—probably the local inhabitants, for as the dust began to clear, Ezio could see the coachman's body lying prone among some rocks.

There was no sign of Ahmet.

Or Sofia.

Vainly, Ezio called her name.

SEVENTY-TWO

When the dust had settled completely, Ezio was able to get his bearings. The startled villagers stood a little way off, eyeing each other uncertainly at the scene of the crash. Ezio's baleful glare was enough to keep them at bay, but he knew he'd have to work fast. It wouldn't be long before the Ottoman troops left in their wake would regroup and follow.

He surveyed the scene. Ahmet lay on his back some dozen feet from the wreck. He was groaning, clearly in great pain. The satchel containing the keys lay nearby. Then, to Ezio's intense relief, Sofia appeared from behind a patch of shrubbery. She was bruised and shaken but otherwise unhurt. They exchanged a reassuring look, as

Ahmet, with an effort, rolled himself onto his stomach and pushed himself up.

Ezio scooped up the satchel and opened it. The keys were undamaged.

Ezio looked at the fallen prince.

"So—what now, Ezio? How does this end?" Ahmet said, catching his breath in pain as he spoke.

Sofia came up behind Ezio and put a hand on his shoulder.

"I am wondering that myself," Ezio told Ahmet.

Ahmet began to laugh, and couldn't stop, even though it clearly hurt him to do so. He managed to struggle to his knees. "Well, if you happen to find the answer . . ."

Out of nowhere, half a dozen Byzantine troops appeared. They were heavily armed and took up protective positions around the prince.

". . . do let us know!"

Ezio grimaced, drawing his sword and signaling Sofia to step back.

"You are a fool, Ezio. Did you really think I'd travel without backup?"

Ahmet was about to laugh again but he was cut off by a hail of arrows, seemingly coming from nowhere, which struck down all the Byzantines in a moment. One arrow struck Ahmet in the thigh, and he fell back, howling in pain.

Ezio was equally taken aback. He knew no Assassins were in the vicinity, and there was no way that another Dilara could have arrived to rescue him.

He whipped round to see, a short distance away, a dozen Janissary cavalry, fitting fresh arrows to their bows. At their head was a regal-looking man of about forty-five, dressed in black and red, with a fur cape and a luxuriant mustache. He held up his hand.

"Hold!" he commanded.

The Janissaries lowered their bows.

The leader and two captains dismounted and made their way toward Ahmet, still writhing on the ground. They paid little heed to Ezio, who watched warily, unsure of his next move. He exchanged another glance with Sofia, who drew close to him again.

With a superhuman effort, Ahmet struggled to his feet, seizing a broken branch to support himself. He drew himself up, but at the same time gave ground to the new arrival.

Noticing the family resemblance between the two men, Ezio began to put two and two together. At the same time, Ahmet began to speak, addressing the Janissaries in a voice he struggled to keep firm and commanding: "Soldiers! Selim is not your master! You serve the sultan! You carry out his command alone! Where is he? Where is our sultan?"

Ahmet had backed his way to a fence on the edge of the cliff overlooking the sea, and there, unable to go any farther, he collapsed against it. The other man had followed and stood over him.

"Your sultan stands before you, brother," said the man. He put his hands on Ahmet's shoulders and leaned in close, speaking quietly. "Our father made his choice. Before he abdicated. It was the best thing."

"What are you going to do, Selim?" Ahmet babbled, noticing the expression in his brother's eyes.

"I think it will be best to remove all possibility of further dissent, don't you?"

Selim's hands leapt to Ahmet's throat, forcing him back against the fence.

"Selim! Stop! Please!" Ahmet cried. Then he started to choke.

Sultan Selim Osman was indifferent to his brother's cries. In fact, they seemed to urge him on. Ezio saw that he was pressing down on Ahmet with far more force than was really necessary. Ahmet scrabbled at his brother's face in a vain attempt to beat him off, and as he did so, the fence, which had been buckling alarmingly under his weight, finally cracked and gave. Selim released his grip at the very moment that Ahmet, with a hollow scream of fear, fell backward over the cliff and down to the black rocks two hundred feet below.

Selim stood looking over the edge for a moment, his face impassive. Then he turned back, and walked over, at an easy pace, to where Ezio remained standing.

"You must be the Assassin, Ezio Auditore."

Ezio nodded.

"I am Selim, Suleiman's father. He speaks quite highly of you."

"He is a remarkable boy, *Ekselânslari*, with a magnificent mind."

But Selim's cordiality had come to an end. His affability had vanished as his eyes narrowed, and his face grew dark. Ezio got a strong sense of the ruthlessness that had got this man to the position of power he now held. "Let us be clear," said Selim, his face close to Ezio's. "Were it not for my son's endorsement, I would have you killed where you stand. We do not need the influence of foreigners here. Leave this land and do not return."

Unable to restrain himself, Ezio felt rage rise in him at this insult. He clenched his fists, something that did not go unnoticed by Selim, but in that moment Sofia saved his life by putting a restraining hand on his arm.

"Ezio," she whispered. "Let it go. This is not your fight."

Selim looked him in the eye once more—challengingly. Then he turned and walked back to where his captains and his troop of cavalry were waiting for him.

Moments later, they had mounted and ridden off in the direction of Constantinople. Ezio and Sofia were left with the dead, and with the gaggle of gawping locals.

"No, it is not my fight," Ezio agreed. "But where does one end, and the next begin?"

SEVENTY-THREE

Ezio stood once again at the foot of the great fortress of Masyaf.

Much had happened since he had last been there, and, in the wake of Ottoman conquests in the region, the castle was deserted. A solitary eagle flew overhead, but there was no sign of any human activity. The castle stood alone and silent, guarding its secrets.

He started up the long, steep path that followed the escarpment sloping up to the outer gates. After he had been walking for some time, he stopped and turned, concerned for his companion, who had fallen a little way behind, out of breath. He waited for her in the shade of an ancient, scarred tamarind.

"Such a climb!" panted Sofia, catching up.

Ezio smiled. "Just imagine if you were a soldier, burdened by a suit of armor, laden with supplies."

"This is tiring enough. But it's more fun than sitting in a bookshop. I just hope Azize is managing OK back there."

"Have no fear. Here." He passed her his water canteen.

She drank, gratefully, then said: "Has it been deserted long?"

"The Templars came and tried to break into its secret places, but they failed. Just as they failed—in the end— to secure the keys which, together, would have given them access. And now . . ."

They were silent for a moment as Sofia took in the grandeur of her surroundings. "It is so beautiful here," she said at last. "And this is where your Brotherhood began?"

Ezio sighed. "The Order began thousands of years ago, but here, it was reborn."

"And its *levatrice* was the man you mentioned— Altaïr?"

Ezio nodded. "Altaïr Ibn-La'Ahad. He built us up, then set us free." He paused. "But he saw the folly of keeping a castle like this. It had become a symbol of arrogance, and a beacon for all our enemies. In the end, he came to understand that the best way to serve justice was to live a just life. Not above the people we protect but *with* them."

Sofia nodded, then said, lightly, "And the mandate for the menacing hoods—was that Altaïr's idea as well?"

Ezio laughed softly.

"You mentioned a Creed, earlier," Sofia went on. "What is it?"

Ezio paused. "Altaïr made a great . . . study, throughout the latter years of his long life, of certain . . . codes, which were vouchsafed him. I remember one passage of his writings by heart. Shall I tell you it?"

"Please."

"Altaïr wrote: Over time, any sentence uttered long and loud enough, becomes fixed. Provided, of course, that you can outlast the dissent and silence your opponents. But should you succeed, and remove all challengers, then what remains? Truth! Is it truth in some objective sense? No. But how does one ever achieve an objective point of view? The answer is that one doesn't. It's literally, physically impossible. Too many variables. Too many fields and formulae to consider. The Socratic method understood this. It provided for an asymptotic approach to truth. The line never meets the curve at any finite point. But the very definition of the asymptote implies an infinite struggle. We inch closer and closer to a revelation, but never reach it. Not ever . . . And so I have realized that, as long as the Templars exist, they will attempt to bend reality to their will. They recognize that there is no such thing as an absolute truth, or, if there is, we are hopelessly underequipped to recognize it. And so, in its place, they seek to create their own explanation. It is the guiding principle of what they call their New World Order: to reshape existence in their 'own' image. It's not about artifacts. It's not about men.

These are merely tools. It's about concepts. Clever of them, for how does one wage war against a concept? It is the perfect weapon. It lacks a physical form yet can alter the world around us in numerous, often violent, ways. You cannot kill a Creed. Even if you kill all its adherents, destroy all its writings—that provides a reprieve at best. Someday, someday, we shall rediscover it. Reinvent it. I believe that even we, the Assassins, have simply rediscovered an Order that predates the Old Man of the Mountain . . . All knowledge is a chimera. It all comes back to time. Infinite. Unstoppable. It begs the question, what hope is there? My answer is this: We must reach a place where that question is no longer relevant. The struggle *itself* is asymptotic. Always approaching a resolution but never reaching it. The best we can hope for is to smooth the line a bit. Bring about stability and peace, however temporary. And understand, Reader, it will always and forever be *only* temporary. For as long as we continue to reproduce, we will give rise to doubters and challengers. Men who will rise up against the status quo for no other reason, sometimes, than that they have nothing better to do. It is Man's nature to disagree. War is but one of the many ways in which we do so. I think many have yet to understand our Creed. But such is the process. To be mystified. To be frustrated. To be educated. To be enlightened. And then at last, to understand. To be at peace."

Ezio fell silent. Then he said: "Does that make sense?"

"*Grazie.* Yes, it does." She gazed at him as he stood, lost in thought, his eyes on the fortress. "Do you regret your decision? To live as an Assassin for so long?"

He sighed. "I do not remember making any decision. This life—it chose me."

"I see," she replied, dropping her eyes to the ground.

"For three decades I have served the memory of my father and my brothers, and fought for those who have suffered the pain of injustice. I do not regret those years, but now—" He took a deep breath, as if some force greater than himself had released him from its grip, and he moved his gaze from the castle to the eagle, still soaring, soaring. "Now it is time to live for myself, and let them go. To let go of all of this."

She took his hand. "Then let go, Ezio. Let go. You will not fall far."

SEVENTY-FOUR

It was late in the afternoon when they arrived at the
outer bailey gate. It stood open, and already, climbing
plants were weaving their way around its pillars. The
winch mechanisms above were festooned with creepers.
They crossed to the inner bailey and there, too, the gates
were open, and within, the courtyard showed signs of a
hasty departure. A half-laden, abandoned supply wagon
stood near a huge, dead plane tree under which a broken
stone bench rested.

Ezio led the way into the keep and down a staircase
into the bowels of the castle, carrying a torch to light
them as he led the way down a series of dismal corridors,
until, at last, they stood before a massive stone door
made of some smooth, green stone. Its surface was

broken by five slots, arranged in a semicircle at shoulder height.

Ezio put down his pack and from it produced the five keys.

He weighed the first one in his hand. "The end of the road," he said, as much to himself as to Sofia.

"Not quite," said Sofia. "First, we have to discover how to open the door."

Ezio studied the keys and the slots into which they must fit. Symbols surrounding the slots gave him his first clue.

"They must—somehow—match the symbols on the keys," he said, thoughtfully. "I know that Altaïr would have taken every precaution to safeguard this archive— there must be a sequence. If I fail to get that right, I fear the door may remain locked forever."

"What do you hope to find behind it?" Sofia sounded breathless, almost—awed.

Ezio's own voice had sunk to a whisper, though there was no one but her to hear him. "Knowledge, above all else. Altaïr was a profound man and a prolific writer. He built this place as a repository for all his wisdom." He looked at her. "I know that he saw many things in his life and learned many secrets, both troubling and deep. He acquired such knowledge as would drive lesser men to despair."

"Then is it wise to tap into it?"

"I am worried, it is true. But then"—he cracked a smile—"I am not, as you should know by now, a lesser man."

"Ezio—always the joker." Sofia smiled back, relieved that the tension had been broken.

He placed the torch he held in a sconce, where it gave them both enough illumination to read by. But he noticed that the symbols on the door had begun to glow with an indefinable light, scarcely perceptible, but clear, and that the keys themselves glowed, seemingly in response. "Have a careful look at the symbols on these keys with me. Try to describe them out loud as I look at the symbols on the door."

She put on her glasses and took the first of the keys he gave her. As she spoke, he studied the markings on the door closely.

Then he gave a gasp of recognition. "Of course. Altaïr spent much time in the East, and gained much wisdom there." He paused. "The Chaldeans!"

"You mean—this might have something to do with the stars?"

"Yes—the constellations. Altaïr traveled in Mesopotamia, where the Chaldeans lived—"

"Yes, but they lived two thousand years ago. We have books—Herodotus, Diodoros Siculus—that tell us they were great astronomers, but no detailed knowledge of their work."

"Altaïr had—and he has passed it on here, encoded. We must apply our weak knowledge of the stars to theirs."

"That is impossible! We all know that they managed to calculate the length of a solar year to within four minutes, and that's pretty accurate, but how they did it is another matter."

"They cared about the constellations and the movement of the heavenly bodies through the sky. They thought, by them, they could predict the future. They built great observatories—"

"That is pure hearsay!"

"It's all we have to go on, and look—look here. Don't you recognize that?"

She looked at a symbol engraved on one of the keys.

"He's made it deliberately obscure—but isn't that"—Ezio pointed—"the constellation of Leo?"

She peered at what he had shown her. "I believe it is!" she said, looking up, excited.

"And here"—Ezio turned to the door and looked at the markings near the slot he had just been examining—"here, if I am not mistaken, is a diagram of the constellation of Cancer."

"But that is the constellation next to Leo, isn't it? And isn't it also the sign which precedes Leo in the Zodiac?"

"Which was invented by—"

"The Chaldeans!"

"Let's see if this theory holds water," said Ezio, looking at the next slot. "Here is Aquarius."

"How apt," Sofia joked, but she looked seriously at the keys. At last she held one up. "Aquarius is flanked by Pisces and Capricorn," she said. "But the one that comes after Aquarius is Pisces. And here—I think—it is!"

"Let's see if the others work out in a similar way."

They worked busily and found, after only a matter of ten minutes more, that their supposition seemed to work. Each key bore the symbol of a constellation corresponding to a sign of the Zodiac, and each key sign corresponded to a slot identified with a constellation immediately preceding it in the Zodiac cycle.

"Quite a man, your Altaïr," said Sofia.

"We're not there yet," Ezio replied. But, carefully, he put the first key into what he hoped was its corresponding slot—and it fit.

As did the other four.

And then—it was almost an anticlimax—slowly, smoothly, and soundlessly, the green door slid down into the stone floor.

Ezio stood in the entrance. A long hallway yawned before him, and, as he looked, two torches within, simultaneously and spontaneously, flared into life.

He took one from its sconce and stepped forward. Then he hesitated, and turned back to Sofia.

"You had better come back out of there alive," she said.

Ezio gave her a mischievous smile and squeezed her hand tightly. "I plan to," he said.

He made his way forward.

As he did so, the door to the vault slid closed again, so fast that Sofia hardly had time to react.

SEVENTY-FIVE

Ezio walked slowly down the hallway, which sloped ever downward and broadened out as he progressed. He scarcely had need of his torch since the walls were lined with them, and they flared alight, by some mysterious process, as he passed them. But he had no sense of unease, or trepidation. In a curious way, he felt as if he were coming home. As if something was nearing its completion.

At length, the hallway debouched into a vast, round chamber, 150 feet across and 150 feet high to the top of its dome, like the circular nave of some wondrous basilica. In the body of the room there were cases that must once have contained artifacts; but they were empty. The multiple galleries that ran round it were lined with bookshelf upon bookshelf—every inch of every wall was covered with them.

Ezio noticed, to his astonishment, that every single one of them was empty.

But he had no time to ponder the phenomenon, as his eye was drawn irresistibly to a huge oak desk on a high podium at the far end of the room, opposite the entrance. It was brightly lit from somewhere far above, and the light fell squarely on the tall figure seated at the desk.

And Ezio did feel something like awe, for in his heart he knew immediately who it was. He approached with reverence, and when he drew near enough to touch the cowled figure in the chair, he fell to his knees.

The figure was dead—he had been dead a long time. But the cloak, and white robes, were undamaged by the passage of centuries, and even in his stillness, the dead man radiated—something. Some kind of power—but no earthly power. Ezio, having made his obeisance, rose again. He did not dare lift the cowl to see the face, but he looked at the long bones of the skeletal hands stretched out on the surface of the desk, as if drawn to them. On the table, there was a pen, together with blank sheets of ancient parchment and a dried-up inkwell. Under the figure's right hand lay a circular stone—not unlike the keys of the door, but more delicately wrought, and made, as Ezio thought, of the finest alabaster he had ever seen.

"No books," said Ezio into the silence. "No artifacts . . . Just you, *fratello mio*." He laid a hand delicately on the dead man's shoulder. They were in no way related by blood, but the ties of the Brotherhood bound them more strongly than those of family ever could have.

"*Requiescat in Pace*, O Altaïr."

He looked down, thinking he had caught a movement out of the corner of his eye. But there was nothing. Except that the stone on the desk was free of the hand that Ezio must have imagined had covered it. A trick of the light. No more.

Ezio knew instinctively what he had to do. He struck a flint to light a candle stump in a stick on the desk to study the stone more closely. He put his own hand out and picked it up.

The moment he had it in his hand, the stone began to glow.

He raised it to his face as familiar clouds swirled, engulfing him . . .

SEVENTY-SIX

"You say Baghdad has been sacked?"

"Yes, Father. Khan Hulagu's Mongols have driven through the city like a conflagration. No one has been spared. He set up a wagon wheel and made the population file past it. Anyone whose head came higher than the wheel's hub, he killed."

"Leaving only the young and malleable?"

"Indeed."

"Hulagu is not a fool."

"He has destroyed the city. Burned all its libraries. Smashed the university. Killed all its intellectuals. Along with the rest. The city has never seen such a holocaust."

"And never will again, I pray."

"Amen to that, Father."

"I commend you, Darim. It is well you took the decision to sail to Alexandria. Have you seen to my books?"

"Yes, Father—those we did not send with the Polo brothers, I have already sent to Latakia on wagons for embarkation."

Altaïr sat hunched by the open doorway of his great, domed library and archive. Empty now, swept clean. Clutched to him was a small wooden box. Darim had more sense than to ask his father what it was.

"Good. Very good," said Altaïr.

"But there is one thing—one fundamental thing—that I do not understand," said Darim. "Why did you build such a vast library and archive, over so many decades, if you did not intend to keep your books?"

Altaïr waved an interrupting hand. "Darim, you know very well that I have long outlived my time. I must soon leave on a journey that requires no baggage at all. But you have answered your own question. What Hulagu did in Baghdad, he will do here. We drove them off once, but they will return, and when they do, Masyaf must be empty."

Darim noticed that his father hugged the small box even more tightly to his chest as he spoke, as if protecting it. He looked at Altaïr, so fragile as to seem made of parchment; but, inside, tough as vellum.

"I see," he said. "This is no longer a library then—but a vault."

His father nodded gravely.

"It must stay hidden, Darim. Far from eager hands. At least until it has passed on the secret it contains."

"What secret?"

Altaïr smiled, and rose. "Never mind. Go, my son. Go and be with your family, and live well."

Darim embraced him. "All that is good in me, began with you," he said.

They drew apart. Then, Altaïr stepped through the doorway. Once within, he braced himself, straining to pull a large lever just inside, up by the lintel. At last it moved and, having completed its arc, clicked into place. Slowly, a heavy green stone door rose from the floor to close the opening.

Father and son watched each other wordlessly as the door came up. Darim tried hard to keep his self-control, but finally could not restrain his tears as the door enveloped his father in his living grave. At last he found himself looking at what was, to all intents and purposes, a blank surface, only the slight change of color distinguishing door from walls, that and the curious grooves cut into it.

Beating his breast in grief, Darim turned and left.

Who were Those Who Came Before? thought Altaïr, as he made his way unhurriedly down the long hallway that led to his great domed chamber underground. As he passed them, the torches on the walls lit his way, fueled by a combustible air that led to them from hidden pipes within the walls, ignited by sprung flints that operated as his weight triggered catches under the floor. They flared for minutes behind him, then went out again.

What brought Them here? What drove Them out? And what of Their artifacts? What we have called Pieces of Eden? Messages in bottles? Tools left behind to aid and guide us? Or do we fight for control over Their refuse, giving divine purpose and meaning to little more than discarded toys?

He shuffled on down the hall, clutching the box, his legs and arms aching with weariness.

At last he gained the great, gloomy room, and crossed it without ceremony until he reached his desk. He reached it with the relief that a drowning man feels when he finds a spar to cling to in the sea.

He sat down, placing the box carefully by him, well within reach, hardly liking to take his hands from it. He pulled paper, pen, and ink toward him, dipped the pen, but did not write. He thought instead of what he *had* written—something from his journal.

The Apple is more than a catalogue of that which preceded us. Within its twisting, sparking interior I have caught glimpses of what will *be. Such a thing should not be possible. Perhaps it isn't. Maybe it is simply a suggestion. I contemplate the consequences of these visions: Are they images of things to come—or simply the* potential *for what* might *be? Can we influence the outcome? Dare we try? And, in so doing, do we merely ensure that which we've seen? I am torn—as always—between action and inaction— unclear as to which—if either—will make a difference. Am I even* meant *to make a difference? Still, I keep this journal. Is that not an attempt to change—or guarantee— what I have seen? . . .*

How naïve to believe that there might be a single answer to every question. Every mystery. That there exists a lone, divine light that rules over everything. They say it is a light that brings truth and love. I say it is a light that blinds us—and forces us to stumble about in ignorance. I long for the day when men will turn away from invisible monsters, and once more embrace a more rational view of the world. But these new religions are so convenient—and promise such terrible punishment should one reject them—I worry that fear shall keep us stuck to what is truly the greatest lie ever told . . .

The old man sat for a while in silence, not knowing whether he felt hope or despair. Perhaps he felt neither. Perhaps he had outgrown, or outlived, both. The silence of the great hall, and its gloom, protected him like a mother's arms. But still he could not shut out his past.

He pushed his writing materials from him and drew the box to him, placing both hands on it, guarding it—from what?

Then it seemed that Al Mualim stood before him. His old Mentor. His old betrayer. Whom he had at last exposed and destroyed. But when the man spoke, it was with menace and authority:

"In much wisdom is much grief. And he that increaseth knowledge, increaseth sorrow." The ghost leaned forward, speaking now in an urgent whisper, close to Altaïr's ear. "Destroy it! Destroy it as you said you would!"

"I—I can't!"

Then another voice. One which caught at his heart as

he turned to it. Al Mualim had disappeared. But where was *she*? He couldn't *see* her!

"You tread a thin line, Altaïr," said Maria Thorpe. The voice was young, firm. As it had been when he'd met her, seven decades ago.

"I have been ruled by curiosity, Maria. As terrible as this artifact is, it contains wonders. I would like to understand, as best I can."

"What does it tell you? What do you see?"

"Strange visions and messages. Of those who came before, of their rise, and their fall . . ."

"And what of us? Where do we stand?"

"We are links in a chain, Maria."

"But what happens to us, Altaïr? To our family? What does the Apple say?"

Altaïr replied, "Who were those who came before? What brought them here? How long ago?" But he was talking more to himself than to Maria, who broke in on his thoughts again:

"Get rid of that thing!"

"This is my duty, Maria," Altaïr told his wife, sadly.

Then she screamed, terribly. And the rattle in her throat followed, as she died.

"Strength. Altaïr." A whisper.

"Maria! Where . . . where are you?" To the great hall he cried: "Where is she?" But the only answer was his echo.

Then a third voice, itself distressed, though trying to calm him.

"Father—she is gone. Don't you remember? She is gone," Darim said.

A despairing howl: "Where is my *wife*?"

"It has been twenty-five years, you old fool! She's *dead*!" his son shouted at him angrily.

"Leave me. Leave me to my work!"

Softer, now: "Father—what is this place? What is it for?"

"It is a library. And an archive. To keep safe all that I have learned. All that They have shown me."

"What have they shown you, Father?" A pause. "What happened at Alamut before the Mongols came? What did you find?"

And then there was silence, and the silence covered Altaïr like a warm sky, and into it he said:

"Their purpose is known to me now. Their secrets are mine. Their motives are clear. But this message is not for me. It is for another."

He looked at the box on the desk before him. *I shall not touch that wretched thing again. Soon I shall pass from this world. It is my time. All the hours of the day are now colored by the thoughts and fears born of this realization. All the revelations that were ever to be vouchsafed me are done. There is no next world. Nor a return to this one. It will simply be—done. Forever.*

And he opened the box. In it, on a bed of brown velvet, lay the Apple. A Piece of Eden.

I have let it be known that this Apple was first hidden in Cyprus, then lost at sea, dropped in the ocean . . . this Apple must not be discovered until it is time . . .

He gazed at it for a moment, then rose and turned to a dark recess in the wall behind him. He pressed a lever, which opened a heavy door, covering a hidden alcove, in which stood a pedestal. Altaïr took the Apple from the box, a thing no bigger than a kickball, and transferred it quickly to the pedestal. He worked fast, before temptation could work on him, and pulled the lever again. The door over the alcove slid shut, snapping into place with finality. Altaïr knew that the lever would not operate again for two-and-a-half centuries. Time for the world to move on, perhaps. For him, though, temptation was over.

He took his seat at his desk again, and took, from a drawer, a white alabaster disc. He lit a candle by him and took the disc in both hands, raising it close to his eyes, and closing them and concentrating, he began to imbue the alabaster with his thoughts—his testament.

The stone glowed, lighting up his face for a long time. Then the glow faded, and it grew dark. All grew dark.

Ezio turned the disc over and over in his hands under the candlelight. How he had come to learn what he now knew, he had no idea. But he felt a deep fellowship, a kinship, even, with the husk that sat at his side.

He looked at Altaïr, incredulous. "Another artifact?" he said. "Another *Apple*?"

SEVENTY-SEVEN

He knew what to do, but he did it almost as if he were still in a dream. He placed the disc carefully back on the desktop and turned to the dark recess behind it. He knew where to look for the lever, and it gave immediately when he tugged gently at it. But as the door slid open, he gasped. *I thought there was only one. The one Machiavelli and I buried forever in the vault under the church of San Nicola in Carcere. And now—its twin!*

He studied the Apple for a moment. It was dark and cold—lifeless. But he could feel his hand, as if independent of his will, reaching out for it.

With a supreme effort, he stopped himself.

"NO! You will stay HERE!"

He took a step back.

"I have seen enough for one lifetime!"

He put his hand on the lever.

But then the Apple flared into life, its light blinding him. He staggered back, turning, to see, in the center of the now-dazzlingly-lit chamber, the world—the world!—turning in space, twenty feet above the floor, a giant, vulgar ball of blue, brown, white, and green.

"NO!" he yelled, hiding his eyes with his hands. "I have done enough! I have lived my life as best I could, not knowing its purpose, but drawn forward like a moth to a distant moon. No more!"

Listen. You are a conduit for a message that is not for you to understand.

Ezio had no idea where the voice was coming from, or whose it was. He took his hands from his eyes and placed them over his ears, turning to the wall, his body wrenched to and fro as if he were being beaten.

And he was pulled round to face the room. Swimming in the air, filling the gaudy brightness, were trillions of numbers and icons, calculations and formulae, and words and letters, some jumbled, some thrown together to make occasional sense, but splitting again to give way to chaos. And from their midst the voice of an old man; old because from time to time it trembled. It was not without authority. It was the most powerful voice Ezio had ever heard.

Do you hear me, cipher? Can you hear me?

And then—something like a man, walking toward him as if from a great distance, walking through the swirling sea of all the symbols Man had ever used to try to make sense of it all; walking on air, on water, but not on land. But Ezio knew that the figure would never break free to reach him. They were on two sides of an unbridgeable abyss.

Ah. There you are.

The numbers around the figure shifted and pulsed. And started to flee from one another without being able to get free—in a kind of nightmarish entropy. But the figure became clearer. A man. Taller and broader than most men. Ezio was reminded of one of the statues of Greek gods Michelangelo had shown him when the Borgias' collection had been seized by Pope Julius. An old god, though. Zeus or Poseidon. A full beard. Eyes that shone with an unearthly wisdom. Around him, the trailing digits and equations ceased to battle with one another and finally began to drift away, faster and faster, until they were gone, and the world was gone, and all that was left was this—man. What else was Ezio to call him?

Jupiter. Jupiter is my name. I think you've met my sisters.

Ezio looked at the creature but it was watching the very last trailing formulae as they scurried away through the ether.

The voice when it next spoke seemed oddly human, a little unsure of itself.

A strange place, this nexus of Time. I am not used to the . . . calculations. That has always been Minerva's domain.

He looked at Ezio quizzically. But there was something else—profound sadness, and a kind of paternal pride.

I see you still have many questions. Who were we? What became of us? What do we desire of you?

Jupiter smiled.

You will have your answers. Only listen and I will tell you.

Light slowly drained from the entire room, and once again a ghostly, blue, revolving globe came into view directly behind Jupiter, and slowly grew in size until it occupied almost the entire chamber.

Both before the end, and after, we sought to save the world.

Small dots began appearing on the huge, revolving globe, one after another.

These mark where we built vaults in which to work, each dedicated to a different manner of salvation.

Ezio saw one of the dots among the many flash brightly. It was near the eastern seaboard of a vast continent he couldn't imagine really existed, except that he knew that his friend Amerigo Vespucci had discovered a coastline there a decade earlier, and he had seen the Waldseemüller map depicting all the discovered world. But all that the map showed was farther south. Could there be more? A great land there? It seemed so unlikely.

They were placed underground to avoid the war that raged above, and also as a precaution, should we fail in our efforts.

And Ezio saw now that beams of light were beginning to stretch like lines across the slowing, spinning globe from all the other points marked on it to the one on the strange new continent, and went on until the entire world was crisscrossed with a filigree of lines of light.

Each vault's knowledge was transmitted to a single place . . .

And then Ezio's point of view seemed to change as he watched the great image of the world; and he seemed to plummet toward it, down through space, until it seemed as if he were about to crash into the ground, which rose to meet him, coming alarmingly close. But then—then it was as if he were lifted up, at the last moment, and was skimming along close to the ground, then down again, down through a shaft like a mineshaft until he emerged in an immense underground building, like a temple or a palace hall.

It was our duty . . . mine, and my sisters, Minerva and Juno—to sort and sample all that was collected. We chose those solutions which held the most promise, and devoted ourselves to testing their merits.

And, indeed, now Ezio was in the great hall, in the mysterious vault in the mysterious land—or seemed to be there—and there, near Jupiter, stood Minerva and Juno, whom Ezio had indeed encountered before . . .

Six we tried in succession, each one more encouraging than the last. But none worked.

And then—the world ended.

The last statement was made in so simple and matter-of-fact a tone that Ezio was taken aback by it. He saw Minerva, heavy-hearted, and Juno, angry, look on as Jupiter put into action a complex mechanism that triggered the great doors of the place to close and seal themselves shut. And then—

Then a great wave of indescribable power hit the

upper vault of heaven and lit up the sky like ten thousand northern lights. Ezio seemed to be standing amid hundreds of thousands of people, in an elegant city and all looking up at the supernatural display above them. But the light breeze that played on them changed, from zephyr to storm, then to hurricane, within less than a minute. The people looked at one another in disbelief, then panic, and they scurried away to safety.

The sky, still ablaze with waves of green fire, began to crackle and spark with lightning. Thunder rolled and crashed, though there was not a cloud to be seen, and bolts smashed from the heavens onto trees, buildings, and people alike. Debris flew through the air, destroying everything in its path.

Next, a colossal tremor caused the ground to shudder. Those left in the open lost their footing and before they could rise were struck down by rocks and stones carried like balls of paper by the wind. The earth shook again, more violently this time, and the screams and cries of the afflicted were drowned by the crack of lightning and the deafening scream of the gale. Survivors in the open strove to find shelter, some fighting to keep their balance by clinging to the sides of whatever buildings still stood, as they clawed their way along.

But, amid the general devastation, great temples stood firm, untouched by the catastrophe around them, bearing tribute to the technical ingenuity of those who had built them. But another great tremor rippled the ground, then another. A broad highway split in two along its length, and people fled from the growing abyss that cleaved it. The sky by then was on fire, arcs of lightning rushing from one horizon to the other, and the upper reaches of the firmament seemed about to implode.

Then it appeared to Ezio that he saw the earth from afar again, engulfed in a gargantuan solar flare, trapped in a web of gigantic fireballs; then, unthinkably, the world shifted from its axis, rolling over. The elegant city, the refined, sophisticated collection of tall buildings and manicured parks, was riven with gaping wounds as the earth split and cracked under it, ripping down previously untouched edifices and smashing them to pieces. The few remaining people in the remains of the streets screamed, one last despairing cry of agony, as the shift in the earth's poles left the planet's surface vulnerable to the deadly radiation of solar flares. The last structures were swept away like houses of cards in the wind.

And then—just as suddenly as it had started—all became quiet. The northern lights ceased just as a candle's flame dies when a man blows it out, and, almost immediately, the wind calmed. But the devastation was complete. Almost nothing had been spared. Fires and smoke, darkness and decay, held illimitable dominion over all.

Through the miasma, Jupiter's voice came to Ezio. Or to someone like him. Nothing was certain anymore:

Listen. You must go there. To the place where we labored . . . Labored, and lost. Take my words. Pass them from your head into your hands. It is how you will open the Way. But be warned. Much still remains in flux. And I do not know how things will end—either in my time, or yours.

The dust storms were clearing, the molten lava was

cooling. Time accelerated as tiny shoots broke through the ground and reestablished themselves. The entrance to an underground vault opened, and people of the First Civilization emerged, and they, in turn, began to rebuild. But their numbers were few and did not increase.

Over many centuries they diminished, until there were only a few hundred left, then a few dozen, then none . . .

What they had rebuilt was claimed by the conquering forests. Their new buildings disappeared in their turn, devoured by time. A low-hilled, richly forested landscape enveloped those great expanses not covered by plains. And then, people—but different from the First Comers. Humans now. Those whom the First Comers had created as slaves would now, free, become their heirs. Some indeed had been taken as lovers by the First Comers, and from them a small line of people with more than human powers had emerged.

But the true inheritors were the humans. The first in this unknown land were men and women with deeply tanned skins and long, straight, black hair. Proud peoples who hunted strange, dark brown, wild cattle, riding bareback on tough ponies, using bows and arrows. People who lived in separate tribes and fought one another but with little bloodshed.

Then more people came. Paler people, whose clothes were different and covered them more fully. People who came on ships from Europe, across the Mare Occidentalis. People who hunted down the others and drove them from their lands, establishing in turn their own farms, villages, and, again at last, towns and cities to rival those of the lost civilization, which had disappeared into the earth many millennia before.

Mark this and remember. It is never your choice to give up the fight for justice. Even when it seems that it can never be won, that all hope is lost, the fight, the fight *ensures the survival of justice, the survival of the world. You live balanced on the edge of a cliff, you cannot help that. Your job is to ensure that the balance never tips too far to the wrong side. And there is one more thing you can do that will make certain it never does: You can love.*

Ezio clung to the desk. Next to him, Altaïr still sat in his chair. Nothing had moved on the desktop, not a sheet of parchment had stirred, and the stump of candle burned with a steady light.

He did not know how he had got from the recess to the desk, but now he retraced the few steps. The Apple still rested on its pedestal within the alcove, cold and dead. He could hardly make out its contours in the gloom. Its dust-covered box, he noticed, lay on the desktop.

He gathered himself together and crossed the great chamber again, making for the corridor that would lead back to the sunlight, and to Sofia.

But at the entrance to the great library, he turned once more. Far away now, as it seemed, he looked for one last time at Altaïr, sitting for eternity in the ghost of his library.

"Farewell, Mentor," he said.

SEVENTY-EIGHT

Reaching the outer doorway, Ezio found the lever by the lintel and pulled it. Obediently, the green door slid down into the ground. And there was Sofia, reading a book, waiting for him.

As he emerged, she smiled at him and stood, and came to him and took his hand.

"You came back," she said, unable to disguise the sheer relief in her voice.

"I promised I would."

"Have you found what you sought?"

"I have found—enough."

She hesitated. "I thought—"

"What?"

"I thought I'd never see you again."

"Sometimes our worst premonitions are the least reliable."

She looked at him. "I must be mad. I think I like you even when you're being pompous." She paused. "What do we do now?"

Ezio smiled. "We go home," he said.

PART III

Eternal light, you sojourn in yourself alone.
Alone, you know yourself. Known to yourself,
you, knowing, love and smile on your own being.

—DANTE, PARADISO

SEVENTY-NINE

Ezio was quiet for much of the journey back to Constantinople. Sofia, remembering Selim's dire warning, questioned the wisdom of his returning there at all, but he merely said, "There is still work to be done."

She wondered about him—he seemed so withdrawn, almost ill. But when the golden domes and white minarets once again appeared on the northern seaboard, his spirits lifted, and she saw the old gleam back in his dark grey eyes.

They returned to her shop. It was almost unrecognizable. Azize had modernized it, and all the books were ranged neatly on their shelves, in impeccable order. Azize was almost apologetic when she handed Sofia back the keys, but Sofia had mostly noticed that the shop was full of customers.

"Dogan wishes to see you, Mentor," Azize said as she greeted Ezio. "And be reassured. Prince Suleiman knows of your return and has provided you with a safe-conduct. But his father is adamant that you should not remain long."

Ezio and Sofia exchanged a look. They had been together awhile, ever since she had insisted on accompanying him on his journey to Masyaf—a request which he'd agreed to, to her surprise, with no objection at all. Indeed, he had seemed to welcome it.

With Dogan, Ezio made sure that the Turkish Assassins had a firm base in the city, with Suleiman's tacit agreement and under his unofficial protection. The work had already started in purging the city and the empire of any last trace of renegade Ottomans and Byzantines, now leaderless, following the deaths of Ahmet and Manuel; and the Janissaries, under Selim's iron hand, knew no more dissent within their ranks. There was no need of any since their preferred prince had made himself their sultan.

As for the Templars, their power bases in Italy and, now, in the East, broken, they had disappeared. But Ezio knew that the volcano was dormant, not extinct. His troubled thoughts turned to the Far East—the Orient—and he wondered what the knowledge imparted to him by Jupiter and the ghostly globe might mean for the undiscovered continents—if they existed—far away across the Western Sea.

*   *   *

Dogan, though lacking Yusuf's élan, made up for this by his organizational skills and his complete devotion to the Creed. He might make a Mentor one day, Ezio thought. But his own feelings seemed to have been cut adrift. He no longer knew what he believed, if he believed in anything at all, and this, with one other thing, was what had preoccupied him during the long voyage home.

Home! What could he call home? Rome? Florence? His work? But he had no real home, and he knew in his heart that his experience in Altaïr's hidden chamber at Masyaf had marked the end of a page in his life. He had done what he could, and he had achieved peace and stability—for the time being—in Italy and in the East. Could he not afford to spend a little time on himself? His days were growing short, he knew, but there were still enough of them left to reap a harvest. If he dared take the risk.

Ezio spent his fifty-third birthday, Midsummer's Day, 1512, with Sofia. The days permitted him by Selim's visa were also growing short in number. His mood seemed somber. They were both apprehensive, as if some great weight were hanging over them. In his honor she had prepared a completely Florentine banquet: *salsicce di cinghiale* and *fettunta*, then *carciofini sott'olio*, followed by *spaghetti allo scoglio* and *bistecca alla fiorentina*; and afterward a good dry *pecorino*. The cake she made was a *castagnaccio*, and she threw in some *brutti ma buoni* for good measure. But the wine, she decided, should come from the Veneto.

It was all far too rich, and she'd made far too much, and he did his best, but she could see that food, even food from home, which had cost her a fortune to get, was the last thing on his mind.

"What will you do?" she asked him.

He sighed. "Go back to Rome. My work here is done." He paused. "And you?"

"Stay here I suppose. Go on as I have always done. Though Azize is a better bookseller than I ever was."

"Maybe you should try something new."

"I don't know if I'd dare to, on my own. This is what I know. Though—" she broke off.

"Though what?"

She looked at him. "I have learned that there is a life outside books."

"All life is outside books."

"Spoken like a true scholar!"

"Life enters books. It isn't the other way round."

Sofia studied him. She wondered how much longer he'd hesitate. Whether he'd ever come to the point at all. Whether he'd dare. Whether he even wanted to—though she tried to keep that thought at bay—and whether she'd dare prompt him. That trip to Adrianopolis without him had been the first time she'd realized what was happening to her, and she was pretty sure it had happened to him as well. They were lovers—of course they were lovers. But what she really longed for hadn't happened yet.

They sat at her table for a long time in silence. A very charged silence.

"Azize, unlike you, has not sprung back from her ordeal at Ahmet's hands," said Ezio, finally, and slowly, pouring them both fresh glasses of Soave. "She has asked me to ask you if she may work here."

"And what is your interest in that?"

"This place would make an excellent intelligence center for the Seljuk Assassins." He corrected himself hastily. "As a secondary function, of course, and it would give Azize a quieter role in the Order. That is, if you . . ."

"And what will become of me?"

He swallowed hard. "I—I wondered if—"

He went down on one knee.

Her heart was going like mad.

EIGHTY

They decided it would be best to marry in Venice. Sofia's uncle was vicar general of Santa Maria Gloriosa dei Frari in the San Polo district and had offered to officiate—as soon as he realized that Ezio's late father had been the eminent banker Giovanni Auditore, he had given the marriage his wholehearted blessing. Ezio's connection with Pietro Bembo didn't do any harm, either, and though Lucrezia Borgia's former lover couldn't attend, being away in Urbino, the guests did include Doge Leonardo Loredan and the up-and-coming young painter Tizian Vecelli, who, smitten by Sofia's beauty, and jealous of Dürer's picture of her, offered, for a friendly price, to do a double portrait of them as a wedding tribute.

The Assassin Brotherhood had paid Sofia a generous price for her bookshop, and under it, in the cistern Ezio had discovered, the five keys of Masyaf were walled up and sealed. Azize, though sad to see them go, was also overjoyed at her new profession.

They stayed in Venice, allowing Sofia to acquaint herself with her scarcely known homeland and to make friends with her surviving relatives. But Ezio began to grow restless. There had been impatient letters from Claudia in Rome. Pope Julius II, long the Assassins' protector, was approaching his sixty-ninth birthday and ailing. The succession was still in doubt, and the Brotherhood needed Ezio there to take charge of things in the interim period that would follow Julius's death.

But Ezio, though worried, still put off making any arrangements for their departure.

"I no longer wish to be part of these things," he told Sofia in answer to her inquiry. "I need to have time to think for myself, at last."

"And to think of yourself, perhaps."

"Perhaps that, too."

"But still, you have a duty."

"I know."

There were other things on his mind. The leader of the North European branch of the Brotherhood, Desiderius Erasmus, had written to Claudia from Queens' College at Cambridge, where the wandering scholar was for the present living and teaching, that there was a newly appointed *Doctor in Bible* at Wittenberg, a young man called Luther, whose religious thinking might need watching, as it seemed to be leading to something very revolutionary indeed—something that might yet again threaten the fragile stability of Europe.

He told Sofia of his concern.

"What is Erasmus doing?"

"He watches. He waits."

"Will you recruit new men to the Order if there is a shift away from the Roman Church in the north?"

Ezio spread his hands. "I will be advised by Desiderius." He shook his head. "Everywhere, always, there is fresh dissent and division."

"Isn't that a feature of life?"

He smiled. "Perhaps. And perhaps it is not my fight anymore."

"That doesn't sound like you." She paused. "One day, you will tell me what really happened in that vault under Masyaf."

"One day."

"Why not tell me now?"

He looked at her. "I will tell you this. I have come to realize that the progress of Mankind toward the goals of peace and unity will always be a journey—there will never be an arrival. It's just like the journey through life of any man or woman. The end is always the interruption of that journey. There is no conclusion. There is always unfinished business." Ezio was holding a book in his hands as he spoke—Petrarch's *Canzoniere*. "It's like this," he continued. "Death doesn't wait for you to finish a book."

"Then read what you can, while you can."

With a new determination, Ezio made arrangements for the journey back to Rome.

By that time, Sofia was pregnant.

EIGHTY-ONE

"What took you so long?" Claudia snapped, then pulled him to her and kissed him hard on both cheeks. "*Fratello mio*. You've put on weight. All that Venetian food. Not good for you."

They were in the Assassins' Headquarters on Tiber Island. It was late in February. Ezio's arrival back in Rome had coincided with the funeral of Pope Julius.

"Some good news, I think," Claudia went on. "Giovanni di Lorenzo de Medici is going to be elected."

"But he's only a deacon."

"Since when has that stopped anyone from becoming pope?"

"Well, it would be good news if he gets it."

"He has the backing of almost the entire College of Cardinals. He's even chosen a name—Leo."

"Will he remember me?"

"He could hardly forget that day back in the *duomo* in Florence when you saved his father's life. And his own, by the way."

"Ah," said Ezio, remembering. "The Pazzi. It seems like a long time ago."

"It is a long time ago. But little Giovanni is all grown-up now—he's thirty-eight, would you believe? And a tough customer."

"As long as he remembers his friends."

"He's strong. That's what counts. And he wants us on his side."

"If he is just, we will stand by him."

"We need him as much as he needs us."

"That is true." Ezio paused, looking round the old hall. So many memories. But it was almost as if they had nothing to do with him any longer. "There is something I need to discuss with you, sister."

"Yes?"

"The question of . . . my successor."

"As Mentor? You are giving up?" But she did not sound surprised.

"I have told you the story of Masyaf. I have done all I can."

"Marriage has softened you up."

"It didn't soften you up, and you've done it twice."

"I do approve of your wife, by the way. Even if she is a Venetian."

"*Grazie.*"

"When's the happy event?"

"May."

She sighed. "It's true. This job wears one out. The Blessed Mother knows, I've only been doing it in your stead for two short years, but I have come to realize what you have been carrying on your shoulders for so long. But have you thought of who might take on the mantle?"

"Yes."

"Machiavelli?"

Ezio shook his head. "He would never accept. He is far too much of a thinker to be a leader. But the job—and I say this in all modesty—needs a strong mind. There is one of our number, never called on to assist us before in anything but his diplomatic missions, whom I have sounded out, and who, I think, is ready."

"And do you think the others—Niccolò himself, Bartolomeo, Rosa, Paola, and Il Volpe—will they elect him?"

"I think so."

"Who have you in mind?"

"Lodovico Ariosto."

"*Him?*"

"He was Ferraran ambassador to the Vatican twice."

"And Julius nearly had him killed."

"That wasn't his fault. Julius was in conflict with Duke Alfonso at the time."

Claudia looked astonished. "Ezio—have you taken leave of your senses? Do you not remember who Alfonso is married to?"

"Lucrezia—yes."

"Lucrezia *Borgia*."

"She's leading a quiet life these days."

"Tell Alfonso that! Besides, Ariosto's a sick man—and, by Saint Sebastian, he's a weekend poet! I hear he's working on some tosh about *Sieur* Roland."

"Dante was a poet. Being a poet doesn't automatically emasculate you, Claudia. And Lodovico is only thirty-eight, he's got all the right contacts, and, above all, he's loyal to the Creed."

Claudia looked sullen. "You might as well have asked Castiglione," she muttered. "He's a weekend *actor*."

"My decision is taken," Ezio told her, firmly. "But we will leave it to the Assassin Council to ratify it."

She was silent a long time, then smiled, and said, "It's true that you need a rest, Ezio. Perhaps we all do. But what are your plans?"

"I'm not sure. I think I'd like to show Sofia Florence."

Claudia looked sad. "There's not much left of the Auditores there to show her. Annetta's dead, did you know?"

"Annetta? When?"

"Two years ago. I thought I wrote to you about it."

"No."

They both fell silent, thinking of their old housekeeper, who had stayed loyal and helped save them after their family and their home were destroyed by Templar agents over thirty years earlier.

"Nevertheless, I'm taking her there."

"And what will you do there? Will you stay?"

"Sister, I really don't know. But I thought . . . If I can find the right place . . ."

"What?"

"I might grow a little wine."

"You don't know the first thing about it!"

"I can learn."

"You—in a vineyard! Cutting bunches of grapes!"

"At least I know how to use a blade."

She looked scornful. "Brunello di Auditore, I suppose! And what else? Between harvests, I mean."

"I thought—I might try my hand at a bit of writing."

Claudia almost exploded.

EIGHTY-TWO

But Claudia would later come to love her visits to the estate in the hills above Florence that Ezio and Sofia found, more or less falling down, but bought and, with the proceeds from the sale of the Constantinople bookshop to the Assassins, and Ezio's own capital, restored and turned into a modest, but quite profitable, vineyard within two years.

Ezio became lean and tanned, wore workmen's clothes during the day, and Sofia scolded him, telling him that his hands were getting too gnarled for lovemaking from working on the vines.

But that hadn't prevented them from producing Flavia in May 1513, and Marcello arrived a year later, in October.

And Claudia loved her new niece and nephew almost more than she thought possible, though she made quite sure, given the twenty-year difference in their ages, that she never became a kind of ersatz mother-in-law to Sofia. She never interfered, and she disciplined herself to visit the Auditore estate near Fiesole no more than half the number of times she would have liked to. Besides, she had a new husband in Rome to think about as well.

But Claudia couldn't love the children as much as Ezio did. In them, and in Sofia, Ezio had at last found the *reason*, which he had spent a lifetime seeking.

EIGHTY-THREE

Machiavelli had had a hard time of it, politically, and even spent a while in prison, but when the white water was past, and he was able to take up the reins of his life in Florence again, he was a frequent visitor to the Villa Auditore.

Ezio missed him when he wasn't there, though he didn't take kindly to his old friend's sometimes acerbic comments on his frequently-put-off attempts to write a memoir. The *raccolto* of 1518 had not been good, and Ezio had caught some kind of chest infection—which he ignored—that had dragged on throughout the winter.

Early one evening, near the beginning of the following spring, Ezio sat alone by the fire in his dining hall, a glass of his own red by him. He had pen and paper, and he was trying to make a start, for the umpteenth time, on Chapter XVI, but he found recollection far less interesting than action, and after a while, as always, he impatiently pushed the manuscript away. Reaching for his glass, he was overcome by a fit of painful coughing, knocking it over. It fell with a terrible clatter, spilling wine all over the olive-wood surface of his table, but it did not break. He stood to retrieve it as it rolled toward the edge of the table, and righted it, as Sofia came in, attracted by the noise.

"Are you all right, *amore*?"

"It's nothing. I'm sorry about the mess. Hand me a cloth."

"Forget the cloth. You need rest."

Ezio groped for a chair as Sofia stood by his side, easing him down. "Sit," she commanded, gently. As he did so, she picked up the unlabeled bottle, small towel wrapped round its neck, and checked the level of wine left in it.

"Best cure for a cold," said Ezio, sheepishly. "Has Niccolò arrived yet?"

"He is right behind me," she replied, adding drily, "I'd better bring you another bottle. This one, I see, is nearly empty."

"A writer needs his fuel."

Machiavelli had entered the room with the lack of ceremony he was entitled to as an old friend and a frequent guest. He took the cloth from Sofia.

"Here, let me." He wiped the glass, then the tabletop. Ezio watched him, a slightly sour look on his face.

"I invited you here to drink, not clean up after me."

Machiavelli finished the job before he replied, with a smile, "I can do both. A tidy room and a good glass of wine are all a man needs to feel content."

Ezio laughed mockingly. "Rubbish! You sound like a character from one of your plays."

"You've never seen one of his plays," put in Sofia, shaking her head.

Ezio was embarrassed. "Well, I can imagine."

"Can you? Then why not put that imagination to work? Why don't you buckle down and get on with this?" He indicated the neglected manuscript.

"We've been over this, Niccolò. I don't write. I'm a father, a husband, a winemaker. I'm quite happy with that."

"Fair enough."

Sofia had fetched a fresh bottle of the red, and placed it by them, with two clean glasses, clean napkins, and a basket of *pandiramerino*. "I'll leave you two to discuss literature together," she said. "Once I've helped Andrea get the children to bed, I've got some writing of my own to do."

"What's that?" asked Machiavelli.

"Never you mind," she said. "I'll just wait to see what you think of the wine. He's been fretting about it. Through several bottles."

"She'll get her book finished well before you do yours," said Machiavelli.

"Never mind that," said Ezio. "Taste this. Last year's harvest. A disaster."

"If you ask for my judgment, you shall have it."

He sipped the wine Ezio had poured him, rolled it round his mouth, savoring it, and swallowed.

"It's delicious." He smiled. "Sangiovese again—or have you changed?"

Sofia's face broke into a grin, as she rubbed Ezio's shoulder. "You see?" she said.

"A blend," said Ezio, pleased. "But mainly my old Sangiovese. I didn't really think it was all that bad. My grapes are the best."

"Of course they are." Machiavelli took another deep draft. Ezio smiled, though Sofia noticed that his hand went to his chest surreptitiously, to massage it.

"Come on," said Ezio. "There's still some light in the sky. I'll show you . . ."

They went outside and walked down the avenue leading to the vineyards.

"Trebbiano for the white," Ezio said, waving his hand at a row of vines. "You must have some with dinner. We're getting *tonno al cartoccio.* Serena's specialty."

"I love the way she cooks tuna," Machiavelli replied. He looked around. "You've done well, Ezio. Leonardo would have been proud to see what you have cultivated here."

"Only because I'm using the tools he gave me," Ezio said, laughing. "He'd be jealous. I sell twice as much wine as he ever does from his vineyards in Porta Vercinella. Still, he should never have sent that rascal Salai back from Amboise to run the place." Then he paused. "What do you mean—he *would have been* proud?"

Machiavelli's face grew grave. "I've had a letter. It's to both of us actually but it takes forever for the post to get out here to Fiesole. Look, Ezio. He's not too well. He'd like to see us."

Ezio squared his shoulders. "When do we start?" he said.

They reached the Clos Lucé, the manor house near the château at Amboise which King Francis had given Leonardo as part of the package of his patronage, in late April. The Loire flowed at an easy pace, the banks of its brown waters crowded with trees in new leaf.

They rode through the gates of the manor, down an avenue lined with cypress trees, to be met by a manservant. Leaving their horses in the care of an ostler, they followed the manservant into the house. In a large, airy room, its open windows overlooking the park to the rear, lay Leonardo on a chaise longue, dressed in a yellow brocade gown and half-covered by a bearskin rug. His long white hair and beard were straggly, and he had gone bald on top, but his eyes still shone brightly, and he half rose to greet them.

"My dear friends—I am so glad you have come! Etienne! Bring us wine and cakes."

"You're not supposed to have cakes. Let alone wine."

"Look here—who pays your wages? Never mind—don't answer that. The same man that pays mine, I know! Just—do as you're told!"

The manservant bowed, and left, soon to return with

a tray, which he placed ceremoniously on a nearby polished table before taking his leave again. But as he did so, he bowed once more, and said to Leonardo's guests: "You must forgive the disorder. It's our way."

Machiavelli and Ezio shared a smile. The polished table and the gleaming tray were an island in a rough sea of chaos. Leonardo's habits hadn't changed.

"How are things, old friend?" asked Ezio, taking a seat near the artist.

"I can't complain, but I'm interested in moving on," Leonardo said, trying to make his voice sound stronger than it was.

"What do you mean?" said Ezio, concerned that his friend was using some kind of euphemism.

"I'm not talking about dying," said Leonardo, irritably. "I'm talking about England. Their new king's very interested in building up his navy. I'd like to get over there and sell him my submarine. The Venetians never did pay me, you know."

"They never built it."

"That's beside the point!"

"Don't you have enough to occupy your mind here?" asked Machiavelli.

Leonardo gave him an outraged look. "If you can call creating a mechanical lion occupying my mind!" he snapped. "That was my liege lord's last commission. I ask you—a mechanical lion, that walks along and roars, and as a finale, his breast opens and reveals a basket of lilies!" he snorted. "Good enough in itself, I suppose; but to

demand such a gewgaw of me! Me! The inventor of flying machines, and tanks!"

"And parachutes," added Ezio, softly.

"Did it come in handy?"

"Very handy."

"Good." Leonardo waved a hand toward the tray.
"Help yourselves. But not me." His voice fell a little.
"Etienne's right—the most I can stomach these days is
warm milk."

They were silent. Then Machiavelli said, "Do you
paint still?"

Leonardo grew sad. "I'd like to . . . But somehow
I've lost the force. Can't seem to finish things anymore.
But I've left Salai the *Gioconda* in my will. It might help
him out in his old age. I think Francis would love to buy
it. Mind you, I wouldn't give you tuppence for it myself.
Not my best work, not by far. I prefer the thing I did of
dear little Salai as John the Baptist . . ." His voice trailed
off, and he looked into the middle distance, at nothing.
"That dear boy. Such a pity I had to let him go. I miss
him so much. But he was wretched here. He's better off
looking after the vineyards."

"I tend vines myself, these days," said Ezio, softly.

"I know! Good for you. Much more sensible for a
man of your age than running around hacking off the
heads of Templars." Leonardo paused. "I'm afraid they
will always be with us, whatever we do. Perhaps it's better to bow to the inevitable."

"Never say that!" cried Ezio.

"Sometimes we have no choice," Leonardo replied sadly.

There was silence again, then Machiavelli said, "What's this talk of wills, Leonardo?"

Leonardo looked at him. "Oh, Niccolò. What's the point of pretense? I'm dying. That's why I asked you to come. We three have been through so much. I wanted to say goodbye."

"I thought you had plans to visit King Henry of England?"

"He's a bullish young puppy, and I'd like to," Leonardo replied. "But I won't. I can't. This room is the last place I'll ever see. And the trees outside. Full of birds, you know, especially now it's spring again." He lay silent for so long, without moving, that the two friends looked at each other in alarm. But then Leonardo stirred. "Did I nod off?" he asked. "I shouldn't. I don't have time for sleep. Be getting enough of that, soon enough."

Then he was silent again. He was asleep once more.

"We'll come back tomorrow," Ezio said gently. He and Machiavelli rose and made for the door.

"Come back tomorrow!" Leonardo's voice stopped them in their tracks. "We'll talk some more."

They turned to him as he raised himself on one elbow. The bearskin fell from his knees, and Machiavelli stooped to replace it.

"Thank you, Niccolò." Leonardo looked at them. "I'll tell you a secret. All my life—while I thought I was learning to live, I have simply been learning how to die."

* * *

They were with him a week later, when he breathed his last, in the small hours of May 2. But he no longer knew them. He was already gone.

"A rumor's already going around," said Machiavelli, as they rode sadly homeward, "that King Francis cradled his head in his arms as he died."

Ezio spat. "Some people—even kings—will do anything for publicity," he said.

EIGHTY-FOUR

The seasons revolved four more times. Little Flavia had turned ten; Marcello was approaching his ninth birthday. Ezio could not believe that he had reached the age of sixty-four. Time seemed to speed up more relentlessly, the less you had left of it, he thought. But he tended his vines and enjoyed it, and still, as Machiavelli and Sofia endlessly pressed him to, continued with his memoir. He had reached Chapter XXIV already!

He still trained, too, despite the nagging cough that had never quite left him. But he had long since handed his Assassin's weapons over to Ariosto. There was no news from Rome or Constantinople, or indeed from Erasmus in Rotterdam, to give him any cause for anxiety, though the predicted split in the Church had occurred, with young Luther at the forefront of the Reformation in the north; and new wars threatened the world once again. Ezio could only watch and wait. Old habits died hard, he thought. And he'd become enough of a countryman to be able to catch the scent of a storm.

It was afternoon, and he looked from his verandah across his vineyards to the south, where he could see three figures on a carriage, silhouetted on the skyline. He did not recognize them, and it was too far away to see what manner of people they were, though he saw that their unfamiliar headgear marked them as foreigners. But they did not stop. He guessed they hoped to make Florence by dusk.

He went back into the villa and made for his room. His den. He had the shutters drawn there to help him concentrate. An oil lamp was burning on a desk scattered with papers. His day's literary efforts. He seated himself reluctantly, put on his glasses, and read what he had written, grimacing slightly. The battle with the Wolfmen! How could he have failed to make *that* interesting?

He was interrupted by a knock at the door.

"Yes?" he said, not displeased to be interrupted.

The door opened halfway, and Sofia stood there though she did not enter.

"I'm taking Marcello into town," she said cheerily.

"What—to see Niccolò's latest?" said Ezio, looking up from his reading and not really paying attention to her. "I shouldn't have though *Mandragola* was a suitable play for an eight-year-old."

"Ezio, Machiavelli's play closed three weeks ago. Besides, I'm not going to Florence, just to Fiesole."

"I missed his play? He'll be furious."

"I'm sure he'll be fine about it. He knows you've got your head down. We'll be back soon. Keep an eye on Flavia, will you? She's playing in the garden."

"Of course. I'm fed up with this anyway. I think I'll do some pruning instead."

"I must say it's a pity to waste such a glorious afternoon cooped up in here." She gave him a slight look of concern. "Some fresh air would do you good."

"I'm not an invalid!"

"Of course you aren't, *amore*. I was just thinking . . ." She gestured toward the crumpled pages scattered over the desk. Ezio pointedly dipped his quill and drew a blank sheet toward him.

"*A presto!* Be safe."

Sofia closed the door softly. Ezio wrote a few words and stopped, scowling at the page.

He put down his quill, took off his glasses, and crumpled the page into a ball. Then he stalked from the room. He *did* need some fresh air.

He went to his toolshed and collected a pair of secateurs and a trug. Then he made his way across the garden toward the nearest row of vines. He looked idly around for Flavia but he could see no sign of her. He wasn't unduly worried. She was a sensible girl.

He was halfway to the vineyard when he heard a

sudden noise from a nearby shrubbery. Flavia in peals of laughter. She had ambushed him!

"Flavia, *tesoro*—stay where I can see you!"

There was more laughter as the bush shook. Then Flavia peeked out. Ezio smiled, shaking his head.

Just then, his attention was caught by someone on the road. He looked up, and, in the far distance, he saw a figure dressed in oddly colored, motley garb. But the sun was behind it, and too bright for him to make it out completely. He held his hand up to shield his eyes, but when he looked again, the figure had disappeared.

He wiped his brow and made his way across to his vines.

A little later, he was deep in the vineyard, pruning the Trebbiano grapes. They didn't really need it, but it gave him something to do while his mind beavered away at the problem of recounting the story of his fight, long ago in Rome, with the group of fanatics who'd called themselves the Sons of Remus. The vines brushed his elbows as he worked. He stopped to examine a bunch of grapes, and he plucked one from the cluster. He examined it, rolling it around. He squeezed it, crushing it, and saw that it was juicy. He smiled, and ate the mangled grape, cleaning his fingers on his coarse linen tunic.

He wiped his brow again, satisfied. A breeze blew up, making the vine leaves rustle. He took a deep breath, scenting the warm air, and closed his eyes for a moment.

Then he felt the hairs on the back of his neck prickle.

He opened his eyes and made his way fast to the edge of the vines, looking in the direction of the villa. There, on the road by it, he saw Flavia, talking to the oddly clothed person he'd seen earlier. The figure wore a peaked hood.

He hurried toward them, his secateurs held like a dagger. The wind freshened, bearing his warning cries away. He broke into a jog, wheezing with the effort. His chest hurt. But he had no time to worry about that. The figure was bending down, toward his daughter.

"Leave her alone!" he shouted, stumbling on.

The figure heard him then, turning its head, but keeping it lowered. At the same moment, Flavia plucked something, which she'd evidently been offered, from its hand.

Ezio was nearly upon them. The figure drew itself erect, head still low. Ezio hurled his secateurs at it, as if they were a throwing knife, but they fell short and clattered harmlessly to the ground.

Ezio drew up to them. "Flavia! Go inside!" he commanded, keeping the fear out of his voice.

Flavia looked at him in surprise. "But, Papa—she's nice."

Ezio stepped between his daughter and the stranger, and took the person by the coat lapels. The stranger's head came up, and Ezio saw the face of a young Chinese woman. He released her, taken aback.

The child held up a small oval coin with a square hole at its center for him to see. The writing on it—if it was writing—looked strange. Pictograms. A Chinese *qián*.

The Chinese woman remained motionless, silent. Ezio, still tense, looked at her closely. He was breathing heavily, winded, but his mind was razor-sharp.

Then he saw that at her neck she wore a familiar emblem.

The emblem of the Brotherhood of the Assassins.

EIGHTY-FIVE

Later, when Sofia had returned, the three of them sat talking in the villa while the children watched curiously from the top of the staircase. Ezio was being as hospitable as he possibly could to his unexpected guest, but he was adamant.

"I don't know what else to say, Shao Jun. I am so sorry."

The Chinese woman did not reply, but she was not angry. She was very calm.

"I am very sorry. But I cannot help you. I don't want any part of this."

Shao Jun raised her eyes to meet his. "I want to understand."

"Understand what?"

"How to lead. How to rebuild my Order."

He sighed, now slightly annoyed. "No. For me, that is over. *Finito*." He paused. "Now, I think you should go."

"Ezio, think!" Sofia scolded him. "Shao Jun has come a long way." She turned to their guest. "Did I pronounce your name correctly?"

Jun nodded.

"Will you stay for dinner?"

Ezio gave his wife a black look and turned to face the fireplace.

"Grah-zie," said Jun, in hesitant Italian.

Sofia smiled. "Good. And we have a bedroom already made up. You are welcome to stay for a few nights—or as long as you like."

Ezio growled but said nothing. Sofia left in the direction of the kitchens, while Ezio slowly turned and observed his guest. Shao Jun sat quietly, but she was completely self-possessed. She surveyed the room.

"I'll be back before dark," he told her in a bad-tempered voice.

He stormed out, throwing his manners to the wind. Jun watched him go, a subtle smile on her lips.

Once outside, Ezio took refuge in his vineyard.

EIGHTY-SIX

Ezio was in the children's room, watching their sleeping figures by candlelight. He stepped up to the window and locked it. He sat on the edge of Flavia's bed, watching her and Marcello with a heavy heart. They looked so peaceful—so angelic.

Suddenly, the room got a little brighter as Sofia entered, holding another candle. He looked up at her and smiled. She smiled back and sat at the foot of Marcello's bed.

Ezio said nothing for a moment.

"Are you all right?" she asked, a little timidly.

He looked down at his children again, lost in thought. "I can't seem to leave my past behind me," he muttered. Then he turned his gaze to his wife. "I started this act of my life so late, Sofia. I knew I wouldn't have time to do everything . . . But now I worry that I won't have time to do *any*thing."

Her eyes were sad but full of understanding.

They heard a faint creaking from above and looked toward the ceiling.

"What is she doing on the roof?" Ezio muttered.

"Leave her be," said Sofia.

Above them, Shao Jun stood on the red tiles high up near the chimneys. She had taken up a pose that was something between an Assassin attack position and simply that of someone relaxing and enjoying herself. She scanned the moonlit countryside as the night wind whispered around her.

The next day, Ezio emerged from the villa early, to grey skies. He glanced up at the roof, but, though the window of her room was open, there was no sign of Shao Jun.

He called her name, but there was no answer. He went to give orders to his foreman, for the time of the *vendange* was approaching, and he prayed for a good harvest this year—the grapes certainly promised it, and the summer weather had been favorable. The *veraison* had been good, too, but he wanted to double-check the sugar and acid levels in the grapes before picking. Then he'd send the foreman into Fiesole and as far as Florence if need be, to recruit the seasonal labor they'd need. It was going to be a busy time, and it was one that Ezio looked forward to every year—lots of physical activity and little time to think about anything else. Shao Jun's arrival had thrown the hard-won security he enjoyed off track. He resented it. He found himself hoping that she had left before dawn.

Once he had finished his meeting with his foreman, he felt an irresistible impulse to return to the villa to see if his prayer had been answered. Somehow, he doubted it, but there was no one about when he entered the house. Grimly, following some instinct that hollowed his stomach, he made his way to his den.

He stopped short at the door. It was open. He swept into the room and discovered the Chinese woman standing behind his desk—still littered with discarded notes and pages from the days before—and reading part of the completed manuscript.

Ezio fell into a red rage. "What do you think you're doing? Get out!"

She put down the sheaf of papers she was reading from and looked at him calmly. "The wind—it opened the door."

"Fuori!"

Jun walked quickly past him and out of the room. He made his way quickly to the desk and shuffled the papers around, picking up one that caught his eye and reading from it. Then, unimpressed, he tossed it back on the pile and turned from the desk to stare blankly out the window. He could see Jun out there, in the yard, her back to him, apparently waiting.

His shoulders slumped. After a few more minutes' hesitation, he left the den and made his way out to her.

She was sitting on a low stone wall. He approached her, coughing lightly in the keen October wind.

She turned. "*Duìbùqǐ*—I'm sorry. It was wrong of me."

"It was." He paused. "I think you should leave."

She sat silently for a moment, then, without warning, she quoted: " 'My name is Ezio Auditore. When I was a young man, I had liberty, but I did not see it; I had time, but I did not know it; and I had love, but I did not feel it. It would be thirty long years before I understood the meaning of all three.' " She paused. "That is beautiful," she said.

Ezio was stunned. He stared past Jun, reflecting. In the distance, they could hear the jingling of a horse's reins.

"I want to understand, like you do," Jun went on. "To help my people."

Ezio looked at her with a friendlier eye. "I was an Assassin for a long time, Jun. And I know that at any moment, someone could come for me. Or my family." He paused. "Do you see? That is why I must be careful."

She nodded, and he could see that she almost felt sorry for him. He looked toward his vineyards. "I should be starting to hire people to help me with the *vendange*, but . . ."

He trailed off. Jun tilted her head, listening.

"Come inside. Let's get something to eat."

She slid off the wall and followed him.

EIGHTY-SEVEN

The market in the great square southwest of the cathedral was as busy as ever. Merchants, businessmen, servants, and peasants jostled each other in a more or less friendly way as they passed between the stalls. Jun stood under one side of the surrounding colonnade, watching the bustle as Ezio, nearby, haggled in the cold sunlight with a stallholder over the price of a grape picker's basket. Jun was rapt, absorbing the sights and sounds of Florence. She stared openly at people just as openly as people stared at her. She was unbothered.

Ezio completed his purchase and came over, tapping her on the shoulder. "I'll be lucky if this lasts three seasons," he said. She looked at him as he showed her the basket, unsure what she should be looking for to judge its quality. Ezio realized this, with a smile.

"Come on," he said. "I want to show you something."

They moved through the crowds in the direction of the Piazza della Signoria, and once there sat down on a bench near the loggia, watching the people come and go, all brightly clad, except for those dressed in expensive black silks and velvets.

"Who are they?" asked Jun.

"They are the bankers," Ezio replied. "It's a kind of uniform, so that they can recognize each other—but it has another advantage—we can see them coming!"

Jun smiled uncertainly.

"It's nice, *no*?" Ezio continued. "Full of life!"

"Yes."

"But not always. Half my family was murdered in this piazza. Executed. Right here. Forty-five years ago. I was nineteen."

He closed his eyes briefly at the memory, then went on: "But now, to see it like this, so *piena di vita*, I can't help but feel content. And satisfied that so much pain has faded away." He looked at her earnestly. "The life of an Assassin is pain, Jun. You suffer it, and you inflict it. You watch it happen—all in the hope that you can help it disappear, in time. It's terribly ironical, I know. But there it is."

They sat in silence for a while. Jun seemed watchful. Then Ezio saw her tense at something. Something she had noticed in the crowd. A flash of a certain color? A uniform perhaps? One of the Signoria guards? But the moment passed, and he let it go.

"All right," he said, rising. "Time to drag this old man back to his villa."

She joined him, and they left, crossing the square and taking the street, so familiar to Ezio, which ran east, just to the north of the Palazzo.

Jun kept casting backward glances.

The street they'd reached was considerably emptier of people, and finally, as they moved along it, they were alone. Suddenly, Ezio heard a noise Jun did not. He turned his head quickly.

He took a backward leap, raising his basket to shield Jun, and in the nick of time—a thrown dagger embedded itself in it. Barely a second later, someone landed Ezio a savage kick in the gut. He staggered backward and fell against a stone wall.

Meanwhile, Jun had reacted with lightning speed. She was already standing between Ezio and his assailant— another Chinese woman, similarly dressed to Jun, but stripped down to combat tunic and trousers.

The two women circled each other, almost balleti-cally, slowly, then lunging at each other like striking snakes, landing slicing blows with the edges of their hands, or kicking so fast that Ezio could barely follow the movement.

But he could see that Jun was getting the worst of it. He sprang forward and struck her attacker on the head with the basket, sending her sprawling.

She lay prone, motionless. Jun stepped forward.

"Jun! She's faking it!"

At the same moment the mysterious woman was back on her feet, falling on Jun with another knife raised. They both fell to the ground, rolling in the dust, fighting with the ferocity and the vicious agility of cats, their limbs and bodies moving so fast that they became blurred.

Then a sudden scream. The assailant broke free, her own knife buried in her chest, just above the sternum. She tottered sideways for a moment, then keeled over, striking her head on a flint buttress, and was still. This time she was not faking.

Ezio looked round. No one in sight.

He grabbed Jun's hand.

"Come on!" he said through clenched teeth.

As they rode home in Ezio's carriage, Jun began to explain. Ezio realized that she might have done so earlier if he'd given her the chance. He listened grimly as she told her tale.

"It was my Mentor's wish to meet you. We left China together, in secret. But we were followed. They caught up with us in Venice. They took my master prisoner there. He bade me flee, complete our mission. I did not see him again."

"Who are they?"

"Servants of Zhu Huocong—the Jiajing Emperor. A young man, scarcely more than a boy, and not born to rule, but fate gave him the throne, and he controls us with a ruthless and bloody hand." She paused. "I was born a concubine, but my Mentor freed me when I was young. We returned later to save more girls, but they were—" She paused. "The emperor thought that if he drank their monthly blood it would give him eternal life." She broke off, swallowing hard before mustering her self-control, with an effort, and continuing:

"Jiajing is a cruel man. He kills all who oppose him, and he prefers *ling chi* to beheading."

"Ling chi?"

Jun made several slicing motions across her palm. "Slow process. Many thousand cuts. Then—dead."

Ezio's face set like granite. He whipped his horses on.

EIGHTY-EIGHT

Sofia was in Ezio's den, stoking a fresh fire, when she heard the carriage tear up to the front of the house. Alarmed, she rose quickly to her feet. A moment later, Ezio burst in, closely followed by Shao Jun. He rushed to the window and closed the shutters, bolting them. Then he turned to his wife.

"Pack some bags. They are putting fresh horses to the coach. Some of our men will go with you."

"What—?"

"You must stay at Machiavelli's tonight."

"What's happened?"

"A misunderstanding."

Sofia looked from him to Jun, who lowered her eyes,

embarrassed at having brought her troubles to their door.

"Give me a moment," she said.

Soon afterward, she and the children were installed in the carriage. Ezio stood at its door.

They looked at each other. Both wanted to say something, but no words came.

Ezio stepped back and nodded to the coachman. He cracked the reins, and the horses moved forward into the gathering gloom.

As they gathered pace, Sofia leaned from the window and blew him a kiss. He raised his arm in farewell, then, without waiting to watch them out of sight, returned to the villa and closed and locked the door.

EIGHTY-NINE

Ezio and Jun sat facing each other on wooden benches, drawn up in front of a roaring fire. Waiting.

"When I first fought the Borgia, it was revenge that drove me, and my first impulse was to aim for the head," Ezio was telling her. "In time, however, I learned that those who inspire fear have more devoted followers than those who preach love. Killing Rodrigo and Cesare would have achieved nothing if I had not been able to replace their reign of terror with one that involved some measure of fraternity." He paused in thought. "So I spent many years teaching men and women to think and act for themselves. First in Rome, then among our Brotherhood in Constantinople."

"I long to read of your deeds. You must finish your book."

"The important thing to realize is this: Love binds our Order together; love of people, of cultures, of the world." He was silent again for a moment. "Fight to preserve that which inspires hope, and you will win back your people, Shao Jun."

Jun stared into the flames, thinking, as the grand scope of her future widened in her imagination. "It will take a long, long time," she said quietly, at last.

"But if you do it right, it will happen."

Jun took a deep breath and straightened up, a determined expression on her face. She looked across at Ezio and nodded. He leaned across and patted her on the shoulder.

"Get some rest," he said.

She rose and bowed slightly, then left the room.

Ezio turned to the fire, its glow reddening his face.

Deep in the night, disturbed by stealthy sounds outside, Ezio made his way to the kitchens. From high in the sky, the moon shone through the barred windows. Ezio approached the knife blocks and pulled several knives out, testing them for balance. Not satisfied, he put them back and cast around for some other weapon. An iron ladle? No. A chopping board? No. A poker, perhaps? Yes! He went over to the stove and picked one out, three feet long and made of heavy steel. He tested it, making two or three practice passes with it.

He tensed at a noise from above. Seconds later, a body dropped past the window. Ezio saw Jun land in a crouch, then bolt into the night. He made for the door and unlocked it, flinging it open.

There was a Chinese man there, poised for attack, who instantly lunged at him with a *dao*. Ezio stepped back and slammed the door on the man's arm, smashing the radius and ulna, and the sword dropped from his hand, as the Chinese howled in agony. Ezio threw the door open again and brought the poker down hard on the man's head, splitting the skull. He jumped over the corpse and dashed outside.

He soon found Jun, engaged in combat with three attackers. It was going badly for her, but he'd arrived in time to turn the tide, and the servants of the Jiajing Emperor retreated in the direction of the vineyard.

There, they took a stand. Jun, fighting with only her fists and feet, took one of their opponents out almost immediately, as Ezio brought down a second with his poker, ramming its point squarely into his attacker's face. But the third Chinese managed to knock the poker from his grasp, and it was only by reaching out fast for a wooden dowel, which he plucked from the vines, that he managed to regain his advantage, beating the man to the ground, then striking him hard on the nape of the neck, crushing the cervical vertebrae.

It was over. Ezio collapsed on the gentle slope where his vines were planted, exhausted but uninjured. He caught Jun's eye and tried to laugh, but his laughter turned into a wheezing cough.

"I sound like a dying cat," he said.

"Come on, I'll help you."

She helped him to his feet, and, together, they returned to the villa.

NINETY

They were awake long before break of day. The morning was cool. Some watery sunlight found its way through the haze.

Shao Jun stood in the road, her pack on her back. Staring into the distance, she was ready to depart. She seemed lost in thought, and only turned when Ezio approached from the villa. His breathing was still labored and heavy.

He came up to her. "It is long way home, *no?*"

"But there is much to see along the way. *Dashi, xièxiè nin*—Thank you, Mentor." She bowed slightly.

Ezio was carrying something. A small, ancient box. He held it out to her. "Here. This may be of use one day."

Jun took it and turned it in her hands. Then she began to open it, but Ezio stopped her.

"No," he said. "Only if you lose your way."

She nodded and packed it away. Ezio squinted past Jun, peering up the road. He saw the banners of approaching soldiers.

"You should go," he said.

Jun followed his gaze, nodded, and set off, toward the vineyards that grew on the other side of the road. Ezio watched her as she made her way quickly over the brow of a nearby hill.

The soldiers rode up soon afterward, and Ezio greeted them. When he looked in Jun's direction once more, she had disappeared.

A few weeks later, the harvest done, and Marcello's ninth birthday behind them, he was back in his den, trying to write again. He had made good progress this time. He stared at the last blank sheet in front of him, then dipped his quill and scribbled a few words, concentrating hard. He read them back, and smiled. Then he dropped his quill as a shooting pain in his chest caught him off guard.

There was a knock at the door.

"Yes?" he said, collecting himself and replacing the quill in its stand by the inkwell.

Sofia entered the room.

"Just taking the kids down to Fiesole. We'll be back just after dark."

"Good."

"Market day tomorrow. Are you coming with us?"

"Yes."

"Sure?"

"I'll be fine."

She closed the door behind her. Ezio sat brooding for a moment, then, satisfied, began gathering the papers on his desk, stacking them neatly, and tying a ribbon round them.

NINETY-ONE

The next day was fine and fresh. They had stayed in Florence for lunch, and Sofia was bent on making just a few more purchases before the journey home. Ezio, walking down the street a few paces behind his wife and children, suddenly winced as a fit of coughing took him. He leaned against a wall for support.

In a moment, Sofia was by his side.

"You should have stayed at home."

He smiled at her. "I am home."

"Sit down, here." She indicated a nearby bench. "Wait for us. We'll be right over there. Only take a minute or two."

He nodded, watching her rejoin the children and

wander off a little farther down the street. He made himself comfortable, letting the pain subside.

He watched the people walking to and fro, going about their daily business. He felt pleased and enjoyed watching them. He breathed in the smells of the market as it broke up around him. He listened to the sound the traders made.

"I love it here," he said to himself. Home. Home at last.

His reverie was interrupted by the peevish voice of a young Italian who plumped himself down on the bench near him. The young man was talking, apparently, to himself. He didn't look at Ezio.

"*Al diavolo!* I hate this damn city. I wish I were in Rome! I hear the women there are . . . mmm . . . like ripe Sangiovese on the vine, you know? Not like here. *Firenze!*" He spat on the ground.

Ezio looked at him. "I don't think Florence is your problem," he remarked, pained at what the young man had said.

"I beg your pardon?"

Ezio was about to reply, but the pain seized him again, and he winced, and started to gasp. The young man turned to him. "Steady, old man."

He grabbed Ezio's wrist as Ezio caught his breath. Looking down at the hand that held him, Ezio thought the grip was uncommonly strong, and there was something strange, almost familiar, about the man's expression. But he was probably imagining it all. He shook his head to clear it.

The young man looked at Ezio closely, and smiled. Ezio returned the look.

"Get some rest, eh?" the young man said.

He rose to his feet and walked away. Ezio nodded in belated agreement, watching him go. Then he leaned back, seeking Sofia in the thinning crowd. And saw her at a stall, buying vegetables. And there beside her were Flavia and Marcello, baiting each other, playing together.

He closed his eyes and took some deep breaths. His breathing calmed. The young man was right. He should get some rest . . .

Sofia was packing the vegetables she'd bought into a basket when something cold crept into her heart. She looked up, then around, back to where Ezio sat. There was something about the way he was sitting.

Confused, not wanting to admit what she feared to herself, she put a hand to her mouth and hurried across to him, leaving the children playing where they were.

As she got closer, she slowed her pace, looking at him. She sat down by his side, taking his hand. And then she leaned forward, pressing her forehead against his hair.

One or two people looked in their direction, then one or two more, with concern; but otherwise, life in the street went on.

NINETY-TWO

Much later that day, back home, and having sent Machiavelli away, Sofia took herself into the den. The children were in bed. She didn't think what had happened had sunk in for them, yet.

In the den, the fire had gone out. She lit a candle. She walked to the desk and picked up the neatly stacked sheaf of papers, tied with a ribbon, that lay on it. And she began to read:

When I was a young man, I had liberty, but I did not see it; I had time, but I did not know it; and I had love, but I did not feel it. Many decades would pass before I understood the meaning of all three. And now, in the twilight of my life, this understanding has passed into contentment. Love, liberty, and time . . . once so much at my disposal, are the fuels that drive me forward; and love, most especially, my dearest, for you, our children, our brothers and sisters . . . and for the vast and wonderful world that gave us life and keeps us guessing. With endless affection, my Sofia, I am forever yours.

Ezio Auditore

LIST OF CHARACTERS

Adad: stonemason

Al Mualim: Mentor of the Brotherhood

Al-Sayf, Malik: Assassin comrade of Altaïr

Al-Sayf, Tazim: Assassin and Malik's son

Al-Scarab: pirate captain

Auditore, Claudia: Ezio's sister

Auditore, Ezio: Master Assassin

Auditore, Federico: Ezio's elder brother

Auditore, Giovanni: Ezio's father

Auditore, Mario: Ezio's uncle

Auditore, Petruccio: Ezio's younger brother

Azize: Assassin in Constantinople

Baglioni, Pantasilea: Bartolomeo d'Alviano's wife

Barleti, Tarik: Janissary captain

Bekir: Larnaka shipping agent

Borgia, Cesare: Rodrigo's son, 1480–1519

Borgia, Rodrigo: Pope Alexander VI, 1451–1503

Buonarroti, Michelangelo: artist, sculptor, etc.,
    1475–1564

Cemal: Assassin in Altaïr's time

d'Alviano, Bartolomeo: Italian captain and Assassin, aka
    Barto, 1455–1515

da Vinci, Leonardo: artist, scientist, sculptor, etc.,
    1452–1519

de Sable, Robert: Templar Grand Master

Dilara: Ottoman spy, Tarik's agent

Dogan: Assassin in Constantinople

Dovizi, Duccio: Claudia's ex-boyfriend

Dürer, *Meister* **Albrecht:** painter, 1471–1528

Erasmus, Desiderius: leader of the Northern European
    Assassins

Evraniki: Assassin in Constantinople

Ferdinand II, King: king of Spain, 1479–1516

Francis I, King: king of France, 1494–1547

Haras: Assassin adept in Altaïr's time

Heyreddin: Assassin in Constantinople

Hulagu, Khan: grandson of Genghis Khan, 1217–65

Ibn-La'Ahad, Altaïr: Master Assassin

Ibn-La'Ahad, Darim: Altaïr's eldest son

Ibn-La'Ahad, Sef: Altaïr's youngest son

Ibn-La'Ahad, Umar: Altaïr's father

Il Volpe: member of the Assassin Council

Irini: Assassin in Constantinople

Janos: Ottoman prisoner

Julius II, Pope: Pope and friend to the Assassins, 1443–1513

Juno: goddess, one of Those Who Came Before

Jupiter: god, one of Those Who Came Before

Kasim: Assassin in Constantinople

Kemal Reis: Piri Reis's uncle

Luther: aka Martin Luther, priest, 1483–1546

Machiavelli, Niccolò di Bernardo dei: philosopher and writer, 1469–1527

Ma'Mun: shipping agent

Mehmed II, Sultan: previous sultan of the Ottoman Empire, 1432–81

Minerva: goddess, one of Those Who Came Before

Nazar: Janissary soldier

Nikolos: guard

Osman, Ahmet: Suleiman's uncle and Bayezid II's eldest son, 1465–1513

Osman, Cem: Bayezid II's brother and pretender to the throne, 1459–95

Osman, Selim I: Suleiman's father and Bayezid II's youngest son, ca. 1465–1520

Osman, Suleiman: the prince and governor of Kefe, 1494–1566

Osman, Sultan Bayezid II: the current sultan, Suleiman's grandfather, 1447–1512

Osman, Tomas: Bayezid II's brother

Palaiologos, Constantine: last Byzantine emperor

Palaiologos, Manuel: heir of the Palaiologos family

Paola: Assassin *madame*, member of the Assassin Council

Petros: soldier

Piri Reis: admiral, cartographer, bomb maker

Polo, Maffeo: Niccolò Polo's brother, 1252–1309

Polo, Niccolò: journal writer, Marco's father, 1252–94

Rosa: member of the Assassin Council

Salai: Leonardo's assistant

Sartor, Sofia: lady in green

Sforza, Caterina: Countess of Forlì

Shahkulu: Manuel's bodyguard

Shao Jun: Chinese Assassin

Sofian, Abbas: Altaïr's former comrade and Master Assassin

Sofian, Ahmad: Abbas's father

Tazim, Yusuf: leader of the Assassins in Constantinople

Teragani: Assassin in Altaïr's time

Thorpe, Maria: Altaïr's wife

Vespucci, Amerigo: explorer and navigator, 1454–1512

Vespucci, Cristina: Ezio's former girlfriend

Villiers de L'Isle-Adam, Philippe: member of the Knights Hospitalier at Rhodes, 1464–1534

Zhu Huocong: the Jiajing Emperor

GLOSSARY OF FOREIGN TERMS

ARABIC
barakallah feek   God bless you
hajj   pilgrimage
masa'il kher   good evening

CHINESE (Mandarin)
dao   knife
dashi, xièxiè nin   thank you, Mentor
duìbùqǐ   I'm sorry
ling chi   death by a thousand cuts
qián   Chinese currency

FRENCH
vendange   vintage
veraison   ripening

GREEK

apistefto unbelievable

edáxi okay

fíye apó brostá mou! get out of my way!

Hristé mou my God

kouráyo courage

poi kalà very good

ti distihìa what misery

ITALIAN

al diavolo to hell

amore love

a presto see you soon

arrocco castling (chess move)

bastardo bastard

bene good, well

bistecca alla fiorentina Florentine steak

brutti ma buoni Italian cookies

buffone jester

buona donna good woman

buona sera good evening

buon giorno good day

canaglia scoundrel

carciofini sott'olio artichokes in oil

castagnaccio chestnut flour cake

cazzo prick, shit

che succede? what's happening?

Dio mio my God

duomo dome

è incredibile it's incredible

fettunta garlic bread

finito finished

fratello mio my brother

fuori out

grazie thank you

il diavolo the devil

kogge ship

levatrice midwife

maccaroin in broddo pasta soup

magnetismo magnetism

meister master

merda shit

messer/e sir

mia cara my dear

mio my

mio bel menestrello my handsome minstrel

moleche soft-shell crab

molto curioso very curious

navigatore navigator

nessun problema no problem

non mi sorprende I'm not surprised

pandiramerino rosemary bread

panzanella Florentine bread

pecorino cheese

perdonate, buon signore pardon me, good sir

perfetto perfect

piena di vita full of life

prego please

presuntuoso   presumptuous

principe   prince

raccolto   harvest

ragazzo   boy

requiescat in pace   rest in peace

rixoto de gò   rice with fish

salame toscano   Tuscan salami

salsicce di cinghiale   wild boar sausages

salute a voi, Assassini   health to you, Assassins

salve   hello

se solo   if only

sì   yes

sì, da molto tempo   yes, a long time

sieur   sire

soldi   money

spaghetti allo scoglio   reef spaghetti

tesoro   treasure

tonno al cartoccio   tuna in foil

una tortura!   torture

va bene   fine

TURKISH

adi herif   bastard, pig

affedersiniz, efendim   excuse me, sir

akçe   Turkish coin

allaha ismarladik   goodbye

Allah ashkina   in God's name

aman Allahim   oh my God

aynen oyle   exactly

bey   lord

beyefendi   gentleman

bir sey degil   you're welcome

çok tesekkür ederim   thank you very much

çok üzüldüm   I am so sorry

efendim   sir

effendi   master

Ekselânslari   His Excellency

evet   yes

gerzek   idiot

ghazi   holy warriors

güle güle   goodbye

güzel   beautiful

haydi rastgele   good luck

inanilmaz   incredible

kanun   law

kardeslerim   brothers and sisters

karesi   square

kargasa   turmoil

kesinlikle   certainly

kofta   meatball

merhaba   hello

pekala   well

pek güzel   very beautiful

prens   prince

sagliginiza   to your health

saray   palace

Sayin   Mr.

sehzadem   prince

serefe   cheers

sharbat   Middle Eastern drink

sinav icin iyi sanslar   good luck on the test

sövalye   knight

tesekkür ederim   thank you

Acknowledgments

Special thanks to
Yves Guillemot
Jean Guesdon
Corey May
Darby McDevitt

And also
Alain Corre
Laurent Detoc
Sébastien Puel
Geoffroy Sardin
Xavier Guilbert
Tommy François
Cecile Russeil
Christele Jalady
The Ubisoft Legal Department
Chris Marcus
Etienne Allonier
Maria Loreto
Alex Clarke
Alice Shepherd
Anton Gill
Guillaume Carmona
Clémence Deleuze